Alexander Pope, George Ravenscroft Dennis

The Poetical Works of Alexander Pope

Vol. III.

Alexander Pope, George Ravenscroft Dennis

The Poetical Works of Alexander Pope
Vol. III.

ISBN/EAN: 9783337031169

Printed in Europe, USA, Canada, Australia, Japan

Cover: Foto ©Andreas Hilbeck / pixelio.de

More available books at **www.hansebooks.com**

THE POETICAL WORKS OF

ALEXANDER POPE

A NEW EDITION IN THREE VOLUMES

REVISED BY G. R. DENNIS, B.A. LOND.

WITH A MEMOIR BY

JOHN DENNIS

AUTHOR OF "STUDIES IN ENGLISH LITERATURE," EDITOR OF
"ENGLISH SONNETS : A SELECTION," ETC.

VOL. III.

LONDON

GEORGE BELL & SONS, YORK ST., COVENT GARDEN

AND NEW YORK

1891

CONTENTS.

MISCELLANEOUS POEMS.

MISCELLANEOUS POEMS.

EPIGRAMS FROM THE GRUB-STREET JOURNAL.[1]

I.

EPIGRAM

OCCASIONED BY SEEING SOME SHEETS OF DR. BENTLEY'S EDITION OF MILTON'S PARADISE LOST.

DID Milton's prose, O Charles, thy
    death defend ?
A furious foe unconscious proves a
    friend.
On Milton's verse does Bentley comment ?—
    Know
A weak officious friend becomes a foe.
While he but sought his Author's fame to
    further,
The murderous critic has avenged thy murder.

[1] The "Grub-Street Journal" was started in January, 1730, and continued weekly for eight years. Carruthers ("Life of Pope," p. 270) says : "Of this periodical Pope was long the animating and presiding spirit. Indeed it seems to have been set on foot for the purpose of enabling the poet to continue his war with the dunces." Although Pope in the Epistle to Arbuthnot (v. 378, note) denied that he had any connection with it, he certainly wrote constantly for it, under the signature " A."

II.

EPIGRAM.

SHOULD D——s [1] print, how once
you robbed your brother,
Traduced your monarch, and de-
bauched your mother;
Say, what revenge on D——s can be had;
Too dull for laughter, for reply too mad?
Of one so poor you cannot take the law;
On one so old your sword you scorn to draw.
Uncaged then let the harmless monster rage,
Secure in dulness, madness, want, and age.

III.

MR. J. M. S——E [2]

CATECHISED ON HIS ONE EPISTLE TO MR. POPE.

WHAT makes you write at this odd
rate?
Why, sir, it is to imitate.
What makes you steal and trifle so?
Why, 'tis to do as others do.
But there's no meaning to be seen.
Why, that's the very thing I mean.

---

[1] Dennis.   [2] James Moore-Smythe.

IV.

EPIGRAM

ON MR. M——RE'S GOING TO LAW WITH MR. GIL-
LIVER : INSCRIBED TO ATTORNEY TIBBALD.

NCE in his life M——re judges right ;
His sword and pen not worth a
straw,
An author that could never write,
A gentleman that dares not fight,
Has but one way to tease—by law.
This suit, dear Tibbald, kindly hatch ;
Thus thou may'st help the sneaking elf ;
And sure a printer is his match,
Who's but a publisher himself.

V.

EPIGRAM.

GOLD watch found on cinder whore,
Or a good verse on J——y M——e,
Proves but what either should con-
ceal.
Not that they're rich, but that they steal.

VI.

EPITAPH.

ERE lies what had nor birth, nor
shape, nor fame ;
No gentleman ! no man ! no-thing !
no name !
For Jamie ne'er grew James ; and what they call

More, shrunk to Smith—and Smith's no name
    at all.
Yet die thou canst not, phantom, oddly fated :
For how can no-thing be annihilated ?

Ex nihilo nihil fit.

VII.

A QUESTION BY ANONYMOUS.

ELL, if you can, which did the worse,
    Caligula or Gr—n's Gr—ce ?[1]
That made a Consul of a horse,
    And *this* a Laureate of an ass.

VIII.

EPIGRAM.

REAT G——[2] such servants since
    thou well canst lack,
Oh ! save the salary, and drink the
    sack.

IX.

EPIGRAM.

EHOLD ! ambitious of the British
    bays,
    Cibber and Duck[3] contend in rival
    lays.
But, gentle Colley, should thy verse prevail,

[1] Grafton's Grace, *i.e.* the Duke of Grafton.
[2] George II.
[3] Stephen Duck. See Imitations of Horace, Bk. ii.
Ep. ii. 140.

Thou hast no fence, alas ! against his flail :
Therefore thy claim resign, allow his right :
For Duck can thresh, you know, as well as
write.

ON MRS. TOFTS,

A CELEBRATED OPERA-SINGER.[1]

O bright is thy beauty, so charming
thy song,
As had drawn both the beasts and
their Orpheus along ;
But such is thy avarice, and such is thy pride,
That the beasts must have starved, and the
poets have died.

EPIGRAM.

OU beat your pate, and fancy wit will
come :
Knock as you please, there's nobody
at home.

[1] This lady, an Englishwoman, maintained her
ground against the Italian singers when the opera
was first introduced to this country. She had a strong
party in her favour, and one night, Feb. 5th, 1703-4,
her Italian rival, Francesca Margherita de l'Epine,
was hissed and pelted by Katharine Tofts' clamorous
admirers. Colley Cibber speaks warmly of the English singer's voice and personal attractions.—*Carruthers.*

EPITAPH.

ELL then, poor G—— [1] lies under-
ground !
So there's an end of honest Jack.
So little justice here he found,
'Tis ten to one he'll ne'er come back.

EPITAPH.

Joannes jacet hic Mirandula—cætera norunt
Et Tagus et Ganges—forsan et Antipodes.

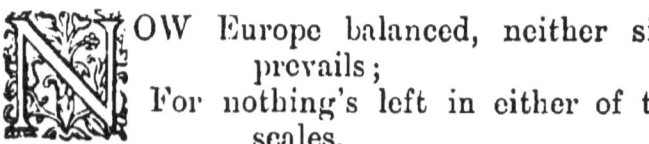ERE Francis C—— [2] lies. Be civil ;
The rest God knows—perhaps the
devil !

THE BALANCE OF EUROPE. [3]

OW Europe balanced, neither side
prevails ;
For nothing's left in either of the
scales.

[1] John Gay.—*Courthope.*
[2] Chartres. See Moral Essays, iii. 20. Spence
applied this epitaph to Coningsby, writing it: "Here
lies Lord Coningsby. Be civil ;" &c.
[3] Written in 1709.

TO A LADY WITH "THE TEMPLE OF FAME."[1]

WHAT'S fame with men, by custom
of the nation,
Is called in women only reputation;
About them both why keep we such
a pother?
Part you with one, and I'll renounce the other.

EPIGRAM

ON THE TOASTS OF THE KIT-CAT CLUB, ANNO 1716.

WHENCE deathless *Kit-Cat* took its
name,[2]
Few critics can unriddle;
Some say from Pastry-cook it came,
And some from Cat and Fiddle.

From no trim beaux its name it boasts,
Gray statesmen or green wits;
But from this pell-mell pack of toasts
Of old " Cats " and young " Kits."

---

[1] " I send you my Temple of Fame, which is just come out; but my sentiments about it you will see better by this epigram."—*Pope to Martha Blount*, 1714.

[2] The Kit-cat Club was formed in the year 1700, and named after Christopher Katt, a pastrycook in Shire-lane, near Temple-bar, at whose house the club met.

A DIALOGUE.

1717.

POPE.

SINCE my old friend is grown so
  great
 As to be Minister of State,
 I'm told, but 'tis not true, I hope,
That Craggs will be ashamed of Pope.

CRAGGS.

Alas! if I am such a creature
To grow the worse for growing greater;
Why, faith, in spite of all my brags,
'Tis Pope must be ashamed of Craggs.

ON DRAWINGS OF THE STATUES OF APOLLO, VENUS, AND HERCULES,

MADE FOR POPE BY SIR GODFREY KNELLER.

WHAT god, what genius, did the pencil
  move,
 When Kneller painted these?
'Twas friendship warm as Phœbus,
  kind as love,
 And strong as Hercules.

UPON THE DUKE OF MARLBOROUGH'S HOUSE AT WOODSTOCK.

"Atria longa patent : sed nec cœnantibus usquam,
Nec somno, locus est : quam bene non habitas."
MARTIAL, Epigr. xii. 50, vv. 7, 8.

EE, sir, here's the grand approach ;
This way is for his Grace's coach :
There lies the bridge, and here's the
    clock,
Observe the lion and the cock,
The spacious court, the colonnade,
And mark how wide the hall is made!
The chimneys are so well designed,
They never smoke in any wind.
This gallery's contrived for walking,
The windows to retire and talk in ;
The council chamber for debate,
And all the rest are rooms of state.
    Thanks, sir, cried I, 'tis very fine,
But where d'ye sleep, or where d'ye dine ?
I find, by all you have been telling,
That 'tis a house, but not a dwelling.

ON BEAUFORT HOUSE GATE AT CHISWICK.[1]

WAS brought from Chelsea last year,
    Battered with wind and weather;
    Inigo Jones put me together ;
    Sir Hans Sloane let me alone ;
Burlington brought me hither.

[1] Beaufort House, Chelsea, was pulled down in
1740, and the gateway, built by Inigo Jones, was
given by Sir Hans Sloane to the Earl of Burlington,
who removed it to his garden at Chiswick, where it
still stands.

ON A PICTURE OF QUEEN CAROLINE,

DRAWN BY LADY BURLINGTON.

EACE, flattering Bishop! lying
    Dean ![1]
This portrait only paints the Queen !

ON CERTAIN LADIES.

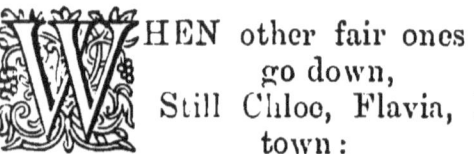HEN other fair ones to the shades
    go down,
    Still Chloe, Flavia, Delia, stay in
    town :
Those ghosts of beauty wandering here reside,
And haunt the places where their honour died.

CELIA.

ELIA, we know, is sixty-five,
    Yet Celia's face is seventeen ;
    Thus winter in her breast must live,
    While summer in her face is seen.

How cruel Celia's fate, who hence
    Our heart's devotion cannot try ;
Too pretty for our reverence,
    Too ancient for our gallantry !

[1] The Bishop was Gilbert; the Dean, Dr. Alured
Clarke, satirised in the Epilogue to the Satires.—
Carruthers.

EPIGRAM.

ENGRAVED ON THE COLLAR OF A DOG WHICH I GAVE TO HIS ROYAL HIGHNESS.[1]

 AM his Highness' dog at Kew;
Pray tell me, sir, whose dog are
you?[2]

INSCRIPTION ON A PUNCH-BOWL,

IN THE SOUTH-SEA YEAR, FOR A CLUB, CHASED WITH JUPITER PLACING CALLISTO IN THE SKIES, AND EUROPA WITH THE BULL.

OME, fill the South Sea goblet full;
The gods shall of our stock take
care;
Europa pleased accepts the *Bull*,
And Jove with joy puts off the *Bear*.

VERBATIM FROM BOILEAU.

Un Jour dit un Auteur, &c.

NCE (says an author; where, I need
not say)
Two travellers found an oyster in
their way;
Both fierce, both hungry, the dispute grew
strong,

[1] Frederick, Prince of Wales, father of George III.
[2] This is taken from Sir William Temple's Heads designed for an Essay on Conversation. " Mr. Grantam's fool's reply to a great man that asked whose fool he was,—'I am Mr. Grantam's fool—pray tell me whose fool are you?'"—*Roscoe.*

While scale in hand Dame Justice passed along.
Before her each with clamour pleads the laws,
Explained the matter, and would win the cause.
Dame Justice, weighing long the doubtful right,
Takes, opens, swallows it, before their sight.
The cause of strife removed so rarely well,
" There, take," says Justice, " take ye each a
    shell.
We thrive at Westminster on fools like you :
'Twas a fat oyster—live in peace—Adieu."

BISHOP HOUGH.[1]

 BISHOP, by his neighbours hated,
Has cause to wish himself translated ;
But why should Hough desire trans-
    lation,
Loved and esteemed by all the nation ?
Yet if it be the old man's case,
I'll lay my life I know the place :
'Tis where God sent some that adore him,
And whither Enoch went before him.

EPIGRAM.

 Y Lord[2] complains that Pope, stark
        mad with gardens,
    Has cut three trees, the value of three
        farthings.
" But he's my neighbour," cries the peer polite :
" And if he visit me, I'll waive the right."
What ! on compulsion, and against my will,
A lord's acquaintance ?   Let him file his bill !

[1] See Epilogue to Satires, ii. 240.
[2] Lord Radnor.—*Warton.*

EPIGRAM.[1]

ES! 'tis the time (I cried), impose
the chain,
Destined and due to wretches self-
enslaved;
But when I saw such charity remain,
I half could wish this people should be saved.
Faith lost, and Hope, our Charity begins;
And 'tis a wise design in pitying Heaven,
If this can cover multitude of sins,
To take the *only* way to be forgiven.

ANSWER TO THE FOLLOWING QUESTION OF MRS. HOWE.[2]

HAT is PRUDERY?
'Tis a beldam,
Seen with wit and beauty seldom,
'Tis a fear that starts at shadows,
'Tis (no, 'tisn't) like Miss Meadows.

[1] The Countess of Hertford, in a letter to the Countess of Pomfret, dated Feb. 20, 1740, says: "The severity of the weather has occasioned greater sums of money to be given in charity than was heard of before. Mr. Pope has written two stanzas on the occasion."

[2] Mary Howe, daughter of Viscount Howe and Maid of Honour to Princess Caroline. She married Lord Pembroke, and afterwards John Mordaunt, brother to the Earl of Peterborough.

"A prude would never have had any charms for Mr. Pope, to whom Mrs. Howe said one day, ' You men call us strange names; some of them I don't understand. Coquetry, indeed, I guess at; but *prudery*,—for Heaven's sake, make me know thoroughly what that prudery is.' Mr. Pope wrote her an answer in the leaf of an ivory book."—AYRE'S *Life of Pope*, vol. ii. p. 48.

'Tis a virgin hard of feature,
Old, and void of all good-nature ;
Lean and fretful, would seem wise ;
Yet plays the fool before she dies.
'Tis an ugly envious shrew,
That rails at dear Lepell, and you.[1]

ON A CERTAIN LADY AT COURT.[2]

 KNOW the thing that's most un-
        common ;
(Envy, be silent, and attend !)
I know a reasonable woman,
Handsome and witty, yet a friend.

Not warped by passion, awed by rumour,
Not grave through pride, or gay through folly,
An equal mixture of good humour,
And sensible soft melancholy.

" Has she no faults then (Envy says), sir ? "
Yes, she has one, I must aver ;
When all the world conspires to praise her,
The woman's deaf, and does not hear.

[1] Miss Meadows and Mary Lepell were also Maids
of Honour to Princess Caroline. See " The Challenge," vv. 6, 25.

[2] Mrs. Howard, afterwards Countess of Suffolk.

LINES TO LORD BATHURST.[1]

 WOOD !" quoth Lewis,[2] and with that
He laughed, and shook his sides of fat.
His tongue, with eye that marked his cunning,
Thus fell a-reasoning, not a-running ;
" Woods are—not to be too prolix—
Collective bodies of straight sticks.
It is, my Lord, a mere conundrum
To call things woods for what grows under 'em,
For shrubs, when nothing else at top is,
Can only constitute a coppice.
But if you will not take my word,
See anno quint. of Richard Third ;
And that's a coppice called, when docked,
Witness an. prim. of Harry Oct.
If this a wood you will maintain,
Merely because it is no plain,
Holland, for all that I can see,
May e'en as well be termed the sea,
Or C——by[3] be fair harangued
An honest man, because not hanged."

---

[1] Sent in a letter to Lord Bathurst, July 5, 1718, but first published by Mr. Mitford in his edition of Gray's correspondence (1843).

[2] Erasmus Lewis. See Imitations of Horace, Sat. i. 64.

[3] Thomas, the first Lord Coningsby, a zealous promoter of the Revolution of 1688.—*Carruthers.*

IMPROMPTU TO LADY WINCHILSEA.[1]

OCCASIONED BY FOUR SATIRICAL VERSES ON WOMEN WITS, IN THE RAPE OF THE LOCK.

N vain you boast poetic names of yore,
    And cite those Sapphos we admire
      no more :
    Fate doomed the fall of every female
wit ;
But doomed it then, when first Ardelia writ.
Of all examples by the world confessed,
I knew Ardelia could not quote the best ;
Who, like her mistress on Britannia's throne,
Fights and subdues in quarrels not her own.
To write their praise you but in vain essay ;
E'en while you write, you take that praise
    away :
Light to the stars the sun does thus restore,
But shines himself till they are seen no more.

OCCASIONED BY SOME VERSES OF HIS GRACE THE DUKE OF BUCKINGHAM.[2]

USE, 'tis enough ; at length thy labour
    ends,
    And thou shalt live, for Buckingham
    commends.
Let crowds of critics now my verse assail,

[1] Lady Winchilsea published a tragedy and a volume of poems, under the name of Ardelia.
[2] Complimenting Pope on his Iliad, and on his merit as a friend. For the Duke of Buckingham, see Essay on Criticism, v. 723.

Let Dennis write, and nameless numbers rail ;
This more than pays whole years of thankless
 pain :
Time, health, and fortune are not lost in vain.
Sheffield approves, consenting Phœbus bends,
And I and Malice from this hour are friends.

TO THE RIGHT HON. THE EARL OF OXFORD.[1]

UPON A PIECE OF NEWS IN MIST (MIST'S JOURNAL),
THAT THE REV. MR. W. REFUSED TO WRITE
AGAINST MR. POPE, BECAUSE HIS BEST PATRON
HAD A FRIENDSHIP FOR THE SAID P.

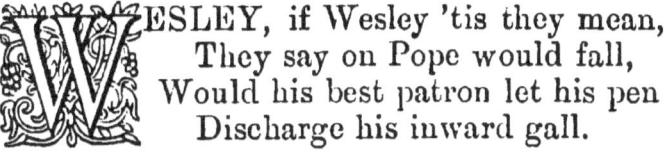ESLEY, if Wesley 'tis they mean,
 They say on Pope would fall,
 Would his best patron let his pen
 Discharge his inward gall.

What patron this, a doubt must be,
 Which none but you can clear,
Or father Francis 'cross the sea,
 Or else Earl Edward here.

That both were good must be confessed ;
 And much to both he owes ;
But which to Him will be the best,
 The Lord of Oxford knows.

---

[1] From Nichols's Literary Anecdotes; the allusions
are to the Rev. Samuel Wesley, and Francis Atterbury, Bishop of Rochester.

LINES IN EVELYN'S BOOK OF COINS.[1]

OM WOOD of Chiswick, deep divine,
To painter Kent gave all this coin.
'Tis the first coin, I'm bold to say,
That ever churchman gave to lay.

LINES ON SWIFT'S ANCESTORS.[2]

ONATHAN SWIFT
Had the gift,
By fatherige, motherige,
And by brotherige,
To come from Gotherige,
But now is spoiled clean
And an Irish Dean.
In this church he has put
A stone of two foot ;
With a cup and can, sir,
In respect to his grandsire ;
So, Ireland, change thy tone,
And cry, O hone ! O hone !
For England hath its own.

[1] Written in Evelyn's Book of Coins, given by Mr. Wood to Kent. Communicated to Notes and Queries, Mar. 13, 1851.

[2] " Swift put up a plain monument to his grandfather, and also presented a cup to the church of Goodrich, or Gotheridge (Herefordshire). He sent a pencilled elevation of the monument (a simple tablet) to Mrs. Howard, who returned it with the following lines inscribed on the drawing by Pope. The paper is indorsed, in Swift's hand, ' Model of a Monument for my grandfather, with Mr. Pope's roguery.' "— SCOTT's *Life of Swift*, p. 3.

LINES SUNG BY DURASTANTI WHEN SHE TOOK LEAVE OF THE ENGLISH STAGE.[1]

THE WORDS WERE IN HASTE PUT TOGETHER BY MR. POPE, AT THE REQUEST OF LORD PETER-BOROUGH.

ENEROUS, gay, and gallant nation,
    Bold in arms, and bright in arts;
    Land secure from all invasion,
      All but Cupid's gentle darts !
From your charms, oh who would run ?
Who would leave you for the sun ?
    Happy soil, adieu, adieu !

Let old charmers yield to new ;
    In arms, in arts, be still more shining ;
All your joys be still increasing ;
    All your tastes be still refining ;
All your jars for ever ceasing :
    But let old charmers yield to new.
    Happy soil, adieu, adieu !

ON THE COUNTESS OF BURLINGTON CUTTING PAPER.

ALLAS grew vapourish once, and
    odd,
    She would not do the least right
    thing,
Either for goddess, or for god,
    Nor work, nor play, nor paint, nor sing.

---

[1] Margarita Durastanti was brought to England by Handel in 1719, and retired in 1723.

Jove frowned, and, "Use," he cried, "those
  eyes
So skilful, and those hands so taper;
Do something exquisite and wise—"
She bowed, obeyed him,—and cut paper.

This vexing him who gave her birth,
  Thought by all heaven a burning shame;
What does she next, but bids, on earth,
  Her Burlington do just the same.

Pallas, you give yourself strange airs;
  But sure you'll find it hard to spoil
The sense and taste of one that bears
  The name of Saville and of Boyle.[1]

Alas! one bad example shown;
  How quickly all the sex pursue!
See, madam, see the arts o'erthrown,
  Between John Overton and you![2]

[1] Her maiden name was Lady Dorothy Saville.
She married Richard Boyle, Earl of Burlington, in
1721.
[2] We may conjecture that the Countess of Burlington had, in an absent mood, amused herself with
cutting to pieces one of the Sibylline leaves of paper
on which Pope had written some verses. Perhaps
John Overton, her servant, had been called to remove the litter, and hence had helped to "o'erthrow
the arts."—*Courthope.*

THE LOOKING-GLASS.

ON MRS. PULTENEY.[1]

WITH scornful mien, and various toss
    of air,
    Fantastic, vain, and insolently fair,
    Grandeur intoxicates her giddy brain,
She looks ambition, and she moves disdain.
Far other carriage graced her virgin life,
But charming G——y's lost in P——y's wife.
Not greater arrogance in him we find,
And this conjunction swells at least her mind:
O could the sire renowned in glass, produce
One faithful mirror for his daughter's use!
Wherein she might her haughty errors trace,
And by reflection learn to mend her face:
The wonted sweetness to her form restore,
Be what she was, and charm mankind once
    more!

ON RECEIVING FROM THE

RIGHT HON. THE LADY FRANCES SHIRLEY

A STANDISH AND TWO PENS.[2]

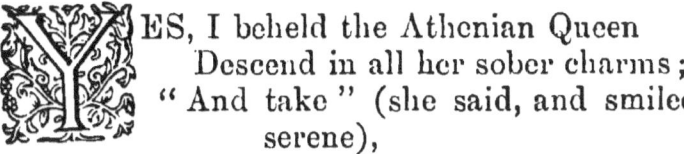

YES, I beheld the Athenian Queen
    Descend in all her sober charms;
    "And take" (she said, and smiled
    serene),
    "Take at this hand celestial arms:

[1] Mrs. Pulteney was the daughter of John Gumley,
a glass manufacturer at Isleworth.
[2] To enter into the spirit of this address, it is neces-

" Secure the radiant weapons wield ;
  This golden lance shall guard Desert,
And if a Vice dares keep the field,
  This steel shall stab it to the heart."

Awed, on my bended knees I fell,
  Received the weapons of the sky ;
And dipped them in the sable well,
  The fount of fame or infamy.

" What *well ?* what *weapons ?* " (Flavia cries)
  " A standish, steel and golden pen !
It came from Bertrand's,[1] not the skies ;
  I gave it you to write again.

" But, friend, take heed whom you attack ;
  You'll bring a House (I mean of Peers),
Red, blue, and green, nay white and black,
  L . . . . . and all about your ears.[2]

sary to premise that the poet was threatened with a
prosecution in the House of Lords for the two poems
entitled the Epilogue to the Satires ; on which, with
great resentment against his enemies for not being
willing to distinguish between

  " Grave Epistles bringing vice to light,"

and licentious libels, he began a *Third Dialogue*,
more severe and sublime than the first and second,
which being no secret, matters were soon compro-
mised. His enemies agreed to drop the prosecution,
and he promised to leave the Third Dialogue unfinished and suppressed. This affair occasioned this
little beautiful poem, to which it alludes throughout,
but more especially in the four last stanzas.—*Warburton.* Lady Frances Shirley was a daughter of
Earl Ferrers, who had at that time a house at
Twickenham. She died unmarried in 1762.—*Bowles.*
  [1] A toy-shop at Bath.
  [2] Lambeth would seem to be here meant. In the
Epilogue to the Satires, Dial. i. 120, Pope had

" You'd write as smooth again on glass,
   And run, on ivory, so glib,
As not to stick at fool or ass,
   Nor stop at flattery or fib.

" *Athenian Queen!* and *sober charms!*
   I tell ye, fool, there's nothing in't :
'Tis Venus, Venus gives these arms ;
   In Dryden's Virgil see the print.

" Come, if you'll be a quiet soul,
   That dares tell neither truth nor lies,
I'll list you in the harmless roll,
   Of those that sing of these poor eyes."

VERSES LEFT BY MR. POPE,

ON HIS LYING IN THE SAME BED WHICH WILMOT,
THE CELEBRATED EARL OF ROCHESTER, SLEPT IN
AT ADDERBURY, THEN BELONGING TO THE DUKE
OF ARGYLL, JULY 9, 1739.

ITH no poetic ardour fired
   I press the bed where Wilmot lay;
That here he loved, or here expired,
   Begets no numbers grave or gay.

Beneath thy roof, Argyll, are bred
   Such thoughts as prompt the brave to lie
Stretched out in honour's nobler bed,
   Beneath a nobler roof—the sky.

hazarded an allusion to a scandal, that the Archbishop of Canterbury had " pocketed " the will of
George I.—*Carruthers.*

Such flames as high in patriots burn,
Yet stoop to bless a child or wife;
And such as wicked kings may mourn,
When freedom is more dear than life.

ON SEEING THE LADIES AT CRUX-EASTON WALK IN THE WOODS BY THE GROTTO.[1]

EXTEMPORE BY MR. POPE.

UTHORS the world and their dull
brains have traced
To fix the ground where Paradise
was placed;
Mind not their learned whims and idle talk;
Here, here's the place where these bright angels
walk.

INSCRIPTION ON A GROTTO, THE WORK OF NINE LADIES.[2]

ERE, shunning idleness at once and
praise,
This radiant pile nine rural sisters
raise;
The glittering emblem of each spotless dame,
Clear as her soul and shining as her frame;
Beauty which nature only can impart,
And such a polish as disgraces art;
But fate disposed them in this humble sort,
And hid in deserts what would charm a Court.

[1] From "The Student," Oxford Miscellany, 1750.
[2] From Dodsley's Miscellany. The nine ladies
were sisters of Dr. Lisle, chaplain to the Factory at
Smyrna.

IMITATION OF TIBULLUS.[1]

Hic jacet immiti consumptus morte Tibullus,
Messalam, terra, dum sequiturque mari.

ERE, stopped by hasty death, Alexis lies,
　　Who crossed half Europe, led by Wortley's eyes.

IMITATION OF MARTIAL.[2]

T length my friend, while Time with still career
　　Wafts on his gentle wing his eightieth year,
Sees his past days safe out of Fortune's power,
Nor dreads approaching Fate's uncertain hour;
Reviews his life, and in the strict survey
Finds not one moment he could wish away,
Pleased with the series of each happy day.

[1] Pope, in a letter to Lady Mary Wortley Montagu, Nov. 10, 1716, expressed a desire to travel abroad to meet her; " But if my fate be such," he says, "that this body of mine be left behind in the journey, let this epitaph of Tibullus be set over it." (Tibullus i. 4, 55-6).

[2] Sir William Trumbull, Jan. 19, 1716, writes to Pope : " On occasion of my being obliged to congratulate the birthday of a friend of mine, finding I had no materials of my own, I very frankly sent him your imitation of Martial's epigram on Antonius Primus, *Jam numerat placido felix Antonius ævo*, &c." (Martial x. 23.)

Such, such a man extends his life's short space,
And from the goal again renews the race ;
For he lives twice, who can at once employ
The present well, and ev'n the past enjoy.

THE TRANSLATOR.

ZELL, at Sanger's[1] call, invoked his
   Muse—
For who to sing for Sanger could
   refuse ?
His numbers such as Sanger's self might use.
Reviving Perrault, murdering Boileau, he
Slandered the ancients first, then Wycherley ;
Which yet not much that old bard's anger
   raised,
Since those were slandered most, whom Ozell
   praised.
Nor had the gentle satire caused complaining,
Had not sage Rowe pronounced it entertaining :
How great must be the judgment of that writer
Who the *Plain-Dealer* damns, and prints the
   Biter ! "[2]

[1] Sanger served his apprenticeship with Jacob Tonson, and succeeded Bernard Lintot in his shop at the Middle Temple Gate, Fleet Street. Lintot printed Ozell's translation of Perrault's Characters, and Sanger his translation of Boileau's Lutrin, which was recommended by Rowe in 1709.—*Warton.* See Dunciad, i. 286.

[2] The " Plain-Dealer " was the most popular of Wycherley's comedies ; the " Biter " an inferior play by Rowe.

THE THREE GENTLE SHEPHERDS.[1]

OF gentle Philips will I ever sing,
With gentle Philips shall the valleys
ring.
My numbers too for ever will I vary,
With gentle Budgell and with gentle Carey.
Or if in ranging of the names I judge ill,
With gentle Carey and with gentle Budgell:
Oh! may all gentle bards together place ye,
Men of good hearts, and men of delicacy.
May satire ne'er befool ye, or beknave ye,
And from all wits that have a knack, God save
ye.

MACER: A CHARACTER.[2]

WHEN simple Macer, now of high re-
nown,
First sought a poet's fortune in the
town,
'Twas all the ambition his high soul could feel,
To wear red stockings, and to dine with Steele.
Some ends of verse his betters might afford,
And gave the harmless fellow a good word.
Set up with these he ventured on the town,
And with a borrowed play, out-did poor Crown.[3]

---

[1] Two of the shepherds are well enough known.
The third would seem to be Henry Carey, the
dramatist (author of "Sally in our Alley"); but
there was also a John Carey, of New College, Oxford,
a contributor to the Tatler and Spectator, and Walter
Carey (Umbra).—*Carruthers.*

[2] The person satirised is Ambrose Philips (1671-
1749).

[3] The borrowed play refers to Philips' "The Dis-

There he stopped short, nor since has writ a tittle,
But has the wit to make the most of little :
Like stunted hide-bound trees, that just have got
Sufficient sap at once to bear and rot.
Now he begs verse, and what he gets com-
    mends,
Not of the wits his foes, but fools his friends.
  So some coarse country wench, almost de-
    cayed,
Trudges to town, and first turns chambermaid ;
Awkward and supple, each devoir to pay ;
She flatters her good lady twice a-day ;
Thought wondrous honest, though of mean
    degree,
And strangely liked for her simplicity :
In a translated suit, then tries the town,
With borrowed pins, and patches not her own :
But just endured the winter she began,
And in four months a battered harridan.
Now nothing left, but withered, pale, and
    shrunk,
To bawd for others, and go shares with Punk.

UMBRA.[1]

LOSE to the best known author
    Umbra sits,
    The constant index to all Button's
    wits.
" Who's here ? " cries Umbra : " only John-
    son," [2]—" Oh !

trest Mother," founded on Racine's Andromaque.
John Crowne, a prolific dramatist, died about 1705.
  [1] Walter Carey, Warden of the Mint, and Clerk of
the Privy Council.
  [2] Charles Johnson, a second-rate dramatist.—
Bowles.

Your slave," and exit; but returns with Rowe:
" Dear Rowe, let's sit and talk of tragedies:"
Ere long Pope enters, and to Pope he flies.
Then up comes Steele: he turns upon his
     heel,
And in a moment fastens upon Steele;
But cries as soon, " Dear Dick, I must be gone,
For, if I know his tread, here's Addison."
Says Addison to Steele, " 'Tis time to go:"
Pope to the closet steps aside with Rowe.
Poor Umbra, left in this abandoned pickle,
E'en sits him down, and writes to honest
     T——.[1]
Fool ! 'tis in vain from wit to wit to roam;
Know, sense, like charity begins at home.

SYLVIA, A FRAGMENT.[2]

YLVIA, my heart in wondrous wise
     alarmed,
     Awed without sense, and without
     beauty charmed:
But some odd graces and some flights she had,
Was just not ugly, and was just not mad:
Her tongue still ran on credit from her eyes,
More pert than witty, more a wit than wise:
Good-nature, she declared it, was her scorn,
Though 'twas by that alone she could be borne:
Affronting all, yet fond of a good name;
A fool to pleasure, yet a slave to fame:
Now coy, and studious in no point to fall,

_____

[1] Tickell.
[2] Introduced, with some alterations, into the Second
of the Moral Epistles, *Of the Characters of Women.*

Now all agog for D——y [1] at a ball:
Now deep in Taylor, and the Book of Martyrs,
Now drinking citron with his Grace and
　　Chartres,[2]
Men, some to business, some to pleasure take;
But every woman is at heart a rake.
Frail, feverish sex; their fit now chills, now
　　burns:
Atheism and superstition rule by turns;
And a mere heathen in her carnal part,
Is still a sad good Christian at her heart.

THE BASSET-TABLE.[3]

AN ECLOGUE.

CARDELIA, SMILINDA.

CARDELIA.

THE Basset-table spread, the tallier
　　come;
　　Why stays Smilinda in the dress-
　　ing-room?
Rise, pensive nymph, the tallier waits for you:

SMILINDA.

Ah, madam, since my Sharper is untrue,
I joyless make my once adored alpeu.

[1] Colonel Disney.—*Carruthers.*
[2] For the Duke of Wharton and Chartres, see
Moral Essays, i. 179, iii. 20, &c.
[3] One of the "Town Eclogues," published anonymously in 1716. They were parodies on the Pastorals
of Pope and Philips, and were written, with the exception of the " Basset Table," by Lady M. W. Montagu. Basset was a card game resembling the modern
" Faro."

I saw him stand behind Ombrelia's chair,
And whisper with that soft deluding air,
And those feigned sighs which cheat the
    listening fair.

CARDELIA.

Is this the cause of your romantic strains?
A mightier grief my heavy heart sustains :
As you by love, so I by fortune crossed ;
One, one bad deal, three septlevas have lost.

SMILINDA.

Is that the grief which you compare with mine?
With ease the smiles of fortune I resign :
Would all my gold in one bad deal were gone,
Were lovely Sharper mine, and mine alone.

CARDELIA.

A lover lost, is but a common care ;
And prudent nymphs against that change pre-
    pare :
The Knave of Clubs thrice lost ; oh ! who could
    guess
This fatal stroke, this unforeseen distress ?

SMILINDA.

See Betty Lovet ! very *à propos*,
She all the cares of love and play does know :
Dear Betty shall the important point decide;
Betty ! who oft the pain of each has tried ;
Impartial, she shall say who suffers most,
By cards' ill usage, or by lovers lost.

LOVET.

Tell, tell your griefs ; attentive will I stay,
Though time is precious, and I want some tea.

III.   D

CARDELIA.

Behold this equipage, by Mathers wrought,
With fifty guineas (a great pen'worth) bought.
See, on the toothpick, Mars and Cupid strive,
And both the struggling figures seem alive.
Upon the bottom shines the Queen's bright
 face;
A myrtle foliage round the thimble-case.
Jove, Jove himself, does on the scissors shine:
The metal, and the workmanship, divine!

SMILINDA.

This snuff-box—once the pledge of Sharper's
 love,
When rival beauties for the present strove;
At Corticelli's he the raffle won;
Then first his passion was in public shown:
Hazardia blushed, and turned her head aside,
A rival's envy (all in vain) to hide.
This snuff-box—on the hinge see brilliants
 shine;
This snuff-box will I stake; the prize is mine.

CARDELIA.

Alas! far lesser losses than I bear,
Have made a soldier sigh, a lover swear.
And oh! what makes the disappointment hard,
'Twas my own lord that drew the fatal card.
In complaisance I took the Queen he gave,
Though my own secret wish was for the
 Knave:
The Knave won sonica, which I had chose,
And, the next pull, my septleva I lose.

SMILINDA.

But ah! what aggravates the killing smart,
The cruel thought, that stabs me to the heart;

This cursed Ombrelia, this undoing fair,
By whose vile arts this heavy grief I bear ;
She, at whose name I shed these spiteful tears,
She owes to me the very charms she wears.
An awkward thing, when first she came to
    town ;
Her shape unfashioned, and her face unknown :
She was my friend ; I taught her first to
    spread
Upon her sallow cheeks enlivening red ;
I introduced her to the park and plays ;
And, by my interest, Cozens made her stays.
Ungrateful wretch, with mimic airs grown
    pert,
She dares to steal my favourite lover's heart.

CARDELIA.

Wretch that I was, how often have I swore,
When Winnall tallied, I would punt no more !
I know the bite, yet to my ruin run ;
And see the folly, which I cannot shun.

SMILINDA.

How many maids have Sharper's vows de-
    ceived ?
How many cursed the moment they believed ?
Yet his known falsehoods could no warning
    prove ;
Ah ! what is warning to a maid in love ?

CARDELIA.

But of what marble must that breast be
    formed,
To gaze on Basset, and remain unwarmed ?
When Kings, Queens, Knaves, are set in decent
    rank ;
Exposed in glorious heaps the tempting bank,

Guineas, half-guineas, all the shining train,
The winner's pleasure, and the loser's pain;
In bright confusion open rouleaux lie,
They strike the soul, and glitter in the eye.
Fired by the sight, all reason I disdain;
My passions rise, and will not bear the rein.
Look upon Basset, you who reason boast,
And see if reason must not there be lost.

SMILINDA.

What more than marble must that heart
    compose,
Can hearken coldly to my Sharper's vows?
Then, when he trembles! when his blushes rise!
When awful Love seems melting in his eyes!
With eager beats his Mechlin cravat moves:
"He loves,"—I whisper to myself, "He loves!"
Such unfeigned passion in his looks appears,
I lose all memory of my former fears;
My panting heart confesses all his charms,
I yield at once, and sink into his arms;
Think of that moment, you who prudence
    boast;
For such a moment, prudence well were lost.

CARDELIA.

At the Groom-Porter's, battered bullies play,
Some dukes at Mary-bone bowl time away;
But who the bowl or rattling dice compares
To Basset's heavenly joys, and pleasing cares?

SMILINDA.

Soft Simplicetta dotes upon a beau;
Prudina likes a man, and laughs at show.
Their several graces in my Sharper meet;
Strong as the footman, as the master sweet.

LOVET.

Cease your contention, which has been too
   long ;
I grow impatient, and the tea's too strong.
Attend, and yield to what I now decide ;
The equipage shall grace Smilinda's side ;
The snuffbox to Cardelia I decree,
Now leave complaining, and begin your tea.

THE CHALLENGE.

A COURT BALLAD.

To the tune of " To all you Ladies now at Land," &c.
[By Dorset.]

WRITTEN ANNO 1717.

I.

O one fair lady out of Court,
      And two fair ladies in,
   Who think the Turk[1] and Pope[2] a
         sport,
   And wit and love no sin !
Come, these soft lines, with nothing stiff in,
To Bellenden, Lepell, and Griffin.[3]
      With a fa, la, la.

II.

What passes in the dark third row,
   And what behind the scene,

[1] Ulric, the little Turk.—*Curll.*
[2] The author.—*Curll.*
[3] Ladies of the Court of Princess Caroline.—*Curll.*
Mary Bellenden married Colonel Campbell (afterwards
Duke of Argyll). Mary Lepell afterwards married
Lord Hervey. Miss Griffin was sister to Lady Rich
mentioned below (stanza vii.).

Conches and crippled chairs I know,
  And garrets hung with green ;
I know the swing of sinful hack,
Where many damsels cry alack.
      With a fa, la, la.

III.

Then why to Courts should I repair,
  Where's such ado with Townshend ? [1]
To hear each mortal stamp and swear,
  And every speech with " Zounds " end ;
To hear them rail at honest Sunderland,[2]
And rashly blame the realm of Blunderland.[3]
      With a fa, la, la.

IV.

Alas ! like Schutz I cannot pun,[4]
  Like Grafton [5] court the Germans ;
Tell Pickenbourg [6] how slim she's grown,
  Like Meadows run to sermons ;
To court ambitious men may roam,
But I and Marlbro' stay at home.
      With a fa, la, la.

V.

In truth, by what I can discern,
  Of courtiers, 'twixt you three,
Some wit you have, and more may learn
  From Court, than Gay or me :

---

[1] Lord Townshend, Secretary of State, was dismissed in 1716.
[2] The Earl of Sunderland, Lord-Lieutenant of Ireland.
[3] Ireland.—*Curll*.
[4] Augustus Schutz, Equerry to Prince George. See Imitations of Horace, Bk. i. Ep. i. 112.
[5] Charles, second Duke of Grafton.
[6] Pickenbourg and Meadows were Maids of Honour.

Perhaps, in time, you'll leave high diet,
To sup with us on milk and quiet.
   With a fa, la, la.

VI.

At Leicester Fields, a house full high,[1]
  With door all painted green,
Where ribbons wave upon the tie,
  (A milliner, I mean ;)
There may you meet us three to three,
For Gay can well make two of me.[2]
   With a fa, la, la.

VII.

But should you catch the prudish itch,
  And each become a coward,
Bring sometimes with you Lady Rich,[3]
  And sometimes Mistress Howard ;[4]
For virgins, to keep chaste, must go
Abroad with such as are not so.
   With a fa, la, la.

VIII.

And thus, fair maids, my ballad ends :
  God send the King safe landing ;[5]
And make all honest ladies friends
  To armies that are standing ;
Preserve the limits of these nations,
And take off ladies' limitations.
   With a fa, la, la.

[1] Leicester House, the residence of the Prince of Wales.
[2] Gay was a large, stout man.
[3] Lady Rich, wife of Sir Robert Rich, a correspondent of Lady Mary Wortley Montagu.
[4] Mrs. Howard, afterwards Countess of Suffolk. See Moral Essays, ii. 157.
[5] This ballad was written anno 1717.

SONG,

BY A PERSON OF QUALITY.

WRITTEN IN THE YEAR 1733.

I.

FLUTTERING spread thy purple
　　pinions,
　　Gentle *Cupid*, o'er my heart;
　　I a slave in thy dominions;
Nature must give way to art.

II.

Mild *Arcadians*, ever blooming,
　　Nightly nodding o'er your flocks,
See my weary days consuming,
　　All beneath yon flowery rocks.

III.

Thus the *Cyprian* goddess, weeping,
　　Mourned *Adonis*, darling youth:
Him the boar, in silence creeping,
　　Gored with unrelenting tooth.

IV.

Cynthia, tune harmonious numbers;
　　Fair *Discretion*, string the lyre;
Soothe my ever-waking slumbers;
　　Bright *Apollo*, lend thy choir.

V.

Gloomy *Pluto*, king of terrors,
　　Armed in adamantine chains,
Lead me to the crystal mirrors,
　　Watering soft Elysian plains.

VI.

Mournful cypress, verdant willow,
Gilding my *Aurelia's* brows,
Morpheus hovering o'er my pillow,
Hear me pay my dying vows.

VII.

Melancholy smooth *Mæander*,
Swiftly purling in a round,
On thy margin lovers wander,
With thy flowery chaplets crowned.

VIII.

Thus when *Philomela*, drooping,
Softly seeks her silent mate,
See the bird of *Juno* stooping ;
Melody resigns to fate.

SANDYS' GHOST;

OR,

A PROPER NEW BALLAD ON THE NEW OVID'S METAMORPHOSES,

AS IT WAS INTENDED TO BE TRANSLATED BY PERSONS OF QUALITY.[1]

E Lords and Commons, men of wit,
And pleasure about town ;
Read this ere you translate one bit
Of books of high renown.

[1] In 1718 Sir Samuel Garth undertook an edition of Ovid's Metamorphoses, translated by several hands : he himself translated the fourteenth and part of the fifteenth books. Sandys' translation of the Metamorphoses was published in 1626.

Beware of Latin authors all!
  Nor think your verses sterling,
Though with a golden pen you scrawl,
  And scribble in a Berlin:

For not the desk with silver nails,
  Nor bureau of expense,
Nor standish well japanned avails
  To writing of good sense.

Hear how a ghost in dead of night,
  With saucer eyes of fire,
In woeful wise did sore affright
  A wit and courtly 'squire.

Rare imp of Phœbus, hopeful youth
  Like puppy tame that uses
To fetch and carry, in his mouth,
  The works of all the Muses.

Ah! why did he write poetry,
  That hereto was so civil;
And sell his soul for vanity,
  To rhyming and the Devil?

A desk he had of curious work,
  With glittering studs about;
Within the same did Sandys lurk,
  Though Ovid lay without.

Now as he scratched to fetch up thought,
  Forth popped the sprite so thin;
And from the key-hole bolted out,
  All upright as a pin.

With whiskers, band, and pantaloon,
  And ruff composed most duly;
This 'squire he dropped his pen full soon,
  While as the light burnt bluely.

" Ho ! Master Sam," quoth Sandys' sprite,
  " Write on, nor let me scare ye ;
Forsooth, if rhymes fall in not right,
  To Budgell seek, or Carey.[1]

" I hear the beat of Jacob's drums,[2]
  Poor Ovid finds no quarter !
See first the merry P—— comes [3]
  In haste, without his garter.

" Then lords and lordlings, 'squires and knights,
  Wits, witlings, prigs, and peers !
Garth at St. James's, and at White's,
  Beats up for volunteers.

" What Fenton will not do, nor Gay,
  Nor Congreve, Rowe, nor Stanyan,
Tom B——t [4] or Tom D'Urfey may,
  John Dunton,[5] Steele, or any one.

" If Justice Philips'[6] costive head
  Some frigid rhymes disburses ;
They shall like Persian Tales be read,
  And glad both babes and nurses.

" Let W—rw—k's muse with Ash—t join,[7]
  And Ozell's with Lord Hervey's :

[1] Eustace Budgell (see Dunciad, ii. 397) and Walter Carey.
[2] Jacob Tonson, the publisher.
[3] The Earl of Pembroke.
[4] Tom Burnet, son of the bishop, one of the authors of " Homerides." See Dunciad, iii. 179.
[5] John Dunton, the bookseller. See Dunciad, ii. 144.
[6] Ambrose Philips was made Registrar (*not* Judge) of the Prerogative Court in Ireland by Bishop Boulter. (See Johnson's Lives of the Poets, ed. Napier, vol. iii. p. 259.) He translated the " Persian Tales " from the French in 1709.
[7] Lord Warwick and Dr. Ashurst.—*Carruthers.*

Tickell and Addison combine,
  And P—pe translate with Jervas.

" L—— himself, that lively lord,¹
  Who bows to every lady,
Shall join with F——² in one accord,
  And be like Tate and Brady.

" Ye ladies too draw forth your pen,
  I pray where can the hurt lie?
Since you have brains as well as men,
  As witness Lady W—l—y.³

" Now Tonson, list thy forces all,
  Review them, and tell Noses;
For to poor Ovid shall befall
  A strange metamorphosis.

" A metamorphosis more strange
  Than all his books can vapour; "
" To   what "   (quoth   'squire)   " shall   Ovid
      change ? "
  Quoth Sandys : " To waste paper."

A FAREWELL TO LONDON.

IN THE YEAR 1715.

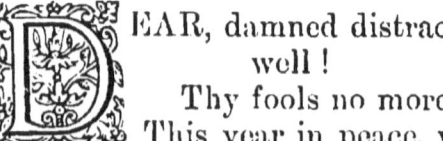EAR, damned distracting town, fare-
      well !
      Thy fools no more I'll tease :
  This year in peace, ye critics, dwell,
  Ye harlots, sleep at ease !

¹ Lord Lansdowne.—*Carruthers.*
 ² Philip Frowde, a dramatic writer and fine scholar.
—*Carruthers.*
 ³ Lady Mary Wortley Montagu.

Soft B——[1] and rough C——s[2] adieu,
   Earl Warwick make your moan,
The lively H——k[3] and you
   May knock up whores alone.

To drink and droll be Rowe allowed
   Till the third watchman's toll ;
Let Jervas gratis paint, and Frowde
   Save three-pence and his soul.

Farewell, Arbuthnot's raillery
   On every learned sot ;
And Garth, the best good Christian he,
   Although he knows it not.   ·

Lintot, farewell ! thy bard must go ;
   Farewell, unhappy Tonson !
Heaven gives thee for thy loss of Rowe,[4]
   Lean Philips, and fat Johnson.[5]

Why should I stay ? Both parties rage ;
   My vixen mistress squalls ;
The wits in envious feuds engage :
   And Homer (damn him !) calls.

The love of arts lies cold and dead
   In Halifax's urn :[6]

[1] Perhaps " Brocas."—*Courthope.*
[2] Craggs.
[3] Lord Hinchinbroke. He was a colonel and a member of Parliament.
[4] Rowe had the year before, on the accession of George I., been made Poet Laureate, one of the land-surveyors of the port of London, Clerk of the Closet to the Prince of Wales, and Secretary of Presentations under the Lord Chancellor. Such an accumulation of offices might well suspend for a season the poetical and publishing pursuits of Rowe.—*Carruthers.*
[5] Charles Johnson, the dramatist. See *Umbra*, v. 3.
[6] Halifax died May 19, 1715.

And not one Muse of all he fed
　　Has yet the grace to mourn.

My friends, by turns, my friends confound,
　　Betray, and are betrayed :
Poor Y——r's sold for fifty pound,
　　And B——ll is a jade.[1]

Why make I friendships with the great,
　　When I no favour seek ?
Or follow girls, seven hours in eight ?
　　I used but once a week.

Still idle, with a busy air,
　　Deep whimsies to contrive ;
The gayest valetudinaire,
　　Most thinking rake, alive.

Solicitous for others' ends,
　　Though fond of dear repose ;
Careless or drowsy with my friends,
　　And frolic with my foes.

Luxurious lobster-nights, farewell,
　　For sober, studious days !
And Burlington's delicious meal,
　　For salads, tarts, and pease !

Adieu to all, but Gay alone,
　　Whose soul, sincere and free,
Loves all mankind, but flatters none,
　　And so may starve with me.

---

[1] Miss Younger and her sister Mrs. Bicknell. They were actresses, and friends of Pope.

TO LADY MARY WORTLEY MONTAGU.[1]

I.

IN beauty, or wit,
    No mortal as yet
To question your empire has dared :
    But men of discerning
    Have thought that in learning,
To yield to a lady was hard.

II.

Impertinent schools,
    With musty dull rules,
Have reading to females denied ;
    So Papists refuse
    The Bible to use,
Lest flocks should be wise as their guide.

III.

'Twas a woman at first
    (Indeed she was cursed)
In knowledge that tasted delight,
    And sages agree
    The laws should decree
To the first possessor the right.

IV.

Then bravely, fair dame,
    Resume the old claim,
Which to your whole sex does belong ;
    And let men receive,
    From a second bright Eve,
The knowledge of right and of wrong.

[1] First published in 1720 in Hammond's Miscellany.

V.

But if the first Eve
Hard doom did receive,
When only one apple had she,
What a punishment new
Shall be found out for you,
Who tasting, have robbed the whole tree ?

EXTEMPORANEOUS LINES,

ON THE PICTURE OF LADY MARY W. MONTAGU,
BY KNELLER.

HE playful smiles around the dimpled
    mouth,
    That happy air of majesty and truth ;
    So would I draw (but oh ! 'tis vain
    to try,
My narrow genius does the power deny ;)
The equal lustre of the heavenly mind,
Where every grace with every virtue's joined ;
Learning not vain, and wisdom not severe,
With greatness easy, and with wit sincere ;
With just description show the work divine,
And the whole princess in my work should shine.

TO MR. GAY,

WHO HAD CONGRATULATED MR. POPE ON FINISHING
HIS HOUSE AND GARDENS.

H, friend ! 'tis true—this truth you
    lovers know—
    In vain my structures rise, my
    gardens grow ;
In vain fair Thames reflects the double scenes

Of hanging mountains, and of sloping greens :
Joy lives not here,—to happier seats it flies,
And only dwells where Wortley casts her eyes.
What are the gay parterre, the chequered shade,
The morning bower, the evening colonnade,
But soft recesses of uneasy minds,
To sigh unheard in, to the passing winds ?
So the struck deer in some sequestered part
Lies down to die, the arrow at his heart ;
He, stretched unseen in coverts hid from day,
Bleeds drop by drop, and pants his life away.

TO MRS. M. B. ON HER BIRTHDAY.[1]

1723.

H be thou blest with all that Heaven
  can send,
  Long health, long youth, long plea-
  sure, and a friend :
Not with those toys the female world admire,
Riches that vex, and vanities that tire.
With added years, if life bring nothing new,

[1] This poem, first published in 1726, was also altered
to form an epitaph on Henry Mordaunt, nephew of
the Earl of Peterborough, who committed suicide in
1724. The first four lines ran as above, and the
remainder of the epitaph was as follows :

If added days of life bring nothing new,
But, like a sieve, let every pleasure through,
Some joy still lost, as each vain year runs o'er,
And all we gain, some pensive notion more ;
Is this a birthday ? ah, 'tis sadly clear,
'Tis but the funeral of the former year.
If there's no hope with kind, though fainter ray,
To gild the evening of our future day ;
If every page of life's long volume tell
The same dull story—Mordaunt ! thou didst well.

But, like a sieve, let every blessing through,
Some joy still lost, as each vain year ruus
   o'er,
And all we gain, some sad reflection more ;
Is that a birthday ? 'tis alas ! too clear,
'Tis but the funeral of the former year.
   Let joy or ease, let affluence or content,
And the gay conscience of a life well spent,
Calm every thought, inspirit every grace,
Glow in thy heart, and smile upon thy face.
Let day improve on day, and year on year,
Without a pain, a trouble, or a fear ;
Till death unfelt that tender frame destroy,
In some soft dream, or extasy of joy,
Peaceful sleep out the Sabbath of the tomb,
And wake to raptures in a life to come.

TO MR. THOMAS SOUTHERN,[1]

ON HIS BIRTHDAY, 1742.

RESIGNED to live, prepared to die,
   With not one sin but poetry,
   This day Tom's fair account has run
   (Without a blot) to eighty-one.
Kind Boyle, before his poet, lays
A table, with a cloth of bays ;[2]
And Ireland, mother of sweet singers,
Presents her harp still to his fingers.[3]

[1] Thomas Southern, the dramatist, born 1660, died 1746.

[2] He was invited to dine on his birthday with this nobleman, Lord Orrery, who had prepared for him the entertainment of which the bill of fare is here set down.—*Warburton.*

[3] The harp is generally wove on the Irish linen, such as table-cloths, &c.—*Warburton.*

The feast, his towering genius marks
In yonder wild goose and the larks !
The mushrooms show his wit was sudden !
And for his judgment, lo a pudden !
Roast beef, though old, proclaims him stout,
And grace, although a bard, devout.
May Tom, whom Heaven sent down to raise
The price of prologues and of plays,[1]
Be every birthday more a winner,
Digest his thirty-thousandth dinner ;
Walk to his grave without reproach,
And scorn a rascal and a coach.

TO MR. JOHN MOORE,[2]

AUTHOR OF THE CELEBRATED WORM-POWDER.

OW much, egregious Moore, are we
Deceived by shows and forms !
Whate'er we think, whate'er we see,
All humankind are worms.

Man is a very worm by birth,
Vile reptile, weak and vain :
Awhile he crawls upon the earth,
Then shrinks to earth again.

---

[1] This alludes to a story Mr. Southern told of Dryden, about the same time, to Mr. P. and Mr. W. When Southern first wrote for the stage, Dryden was so famous for his prologues, that the players would act nothing without that decoration. His usual price till then had been four guineas ; but when Southern came to him for the prologue he had bespoke, Dryden told him he must have six guineas for it; "which," said he, "young man, is out of no disrespect to you ; but the players have had my goods too cheap."—*Warburton.*

[2] First published, anonymously, in 1716.

That woman is a worm—we find
  E'er since our grandam's evil;
She first conversed with her own kind,
  That ancient worm, the Devil.

The learned themselves we book-worms name,
  The blockhead is a slow-worm;
The nymph whose tail is all on flame,
  Is aptly termed a glow-worm.

The fops are painted butterflies,
  That flutter for a day;
First from a worm they take their rise,
  And in a worm decay.

The flatterer an ear-wig grows;
  Thus worms suit all conditions;
Misers are muck-worms, silk-worms beaux,
  And death-watches physicians.

That statesmen have the worm, is seen
  By all their winding play;
Their conscience is a worm within,
  That gnaws them night and day.

Ah Moore! thy skill were well employed,
  And greater gain would rise,
If thou could'st make the courtier void
  The worm that never dies!

O learned friend of Abchurch-lane,
  Who sett'st our entrails free;
Vain is thy art, thy powder vain,
  Since worms shall eat ev'n thee.

Our fate thou only canst adjourn
  Some few short years, no more!
Ev'n Button's wits to worms shall turn,
  Who maggots were before.

VERSES TO MR. C.

ST. JAMES'S PLACE.[1]

LONDON, OCT. 22.

EW words are best; I wish you well:
Bethel, I'm told, will soon be here;
Some morning walks along the Mall,
And evening friends, will end the
year.

If, in this interval, between
The falling leaf and coming frost,
You please to see, on Twit'nam green,
Your friend, your poet, and your host :

For three whole days you here may rest
From office business, news and strife;
And (what most folks would think a jest)
Want nothing else, except your wife.

LINES WRITTEN IN WINDSOR FOREST.[2]

LL hail, once pleasing, once inspiring
shade !
Scene of my youthful loves and
happier hours !
Where the kind Muses met me as I strayed,

---

[1] Mr. Cleland, whose residence was in St. James's-place, where he died in 1741. – *Carruthers.*
[2] Sent in an undated letter to Martha Blount.

And gently pressed my hand, and said " Be
　　ours !—
Take all thou e'er shalt have, a constant Muse:
　At Court thou may'st be liked, but nothing
　　gain :
Stock thou may'st buy and sell, but always lose,
　And love the brightest eyes, but love in vain."

ON HIS GROTTO AT TWICKENHAM,

COMPOSED OF MARBLES, SPARS, GEMS, ORES, AND MINERALS.[1]

HOU who shalt stop, where Thames'
　　　　translucent wave
　　　Shines a broad mirror through the
　　　　shadowy cave ;
Where lingering drops from mineral roofs
　　distill,
And pointed crystals break the sparkling rill,
Unpolished gems no ray on pride bestow,
And latent metals innocently glow :
Approach !　Great Nature studiously behold ;
And eye the mine without a wish for gold.
Approach : but awful !　Lo ! the Egerian grot,
Where, nobly-pensive, St. John sat and thought;
Where British sighs from dying Wyndham stole,
And the bright flame was shot through March-
　　mont's soul.
Let such, such only tread this sacred floor,
Who dare to love their country, and be poor.

----

[1] Sent in a letter to Bolingbroke, September 3,
1740.

TO THE AUTHOR OF A POEM
ENTITLED " SUCCESSIO." [1]

BEGONE, ye critics, and restrain your
  spite,
Codrus writes on, and will for ever
  write.
The heaviest Muse the swiftest course has gone,
As clocks run fastest when most lead is on ;
What though no bees around your cradle flew,
Nor on your lips distilled their golden dew ;
Yet have we oft discovered in their stead
A swarm of drones that buzzed about your head.
When you, like Orpheus, strike the warbling
  lyre,
Attentive blocks stand round you and admire.
Wit passed through thee no longer is the same,
As meat digested takes a different name :
But sense must sure thy safest plunder be,
Since no reprisals can be made on thee.
Thus thou may'st rise, and in thy daring flight
(Though ne'er so weighty) reach a wondrous
  height.
So, forced from engines, lead itself can fly,
And ponderous slugs move nimbly through the
  sky.
Sure Bavius copied Mævius to the full,
And Chærilus taught Codrus to be dull ;
Therefore, dear friend, at my advice give o'er
This needless labour ; and contend no more
To prove a *dull succession* to be true,
Since 'tis enough we find it so in you.

---

[1] Elkanah Settle. In a note on the Dunciad, Bk. i.
181, Warburton says that this poem was written by
Pope when fourteen years old.

ARGUS.[1]

WHEN wise Ulysses, from his native
    coast
    Long kept by wars, and long by
    tempests tossed,
Arrived at last, poor, old, disguised, alone,
To all his friends and ev'n his Queen unknown;
Changed as he was, with age, and toils, and cares,
Furrowed his reverend face, and white his hairs,
In his own palace forced to ask his bread,
Scorned by those slaves his former bounty fed,
Forgot of all his own domestic crew;
The faithful dog alone his rightful master knew!
Unfed, unhoused, neglected, on the clay,
Like an old servant, now cashiered, he lay;
Touched with resentment of ungrateful man,
And longing to behold his ancient lord again.
Him when he saw—he rose, and crawled to meet,
('Twas all he could) and fawned and kissed his
    feet,
Seized with dumb joy—then falling by his side,
Owned his returning lord, looked up, and died!

PRAYER OF ST. FRANCIS XAVIER.[2]

THOU art my God, sole object of my
    love;
    Not for the hope of endless joys
    above;
Not for the fear of endless pains below,
Which they who love Thee not must undergo.

[1] These lines were sent by Pope in a letter to
Henry Cromwell, dated Oct. 19, 1709.
[2] First published in the Gentleman's Magazine,

For me, and such as me, Thou deign'st to bear
An ignominious cross, the nails, the spear:
A thorny crown transpierced Thy sacred brow,
While bloody sweats from every member flow.

For me in tortures Thou resign'st Thy breath,
Embraced me on the cross, and saved me by
    Thy death.
And can these sufferings fail my heart to move?
What but Thyself can now deserve my love?

Such as then was, and is, Thy love to me,
Such is, and shall be still, my love to Thee—
To Thee, Redeemer! mercy's sacred spring!
My God, my Father, Maker, and my King!

TRANSLATION OF A PRAYER OF BRUTUS.[1]

ODDESS of woods, tremendous in
    the chase,
    To mountain wolves and all the
    savage race,
Wide o'er the aërial vault extend thy sway,

October, 1891, where it is said that Pope was re-
quested by Mr. Brown, domestic chaplain in the
family of Mr. Caryll, to change the subject of his
compositions, and to devote his talents to the translating of the Latin hymn composed by Francis Xavier,
and beginning, " O Deus ! ego amo te," &c.

[1] The Rev. Aaron Thompson, of Queen's College,
Oxon., translated the Chronicle of Geoffrey of Mon-
mouth. He submitted the translation to Pope, 1717,
who gave him the following lines, being a translation
of a prayer of Brutus.—*Carruthers.*

And o'er the infernal regions void of day.
On thy third reign look down; disclose our fate,
In what new station shall we fix our seat ?
When shall we next thy hallowed altars raise,
And choirs of virgins celebrate thy praise ?

A PARAPHRASE.

(ON THOMAS À KEMPIS, l. iii. c. 2.)

Done by the Author at Twelve Years old.[1]

PEAK, gracious Lord, oh, speak ;
 Thy servant hears :
  For I'm Thy servant and I'll still
  be so :
Speak words of comfort in my willing ears;
 And since my tongue is in Thy praises slow,
And since that Thine all rhetoric exceeds;
Speak Thou in words, but let me speak in deeds!

Nor speak alone, but give me grace to hear
 What Thy celestial sweetness does impart;
Let it not stop when entered at the ear,
 But sink and take deep rooting in my heart.
As the parched earth drinks rain (but grace
 afford)
With such a gust will I receive Thy word.

Nor with the Israelites shall I desire
 Thy heavenly word by Moses to receive,
Lest I should die : but Thou who didst inspire
 Moses himself, speak Thou, that I may live.

---

[1] First published from the Caryll Papers, in the
Athenæum, July 15, 1854.

Rather with Samuel I beseech with tears,
Speak, gracious Lord, oh, speak, Thy servant
    hears.

Moses, indeed, may say the words, but Thou
    Must give the spirit and the life inspire
Our love to Thee his fervent breath may blow,
    But 'tis Thyself alone can give the fire :
Thou without them may'st speak and profit too;
But without Thee what could the prophets do ?

They preach the doctrine, but Thou mak'st us
    do't ;
They teach the mysteries Thou dost open lay;
    The trees they water, but Thou giv'st the fruit ;
    They to salvation show the arduous way,
But none but You can give us strength to walk ;
You give the practice, they but give the talk.

Let them be silent then ; and Thou alone,
    My God ! speak comfort to my ravished ears;
Light of my eyes, my consolation,
    Speak when Thou wilt, for still Thy servant
        hears.
Whate'er Thou speak'st, let this be understood :
Thy greater glory, and my greater good !

OCCASIONED BY READING THE TRAVELS
OF CAPTAIN LEMUEL GULLIVER.

I.

TO QUINBUS FLESTRIN, THE MAN-MOUNTAIN.

AN ODE BY TILLY-TIT, POET LAUREATE TO HIS
MAJESTY OF LILLIPUT.

Translated into English.

N amaze,
Lost, I gaze,
Can our eyes
Reach thy size ?
May my lays
Swell with praise,
Worthy thee !
Worthy me !
Muse, inspire,
All thy fire !
Bards of old
Of him told,
When they said
Atlas' head
Propped the skies :
See ! and believe your eyes !
See him stride
Valleys wide,
Over woods
Over floods !
When he treads,
Mountains' heads
Groan and shake :
Armies quake :
Let his spurn
Overturn

Man and steed :
Troops take heed !
Left and right,
Speed your flight !
Lest an host
Beneath his foot be lost.
Turned aside,
From his hide,
Safe from wound,
Darts rebound.
From his nose
Clouds he blows :
When he speaks,
Thunder breaks !
When he eats,
Famine threats !
When he drinks,
Neptune shrinks !
Nigh thy ear,
In mid air,
On thy hand,
Let me stand ;
So shall I,
Lofty Poet, touch the sky.

II.

THE LAMENTATION OF GLUMDAL-CLITCH FOR THE LOSS OF GRILDRIG.

A PASTORAL.

SOON as Glumdalclitch missed her
　　pleasing care,
　She wept, she blubbered, and she
　　tore her hair.
No British miss sincerer grief has known,

Her squirrel missing, or her sparrow flown.
She furled her sampler, and hauled in her
  thread,
And stuck her needle into Grildrig's bed;
Then spread her hands, and with a bounce let
  fall
Her baby, like the giant in Guildhall.
In peals of thunder now she roars, and now
She gently whimpers like a lowing cow:
Yet lovely in her sorrow still appears,
Her locks dishevelled, and her flood of tears
Seem like the lofty barn of some rich swain,
When from the thatch drips fast a shower of
  rain.
  In vain she searched each cranny of the
  house,
Each gaping chink impervious to a mouse.
"Was it for this (she cried) with daily care
Within thy reach I set the vinegar!
And filled the cruet with the acid tide,
While pepper-water worms thy bait supplied;
Where twined the silver eel around thy hook,
And all the little monsters of the brook.
Sure in that lake he dropped; my Grilly's
  drowned."
She dragged the cruet, but no Grildrig found.
  "Vain is thy courage, Grilly, vain thy boast;
But little creatures enterprise the most.
Trembling, I've seen thee dare the kitten's paw,
Nay, mix with children, as they played at taw,
Nor fear the marbles, as they bounding flew;
Marbles to them, but rolling rocks to you.
  "Why did I trust thee with that giddy youth?
Who from a page can ever learn the truth?
Versed in Court tricks, that money-loving boy
To some lord's daughter sold the living toy;
Or rent him limb from limb in cruel play,

As children tear the wings of flies away.
From place to place o'er Brobdignag I'll roam,
And never will return or bring thee home.
But who has eyes to trace the passing wind ?
How, then, thy fairy footsteps can I find ?
Dost thou bewildered wander all alone,
In the green thicket of a mossy stone ;
Or tumbled from the toadstool's slippery round,
Perhaps all maimed, lie grovelling on the
    ground ?
Dost thou, embosomed in the lovely rose,
Or sunk within the peach's down, repose ?
Within the king-cup if thy limbs are spread,
Or in the golden cowslip's velvet head :
O show me, Flora, midst those sweets the flower
Where sleeps my Grildrig in his fragrant bower.
    " But ah ! I fear thy little fancy roves
On little females, and on little loves ;
Thy pigmy children, and thy tiny spouse,
Thy baby playthings that adorn thy house,
Doors, windows, chimneys, and the spacious
    rooms,
Equal in size to cells of honeycombs,
Hast thou for these now ventured from the shore,
Thy bark a bean-shell, and a straw thy oar ?
Or in thy box, now bounding on the main,
Shall I ne'er bear thyself and house again ?
And shall I set thee on my hand no more,
To see thee leap the lines and traverse o'er
My spacious palm ?   Of stature scarce a span,
Mimic the actions of a real man ?
No more behold thee turn my watch's key,
As seamen at a capstern anchors weigh ?
How wert thou wont to walk with cautious
    tread,
A dish of tea like milk-pail on thy head !
How chase the mite that bore thy cheese away ?

And keep the rolling maggot at a bay!"
She said, but broken accents stopped her voice,
Soft as the speaking-trumpet's mellow noise:
She sobbed a storm, and wiped her flowing eyes,
Which seemed like two broad suns in misty skies
O squander not thy grief; those tears command
To weep upon our cod in Newfoundland:
The plenteous pickle shall preserve the fish,
And Europe taste thy sorrows in a dish.

III.

TO MR. LEMUEL GULLIVER,

THE GRATEFUL ADDRESS OF THE UNHAPPY HOU-
YHNHNMS, NOW IN SLAVERY AND BONDAGE IN
ENGLAND.

O thee, we wretches of the Houyhnhnm
      band,
      Condemned to labour in a barbarous
      land,
Return our thanks. Accept our humble lays,
And let each grateful Houyhnhnm neigh thy
      praise.

O happy Yahoo! purged from human crimes,
By thy sweet sojourn in those virtuous climes.
Where reign our sires; there, to thy country's
      shame,
Reason, you found, and virtue were the same.
Their precepts razed the prejudice of youth,
And even a Yahoo learned the force of truth.

Art thou the first who did the coast explore;
Did never Yahoo tread that ground before?
Yes, thousands! But in pity to their kind,
Or swayed by envy, or through pride of mind,

They hid their knowledge of a nobler race,
Which owned, would all their sires and sons
    disgrace.

You, like the Samian, visit lands unknown,
And by their wiser morals mend your own.
Thus Orpheus travelled to reform his kind,
Came back, and tamed the brutes he left
    behind.

You went, you saw, you heard; with virtue
    fought,
Then spread those morals which the Houyhnhnms
    taught.
Our labours here must touch thy generous
    heart,
To see us strain before the coach and cart;
Compelled to run each knavish jockey's heat!
Subservient to Newmarket's annual cheat!

With what reluctance do we lawyers bear,
To fleece their country clients twice a year?
Or managed in your schools, for fops to ride,
How foam, how fret beneath a load of pride!
Yes, we are slaves—but yet, by reason's force,
Have learned to bear misfortune, like a horse.

O would the stars, to ease my bonds, ordain,
That gentle Gulliver might guide my rein!
Safe would I bear him to his journey's end,
For 'tis a pleasure to support a friend.
But if my life be doomed to serve the bad,
O! may'st thou never want an easy pad!
                              HOUYHNHNM.

IV.

MARY GULLIVER TO CAPTAIN LEMUEL GULLIVER.

AN EPISTLE.

ARGUMENT.

The Captain, some time after his return, being retired to Mr. Sympson's in the country, Mrs. Gulliver,
apprehending from his late behaviour some estrange-
ment of his affections, writes him the following ex-
postulating, soothing, and tenderly complaining
epistle.

ELCOME, thrice welcome, to thy
native place !
—What, touch me not ? what, shun
a wife's embrace ?
Have I for this thy tedious absence borne,
And waked, and wished whole nights for thy
return ?
In five long years I took no second spouse ;
What Redriff wife so long hath kept her vows?
Your eyes, your nose, inconstancy betray ;
Your nose you stop ; your eyes you turn away.
'Tis said, that thou shouldst cleave unto thy
wife ;
Once thou didst cleave, and I could cleave for
life.
Hear, and relent ! hark how thy children moan ;
Be kind at least to these : they are thy own ;
Be bold, and count them all ; secure to find
The honest number that you left behind.
See how they pat thee with their pretty paws :
Why start you? are they snakes? or have they
claws ?

Thy Christian seed, our mutual flesh and bone:
Be kind at least to these, they are thy own.
  Biddel, like thee, might farthest India rove ;
He changed his country, but retained his love.
There's Captain Pennell, absent half his life,
Comes back, and is the kinder to his wife.
Yet Pennell's wife is brown, compared to me ;
And Mrs. Biddel sure is fifty-three.
  Not touch me ! never neighbour called me
    slut :
Was Flimnap's dame more sweet in Lilliput ?
I've no red hair to breathe an odious fume ;
At least thy consort's cleaner than thy groom.
Why then that dirty stable-boy thy care ?
What mean those visits to the sorrel mare ?
Say, by what witchcraft or what demon led,—
Preferr'st thou litter to the marriage bed ?
  Some say the devil himself is in that mare :
If so, our dean shall drive him forth by prayer.
Some think you mad, some think you are pos-
    sessed ;
That Bedlam and clean straw will suit you best.
Vain means, alas ! this frenzy to appease,
That straw, that straw, would heighten the
    disease.
  My bed (the scene of all our former joys,
Witness two lovely girls, two lovely boys,)
Alone I press ; in dreams I call my dear,
I stretch my hand, no Gulliver is there !
I wake, I rise, and shivering with the frost,
Search all the house,—my Gulliver is lost !
Forth in the street I rush with frantic cries ;
The windows open, all the neighbours rise ;
" Where sleeps my Gulliver ? O tell me where !"
The neighbours answer, " With the sorrel mare."
  At early morn, I to the market haste,
(Studious in everything to please thy taste) ;

A curious fowl and sparagrass I chose
(For I remember you were fond of those);
Three shillings cost the first, the last seven
    groats;
Sullen you turn from both, and call for oats.
    Others bring goods and treasure to their
        houses,
Something to deck their pretty babes and
    spouses;
My only token was a cup like horn,
That's made of nothing but a lady's corn.
'Tis not for that I grieve; no, 'tis to see
The groom and sorrel mare preferred to me!
    These for some moments when you deign to
        quit,
And (at due distance) sweet discourse admit,
'Tis all my pleasure thy past toil to know,
For pleased remembrance builds delight on woe.
At every danger pants thy consort's breast,
And gaping infants squall to hear the rest.
How did I tremble, when, by thousands bound,
I saw thee stretched on Lilliputian ground?
When scaling armies climbed up every part,
Each step they trod, I felt upon my heart.
But when thy torrent quenched the dreadful
    blaze,
King, Queen, and nation, staring with amaze,
Full in my view how all my husband came,
And what extinguished theirs, increased my
    flame.
Those spectacles, ordained thine eyes to save,
Were once my present; Love that armour gave.
How did I mourn at Bolgolam's decree!
For when he signed thy death, he sentenced me.
    When folks might see thee all the country
        round
For sixpence, I'd have given a thousand pound.

Lord! when the giant-babe that head of thine
Got in his mouth, my heart was up in mine!
When in the marrow-bone I see thee rammed;
Or on the house-top by the monkey crammed,
The piteous images renew my pain,
And all thy dangers I weep o'er again.
But on the maiden's nipple when you rid,
Pray Heaven, 'twas all a wanton maiden did!
Glumdalclitch too—with thee I mourn her case:
Heaven guard the gentle girl from all disgrace!
O may the King that one neglect forgive,
And pardon her the fault by which I live!
Was there no other way to set him free?
My life, alas! I fear proved death to thee.
   O teach me, dear, new words to speak my
      flame!
Teach me to woo thee by thy best-loved name!
Whether the style of Grildrig please the most,
So called on Brobdignag's stupendous coast,
When on the monarch's ample hand you sate,
And hollooed in his ear intrigues of state;
Or Quinbus Flestrin more endearment brings;
When like a mountain you looked down on
      kings:
If ducal Nardac, Lilliputian peer,
Or Glumglum's humbler title soothe thy ear:
Nay, would kind Jove my organs so dispose,
To hymn harmonious Houyhnhnm through the
      nose,
I'd call thee Houyhnhnm, that high-sounding
      name;
Thy children's noses all should twang the same.
So might I find my loving spouse of course
Endued with all the virtues of a horse.

THE DUNCIAD.

IN FOUR BOOKS.

WITH

THE PROLEGOMENA OF SCRIBLERUS,

THE HYPERCRITICS OF ARISTARCHUS,

AND

NOTES VARIORUM.

VENDENTEM THVS ET ODORES

FACSIMILE OF THE FRONTISPIECE TO THE DUNCIAD,
A.D. 1729.

A LETTER TO THE PUBLISHER,

OCCASIONED BY THE FIRST CORRECT EDITION OF

THE DUNCIAD.

T is with pleasure I hear that you have procured a correct copy of the DUNCIAD, which the many surreptitious ones have rendered so necessary; and it is yet with more, that I am informed it will be attended with a COMMENTARY; a Work so requisite, that I cannot think the Author himself would have omitted it, had he approved of the first appearance of this Poem.

Such *Notes* as have occurred to me I herewith send you : you will oblige me by inserting them amongst those which are, or will be, transmitted to you by others ; since not only the Author's friends, but even strangers, appear engaged by humanity, to take some care of an Orphan of so much genius and spirit, which its parent seems to have abandoned from the very beginning, and suffered to step into the world naked, unguarded, and unattended.

It was upon reading some of the abusive papers lately published, that my great regard to a Person, whose Friendship I esteem as one of

the chief honours of my life, and a much greater
respect to Truth, than to him or any man living,
engaged me in enquiries, of which the enclosed
Notes are the fruit.

I perceived that most of these Authors had
been (doubtless very wisely) the first aggressors.
They had tried, till they were weary, what was
to be got by railing at each other : Nobody was
either concerned or surprised if this or that
scribbler was proved a dunce. But every one was
curious to read what could be said to prove
Mr. POPE one, and was ready to pay something
for such a discovery ; a stratagem, which would
they fairly own, it might not only reconcile
them to me, but screen them from the resentment of their lawful Superiors, whom they daily
abuse, only (as I charitably hope) to get that
by them, which they cannot get *from* them.

I found this was not all : ill success in that
had transported them to Personal abuse, either
of himself, or (what I think he could less forgive)
of his Friends.   They had called Men of virtue
and honour bad Men, long before he had either
leisure or inclination to call them bad Writers ;
and some of them had been such old offenders,
that he had quite forgotten their persons, as
well as their slanders, till they were pleased to
revive them.

Now what had Mr. POPE done before to
incense them ?   He had published those works
which are in the hands of every body, in which
not the least mention is made of any of them.
And what has he done since ?   He has laughed,
and written the DUNCIAD.   What has that said
of them ?   A very serious truth, which the
public had said before, that they were dull ;
and what it had no sooner said, but they them-

selves were at great pains to procure, or even
purchase room in the prints, to testify under
their hands to the truth of it.

I should still have been silent, if either I had
seen any inclination in my friend to be serious
with such accusers, or if they had only meddled
with his Writings; since whoever publishes,
puts himself on his trial by his Country. But
when his Moral character was attacked, and in
a manner from which neither truth nor virtue
can secure the most innocent,—in a manner,
which, though it annihilates the credit of the
accusation with the just and impartial, yet
aggravates very much the guilt of the accusers;
I mean by Authors *without names;* then I
thought, since the danger was common to all,
the concern ought to be so; and that it was an
act of justice to detect the Authors, not only on
this account, but as many of them are the same
who, for several years past, have made free with
the greatest names in Church and State, exposed
to the world the private misfortunes of Families,
abused all, even to Women, and whose pros-
tituted papers (for one or other Party, in the
unhappy divisions of their Country) have insulted the Fallen, the Friendless, the Exiled,
and the Dead.

Besides this, which I take to be a public
concern, I have already confessed I had a private
one. I am one of that number who have long
loved and esteemed Mr. POPE; and had often
declared it was not his capacity or writings
(which we ever thought the least valuable part
of his character) but the honest, open, and
beneficent man, that we most esteemed and
loved in him. Now, if what these people say
were believed, I must appear to all my friends

either a fool or a knave; either imposed on myself, or imposing on them; so that I am as much interested in the confutation of these calumnies, as he is himself.

I am no Author, and consequently not to be suspected either of jealousy or resentment against any of the Men, of whom scarce one is known to me by right; and as for their Writings, I have sought them (on this one occasion) in vain, in the closets and libraries of all my acquaintance. I had still been in the dark, if a Gentleman had not procured me (I suppose from some of themselves, for they are generally much more dangerous friends than enemies) the passages I send you. I solemnly protest I have added nothing to the malice or absurdity of them; which it behoves me to declare, since the vouchers themselves will be so soon and so irrecoverably lost. You may, in some measure, prevent it, by preserving at least their Titles,[1] and discovering (as far as you can depend on the truth of your information) the Names of the concealed authors.

The first objection I have heard made to the Poem is, that the persons are too *obscure* for satire. The persons themselves, rather than allow the objection, would forgive the satire; and if one could be tempted to afford it a serious answer, were not all assassinates, popular insurrections, the insolence of the rabble without doors, and of domestics within, most wrongfully chastised, if the Meanness of offenders indemnified them from punishment? On the contrary, Obscurity renders them more dangerous, as less

---

[1] Which we have done in a List printed in the Appendix.—P.

thought of ; Law can pronounce judgment only on open facts : Morality alone can pass censure on intentions of mischief ; so that for secret calumny, or the arrow flying in the dark, there is no public punishment left, but what a good Writer inflicts.

The next objection is, that these sort of authors are *poor*. That might be pleaded as an excuse at the Old Bailey for lesser crimes than Defamation (for it is the case of almost all who are tried there), but sure it can be none here : for who will pretend that the robbing another of his Reputation supplies the want of it in himself ? I question not but such authors are poor, and heartily wish the objection were removed by any honest livelihood. But Poverty is here the accident, not the subject : He who describes Malice and Villany to be pale and meagre, expresses not the least anger against Paleness or Leanness, but against Malice and Villany. The Apothecary in *Romeo and Juliet* is poor ; but is he therefore justified in vending poison ? Not but Poverty itself becomes a just subject of satire, when it is the consequence of vice, prodigality, or neglect of one's lawful calling ; for then it increases the public burden, fills the streets and highways with Robbers, and the garrets with Clippers, Coiners, and Weekly Journalists.

But admitting that two or three of these offend less in their morals, than in their writings; must Poverty make nonsense sacred ? If so, the fame of bad authors would be much better consulted than that of all the good ones in the world ; and not one of an hundred had ever been called by his right name.

They mistake the whole matter : It is not

charity to encourage them in the way they
follow, but to get them out of it; for men are
not bunglers because they are poor, but they
are poor because they are bunglers.

Is it not pleasant enough to hear our authors
crying out on the one hand, as if their persons
and characters were too sacred for Satire; and
the public objecting, on the other, that they are
too mean even for Ridicule? But whether Bread
or Fame be their end, it must be allowed, our
Author, by and in this Poem, has mercifully
given them a little of both.

There are two or three who, by their rank and
fortune, have no benefit from the former objec-
tions, supposing them good, and these I was
sorry to see in such company. But if, without
any provocation, two or three Gentlemen will
fall upon one, in an affair wherein his interest
and reputation are equally embarked; they cannot, certainly, after they have been content to
print themselves his enemies, complain of being
put into the number of them.

Others, I am told, pretend to have been once
his Friends. Surely they are their enemies who
say so, since nothing can be more odious than
to treat a friend as they have done. But of this
I cannot persuade myself, when I consider the
constant and eternal aversion of all bad writers
to a good one.

Such as claim a merit from being his Admirers, I would gladly ask, if it lays him under
a personal obligation? At that rate, he would
be the most obliged humble servant in the
world. I dare swear for these in particular,
he never desired them to be his admirers, nor
promised in return to be theirs. That had
truly been a sign he was of their acquaintance;

but would not the malicious world have suspected such an approbation of some motive
worse than ignorance, in the author of the
Essay on Criticism ?   Be it as it will, the reasons of their Admiration and of his Contempt
are equally subsisting, for his works and theirs
are the very same that they were.

One, therefore, of their assertions I believe
may be true, "That he has a contempt for their
writings."   And there is another which would
probably be sooner allowed by himself than by
any good judge beside, "That his own have
found too much success with the public."   But
as it cannot consist with his modesty to claim
this as a justice, it lies not on him, but entirely
on the public, to defend his own judgment.

There remains what in my opinion might
seem a better plea for these people than any
they have made use of.   If Obscurity or Poverty
were to exempt a man from satire, much more
should Folly or Dulness, which are still more
involuntary; nay, as much so as personal Deformity.   But even this will not help them:
Deformity becomes an object of Ridicule when
a man sets up for being handsome; and so must
Dulness, when he sets up for a Wit.   They are
not ridiculed because Ridicule in itself is, or
ought to be, a pleasure; but because it is just
to undeceive and vindicate the honest and un-
pretending part of mankind from imposition;
because particular interest ought to yield to
general, and a great number who are not
naturally Fools, ought never to be made so, in
complaisance to a few who are.   Accordingly
we find that in all ages, all vain pretenders,
were they ever so poor, or ever so dull, have
been constantly the topics of the most candid

satirists, from the Codrus of JUVENAL to the Damon of BOILEAU.

Having mentioned BOILEAU, the greatest Poet and most judicious Critic of his age and country, admirable for his Talents, and yet perhaps more admirable for his Judgment in the proper application of them; I cannot help remarking the resemblance betwixt him and our Author, in Qualities, Fame, and Fortune; in the distinctions shown them by their Superiors, in the general esteem of their Equals, and in their extended reputation amongst Foreigners; in the latter of which ours has met with the better fate, as he has had for his Translators persons of the most eminent rank and abilities in their respective nations.[1] But the resemblance holds in nothing more, than in their being equally abused by the ignorant pretenders to Poetry of their times; of which not the least memory will remain but in their own Writings, and in the Notes made upon them. What BOILEAU has done in almost all his poems, our Author has only in this: I dare answer for him he will do it in no more; and on this principle, of attacking few but who had slandered

[1] Essay on Criticism, in French verse, by General Hamilton; the same, in verse also, by Monsieur Roboton, Counsellor and Privy Secretary to King George I. after by the Abbé Reynel, in verse, with notes. Rape of the Lock, in French, by the Princess of Conti, Paris, 1728; and in Italian verse by the Abbé Conti, a noble Venetian; and by the Marquis Rangoni, Envoy Extraordinary from Modena to King George II. Others of his works by Salvini of Florence, &c. His Essays and Dissertations on Homer, several times translated into French. Essay on Man, by the Abbé Reynel, in verse; by Monsieur Silhouet, in prose, 1737; and since by others in French, Italian, and Latin.—P.

him, he could not have done it at all, had he
been confined from censuring obscure and
worthless persons, for scarce any other were his
enemies. However, as the parity is so remarkable, I hope it will continue to the last; and if
ever he should give us an edition of this Poem
himself, I may see some of them treated as
gently, on their repentance or better merit, as
Perrault and Quinault were at last by BOILEAU.

In one point I must be allowed to think the
character of our English Poet the more amiable.
He has not been a follower of Fortune or Success; he has lived with the Great without flattery; been a friend to Men in power, without
pensions, from whom, as he asked, so he received, no favour, but what was done him in
his Friends. As his Satires were the more just
for being delayed, so were his Panegyrics;
bestowed only on such persons as he had fami-
liarly known, only for such virtues as he had
long observed in them, and only at such times
as others cease to praise, if not begin to
calumniate them—I mean when out of power,
or out of fashion.[1] A satire, therefore, on
writers so notorious for the contrary practice,
became no man so well as himself; as none, it
is plain, was so little in their friendships, or so
much in that of those whom they had most
abused, namely, the Greatest and Best of all
Parties. Let me add a further reason, that,

[1] As Mr. Wycherley, at the time the Town declaimed against his book of Poems ; Mr. Walsh, after
his death ; Sir William Trumbull, when he had resigned the office of Secretary of State ; Lord Boling-
broke, at his leaving England, after the Queen's
death ; Lord Oxford, in his last decline of life ; Mr.
Secretary Craggs, at the end of the South-Sea year,
and after his death : Others only in Epitaphs.—P.

though engaged in their Friendships, he never
espoused their Animosities ; and can almost
singly challenge this honour, not to have written a line of any man, which, through Guilt,
through Shame, or through Fear, through
variety of Fortune, or change of Interests, he
was ever unwilling to own.

I shall conclude with remarking what a pleasure it must be to every reader of Humanity,
to see all along that our Author in his very
laughter is not indulging his own ill-nature,
but only punishing that of others. As to his
Poem, those alone are capable of doing it justice,
who, to use the words of a great writer, know
how hard it is (with regard both to his subject
and his manner) VETUSTIS DARE NOVITATEM,
OBSOLETIS NITOREM, OBSCURIS LUCEM, FASTIDITIS
GRATIAM. I am
Your most humble servant,
WILLIAM CLELAND.[1]

St. James's, Dec. 22, 1728.

[1] This Gentleman was of Scotland, and bred at the
University of Utrecht, with the Earl of Mar. He
served in Spain under Earl Rivers. After the Peace,
he was made one of the Commissioners of the Customs
in Scotland, and then of Taxes in England ; in which,
having shown himself for twenty years diligent, punctual, and incorruptible, though without any other
assistance of Fortune ; he was suddenly displaced by
the Minister, in the sixty-eighth year of his age ; and
died two months after, in 1741. He was a person of
Universal Learning, and an enlarged Conversation ;
no man had a warmer heart for his Friend, or a sincerer attachment to the Constitution of his Country.
—P.

And yet, for all this, the public will not allow him
to be the Author of this Letter.—*Warburton.*

MARTINUS SCRIBLERUS

HIS PROLEGOMENA AND ILLUSTRATIONS

TO

THE DUNCIAD.

WITH THE HYPERCRITICS OF ARISTARCHUS.

DENNIS, *Remarks on Pr. Arthur.*

I CANNOT but think it the most reasonable thing in the world, to distinguish good writers, by discouraging the bad.   Nor is it an ill-natured thing, in relation even to the very persons upon whom the reflections are made.   It is true, it may deprive them, a little the sooner, of a short profit and a transitory reputation ; but then it may have a good effect, and oblige them (before it be too late) to decline that for which they are so very unfit, and to have recourse to something in which they may be more successful.

Character of Mr. P. 1716.

The Persons whom Boileau has attacked in his writings have been for the most part *Authors,* and most of those authors, *Poets :* And the censures he hath passed upon them have been confirmed by all Europe.

GILDON, *Pref. to his New Rehearsal.*

It is the common cry of the poetasters of the town, and their fautors, that it is an ill-natured thing to expose the pretenders to wit and poetry. The judges and magistrates may with full as good reason be reproached with ill-nature for putting the laws in execution against a thief or impostor.—The same will hold in the Republic of Letters, if the critics and judges will let every ignorant pretender to scribbling pass on the world.

THEOBALD, *Letter to* MIST, *June* 22, 1728.

Attacks may be levelled either against *failures in genius,* or against the *pretensions of writing without one.*

CONCANEN, *Ded. to the Author of the Dunciad.*

A satire upon Dulness is a thing that has been used and allowed in all ages.

Out of thine own mouth will I judge thee, wicked Scribbler!

TESTIMONIES OF AUTHORS

CONCERNING

OUR POET AND HIS WORKS.

M. SCRIBLERUS LECTORI S.

BEFORE we present thee with our exercitations on this most delectable Poem (drawn from the many volumes of our Adversaria on modern Authors) we shall here, according to the laudable usage of editors, collect the various judgments of the Learned concerning our Poet : Various indeed, not only of different authors, but of the same author at different seasons. Nor shall we gather only the Testimonies of such eminent Wits as would of course descend to posterity, and consequently be read without our collection ; but we shall likewise, with incredible labour, seek out for divers others, which, but for this our diligence, could never, at the distance of a few months, appear to the eye of the most curious. Hereby thou mayst not only receive the delectation of Variety, but also arrive at a more certain judgment, by a grave and circumspect comparison of the witnesses with each other, or of each with himself. Hence, also, thou wilt be enabled to draw reflections, not only of a critical, but a moral nature, by being let into many particulars of the Person as well as Genius, and of the Fortune as well as Merit, of our Author : In which if I relate some things of little concern peradventure to thee, and some of as little even to him ; I entreat thee to consider how minutely all true critics and

commentators arc wont to insist upon such, and
how material they seem to themselves, if to nono
other. Forgive me, gentle reader, if (following
learned example) I ever and anon become
tedious: allow me to take the same pains to
find whether my author were good or bad, well
or ill-natured, modest or arrogant ; as another,
whether his author was fair or brown, short or
tall, or whether he wore a coat or a cassock.
    We purposed to begin with his Life, Paren-
tage, and Education ; But as to these, even his
contemporaries do exceedingly differ. One
saith,[1] he was educated at home ; another,[2] that
he was bred at St. Omer's by Jesuits ; a third,[3]
not at St. Omer's, but at Oxford ; a fourth,[4]
that he had no university education at all.
Those who allow him to be bred at home, differ
as much concerning his tutor : One saith,[5] he
was kept by his father on purpose ; a second,[6]
that he was an itinerant priest ; a third,[7] that
he was a parson ; one[8] calleth him a secular
clergyman of the Church of Rome ; another[9] a
monk. As little do they agree about his Father,
whom one[10] supposeth, like the father of Hesiod,
a tradesman or merchant ; another,[11] a husband-

---

[1] Giles Jacob's Lives of the Poets, vol. ii. in his
Life.—P.
[2] Dennis's Reflections on the Essay on Crit. p. 4.
—P.
[3] Dunciad dissected, p. 4.—P.
[4] Guardian, No. 40.—P.
[5] Jacob's Lives, &c. vol. ii.—P.
[6] Dunciad dissected, p. 4.—P.
[7] Farmer P. and his son.—P.
[8] Dunciad dissected.—P.
[9] Characters of the Times, p. 45.—P.
[10] Female Dunc., p. ult.—P.
[11] Dunciad dissected.—P.

man; another,[1] a hatter, &c. Nor has an author been wanting to give our Poet such a father, as Apuleius hath to Plato, Jamblichus to Pythagoras, and divers to Homer, namely a Dæmon: For thus Mr. Gildon :[2] " Certain it is, that his original is not from Adam, but the Devil; and that he wanteth nothing but horns and tail to be the exact resemblance of his infernal Father." Finding, therefore, such contrariety of opinions, and (whatever be ours of this sort of generation) not being fond to enter into controversy, we shall defer writing the life of our Poet, till authors can determine among themselves what Parents or Education he had, or whether he had any Education or Parents at all.

Proceed we to what is more certain, his Works, though not less uncertain the judgments concerning them; beginning with his ESSAY on CRITICISM, of which hear first the most ancient of Critics,

MR. JOHN DENNIS.

" His precepts are false or trivial, or both; his thoughts are crude and abortive; his expressions absurd, his numbers harsh and unmusical, his rhymes trivial and common ;— instead of majesty, we have something that is

---

[1] Roome, Paraphrase on the 4th of Genesis, printed 1729.—P.

[2] Character of Mr. P. and his Writings, in a Letter to a Friend, printed for S. Popping, 1716, p. 10. Curl, in his Key to the Dunciad (first edit. said to be printed for A. Dodd), in the 10th page, declared Gildon to be author of that libel; though, in the subsequent editions of his Key, he left out this assertion, and affirmed (in the Curliad, pp. 4 and 8) that it was written by Dennis only.—P.

very mean ; instead of gravity, something that
is very boyish ; and instead of perspicuity and
lucid order, we have but too often obscurity and
confusion." And in another place : " What
rare *numbers* are here ! Would not one swear
that this youngster had espoused some anti-
quated Muse, who had sued out a divorce from
some superannuated sinner, upon account of
impotence, and who, being poxed by her former
spouse, has got the gout in her decrepit age,
which makes her *hobble so damnably ?*"[1]

No less peremptory is the censure of our
hypercritical Historian,

MR. OLDMIXON.

" I dare not say any thing of the Essay on
Criticism in verse ; but if any more curious
reader has discovered in it something *new*
which is not in Dryden's Prefaces, Dedications,
and his Essay on Dramatic Poetry, not to
mention the French critics, I should be very
glad to have the benefit of the discovery."[2]

He is followed (as in fame, so in judgment)
by the modest and simple-minded

MR. LEONARD WELSTED,

who, out of great respect to our poet not
naming him, doth yet glance at his Essay,
together with the Duke of Buckingham's, and
the Criticisms of Dryden, and of Horace, which
he more openly taxeth :[3] " As to the numerous
treatises, essays, arts, &c. both in verse and

---

[1] Reflections critical and satirical on a Rhapsody,
called, An Essay on Criticism. Printed for Bernard
Lintot, octavo.—P.
[2] Essay on Criticism in prose, octavo, 1728, by the
author of the Critical History of England.—P.
[3] Preface to his Poems, pp. 18, 53.—P.

prose, that have been written by the moderns on this groundwork, they do but *hackney the same thoughts over again*, making them still more *trite*. Most of their pieces are nothing but a pert insipid heap of *commonplace*. Horace has even in his Art of Poetry thrown out several things which plainly show he thought an Art of Poetry was of no use, even while he was writing one."

To all which great authorities we can only oppose that of

MR. ADDISON.

"The Art of Criticism," saith he,[1] "which was published some months since, is a master-piece in its kind. The observations follow one another like those in Horace's Art of Poetry, without that methodical regularity which would have been requisite in a prose writer. They are some of them *uncommon*, but such as the reader must assent to, when he sees them explained with that ease and perspicuity in which they are delivered. As for those which are the *most known*, and the most *received*, they are placed in so beautiful a light, and illustrated with such apt allusions, that they have in them all the graces of novelty; and make the reader, who was before acquainted with them, still more convinced of their truth and solidity. And here give me leave to mention what Monsieur Boileau has so well enlarged upon in the preface to his works; that wit and fine writing doth not consist so much in advancing things that are new, as in giving things that are known an agreeable turn. It is impossible for us, who live in the latter ages of the world, to make observations in criticism, morality, or any art or science, which have not been touched upon by others; we have little else left us, but to represent the common sense of mankind in more strong, more beautiful, or more uncommon lights. If a reader examines Horace's Art of Poetry, he will find but few precepts in it which he may not meet with in Aristotle, and which were not commonly known by all the poets of the Augustan age. His way of expressing and applying them, not his invention of them, is what we are chiefly to admire.

"Longinus, in his Reflexions, has given us the same kind of sublime, which he observes in the several passages that occasioned them : I cannot but take notice that our English author has, after the same manner, exemplified several of the precepts in the very precepts themselves." He then produces some instances of a particular beauty in the numbers, and concludes with saying, that "there are three poems in our tongue of the same nature, and each a masterpiece in its kind; the Essay on Translated Verse; the Essay on the Art of Poetry; and the Essay on Criticism."

Of WINDSOR FOREST, positive is the judgment of the affirmative

MR. JOHN DENNIS.

"That [1] it is a wretched rhapsody, impudently writ in emulation of the Cooper's Hill of Sir John Denham : The author of it is obscure, is ambiguous, is affected, is temerarious, is barbarous." [2]

[1] Letter to B. B. at the end of the Remarks on Pope's Homer, 1717.—P.
[2] Printed 1728, p. 12.—P.

But the author of the Dispensary,

DR. GARTH,

in the preface to his poem of Claremont, differs from this opinion : " Those who have seen these two excellent poems of Cooper's Hill, and Windsor Forest, the one written by Sir John Denham, the other by Mr. Pope, will show a great deal of candour if they approve of this."

Of the Epistle of ELOISA, we are told by the obscure writer of a poem called Sawney, " That because Prior's Henry and Emma charmed the finest tastes, our author writ his Eloise, *in opposition to it;* but forgot innocence and virtue : if you take away her tender thoughts, and her fierce desires, all the rest is of no value." In which, methinks, his judgment resembles that of a French tailor on a villa and gardens by the Thames : " All this is very fine ; but take away the river, and it is good for nothing."

But very contrary hereunto was the opinion of

MR. PRIOR

himself, saying in his *Alma,*[1]

> O *Abelard!* ill fated youth,
> Thy tale will justify this truth.
> But well I weet thy cruel wrong
> Adorns a nobler Poet's song :
> Dan *Pope*, for thy misfortune griev'd,
> With kind concern and skill has weav'd
> A silken web ; and ne'er shall fade
> Its colours : gently has he laid
> The mantle o'er thy sad distress,
> And Venus shall the texture bless.   &c.

Come we now to his translation of the

[1] Alma, Cant. 2.—P.

ILIAD, celebrated by numerous pens, yet it shall suffice to mention the indefatigable

SIR RICHARD BLACKMORE, KT.,

who (though otherwise a severe censurer of our author) yet styleth this " a laudable translation." [1] That ready writer

MR. OLDMIXON,

in his forementioned Essay, frequently commends the same.   And the painful

MR. LEWIS THEOBALD

thus extols it : [2] "The spirit of Homer breathes all through this translation.—I am in doubt whether I should most admire the justness to the original, or the force and beauty of the language, or the sounding variety of the numbers ; But when I find all these meet, it puts me in mind of what the poet says of one of his heroes, That he alone raised and flung with ease a weighty stone that two common men could not lift from the ground ; just so, one single person has performed, in this translation, what I once despaired to have seen done by the force of several masterly hands."   Indeed the same gentleman appears to have changed his sentiment in his Essay on the Art of Sinking in Reputation, (printed in Mist's Journal, March 30, 1728,) where he says thus: " In order to sink in reputation, let him take it into his head to descend into Homer (let the world wonder, as it will, how the devil he got there), and pretend to do him into English, so

---

[1] In his Essays, vol. i. printed for E. Curl.—P.
[2] Censor, vol. ii. n. 33.—P.

his version denote his neglect of the manner how." Strange variation ! We are told in

MIST'S JOURNAL, JUNE 8,

" That this translation of the Iliad was not in all respects conformable to the fine taste of his friend Mr. Addison ; insomuch that he employed a *younger muse*, in an undertaking of this kind, which he supervised himself." Whether Mr. Addison did find it conformable to his taste, or not, best appears from his own testimony the year following its publication, in these words :

MR. ADDISON, FREEHOLDER, NO. 40.

" When I consider myself as a British freeholder, I am in a particular manner pleased with the labours of those who have improved our language with the translations of old Greek and Latin authors.—We have already most of their Historians in our own tongue, and, what is more for the honour of our language, it has been taught to express with elegance the greatest of their poets in each nation. The illiterate among our own countrymen may learn to judge from Dryden's Virgil of the most perfect Epic performance. And those parts of Homer which have been published already by Mr. Pope, give us reason to think that the Iliad will appear in English with as little disadvantage to that immortal poem."

As to the rest, there is a slight mistake ; for this *younger muse* was an *elder :* Nor was the gentleman (who is a friend of our author) employed by Mr. Addison to translate it *after him,* since he saith himself that he did it *before.*[1]

[1] Vide Pref. to Mr. Tickel's translation of the first book of the Iliad, 4to.—P.

Contrariwise that Mr. Addison engaged our author in this work appeareth by declaration thereof in the preface to the Iliad, printed some time before his death, and by his own letters of October 26, and November 2, 1713, where he declares it is his opinion, that no other person was equal to it.

Next comes his Shakespear on the stage: "Let him" (quoth one, whom I take to be

MR. THEOBALD, MIST'S JOURNAL, JUNE 8, 1728)

"publish such an author as he has least studied, and forget to discharge even the dull duty of an editor. In this project let him lend the bookseller his name (for a competent sum of money) to promote the credit of an exorbitant subscription." Gentle reader, be pleased to cast thine eye on the *Proposal* below quoted, and on what follows (some months after the former assertion) in the same Journalist of June 8: "The bookseller proposed the book by subscription, and raised some thousands of pounds for the same: I believe the gentleman did *not* share in the profits of this extravagant subscription.

"After the Iliad, he undertook (saith

MIST'S JOURNAL, JUNE 8, 1728)

the sequel of that work, the Odyssey; and having secured the success by a numerous subscription, he employed some *underlings* to perform what, according to his proposals, should come from his own hands." To which heavy charge we can in truth oppose nothing but the words of

MR. POPE'S PROPOSAL FOR THE ODYSSEY.

(printed by J. Watts, Jan. 10, 1724.)

"I take this occasion to declare that the

subscription for Shakespear belongs wholly to Mr. Tonson ; and that the benefit of *this Pro-posal* is not solely for my own use, but for that of *two of my friends,* who have *assisted me in this work.*" But these very gentlemen are extolled above our poet himself in another of Mist's Journals, March 30, 1728, saying, " That he would not advise Mr. Pope to try the experiment again of getting a great part of a book done by assistants, lest those extraneous parts should unhappily ascend to the sublime, and retard the declension of the whole." Behold ! these *Underlings* are become good writers !

If any say, that before the said proposals were printed, the subscription was begun without declaration of such assistance ; verily those who set it on foot, or (as the term is) secured it, to wit, the right honourable the Lord Viscount HARCOURT, were he living, would testify, and the right honourable the Lord BATHURST, now living, doth testify, the same is a falsehood.

Sorry I am, that persons professing to be learned, or of whatever rank of authors, should either falsely tax, or be falsely taxed. Yet let us, who are only reporters, be impartial in our citations, and proceed.

MIST'S JOURNAL, JUNE 8, 1728.

" Mr. Addison raised this author from obscurity, obtained him the acquaintance and friendship of the *whole body of our nobility*, and transferred his powerful interests with those great men to this rising bard, who frequently levied, by that means, unusual contributions on the public." Which surely cannot be, if, as

the author of the Dunciad Dissected reporteth,
"Mr. Wycherley had before introduced him
into a familiar acquaintance with the *greatest
Peers* and *brightest Wits* then living."

"No sooner (saith the same Journalist) was
his body lifeless, but this author, reviving his
resentment, libelled the memory of his departed
friend; and, what was still more heinous,
made the scandal public." Grievous the accusation! unknown the accuser! the person accused no witness in his own cause; the person,
in whose regard accused, dead! But if there
be living any one nobleman whose friendship,
yea any one gentleman whose subscription
Mr. Addison procured to our author; let him
stand forth, that truth may appear! *Amicus
Plato, amicus Socrates, sed magis amica veritas.*
In verity, the whole story of the libel is a lie;
witness those persons of integrity who, several
years before Mr. Addison's decease, did see and
approve of the said verses, in no wise a libel,
but a friendly rebuke sent privately in our
author's own hand to Mr. Addison himself,
and never made public, till after their own
Journals, and Curl had printed the same. One
name alone, which I am here authorised to
declare, will sufficiently evince this truth, that
of the right honourable the Earl of BUR-
LINGTON.

Next is he taxed with a crime (in the opinion
of some authors, I doubt, more heinous than
any in morality) to wit Plagiarism, from the
inventive and quaint-conceited

JAMES MOORE SMITH, GENT.

"Upon[1] reading the third volume of Pope's

[1] Daily Journal, March 18, 1728.—P.

Miscellanies, I found five lines which I thought excellent; and happening to praise them, a gentleman produced a modern comedy (the Rival Modes) published last year, where were the same verses to a tittle.

"These gentlemen are undoubtedly the first plagiaries, that pretend to make a reputation by stealing from a man's works in his own lifetime, and out of a public print." Let us join to this what is written by the author of the Rival Modes, the said Mr. James Moore Smith, in a letter to our author himself, who had informed him, a month before that play was acted, Jan. 27, 1726-7, "That these verses, which he had before given him leave to insert in it, would be known for his, some copies being got abroad. He desires, nevertheless, that since the lines had been read in his comedy to several, Mr. P. would not deprive it of them," &c. Surely, if we add the testimonies of the Lord BOLING-BROKE, of the lady to whom the said verses were originally addressed, of Hugh Bethel, Esq. and others, who knew them as our author's long before the said gentleman composed his play; it is hoped the ingenuous that affect not error, will rectify their opinion by the suffrage of so honourable personages.

And yet followeth another charge, insinuating no less than his enmity both to Church and State, which could come from no other informer than the said

MR. JAMES MOORE SMITH.

"The[1] Memoirs of a Parish Clerk was a very dull and unjust abuse of a person who wrote in

[1] Daily Journal, April 3, 1728.—P.

defence of our Religion and Constitution, and
who has been dead many years." This seemeth
also most untrue; it being known to divers that
these Memoirs were written at the seat of the
Lord Harcourt, in Oxfordshire, before that
excellent person (Bishop Burnet's) death, and
many years before the appearance of that history of which they are pretended to be an
abuse. Most true it is that Mr. Moore had
such a design, and was himself the man who
pressed Dr. Arbuthnot and Mr. Pope to assist
him therein; and that he borrowed those
Memoirs of our author, when that history
came forth, with intent to turn them to such
abuse. But being able to obtain from our
author but one single hint, and either changing
his mind, or having more mind than ability,
he contented himself to keep the said Memoirs,
and read them as his own to all his acquaintance. A noble person there is into whose company Mr. Pope once chanced to introduce him,
who well remembereth the conversation of Mr.
Moore to have turned upon the "contempt he
had for the work of that reverend prelate, and
how full he was of a design he declared himself to have of exposing it." This noble person
is the Earl of PETERBOROUGH.

Here, in truth, should we crave pardon of
all the aforesaid right honourable and worthy
personages, for having mentioned them in the
same page with such weekly riff-raff railers and
rhymers; but that we had their ever-honoured
commands for the same; and that they are
introduced not as witnesses in the controversy,
but as witnesses that cannot be controverted;
not to dispute, but to decide.

Certain it is, that dividing our writers into

two classes, of such who were acquaintance,
and of such who were strangers to our author;
the former are those who speak well, and the
other those who speak evil of him. Of the first
class, the most noble

JOHN DUKE OF BUCKINGHAM

sums up his character in these lines:

> And yet so wondrous, so sublime a thing,[1]
> As the great Iliad, scarce could make me sing.
> Unless I justly could at once commend
> A *good companion*, and as *firm a friend*:
> One *moral*, or a mere *well-natur'd deed*,
> Can all desert in sciences exceed.

So also is he deciphered by the honourable

SIMON HARCOURT.

> Say,[2] wondrous youth, what column wilt thou
>   choose,
> What laurel'd arch for thy triumphant Muse?
> Though each great ancient court thee to his shrine,
> Though every laurel through the dome be thine—
> Go to the *good* and *just*, an awful train!
> *Thy soul's delight.*——

Recorded in like manner for his virtuous disposition, and gentle bearing, by the ingenious

MR. WALTER HART,

in this apostrophe:

> O![3] ever worthy, ever crown'd with praise!
> Blest in thy *life*, and blest in all thy *lays*,
> Add, that the Sisters every thought refine,
> And ev'n thy *life* be *faultless* as thy line.
> Yet Envy still with fiercer rage pursues,
> Obscures the *virtue*, and defames the Muse.
> A soul like thine, in pain, in grief, resign'd,
> Views with just scorn the malice of mankind.

[1] Verses to Mr. P. on his translation of Homer.—P.
[2] Poems prefixed to his Works.—P.
[3] In his Poems, printed for B. Lintot.—P.

The witty and moral satirist

DR. EDWARD YOUNG,

wishing some check to the corruption and evil manners of the times, calleth out upon our poet to undertake a task so worthy of his virtue :

Why[1] slumbers Pope, who leads the Muses' train,
Nor hears that *Virtue*, which he *loves*, complain?

MR. MALLET,

in his epistle on Verbal Criticism :

Whose life, severely scann'd, transcends his lays ;
For wit supreme is but his second praise.

MR. HAMMOND,

that delicate and correct imitator of Tibullus, in his Love Elegies, Elegy xiv.

Now fir'd by Pope and *Virtue*, leave the age,
  In low pursuit of self-undoing wrong,
And trace the author through his moral page,
  Whose blameless life still answers to his song.

MR. THOMSON,

in his elegant and philosophical poem of the Seasons :

Although not sweeter his own Homer sings,
Yet is his *life* the more endearing song.

To the same tune also singeth that learned clerk of Suffolk,

MR. WILLIAM BROOME :

Thus[2] nobly rising in fair *Virtue's* cause,
From thy own *life* transcribe th' *unerring laws*.

And, to close all, hear the reverend Dean of St. Patrick's :

[1] Universal Passion, Sat. 1.—P.
[2] In his poems, and at the end of the Odyssey.—P.

A soul with every virtue fraught,
By Patriots, Priests, and Poets taught :
Whose filial piety excels
Whatever Grecian story tells.
A genius for each business fit,
Whose meanest talent is his wit, &c.

Let us now recreate thee by turning to the other side, and showing his character drawn by those with whom he never conversed, and whose countenances he could not know, though turned against him ; First again commencing with the high-voiced and never· enough quoted

MR. JOHN DENNIS ;

who, in his Reflections on the Essay on Criticism, thus describeth him: "A little affected hypocrite, who has nothing in his mouth but candour, truth, friendship, goodnature, humanity, and magnanimity. He is so great a lover of falsehood, that, whenever he has a mind to calumniate his contemporaries, he brands them with some defect which is just *contrary to some good quality* for which all their *friends and their acquaintance* commend them. He seems to have a particular pique to *People of Quality*, and authors of that rank. He must derive his religion from St. Omer's."—But in the Character of Mr. P. and his Writings (printed by S. Popping, 1716), he saith, " Though he is a professor of the worst religion, yet he *laughs at it ;* " but that " nevertheless, he is a virulent Papist ; and yet a Pillar for the Church of England." Of both which opinions

MR. LEWIS THEOBALD

seems also to be ; declaring, in Mist's Journal of June 22, 1728, " That, if he is not shrewdly abused, he made it his business to cackle to both *parties* in their own sentiments." But as to his *pique* against *People of Quality*, the same Journalist doth not agree, but saith (May 8, 1728), "He had, by some means or other, the *acquaintance* and *friendship* of the *whole body of our nobility.*"

However contradictory this may appear, Mr. Dennis and Gildon, in the character last cited, make it all plain, by assuring us, "That he is a creature that reconciles all contradictions: he is a beast, and a man; a Whig and a Tory; a writer (at one and the same time) of Guardians and Examiners;[1] an Assertor of liberty, and of the dispensing power of kings; a Jesuitical professor of truth; a base and a foul pretender to candour." So that upon the whole account, we must conclude him either to have been a great hypocrite, or a very honest man; a terrible imposer upon both parties, or very moderate to either.

Be it as to the judicious reader shall seem good. Sure it is, he is little favoured of certain authors whose wrath is perilous: for one declares he ought to have a *price set on his head*, and to be hunted down as a *wild beast.*[2] Another protests that he does not know *what may happen;* advises him to *insure his person;* says he has *bitter enemies*, and expressly declares it will be well if he *escapes with his life.*[3] One desires he would *cut his own throat, or hang himself.*[4] But Pasquin seemed rather inclined it should be done by the government, repre-

---

[1] The names of two weekly papers.—P.
[2] Theobald, Letter in Mist's Journal, June 22, 1728.—P.
[3] Smedley, Pref. to Gulliveriana, pp. 14, 16.—P.
[4] Gulliveriana, p. 332.

senting him engaged in grievous designs with a Lord of Parliament, then under prosecution.[1] Mr. Dennis himself hath written to a *Minister*, that he is one of the most *dangerous persons in this kingdom ;*[2] and assureth the public that he is an *open* and *mortal enemy* to his *country ;* a monster that *will*, one day, show as *daring a soul* as a *mad Indian*, who runs *a muck* to kill the first Christian he meets.[3] Another gives information of *Treason* discovered in his poem.[4] Mr. Curl boldly supplies an imperfect verse with *Kings* and *Princesses*.[5] And one Matthew Concanen, yet more impudent, publishes at length the Two most SACRED NAMES in this nation, as members of the Dunciad ![6]

This is prodigious! yet it is almost as strange that in the midst of these invectives his greatest enemies have (I know not how) borne testimony to some merit in him.

MR. THEOBALD,

in censuring his Shakespear, declares, " He has so great an *esteem* for Mr. Pope, and so high an *opinion* of his *genius* and *excellencies;* that notwithstanding he professes a *veneration almost rising to Idolatry* for the writings of this inimitable poet, he would be very loth even to do

---

[1] Anno 1723.—P.   [2] Anno 1729.—P.

[3] Preface to Rem. on the Rape of the Lock, p. 12, and in the last page of that treatise.—P.

[4] Pages 6, 7, of the Preface, by Concanen, to a book entitled, A Collection of all the Letters, Essays, Verses, and Advertisements, occasioned by Pope and Swift's Miscellanies. Printed for A. Moore, octavo, 1712.—P.

[5] Key to the Dunciad, 3rd edition, p. 18.—P.

[6] A List of Persons, &c. at the end of the forementioned Collection of all the Letters, Essays, &c. —P. The two names were George and Caroline.

him justice at the expense of that *other gentleman's* character."[1]

MR. CHARLES GILDON,

after having violently attacked him in many
pieces, at last came to wish from his heart,
"that Mr. Pope would be prevailed upon to
give us Ovid's Epistles by his hand, for it is
certain we see the original of Sappho to Phaon
with much more life and likeness in his version
than in that of Sir Car. Scrope. And this (he
adds) is the more to be wished, because in the
English tongue we have scarce any thing truly
and naturally written upon Love."[2] He also,
in taxing Sir Richard Blackmore for his hete-
rodox opinions of Homer, challenges him to
answer what Mr. Pope hath said in his preface
to that poet.

MR. OLDMIXON

calls him a great master of our tongue; declares "the purity and perfection of the English language to be found in his Homer; and,
saying there are more good verses in Dryden's
Virgil than in any other work, excepts this of
our author only."[3]

THE AUTHOR OF A LETTER TO MR. CIBBER

says,[4] "Pope was so good a versifier [*once*]
that his predecessor Mr. Dryden, and his co-
temporary Mr. Prior excepted, the harmony of
his numbers *is* equal to any body's. And that

[1] Introduction to his Shakespear Restored, in
quarto, p. 3.—P.
[2] Commentary on the Duke of Buckingham's Essay,
8vo. 1721, pp. 97, 98.—P.
[3] In his prose Essay on Criticism.—P.
[4] Printed by J. Roberts, 1742, p. 11.—P.

he *had* all the merit that a man can have that way." And

MR. THOMAS COOKE,

after much blemishing our author's Homer, crieth out,

But in his other works what beauties shine,
While sweetest music dwells in ev'ry line!
These he admir'd, on these he stamp'd his praise,
And bade them live to brighten future days.[1]

So also one who takes the name of

H. STANHOPE,

the maker of certain verses to Duncan Camp-bell, in that poem,[2] which is wholly a satire on Mr. Pope, confesseth,

'Tis true, if finest notes alone could show
(Tun'd justly high, or regularly low)
That we should fame to these mere vocals give;
Pope more than we can offer should receive:
For when some gliding river is his theme,
His lines run smoother than the smoothest stream, &c.

MIST'S JOURNAL, JUNE 8, 1728.

Although he says, " The smooth numbers of the Dunciad are all that recommend it, nor has it any other merit;" yet that same paper hath these words: " The author is allowed to be a perfect master of an easy and elegant versifica-tion. *In all his works* we find the most *happy turns*, and *natural similes*, wonderfully short and thick sown."

The Essay on the Dunciad also owns, p. 25, it is very full of *beautiful images.* But the

[1] Battle of Poets, folio, p. 15.—P.
[2] Printed under the title of the Progress of Dulness duodecimo, 1728.—P.

panegyric, which crowns all that can be said
on this Poem, is bestowed by our Laureate,

MR. COLLEY CIBBER,

who " grants it to be a better poem of its kind
that ever was writ:" but adds, " it was a victory over a parcel of poor wretches, whom it
was almost cowardice to conquer.—A man
might as well triumph for having killed so
many silly flies that offended him. Could he
have let them alone, by this time, poor souls !
they had all been buried in oblivion." [1]   Here
we see our excellent Laureate allows the justice
of the satire on every man in it but *himself*, as
the great Mr. Dennis did before him.

The said

MR. DENNIS AND MR. GILDON,

in the most furious of all their works (the
fore-cited Character, p. 5), do in concert [2] con-

[1] Cibber's Letter to Mr. Pope, pp. 9, 12.—P.

[2] Hear how Mr. Dennis hath proved our mistake in
this place : " As to my writing in *concert* with Mr.
Gildon, I declare upon the honour and word of a gentleman, that I never wrote so much as one line in
concert with any one man whatsoever : and these two
Letters from Gildon will plainly show that we are not
writers in *concert* with each other.

Sir,
——The height of my ambition is to please Men of
the best Judgment ; and finding that I have entertained my Master agreeably, I have the extent of the
Reward of my Labour.

Sir,
I had not the opportunity of hearing of your excellent
Pamphlet till this day.   I am infinitely satisfied and
pleased with it, and hope you will meet with that en-
couragement your admirable performance deserves, &c.
CH. GILDON.

" Now is it not plain that any one who sends such

fess, "that some men of *good understanding*
value him for his rhymes." And (p. 17) "That
he has got, like Mr. Bays in the Rehearsal
(that is, like Mr. Dryden), a notable knack at
rhyming, and writing smooth verse."

Of his Essay on Man, numerous were the
praises bestowed by his avowed enemies, in the
imagination that the same was not written by
him, as it was printed anonymously.

Thus sang of it even

BEZALEEL MORRIS.

Auspicious bard ! while all admire thy strain,
All but the selfish, ignorant, and vain ;
I, whom no bribe to servile flatt'ry drew,
Must pay the tribute to thy merit due :
Thy Muse sublime, significant, and clear,
Alike informs the Soul, and charms the Ear.

And

MR. LEONARD WELSTED

thus wrote[1] to the unknown author on the first
publication of the said Essay : "I must own,
after the reception which the vilest and most
immoral ribaldry hath lately met with, I was
surprised to see what I had long despaired, a
performance deserving the name of a poet.
Such, Sir, is your work. It is, indeed, above
all commendation, and ought to have been
published in an age and country more worthy
of it. If my testimony be of weight any where,

compliments to another, has not been used to write
in partnership with him to whom he sends them ? "
Dennis, Rem. on the Dunc., p. 50. Mr. Dennis
is therefore welcome to take this piece to himself.
—P.

[1] In a letter under his hand, dated March 12, 1733.
—P.

you are sure to have it in the amplest manner,"
&c. &c. &c.

Thus we see every one of his works hath
been extolled by one or other of his most
inveterate enemies ; and to the success of them
all they do unanimously give testimony. But
it is sufficient, *instar omnium*, to behold the
great critic, Mr. Dennis, sorely lamenting it,
even from the Essay on Criticism to this day
of the Dunciad ! "A most notorious instance
(quoth he) of the depravity of genius and taste,
the *approbation* this essay meets with.[1]—I can
safely affirm, that I never attacked any of these
writings, unless they had *success* infinitely
beyond their merit.—This, though an empty,
has been a *popular* scribbler. The epidemic
madness of the times has given him *reputation.*[2]—If, after the cruel treatment so many
extraordinary men (Spenser, Lord Bacon, Ben
Jonson, Milton, Butler, Otway, and others)
have received from this country for these last
hundred years, I should shift the scene, and
show all that penury changed at once to riot
and profuseness ; and more squandered away
upon *one object* than would have satisfied the
greater part of those extraordinary men ; the
reader, to whom this one creature should be
unknown, would fancy him a prodigy of art
and nature ; would believe that all the great
qualities of these persons were centred in him
alone.—But if I should venture to assure him
that the PEOPLE of ENGLAND had made such a
choice—the reader would either believe me a
malicious enemy and *slanderer*, or that the reign

[1] Dennis, Pref. to his Reflect. on the Essay on Criticism. — P.
[2] Pref. to his Rem. on Homer. — P.

of the last (Queen Anne's) *Ministry* was designed by fate to encourage *Fools*."[1]

But it happens that this our Poet never had any Place, Pension, or Gratuity, in any shape, from the said glorious Queen, or any of her ministers. All he owed, in the whole course of his life, to any court, was a subscription for his Homer, of 200*l.* from King George I, and 100*l.* from the Prince and Princess.

However, lest we imagine our Author's Success, was constant and universal, they acquaint us of certain works in a less degree of repute, whereof, although owned by others, yet do they assure us he is the writer. Of this sort Mr. DENNIS[2] ascribes to him *two Farces*, whose names he does not tell, but assures us that *there is not one jest in them;* And an imitation of Horace, whose title he does not mention, but assures us *it is much more execrable than all his works*.[3] The DAILY JOURNAL, May 11, 1728, assures us, "He is below Tom Durfey in the Drama, because (as that writer thinks) the Marriage-Hater matched, and the Boarding School, are better than the What-d'ye-call-it : " which is not Mr. P's. but Mr. Gay's. Mr. Gildon assures us, in his New Rehearsal, p. 48, "That he was writing a Play of the Lady Jane Grey;" but it afterwards proved to be Mr. Rowe's. We are assured by another, "He wrote a pamphlet called Dr. Andrew Tripe;"[4] which proved to be one Dr. Wagstaff's. Mr. THEOBALD assures us, in Mist of the 27th of April, "That the treatise of the *Profound* is very

---

[1] Rem. on Homer, pp. 8, 9.—P.
[2] *Ibid.* p. 8.—P.
[3] Character of Mr. Pope, p. 7.—P.
[4] *Ibid.* p. 6.—P.

dull, and that Mr. Pope is the author of it,"
The writer of Gulliveriana is of another opinion;
and says, " the whole, or greatest part, of the
merit of this treatise must and can only be
ascribed to Gulliver." [1] [Here, gentle reader !
cannot I but smile at the strange blindness and
positiveness of men, knowing the said treatise
to appertain to none other but to me, Martinus
Scriblerus.]

We are assured, in Mist of June 8, " That his
own *Plays* and *Farces* would better have adorned
the Dunciad than those of Mr. Theobald ; for
he had neither genius for Tragedy nor Comedy."
Which, whether true or not, it is not easy to
judge, in as much as he had attempted neither.
Unless we will take it for granted, with Mr.
Cibber, that his being once very angry at hearing a friend's Play abused, was an infallible
proof the Play was his own ; the said Mr. Cibber
thinking it impossible for a man to be much
concerned for any but himself : " Now let any
man judge (saith he) by this concern, who was
the true mother of the child ? " [2]

But from all that hath been said, the discern-
ing reader will collect, that it little availed
our author to have any Candour, since, when
he declared he did not write for others, it was
not credited ; as little to have any Modesty,
since, when he declined writing in any way
himself, the presumption of others was imputed
to him.   If he singly enterprised one great
work, he was taxed of Boldness and Madness
to a prodigy : [3] If he took assistants in another,

[1] Gulliv. p. 336.—P.
[2] Cibber's Letter to Mr. Pope, p. 19.—P.
[3] Burnet's Homerides, p. 1, of his translation of the
Iliad.—P.

it was complained of, and represented as a great
injury to the public.[1] The loftiest heroics, the
lowest ballads, treatises against the state or
church, satires on lords and ladies, raillery on
wits and authors, squabbles with booksellers,
and even full and true accounts of monsters,
poisons, and murders; of any hereof was there
nothing so good, nothing so bad, which had not,
at one or other season, been to him ascribed.
If it bore no author's name, then lay he concealed; if it did, he fathered it upon that author
to be yet better concealed: If it resembled any
of his styles, then was it evident; if it did not,
then disguised he it on set purpose. Yea, even
direct oppositions in religion, principles, and
politics, have equally been supposed in him
inherent. Surely a most rare and singular
character! Of which let the reader make what
he can.

Doubtless most Commentators would hence
take occasion to turn all to their Author's
advantage, and, from the testimony of his very
enemies, would affirm, that his Capacity was
boundless as well as his Imagination; that he
was a perfect master of all Styles, and all
Arguments; and that there was in those times
no other Writer, in any kind, of any degree of
excellence, save he himself. But as this is not
our own sentiment, we shall determine on
nothing; but leave thee, gentle reader, to steer
thy judgment equally between various opinions,
and to choose whether thou wilt incline to the
Testimonies of Authors avowed, or of Authors
concealed; of those who knew him, or of those
who knew him not.

[1] The London and Mist's Journals, on his undertaking the Odyssey.—P.

MARTINUS SCRIBLERUS

OF THE POEM.

THIS poem, as it celebrateth the most grave and ancient of things, Chaos, Night, and Dulness; so is it of the most grave and ancient kind. Homer (saith Aristotle) was the first who gave the *Form*, and (saith Horace) who adapted the *Measure*, to heroic poesy. But even before this, may be rationally presumed, from what the Ancients have left written, was a piece by Homer, composed of like nature and matter with this of our Poet. For of Epic sort it appeareth to have been, yet of matter surely not unpleasant, witness what is reported of it by the learned Archbishop Eustathius, in Odyss. X. And accordingly Aristotle, in his Poetic, chap. iv. doth further set forth, that as the Iliad and Odyssey gave an example to Tragedy, so did this poem to Comedy its first idea.

From these authors also it should seem, that the Hero, or chief personage of it, was no less *obscure*, and his understanding and sentiments no less quaint and strange (if indeed not more so) than any of the actors of our poem. MARGITES was the name of this personage, whom Antiquity recordeth to have been *Dunce the first;* and surely, from what we hear of him, not unworthy to be the root of so spreading a tree, and so numerous a posterity. The poem, therefore, celebrating him, was properly and absolutely a Dunciad; which though now unhappily lost, yet is its nature sufficiently known by the infallible tokens aforesaid. And thus it doth appear that the first Dunciad was the first Epic poem, written by Homer himself, and anterior even to the Iliad or Odyssey.

Now, forasmuch as our poet had translated those two famous works of Homer which are yet left, he did conceive it in some sort his duty to imitate that also which was lost; and was therefore induced to bestow on it the same form which Homer's is reported to have had, namely that of Epic poem; with a title also framed after the ancient Greek manner, to wit, that of *Dunciad*.

Wonderful it is that so few of the moderns have been stimulated to attempt some Dunciad! since, in the opinion of the multitude, it might cost less pain and toil than an imitation of the greater Epic. But possible it is also that, on due reflection, the maker might find it easier to paint a Charlemagne, a Brute, or a Godfrey, with just pomp and dignity heroic, than a Margites, a Codrus, or a Flecknoe.

We shall next declare the occasion and the cause which moved our poet to this particular work. He lived in those days, when (after Providence had permitted the invention of Printing as a scourge for the sins of the learned) Paper also became so cheap, and Printers so numerous, that a deluge of Authors covered the land: whereby not only the peace of the honest unwriting subject was daily molested, but unmerciful demands were made of his applause, yea, of his money, by such as would neither earn the one, nor deserve the other. At the same time, the license of the Press was such, that it grew dangerous to refuse them either; for they would forthwith publish slanders unpunished, the authors being anonymous, and skulking under the wings of Publishers, a set of men who never scrupled to vend either calumny or blasphemy, as long as the Town would call for it.

Now [1] our author, living in those times, did conceive it an endeavour well worthy an honest Satirist, to dissuade the dull, and punish the wicked, *the only way that was left.* In that public-spirited view he laid the plan of this poem, as the greatest service he was capable (without much hurt, or being slain) to render his dear country. First, taking things from their original, he considereth the causes creative of such Authors, namely, *Dulness* and *Poverty;* the one born with them, the other contracted by neglect of their proper talents, through self-conceit of greater abilities. This truth he wrappeth in an *Allegory* [2] (as the construction of Epic poesy requireth) and feigns that one of these Goddesses had taken up her abode with the other, and that they jointly inspired all such writers and such works. [3] He proceedeth to show the *qualities* they bestow on these authors, and the *effects* they produce; [4] then the *materials*, or *stock*, with which they furnish them; [5] and (above all) that *self-opinion* [6] which causeth it to seem to themselves vastly greater than it is, and is the prime motive of their setting up in this sad and sorry merchandise. The great power of these Goddesses acting in alliance (whereof as the one is the mother of Industry, so is the other of Plodding) was to

---

[1] Vide Bossu, Du Poëme Epique, chap. viii.—P.
[2] Bossu, chap. vii.—P.
[3] Book i. ver. 32, &c.—P.
[4] Ver. 45 to 54. P.
[5] Ver. 57 to 77.—P.   [6] Ver. 80.—P.

be exemplified in some *one, great,* and *remarkable Action;* [1] And none could be more so than that which our poet hath chosen, viz. the restoration of the reign of Chaos and Night, by the ministry of Dulness their daughter, in the removal of her imperial seat from the City to the polite World; as the Action of the Æneid is the restoration of the empire of Troy, by the removal of the race from thence to Latium. But as Homer singing only the *Wrath* of Achilles, yet includes in his Poem the whole history of the Trojan War; in like manner, our author has drawn into this *single Action* the whole history of Dulness and her children.

A *Person* must next be fixed upon to support this Action. This *Phantom,* in the poet's mind, must have a *Name ;* [2] He finds it to be —— ; and he becomes of course the Hero of the Poem.

The *Fable* being thus, according to the best Example, one and entire, as contained in the proposition; the *Machinery* is a continued chain of Allegories, setting forth the whole Power, Ministry, and Empire of Dulness, extended through her subordinate instruments, in all her various operations.

This is branched into *Episodes,* each of which hath its Moral apart, though all conducive to the main end. The Crowd assembled in the Second Book demonstrates the design to be more extensive than to bad poets only, and that we may expect other Episodes of the Patrons, Encouragers, or Paymasters of such authors, as occasion shall bring them forth. And the Third Book, if well considered, seemeth

[1] Bossu, chap. vii. viii.—P.
[2] Bossu, chap. viii. Vide Aristot. Poetic. cap. ix. —P.

to embrace the whole World. Each of the
Games relateth to some or other vile class of
writers : The first concerneth the Plagiary, to
whom he giveth the name of More; the second
the libellous Novelist, whom he styleth Eliza ;
the third, the flattering Dedicator ; the fourth,
the bawling Critic, or noisy Poet; the fifth, the
dark and dirty Party-writer ; and so of the
rest ; assigning to each some *proper name* or
other, such as he could find.

As for the *Characters,* the public hath already
acknowledged how justly they are drawn :
The manners are so depicted, and the sentiments so peculiar to those to whom applied,
that surely to transfer them to any other or
wiser personages would be exceeding difficult ;
And certain it is that every person concerned,
being consulted apart, hath readily owned the
resemblance of every portrait, his own excepted. So Mr. Cibber calls them " a parcel of
poor wretches, so many *silly flies;* " [1] but adds,
" our Author's Wit is remarkably more bare
and barren whenever it would fall foul on
Cibber than upon any other person whatever."

The *Descriptions* are singular, the *Compari-
sons* very quaint, the *Narration* various, yet of
one colour; The purity and chastity of *Diction*
is so preserved, that in the places most sus-
picious, not the *words,* but only the *images,*
have been censured, and yet are those images
no other than have been sanctified by ancient
and classical Authority (though, as was the
manner of those good times, not so curiously
wrapped up), yea, and commented upon by the
most grave Doctors and approved Critics.

[1] Cibber's Letter to Mr. P. pp. 9, 12, 41. — P.

As it beareth the name of *Epic*, it is thereby
subjected to such severe indispensable rules as
are laid on all Neoterics, a strict imitation of
the Ancients ; insomuch that any deviation,
accompanied with whatever poetic beauties,
hath always been censured by the sound Critic.
How exact that Imitation hath been in this
piece, appeareth not only by its general structure, but by particular allusions infinite, many
whereof have escaped both the commentator
and poet himself ; yea divers by his exceeding
diligence, are so altered and interwoven with
the rest, that several have already been, and
more will be, by the ignorant abused, as alto-
gether and originally his own.

In a word, the whole poem proveth itself to
be the work of our Author, when his faculties
were in full vigour and perfection ; at that
exact time when years have ripened the Judgment, without diminishing the Imagination ;
which, by good critics, is held to be punctually
at *forty*. For at that season it was that Virgil
finished his Georgics ; and Sir Richard Blackmore, at the like age composing his Arthurs,
declared the same to be the very *acme* and
pitch of life for Epic poesy ; Though since he
hath altered it to *sixty*, the year in which he
published his Alfred.[1] True it is that the
talents for *Criticism*, namely, smartness, quick
censure, vivacity of remark, certainty of as-
severation, indeed all but acerbity, seem rather
the gifts of youth than of riper Age : but it is
far otherwise in *Poetry ;* witness the works of
Mr. Rymer and Mr. Dennis, who, beginning
with Criticism, became afterwards such poets

[1] See his Essays.—P.

as no age hath paralleled. With good reason,
therefore, did our author choose to write his
Essay on that subject at twenty, and reserve
for his maturer years this great and wonderful
work of the Dunciad.—P.

RICARDUS ARISTARCHUS

OF THE

HERO OF THE POEM.

Of the Nature of Dunciad in general, whence
derived, and on what authority founded, as well
as of the Art and conduct of this our poem in
particular, the learned and laborious Scriblerus
hath, according to his manner, and with tolerable
share of judgment, dissertated. But when he
cometh to speak of the *Person* of the Hero fitted
for such poem, in truth he miserably halts and
hallucinates. For, misled by one Monsieur
Bossu, a Gallic critic, he prateth of I cannot
tell what phantom of a Hero, only raised up
to support the fable. A putid conceit! As
if Homer and Virgil, like modern Undertakers,
who first build their house, and then seek out
for a tenant, had contrived the story of a war
and a wandering before they once thought
either of Achilles or Æneas. We shall therefore set our good brother, and the world also,
right in this particular, by assuring them that,
in the greater Epic, the prime intention of the
Muse is to exalt Heroic Virtue, in order to
propagate the love of it among the *children* of
men ; and, consequently, that the poet's first

thought must needs be turned upon a real subject meet for laud and celebration; not one whom he is to make, but one whom he may find truly illustrious. This is the *primum mobile* of his poetic world, whence every thing is to receive life and motion. For this subject being found, he is immediately ordained, or rather acknowledged, a *Hero*, and put upon such action as befitteth the dignity of his character.

But the Muse ceaseth not here her eagle flight: for sometimes, satiated with the contemplation of these *Suns of glory*, she turneth downward on her wing; and darts, with Jove's lightning, on the *Goose* and *Serpent* kind. For we may apply to the Muse, in her various moods, what an ancient master of wisdom affirmeth of the Gods in general: *Si Dii non irascuntur impiis et injustis, nec pios utique justosque diligunt. In rebus enim diversis, aut in utramque partem moveri necesse est, aut in neutram. Itaque qui bonos diligit, et malos odit; et qui malos non odit, nec bonos diligit. Quin et diligere bonos ex odio malorum venit; et malos odisse ex bonorum caritate descendit.* Which in our vernacular idiom may be thus interpreted: "If the Gods be not provoked at evil men, neither are they delighted with the good and just. For contrary objects must either excite contrary affections or no affections at all. So that he who loveth good men must at the same time hate the bad; and he who hateth not bad men cannot love the good; because to love good men proceedeth from an aversion to evil; and to hate evil men from a tenderness to the good." From this delicacy of the Muse arose the *little Epic* (more lively and choleric than her elder sister, whose bulk and complexion incline her to the phleg-

matic) ; and for this some notorious vehicle of
vice and folly was sought out, to make thereof an
EXAMPLE. An early instance of which (nor could
it escape the accurate Scriblerus) the Father of
Epic-poem himself affordeth us. From him the
practice descended to the Greek dramatic Poets,
his offspring ; who, in the composition of their
Tetralogy, or set of four pieces, were wont to
make the last a *Satiric Tragedy*. Happily one
of these ancient *Dunciads* (as we may term it)
is come down unto us, amongst the Tragedies of
the poet Euripides. And what doth the reader
suppose may be the subject thereof ? Why, in
truth, and it is worthy observation, the unequal
Contest of an *old, dull, debauched buffoon, Cyclops,*
with the heaven-directed *Favourite of Minerva:*
who, after having quietly borne all the monster's
obscene and impious ribaldry, endeth the farce
in punishing him with the mark of an indelible
brand in his *forehead.* May we not then be
excused if, for the future, we consider the Epics
of Homer, Virgil, and Milton, together with
this our poem, as a complete *Tetralogy*, in which
the last worthily holdeth the place or station of
the *satiric* piece ?

Proceed we therefore in our subject. It hath
been long, and alas for pity ! still remaineth a
question, whether the Hero of the *greater Epic*
should be an *honest Man;* or, as the French
critics express it, *un honnête homme:*[1] but it
never admitted of any doubt but that the Hero
of the *little Epic* should be just the contrary.
Hence, to the advantage of our Dunciad, we
may observe how much juster the Moral of

---

[1] Si un Héros Poëtique doit être un honnête homme.
Bossu, Du Poëme Epique, liv. v. ch. 5.—P.

that poem must needs be, where so important
a question is previously decided.

But then it is not every Knave, nor (let me
add) every Fool, that is a fit subject for a
Dunciad. There must still exist some analogy,
if not resemblance of Qualities between the
Heroes of the two poems; and this, in order
to admit what Neoteric critics call the *Parody*,
one of the liveliest graces of the little Epic.
Thus it being agreed that the constituent
qualities of the greater Epic Hero are *Wisdom, Bravery*, and *Love*, from whence springeth
heroic Virtue; it followeth that those of the lesser
Epic Hero should be *Vanity, Assurance*, and
Debauchery, from which happy assemblage re-
sulteth *heroic Dulness*, the never-dying subject
of this our Poem.

This being settled, come we now to particulars. It is the character of true *Wisdom* to seek
its chief support and confidence within itself;
and to place that support in the resources which
proceed from a conscious rectitude of Will.—
And are the advantages of *Vanity*, when arising
to the heroic standard, at all short of this self-
complacence? Nay, are they not, in the opinion
of the enamoured owner, far beyond it? "Let
the world (will such an one say) impute to me
what *Folly* or weakness they please; but till
Wisdom can give me something that will make
me more heartily happy, I am content to be
gazed at."[1] This, we see, is *Vanity*, according
to the *heroic* gage or measure; not that low and
ignoble species which pretendeth to *virtues* we
have not; but the laudable ambition of being
gazed at for glorying in those *vices* which every

---

[1] Ded. to the Life of C. C.—P.

body knows *we have.* "The world may ask (says he) why I make my follies public? Why not? I have passed my time very pleasantly with them."[1] In short, there is no sort of Vanity such a Hero would scruple, but that which might go near to degrade him from his high station in this our Dunciad; namely, "Whether it would not be *Vanity* in him to take shame to himself for *not being a wise man?*"[2]

Bravery, the second attribute of the true Hero, is Courage manifesting itself in every limb; while its correspondent virtue in the mock Hero is that same Courage all collected into the Face. And as Power, when drawn together, must needs have more force and spirit than when dispersed, we generally find this kind of courage in so high and heroic a degree, that it insults not only Men, but Gods. Mezentius is, without doubt, the bravest character in all the Æneis: but how? His bravery, we know, was a high courage of blasphemy. And can we say less of this brave man's, who, having told us that he placed "his *summum bonum* in those follies which he was not content barely to possess, but would likewise glory in," adds, "If I am misguided, 'tis Nature's fault, and I follow her."[3] Nor can we be mistaken in making this happy quality a species of *Courage,* when we consider those illustrious marks of it which made his Face "more known (as he justly boasteth) than most in the kingdom;" and his *Language* to consist of what we must allow to be the most *daring* Figure of Speech, that which is taken from the *Name of God.*

Gentle Love, the next ingredient in the true

Life of C. C., p. 2, octavo edit.—P.   [2] *Ibid.* P.
Ibid. p. 23, octavo.— P.

Hero's composition, is a mere bird of passage, or (as Shakespear calls it) *summer-teeming Lust*, and evaporates in the heat of *Youth;* doubtless by that refinement it suffers in passing through those *certain strainers* which our poet somewhere speaketh of. But when it is let alone to work upon the *Lees*, it acquireth strength by *Old age*, and becometh a lasting ornament to the little Epic. It is true, indeed, there is one objection to its fitness for such an use ; For not only the ignorant may think it common, but it is admitted to be so even by him who best knoweth its value. "Don't you think (argueth he) to say only *a man has his Whore*,[1] ought to go for little or nothing? Because, *defendit numerus*, take the first ten thousand men you meet, and, I believe, you would be no loser if you betted ten to one that every single sinner of them, one with another, had been guilty of the same frailty."[2] But here he seemeth not to have done justice to himself: The man is sure enough a Hero who hath his Lady at fourscore. How doth his modesty herein lessen the merit of a *whole well-spent Life:* not taking to himself the commendation (which *Horace* accounted the greatest in a theatrical character) of continuing to the very *dregs* the same he was from the beginning,

―――*Servetur ad imum*
Qualis ab incepto processerat.―――

But here, in justice both to the Poet and the

―――
[1] Alluding to these lines in the Epist. to Dr. Arbuthnot :
And has not Colley still his lord and whore,
His butchers Henley, his free-masons Moore ?—P.
[2] Letter to Mr. P. p. 46.—P.

Hero, let us farther remark, that the calling her *his* Whore implieth she was *his own*, and not *his neighbour's*. Truly, a commendable Continence! and such as Scipio himself must have applauded : for how much Self-denial was exerted not to covet his neighbour's whore! and what disorders must the coveting her have occasioned in that Society, where (according to this political calculator) *nine* in *ten* of all ages have their *concubines!*

We have now, as briefly as we could devise, gone through the three constituent qualities of either Hero. But it is not in any, nor in all of these, that Heroism properly or essentially resideth. It is a lucky result rather from the collision of these lively qualities against one another. Thus, as from Wisdom, Bravery, and Love, ariseth *Magnanimity*, the object of *Admiration*, which is the aim of the greater Epic ; so from Vanity, Impudence, and Debauchery, springeth *Buffoonery*, the source of *Ridicule*, that "laughing ornament," as the owner well termeth it[1] of the little Epic.

He is not ashamed (God forbid he ever should be ashamed!) of this character ; who deemeth that not *Reason*, but *Risibility* distinguisheth the human species from the brutal. "As Nature (saith this profound philosopher) distinguisheth our species from the mute creation by our Risibility, her design must have been by that faculty as evidently to raise our *happiness*, as by *our Os sublime* (our Erected Faces) to lift the dignity of our form above them."[2] All this considered, how complete a Hero must he be, as well as how happy a Man,

[1] Letter to Mr. P. p. 31.—P.
[2] Life, pp. 23, 24.—P.

whose Risibility lieth not barely in his *muscles,*
as in the common sort, but (as himself in-
formeth us) in his very *spirits?* And whose *Os
sublime* is not simply an Erect Face, but a
brazen head; as should seem by his preferring
it to one of *Iron,* said to belong to the late
King of Sweden.[1]

But whatever personal qualities a Hero may
have, the examples of Achilles and Æneas show
us that all these are of small avail without the
constant *assistance of the* Gods : for the subversion and erection of Empires have never been
adjudged the work of Man. How greatly so-
ever then we may esteem of his high talents,
we can hardly conceive his personal prowess
alone sufficient to restore the decayed empire of
Dulness. So weighty an achievement must re-
quire the particular favour and protection of
the GREAT : who, being the natural patrons and
supporters of *Letters* as the ancient Gods were
of *Troy,* must first be drawn off, and engaged
in another Interest, before the total subversion
of them can be accomplished. To surmount,
therefore, this last and greatest difficulty, we
have, in this excellent man, a professed Favourite and Intimado of the GREAT. And look
of what force ancient piety was to draw the
Gods into the party of Æneas, that, and much
stronger is modern Incense, to engage the
Great in the party of Dulness.

Thus have we essayed to portray or shadow
out this noble Imp of Fame. But now the
impatient reader will be apt to say, if so many
and various graces go to the making up a Hero,
what mortal shall suffice to bear his character?

[1] Letter, p. 8.—P.

Ill hath he read, who seeth not, in every trace
of this picture, that *individual*, ALL-ACCOM-
PLISHED PERSON, in whom these rare virtues and
lucky circumstances have agreed to meet and
concentre, with the strongest lustre and fullest
harmony.

The good Scriblerus, indeed, nay, the World
itself might be imposed on, in the late spurious
editions, by I cannot tell what *Sham Hero* or
Phantom; But it was not so easy to impose on
HIM whom this egregious error most of all concerned. For no sooner had the Fourth Book
laid open the high and swelling scene, but he
recognised his own heroic Acts; and when he
came to the words,

> '*Soft on her lap her Laureat son reclines,*'

(though *Laureat* imply no more than *one
crowned with laurel*, as befitteth any associate
or Consort in Empire) he loudly resented this
indignity to violated Majesty. Indeed not
without cause, he being there represented as
fast asleep; so misbeseeming the Eye of Empire;
which, like that of Jove, should never doze nor
slumber. "Hah! (saith he) fast asleep it
seems! that is a little too strong. Pert and
dull at least you might have allowed me, but
as seldom asleep as any fool." [1] However, the
injured Hero may comfort himself with this
reflection, that though it be a *sleep*, yet it is
not the *sleep of Death*, but of *immortality*.
Here he will [2] *live* at least, though not *awake*,
and in no worse condition than many an en-
chanted Warrior before him. The famous
Durandarte, for instance, was, like him, cast

[1] Letter, p. 53.—P.   [2] *Ibid.* p. 1.—P.

into a long slumber by *Merlin* the *British Bard*
and Necromancer; and his example, for sub-
mitting to it with a good grace, might be of
use to our Hero. For that disastrous knight,
being sorely pressed or driven to make his
answer by several *persons* of *Quality*, only replied with a sigh, " Patience, and shuffle the
cards." [1]

But now, as nothing in this world, no, not
the most sacred and perfect things either of
Religion or Government, can escape the stings
of Envy, methinks I already hear these carpers
objecting to the clearness of our Hero's title.

It would never (say they) have been esteemed sufficient to make a Hero for the Iliad
or Æneis, that Achilles was brave enough to
overturn one Empire, or Æneas pious enough
to raise another, had they not been Goddess-
born, and Princes bred. What then did this
Author mean by erecting a Player, instead of
one of his Patrons (a person "never a Hero
even on the stage," [2]) to this dignity of Colleague in the empire of Dulness ; and Achiever
of a work that neither old Omar, Attila, nor
John of Leyden, could entirely bring to pass ?

To all this we have, as we conceive, a sufficient answer from the Roman historian, *Fabrum
esse suæ quemque fortunæ:* " that every man is
the *smith* of his own fortune." The politic
Florentine, Nicholas Machiavel, goeth still
further, and affirmeth, that a man needeth but to
believe himself a Hero to be one of the worthiest
that ever lived. " Let him (saith he) but
fancy himself capable of high things, and he
will of course be able to achieve them." From

---

[1] Don Quixote, Part ii. Book ii. ch. 22.—P.
[2] See Life, p. 148.—P.

this principle it followeth that nothing can
exceed our Hero's prowess, as nothing ever
equalled the greatness of his conceptions.
Hear how he constantly paragons himself; at
one time to Alexander the Great and Charles XII.
of Sweden, for the excess and delicacy of his
Ambition;[1] to Henry IV. of France, for honest
Policy;[2] to the first Brutus for love of Liberty;[3]
and to Sir Robert Walpole, for good Government while in power.[4]   At another time to the
godlike Socrates, for his Diversions and Amuse-
ments;[5] to Horace, Montaigne, and Sir William
Temple, for an elegant vanity that maketh
them for ever read and admired;[6] to two Lord
Chancellors, for Law, from whom, when con-
federate against him at the bar, he carried away
the prize of Eloquence;[7] and to say all in a
word, to the Right Reverend the Lord Bishop
of London himself, in the art of writing *Pastoral
letters.*[8]

Nor did his *Actions* fall short of the sublimity
of his Conceit.   In his early youth he *met the
Revolution*[9] face to face in Nottingham, at a time
when his Betters contented themselves with
following her.   It was here he got acquainted
with *Old Battle-array*, of whom he hath made
so honourable mention in one of his immortal
Odes.[10]   But he shone in Courts as well as in
Camps; he was *called up*, when *the Nation fell*

---

[1] See Life, p. 149.—P.
[2] P. 424.—P.
[3] P. 366.—P.
[4] P. 457.—P.
[5] P. 18.—P.
[6] P. 425.—P.
[7] Pp. 436, 437.—P.
[8] P. 52.—P.
[9] P. 47.—P.

[10] Old Battle-array in confusion is fled;
    And olive-rob'd Peace is come in his stead, &c.
        CIBBER'S *Birthday, or, New Year's Day Ode.*

in labour of this *Revolution*,[1] and was a gossip at her christening, with the Bishop and the Ladies.[2]

As to his *Birth*, it is true he pretendeth no relation either to heathen God or Goddess ; but, what is as good, he was descended from a *Maker* of both.[3] And that he did not pass himself on the world for a *Hero, as well by birth as education, was his own fault; for his lineage he bringeth into his life as an Anecdote, and is sensible he had it in his power *to be thought no body's son at all :*[4] And what is that but coming into the world a hero ?

But be it (the punctilious Laws of Epic Poesy so requiring) that a Hero of more than mortal birth must needs be had ; even for this we have a remedy. We can easily derive our Hero's pedigree from a Goddess of no small power and authority amongst men ; and legitimate and install him after the right classical and authentic fashion : For, like as the ancient Sages found a son of Mars in a mighty warrior ; a son of Neptune in a skilful seaman; a son of Phœbus in a harmonious poet; so have we here, if need be, a son of FORTUNE in an artful *Gamester*. And who fitter than the Offspring of *Chance* to assist in restoring the Empire of *Night* and *Chaos?*

There is, in truth, another objection of greater weight, namely, " That this Hero still existeth, and hath not yet finished his earthly course. For, if Solon said well, that no man could be called happy till his death, surely much less can any one, till then, be pronounced a Hero ; this species of men being far more subject than

---

[1] Life, p. 57. [2] Pp. 58, 59.—P.
[3] A Statuary.—P. [4] Life, p. 6.—P.

others to the caprices of Fortune and Humour."
But to this also we have an answer, that will
(we hope) be deemed decisive. It cometh from
himself, who, to cut this matter short, hath
solemnly protested that *he will never change or
amend*.

With regard to his *Vanity*, he declareth that
nothing shall ever part them. " Nature (saith
he) hath amply supplied me in *Vanity;* a
pleasure which neither the pertness of Wit, nor
the gravity of Wisdom will ever persuade me
to part with."[1] Our poet had charitably
endeavoured to administer a cure to it; But he
telleth us plainly, " My superiors, perhaps, may
be mended by him; but, for my part, I own
myself incorrigible. I look upon my *Follies* as
the best part of my Fortune."[2] And with
good reason : we see to what they have brought
him !

Secondly, as to *Buffoonery*, "Is it (saith he) a
time of day for me to leave off these fooleries,
and set up a new character ? I can no more put
off my *Follies* than my Skin : I have often tried,
but they stick too close to me; nor am I sure
my friends are displeased with them, for in this
light I afford them frequent matter of mirth,"
&c. &c.[3] Having then so publicly declared
himself *incorrigible*, he is become *dead in law*,
(I mean the *law Epopœian*) and devolveth upon
the Poet as his property; who may take him
and deal with him as if he had been dead as
long as an old Egyptian Hero; that is to say,
embowel and *embalm* him for Posterity.

Nothing therefore (we conceive) remaineth to
hinder his own prophecy of himself from taking

[1] Life, p. 424.   [2] P. 19.
[3] P. 17.—P.

immediate effect. A rare felicity! and what few prophets have had the satisfaction to see, alive! Nor can we conclude better than with that extraordinary one of his, which is conceived in these Oraculous words, MY DULNESS WILL FIND SOMEBODY TO DO IT RIGHT.[1]

Tandem Phœbus adest, morsusque inferre parantem
Congelat, et patulos, ut erant, indurat hiatus.[2]

[1] Life, p. 243, octavo edit.—P.
[2] *Ovid*, of the serpent biting at Orpheus's head.—P.

THE DUNCIAD.

IN FOUR BOOKS.

BY AUTHORITY.

By virtue of the Authority in Us vested by the Act for subjecting Poets to the power of a Licenser, we have revised this Piece; where, finding the style and appellation of King to have been given to a certain Pretender, Pseudo-Poet, or Phantom, of the name of TIBBALD; and apprehending the same may be deemed in some sort a Reflection on Majesty, or at least an insult on that legal authority which has bestowed on another person the Crown of Poesy: we have ordered the said Pretender, Pseudo-Poet, or Phantom, utterly to vanish and evaporate out of this work: And do declare the said Throne of Poesy from henceforth to be abdicated and vacant, unless duly and lawfully sup=plied by the LAUREATE himself. And it is hereby enacted, that no other person do presume to fill the same.

C. CII.

THE DUNCIAD:

TO

DR. JONATHAN SWIFT.

BOOK THE FIRST.

ARGUMENT.

The proposition, the invocation, and the inscription. Then the original of the great Empire of Dulness, and cause of the continuance thereof. The
College of the Goddess in the city, with her private
academy for poets in particular ; the governors of it,
and the four cardinal virtues. Then the poem hastes
into the midst of things, presenting her, on the
evening of a Lord Mayor's day, revolving the long
succession of her sons, and the glories past and to
come. She fixes her eye on Bays to be the instru-
ment of that great event which is the subject of the
poem. He is described pensive among his books,
giving up the cause, and apprehending the period of
her Empire : After debating whether to betake himself to the Church, or to gaming, or to party-writing,
he raises an altar of proper books, and (making first
his solemn prayer and declaration) purposes thereon
to sacrifice all his unsuccessful writings. As the pile
is kindled, the Goddess beholding the flame from her
seat, flies and puts it out by casting upon it the poem
of Thulé. She forthwith reveals herself to him,
transports him to her temple, unfolds her arts, and
initiates him into her mysteries ; then announcing
the death of Eusden the Poet Laureate, anoints him,
carries him to Court, and proclaims him successor.

THE DUNCIAD.[1]

BOOK I.

THE Mighty Mother, and her Son, who brings
The Smithfield Muses[2] to the ear of Kings,
I sing.   Say you, her instruments the Great!

[1] The *Dunciad*, sic MS.   It may well be disputed whether this be a right reading : Ought it not rather to be spelled *Dunceiad*, as the Etymology evidently demands?   *Dunce* with an *e*, therefore *Dunceiad* with an *e*.   That accurate and punctual Man of Letters, the restorer of *Shakespear*, constantly observes the preservation of this very Letter *e*, in spelling the Name of his beloved Author, and not like his common careless Editors, with the omission of one, nay, sometimes of two *ee's* (as *Shakspear*) which is utterly unpardonable.   " Nor is the neglect of a *Single Letter* so trivial as to some it may appear ; the alteration whereof in a learned language is an Achievement that brings honour to the Critic who advances it ; and Dr. Bentley will be remembered to posterity for his performances of this sort, as long as the world shall have any esteem for the remains of Menander and Philemon."—*Theobald.*—P.

This poem was written in 1726.   In the next year an imperfect Edition was published at Dublin, and reprinted at London in 12mo ; another at Dublin, and

Called to this work by Dulness, Jove, and Fate;[3]
You by whose care, in vain decried and cursed,
Still Dunce the second reigns like Dunce the
    first;[4]   6
Say, how the Goddess bade Britannia sleep,
And poured her Spirit o'er the land and deep.
  In eldest time, ere mortals writ or read,
Ere Pallas issued from the Thunderer's head, 10
Dulness o'er all possessed her ancient right,
Daughter of Chaos and eternal Night:[5]

another at London in 8vo ; and three others in 12mo
the same year. But there was no perfect Edition
before that of London in 4to ; which was attended
with Notes. We are willing to acquaint Posterity,
that this Poem was presented to King George II.
and his Queen, by the hands of Sir Robert Walpole,
on the 12th of March, 1728-9.—*Schol. Vet.*—P. W.
(*Pope and Warburton.*)
  For some account of the Dunciad see the Memoir
prefixed to these volumes, pp. xxx-xxxiii. It may
here be remarked that the commentary which accom-
panies the poem was intended to parody the criticisms
of Bentley and his school. This commentary has
been considerably curtailed in the present edition.
  [2] *Smithfield* is the place where Bartholomew Fair
was kept, whose shows, machines, and dramatical
entertainments, formerly agreeable only to the taste
of the rabble, were, by the Hero of this poem and
others of equal genius, brought to the theatres of
Covent Garden, Lincoln's-inn-fields, and the Hay-
market, to be the reigning pleasures of the Court and
Town. This happened in the reigns of King George
I. and II. See Book iii.—P.
  [3] *i.e.* by their *Judgments*, their *Interests* and their
Inclinations.—*Warburton.*
  [4] Alluding to a verse of Mr. Dryden, not in Mac
Fleckno (as is said ignorantly in the Key to the Dunciad, p. i.), but in his verses to Mr. Congreve,

"And Tom the second reigns like Tom the first."—P.

  [5] The beauty of this whole Allegory being purely
of the poetical kind, we think it not our proper busi-

Fate in their dotage this fair Idiot gave,
Gross as her sire, and as her mother grave,[1]
Laborious, heavy, busy, bold, and blind,   15
She ruled, in native Anarchy, the mind.
   Still her old Empire to restore she tries,
For, born a Goddess, Dulness never dies.
   O Thou! whatever title please thine ear,
Dean, Drapier, Bickerstaff, or Gulliver![2]   20
Whether thou choose Cervantes' serious air,
Or laugh and shake in Rabelais' easy chair,
Or praise the Court, or magnify Mankind,[3]
Or thy grieved Country's copper chains un-
   bind;
From thy Bœotia though her Power retires,   25
Mourn not, my Swift, at aught our Realm
   acquires.
Here pleased behold her mighty wings out-
   spread
To hatch a new Saturnian age of Lead.[4]

ness, as a Scholiast, to meddle with it; but leave it
(as we shall in general all such) to the reader, remarking only that *Chaos* (according to *Hesiod's
Θεογονία*) was the Progenitor of all the Gods.—*Scriblerus.*—P.
   [1] A parody on a verse of Dryden, Æn. vii. 1044:
    "Famed as his sire, and as his mother fair."—
                   Wakefield.
   [2] The several Names and Characters he assumed in
his ludicrous, his splenetic, or his Party-writings;
which take in all his works.—*Warburton.*
   [3] *Ironicè,* alluding to *Gulliver's* representations of
both.—The next line relates to the papers of the
Drapier against the currency of *Wood's* Copper coin
in *Ireland,* which, upon the great discontent of the
People, his Majesty was graciously pleased to recall.
—P.
   [4] The ancient Golden Age is by Poets styled *Saturnian,* as being under the reign of Saturn; but in the
Chemical language *Saturn* is lead.—P. W.

Close to those walls where Folly holds her
   throne,
And laughs to think Monroe would take her
   down,[1]   30
Where o'er the gates, by his famed father's
   hand,[2]
Great Cibber's brazen, brainless brothers stand;
One cell there is, concealed from vulgar eye,
The Cave of Poverty and Poetry.[3]
Keen, hollow winds howl through the bleak
   recess,   35
Emblem of Music caused by Emptiness.
Hence Bards, like Proteus long in vain tied
   down,
Escape in Monsters, and amaze the town.
Hence Miscellanies spring, the weekly boast
Of Curl's chaste press, and Lintot's rubric post:[4]

[1] A physician at Bedlam.

[2] Mr. Caius Gabriel Cibber, father of the Poet
Laureate. The two Statues of the Lunatics over the
gates of Bedlam Hospital were done by him, and (as
the son justly says of them) are no ill monuments of
his fame as an Artist.—P. W.

[3] I cannot here omit a reflection that will greatly
endear the Author to every one, who shall attentively
observe that Humanity and Candour, which every-
where appears in him towards those unhappy objects
of the ridicule of all mankind, the bad Poets. He
here imputes all scandalous rhymes, scurrilous weekly
papers, base flatteries, wretched elegies, songs, and
verses (even from those sung at Court to ballads in
the streets), not so much to malice or servility as
to Dulness ; and not so much to Dulness as to
Necessity. And thus, at the very commencement
of his Satire, makes an apology for all that are to be
satirized.—P. W.

[4] Two booksellers, of whom see Book ii. The former was fined by the Court of King's Bench for publishing obscene Books ; the latter usually adorned his
shop with titles in red letters.—P.

Hence hymning Tyburn's elegiac lines,[1]   41
Hence Journals, Medleys, Merc'ries, MAGA-
ZINES:[2]
Sepulchral Lies,[3] our holy walls to grace,
And New-year Odes, and all the Grub-street
race.
In clouded Majesty[4] here Dulness shone;   45
Four guardian Virtues, round, support her
throne:
Fierce champion Fortitude, that knows no fears
Of hisses, blows, or want, or loss of ears:[5]
Calm Temperance, whose blessings those par-
take
Who hunger and who thirst for scribbling sake:

[1]   "Genus unde Latinum,
Albanique patres, atque altæ mœnia Romæ."—
                                    Virg. Æn. i.
It is an ancient English custom for the Malefactors
to sing a Psalm at their execution at Tyburn; and no
less customary to print Elegies on their deaths, at the
same time, or before.—P.
[2] The common name of those upstart collections in
prose and verse; in which, at some times,

     "New-born nonsense first is taught to cry;"

at others, dead-born Scandal has its monthly funeral;
where Dulness assumes all the various shapes of Folly
to draw in and cajole the Rabble. The eruption of
every miserable Scribbler; the scum of every dirty
News-paper; or fragments of fragments, picked up
from every dunghill, under the title of *Papers, Essays,
Reflections, Confutations, Queries, Verses, Songs, Epigrams, Riddles,* &c., equally the disgrace of human
Wit, Morality, Decency, and Common Sense.—P. W.
[3] Is a just satire on the Flatteries and Falsehoods
admitted to be inscribed on the walls of Churches in
Epitaphs.—P. W.
[4]   "The moon
Rising in clouded majesty."—*Milton,* Book iv.—P.
[5] "Quem neque pauperies, neque mors, neque vin-
     cula terrent."—*Hor.*—P.

Prudence, whose glass presents the approaching
    jail :   51
Poetic Justice, with her lifted scale,
Where, in nice balance, truth with gold she
    weighs,
And solid pudding against empty praise.
  Here she beholds the Chaos dark and deep,[1]
Where nameless Somethings in their causes
    sleep,   56
'Till genial Jacob,[2] or a warm Third day,[3]
Call forth each mass, a Poem, or a Play:
How hints, like spawn, scarce quick in embryo
    lie,
How new-born nonsense first is taught to
    cry,   60
Maggots half formed in rhyme exactly meet,
And learn to crawl upon poetic feet.
Here one poor word an hundred clenches makes,[4]

[1] That is to say, unformed things, which are either
made into Poems or Plays, as the Booksellers or the
Players bid most. These lines allude to the following
in Garth's Dispensary, cant. vi. :
  " Within the chambers of the globe they spy
  The beds where sleeping vegetables lie,
  Till the glad summons of a genial ray
  Unbinds the glebe, and calls them out to day."—P.

[2] Jacob Tonson, the bookseller.

[3] When a new play was produced, it was usual for
the author to receive the whole of the profits of the
third, sixth, and ninth nights.

[4] It may not be amiss to give an instance or two of
these operations of *Dulness* out of the Works of her
Sons, celebrated in the Poem.   A great Critic formerly held these clenches in such abhorrence that he
declared, " he that would pun, would pick a pocket."
Yet Mr. Dennis's works afford us notable examples in
this kind : "*Alexander Pope* hath sent abroad into
the world as many *bulls* as his namesake Pope *Alexander*. Let us take the initial and final letters of his

And ductile Dulness new mæanders takes;[1]
There motley images her fancy strike,   65
Figures ill paired, and Similes unlike.
She sees a Mob of Metaphors advance,
Pleased with the madness of the mazy dance;
How Tragedy and Comedy embrace;
How Farce and Epic get a jumbled race;[2]   70
How Time himself stands still at her command,
Realms shift their place, and Ocean turns to
    land.
Here gay Description Egypt glads with showers,[3]
Or gives to Zembla fruits, to Barca flowers;
Glittering with ice here hoary hills are seen, 75
There painted valleys of eternal green;
In cold December fragrant chaplets blow,
And heavy harvests nod beneath the snow.
    All these, and more, the cloud compelling
        Queen[1]
Beholds through fogs, that magnify the scene.

name, viz., *A. P—E.* and they give you the idea of
an *Ape.*—*Pope* comes from the Latin word *Popa*, which
signifies a little wart; or from *poppysma*, because he
was continually *popping* out squibs of wit, or rather
popysmata, or *popisms.*"—*Dennis on Hom.* and *Daily
Journal,* June 11, 1728.—P.

    [1] A parody on a verse in Garth's Dispensary, cant. i.:

    " How ductile matter new meanders takes."—P.

    [2] Alludes to the transgressions of the *Unities* in the
plays of such poets. For the miracles wrought upon
Time, and *Place,* and the mixture of Tragedy and
Comedy, Farce and Epic, see Pluto and Proserpine,
Penelope, &c., if yet extant.—P.

    [3] In the Lower Egypt Rain is of no use, the over-
flowing of the Nile being sufficient to impregnate the
soil.—These six verses represent the inconsistencies in
the descriptions of poets, who heap together all glittering and gaudy images, though incompatible in one
season, or in one scene.— P.

    [4] From Homer's Epithet of Jupiter, νεφεληγερέτα
Ζεύς.—P.

She, tinselled o'er in robes of varying hues,   81
With self-applause her wild creation views;
Sees momentary monsters rise and fall,
And with her own fool's-colours gilds them all.
'Twas on the day, when * * rich and
    grave,[1]   85
Like Cimon, triumphed both on land and wave:
(Pomps without guilt, of bloodless swords and
    maces,
Glad chains, warm furs, broad banners, and
    broad faces)
Now Night descending, the proud scene was
    o'er,   89
But lived, in Settle's numbers, one day more.[2]
Now Mayors and Shrieves all hushed and satiate
    lay,

[1] In the former editions:

" 'Twas on the day when Thorold, rich and grave."

Sir George Thorold, Lord Mayor of London in the
year 1720.   The procession of a Lord Mayor is made
partly by land, and partly by water.—Cimon, the
famous Athenian General, obtained a victory by sea,
and another by land, on the same day, over the Per-
sians and Barbarians.—P.

[2] A beautiful manner of speaking, usual with poets
in praise of poetry, in which kind nothing is finer than
those lines of Mr. Addison:

"Sometimes, misguided by the tuneful throng,
I look for streams immortalised in song,
That lost in silence and oblivion lie,
Dumb are their fountains, and their channels dry;
Yet run for ever by the Muses' skill,
And in the smooth description murmur still."

Settle was poet to the City of London.   His office
was to compose yearly panegyrics upon the Lord
Mayors, and verses to be spoken in the Pageants.   But
that part of the shows being at length frugally
abolished, the employment of City-Poet ceased; so
that upon Settle's demise there was no successor to
that place.—P.

Yet ate, in dreams, the custard of the day;
While pensive Poets painful vigils keep,
Sleepless themselves, to give their readers sleep.
Much to the mindful Queen the feast recalls 95
What City Swans once sung within the walls;
Much she revolves their arts, their ancient
 praise,
And sure succession down from Heywood's
 days.[1]
She saw, with joy, the line immortal run,
Each sire impressed, and glaring in his son : 100
So watchful Bruin forms, with plastic care,
Each growing lump, and brings it to a Bear.
She saw old Prynne in restless Daniel shine,[2]
And Eusden eke out Blackmore's endless line;[3]
She saw slow Philips creep like Tate's poor
 page,[4]   105

[1] *John Heywood*, whose Interludes were printed in
the time of Henry VIII.—P.
 [2] The first edition had it,

   "She saw in Norton all his father shine :"

a great mistake ! for Daniel De Foe had parts, but
Norton De Foe was a wretched writer, and never
attempted Poetry. Much more justly is Daniel himself made successor to W. Pryn, both of whom wrote
Verses as well as Politics. And both these authors
had a resemblance in their fates as well as writings,
having been alike sentenced to the Pillory.—P.
 William Prynne (1600-1669), was a most voluminous
writer. He was placed in the pillory and fined £5,000
for his "Histriomastix."
 [3] Laurence Eusden, Poet Laureate. Mr. Jacob gives
a catalogue of some few only of his works, which
were very numerous. Of Blackmore, see Book ii. ;
of Philips, Book i. 258, and Book iii. *prope fin.*—P.
 [4] Nahum Tate was Poet Laureate, a cold writer, of
no invention ; but sometimes translated tolerably
when befriended by Mr. Dryden. In his second part
of Absalom and Achitophel are above two hundred
admirable lines together of that great hand, which

And all the mighty Mad in Dennis rage.[1]

strongly shine through the insipidity of the rest.
Something parallel may be observed of another author
here mentioned.—P.　The other author was Ambrose
Philips, who was supposed to have received assistance
from Addison.

[1] This is by no means to be understood literally, as
if Mr. Dennis were really mad, according to the
Narrative of Dr. Norris in Swift and Pope's Miscellanies, vol. iii.　No—it is spoken of that *excellent* and
divine Madness, so often mentioned by Plato; that
poetical rage and enthusiasm, with which Mr. D.
hath, in his time, been highly possessed; and of those
extraordinary hints and motions whereof he himself
so feelingly treats in his preface to the Rem. on Pr.
Arth. [See Notes on Book ii. ver. 268.]—*Scriblerus.*
—P.

Mr. Theobald, in the Censor, vol. ii. N. 33, calls Mr.
Dennis by the name of Furius. " The modern Furius
is to be looked upon as more an object of pity, than
of that which he daily provokes, laughter and contempt.　Did we really know how much this *poor* man
(I wish that reflection on poverty had been spared)
suffers by being contradicted, or, which is the same
thing in effect, by hearing another praised; we should,
in compassion, sometimes attend to him with a silent
nod, and let him go away with the triumphs of his
ill-nature.　*Poor* Furius (again) when any of his contemporaries are spoken well of, quitting the ground
of the present dispute, steps back a thousand years
to call in the succour of the Ancients. His very panegyric is spiteful, and he uses it for the same reason as
some ladies do their commendations of a dead beauty,
who would never have had their good word, but that
a living one happened to be mentioned in their company.　His applause is not the tribute of his *Heart*,
but the sacrifice of his *Revenge*," &c.　Indeed, his
pieces against our poet are somewhat of an angry
character, and as they are now scarce extant, a taste
of his style may be satisfactory to the curious.　" A
young, squab, short gentleman, whose outward form,
though it should be that of downright monkey, would
not differ so much from human shape as his unthinking
immaterial part does from human understanding.—
He is as stupid and as venomous as a hunch-backed

In each she marks her Image full expressed,

toad.—A book through which folly and ignorance, those brethren so lame and impotent, do ridiculously look very big and very dull, and strut and hobble, cheek by jowl, with their arms on kimbo, being led and supported, and bully-backed by that blind Hector, Impudence."—*Reflect. on the Essay on Criticism*, pp. 26, 29, 30.

It would be unjust not to add his reasons for this fury, they are so strong and so coercive: "I regard him," saith he, "as an *Enemy*, not so much to me, as to my King, to my Country, to my Religion, and to that Liberty which has been the sole felicity of my life. A vagary of Fortune, who is sometimes pleased to be frolicsome, and the epidemic *Madness of the Times*, have given him *Reputation*, and Reputation (as Hobbes says) is *Power*, and *that has made him dangerous*. Therefore I look on it as my duty to *King George*, whose faithful subject I am ; to my *Country*, of which I have appeared a constant lover ; to the laws, under whose protection I have so long lived ; and to the *Liberty* of my *Country*, more dear to me than life, of which I have now for forty years been a constant assertor, &c. I look upon it as my duty, I say, to do—*you shall see what*—to pull the lion's skin from this little Ass, which popular error has thrown round him ; and to show that this Author, who has been lately so much in vogue, has neither sense in his thoughts, nor English in his expressions."—*Dennis, Rem. on Hom. Pref.* pp. 2, 91, &c.

Besides these public-spirited reasons, Mr. D. had a private one ; which, by his manner of expressing it in p. 92, appears to have been equally strong. He was even in bodily fear of his life from the machinations of the said Mr. P. " The story (says he) is too long to be told, but who would be acquainted with it, may hear it from Mr. Curl, my Bookseller.—However, what my reason has suggested to me, that I have with a just confidence said, in defiance of his two clandestine weapons, his *Slander* and his *Poison*." Which last words of his book plainly discover Mr. D.'s suspicion was that of being *poisoned*, in like manner as Mr. Curl had been before him : Of which fact see *A full and true Account of a Horrid and Barbarous Revenge, by Poison, on the Body of Ed-*

But chief in BAYS's monster-breeding breast:[1]

mund Curl, printed in 1716, the year antecedent to that wherein these remarks of Mr. Dennis were published. But what puts it beyond all question, is a passage in a very warm treatise, in which Mr. D. was also concerned, price twopence, called *A true Character of Mr. Pope, and his Writings*, printed for S. Popping, 1716 ; in the tenth page whereof he is said " to have insulted people on those calamities and diseases which he himself gave them, by administering *Poison* to them ;" and is called (p. 4) " a lurking waylaying coward, and a stabber in the dark." Which (with many other things most lively set forth in that piece) must have rendered him a terror, not to Mr. Dennis only, but to all Christian people.

For the rest : Mr. John Dennis was the son of a Saddler in London, born in 1657. He paid court to Mr. Dryden ; and having obtained some correspondence with Mr. Wycherly and Mr. Congreve, he immediately obliged the public with their Letters. He made himself known to the Government by many admirable schemes and projects ; which the Ministry, for reasons best known to themselves, constantly kept private. For his character, as a writer, it is given us as follows: "Mr. Dennis is *excellent* at Pindaric writings, *perfectly regular* in all his performances, and a person of *sound Learning*. That he is master of a great deal of *Penetration* and *Judgment*, his criticisms (particularly on *Prince Arthur*) do sufficiently demonstrate." From the same account it also appears that he writ plays " more to get *Reputation* than *Money*."—*Dennis* of himself. See *Giles Jacob's Lives of Dram. Poets*, pp. 68, 69, compared with p. 286.—P.

[1] In the editions before 1743, these lines ran as follows :

" But chief, in Tibbald's monster-breeding-breast ;
See gods with demons in strange league engage,
And earth, and heaven, and hell her battles wage.

    She eyed the bard, where supperless he sate,
And pined, unconscious of his rising fate ;
Studious he sate, with all his books around,
Sinking from thought to thought," &c.

Tibbald. Author of a pamplet entitled Shakespear Restored. During two whole years while Mr.

Bays, formed by nature Stage and Town to
  bless,[1]
And act, and be, a Coxcomb with success.   110
Dulness with transport eyes the lively Dunce,
Remembering she herself was Pertness once.

Pope was preparing his edition of Shakespear, he
published Advertisements, requesting assistance, and
promising satisfaction to any who could contribute to
its greater perfection. But this Restorer, who was at
that time soliciting favours of him by letters, did
wholly conceal his design till after its publication
(which he was since not ashamed to own, in a *Daily
Journal* of *Nov.* 26, 1728). And then an outcry was
made in the Prints, that our Author had joined with
the booksellers to raise an *extravagant subscription ;*
in which he had no share, of which he had no knowledge, and against which he had publicly advertised
in his own proposals for *Homer.* Probably that proceeding elevated *Tibbald* to the dignity he holds in
this Poem, which he seems to deserve no other way
better than his brethren ; unless we impute it to the
share he had in the Journals, cited among the *Testimonies of Authors* prefixed to this work.—P.
    Lewis Theobald was the exact contemporary of
Pope, being born in 1688, and dying in 1744. His
edition of Shakespeare, published in 1733, was greatly
superior to Pope's edition, published five years earlier.
Theobald was hero of the Dunciad from 1728 till 1743,
when he was replaced by Cibber. See Memoir, p.
xxxii.
    [1] It is hoped the poet here hath done full justice to
his Hero's character, which it were a great mistake
to imagine was wholly sunk in stupidity ; he is
allowed to have supported it with a wonderful mixture of Vivacity. This character is heightened, according to his own desire, in a Letter he wrote to our
author.   " Pert and dull at least you might have
allowed me. What! am I only to be dull, and dull still,
and again, and for ever ? " He then solemnly appealed
to his own conscience, that "he could not think himself so, nor believe that our Poet did ; but that he
spoke worse of him than he could possibly think; and
concluded it must be merely to show his *Wit*, or for

Now (shame to Fortune !)[1] an ill Run at
Play
Blanked his bold visage, and a thin Third
day :
Swearing and supperless the Hero sate,   115
Blasphemed his Gods, the Dice, and damned
his Fate.
Then gnawed his pen, then dashed it on the
ground,
Sinking from thought to thought, a vast pro-
found !
Plunged for his sense, but found no bottom
there,
Yet wrote and floundered on, in mere despair. 120
Round him much Embryo, much Abortion
lay,
Much future Ode, and abdicated Play ;
Nonsense precipitate, like running Lead,
That slipped through Cracks and Zig-zags of
the head ;
All that on Folly Frenzy could beget,   125
Fruits of dull Heat, and Sooterkins [2] of Wit.
Next, o'er his Books his eyes began to roll,
In pleasing memory of all he stole,
How here he sipped, how there he plundered
snug,
And sucked all o'er, like an industrious Bug. 130
Here lay poor Fletcher's half-eat scenes,[3] and
here

some *Profit* or *Lucre* to himself."—*Life of C. C.*,
chap. vii. and *Letter to Mr. P.*, pp. 15, 40, 53.—P.
  [1] Because she usually shows favour to persons of this
character, who have a threefold pretence to it.—P. W.
  [2] Abortions.
  [3] A great number of them taken out to patch up
his plays.—P. W. Alluding to Cibber's thefts from
Fletcher in his "Cæsar in Egypt."—*Courthope.*

The Frippery of crucified Moliere ;[1]
There hapless Shakespear, yet of Tibbald sore,[2]
Wished he had blotted for himself before.[3]
The rest on Out-side merit but presume,[4]   135
Or serve (like other Fools) to fill a room ;
Such with their shelves as due proportion hold,

---

[1] " When I fitted up an old play, it was as a good
housewife will mend old linen, when she has not
better employment."— *Life*, p. 217, 8vo.—P. W.
Cibber's "Non-juror" was founded on the "Tartuffe " of Molière.

[2] It is not to be doubted but Bays was a subscriber
to Tibbald's Shakespear. He was frequently liberal
this way ; and, as he tells us, " subscribed to Mr.
Pope's Homer, out of pure Generosity and Civility ;
but when Mr. Pope did so to his Nonjuror, he concluded it could be nothing but a joke."—*Letter to
Mr. P.*, p. 24. This Tibbald, or Theobald, published
an edition of Shakespear, of which he was so proud
himself as to say, in one of Mist's Journals, June 8,
" That to expose any Errors in it was impracticable."
And in another, April 27, " That whatever care might
for the future be taken by any other Editor, he would
still give above five hundred emendations, that *shall*
escape them all."— P. W.

[3] It was a ridiculous praise which the Players gave
to Shakespear, " that he never blotted a line." Ben
Jonson honestly wished he had blotted a thousand ;
and Shakespear would certainly have wished the
same, if he had lived to see those alterations in his
works, which, not the Actors only (and especially the
daring Hero of this poem) have made on the *Stage*,
but the presumptuous Critics of our days in their
Editions.—P. W.

[4] This library is divided into three parts ; the first
consists of those authors from whom he stole, and
whose works he mangled ; the second, of such as
fitted the shelves, or were gilded for show, or adorned
with pictures ; the third class our author calls solid
learning, old Bodies of Divinity, old Commentaries,
old English Printers, or old English Translations ; all
very voluminous, and fit to erect altars to Dulness.
—P. W.

Or their fond parents dressed in red and gold;
Or where the pictures for the page atone,
And Quarles [1] is saved by Beauties not his
    own.   140
Here swells the shelf with Ogilby the great; [2]
There, stamped with arms, Newcastle shines
    complete : [3]
Here all his suffering brotherhood retire,
And 'scape the martyrdom of jakes and fire :
A Gothic Library ! of Greece and Rome   145
Well purged, and worthy Settle, Banks, and
    Broome. [4]

[1] See Imitations of Horace, Bk. ii. Ep. i. 387.

[2] " John Ogilby was one who, from a late initiation
into literature, made such a progress as might well
style him the prodigy of his time, in sending into the
world so many *Large Volumes!* His translations of
Homer and Virgil, done *to the life*, and *with such
excellent sculptures!* And (what added great grace to
his works) he printed them all on *special good paper*,
and in a *very good letter.*"—*Winstanley, Lives of
Poets.*—P. Ogilby (1600-1676) translated the Æneid,
the Iliad and Odyssey, and Æsop.

[3] "The *Duchess of Newcastle* was one who busied
herself in the ravishing delights of Poetry ; leaving
to posterity in print three *ample Volumes* of her
studious endeavours."—*Winstanley, ibid.* Langbaine
reckons up *eight* Folios of her Grace's, which were
usually adorned with gilded covers, and had her coat
of arms upon them.—P. Margaret, Duchess of Newcastle (1624-1673), a voluminous writer of plays,
poems, and philosophical and other works.

[4] The Poet has mentioned these three authors in
particular, as they are parallel to our Hero in his
three capacities : 1. Settle was his brother Laureate ;
only indeed upon half-pay, for the City instead of the
Court ; but equally famous for unintelligible flights
in his poems on public occasions, such as Shows,
Birth-days, &c. 2. Banks was his Rival in *Tragedy*
(though more successful) in one of his Tragedies, the
Earl of Essex, which is yet alive ; *Anna Boleyn*, the
Queen of Scots, and *Cyrus the Great*, are dead and

But, high above, more solid Learning shone,[1]
The Classics of an Age that heard of none;
There Caxton[2] slept, with Wynkyn at his side,
One clasped in wood, and one in strong cow-
    hide;   150
There saved by spice, like mummies, many a
    year,
Dry Bodies of Divinity appear;
De Lyra there a dreadful front extends,[3]
And here the groaning shelves Philemon bends.[4]
Of these twelve volumes, twelve of amplest
    size,   155
Redeemed from tapers and defrauded pies,
Inspired he seizes: these an altar raise:

gone. Those he dressed in a sort of *Beggar's Velvet*,
or a happy Mixture of the *thick Fustian* and *thin
Prosaic*; exactly imitated in *Perolla and Isidora,
Cæsar in Egypt*, and the *Heroic Daughter*. 3. Broome
was a serving-man of Ben Jonson, who once picked up
a *Comedy* from his Betters, or from some cast scenes
of his Master, not entirely contemptible.—P. W.

[1] Some have objected, that books of this sort suit
not so well the library of our Bays, which they
imagine consisted of Novels, Plays, and obscene
books; but they are to consider, that he furnished
his shelves only for ornament, and read these books
no more than the *Dry Bodies of Divinity*, which, no
doubt, were purchased by his father when he designed
him for the Gown. See the note on verse 200.—P. W.

[2] A printer in the time of Edward IV., Richard
III., and Henry VII.; Wynkyn de Word, his successor, in that of Henry VII. and VIII.—P.

[3] *Nich. de Lyra*, or Harpsfield, a very voluminous
commentator, whose works, in five vast folios, were
printed in 1472.—P.

[4] *Philemon Holland*, Doctor in Physic. " He translated so *many books*, that a man would think he had
done *nothing else*; insomuch that he might be called
Translator general of his age. The books alone of his
turning into English are sufficient to make a *Country
Gentleman a complete library*."—*Winstanley*.—P.

An hecatomb of pure, unsullied lays
That altar crowns : A folio Common-place
Founds the whole pile, of all his works the
    base :   160
Quartos, octavos, shape the lessening pyre ;
A twisted Birth-day Ode completes the spire.
    Then he : " Great Tamer of all human art !
First in my care, and ever at my heart ;
Dulness ! whose good old cause I yet defend, 165
With whom my Muse began, with whom shall
    end.[1]
E'er since Sir Fopling's Periwig was Praise,[2]
To the last honours of the Butt and Bays :
O thou ! of Business the directing soul !
To this our head like bias to the bowl,   170
Which, as more ponderous, made its aim more
    true,
Obliquely waddling to the mark in view :
O ! ever gracious to perplexed mankind,
Still spread a healing mist before the mind ;
And, lest we err by Wit's wild dancing light,
Secure us kindly in our native night.   176
Or, if to Wit a coxcomb make pretence,
Guard the sure barrier between that and Sense ;
Or quite unravel all the reasoning thread,
And hang some curious cobweb in its stead ! 180

---

[1] "A te principium, tibi desinet."—*Virg. Ecl.* viii.
Ἐκ Διὸς ἀρχώμεσθα, καὶ εἰς Δία λήγετε, Μοῦσαι.—*Theor.*
" Prima dicte mihi, summa dicende Camœna."—
                                  Hor.—P.

[2] The first visible cause of the passion of the Town
for our Hero, was a fair flaxen full-bottomed periwig,
which, he tells us, he wore in his first play of the *Fool
in Fashion.* This remarkable periwig usually made
its entrance upon the stage in a sedan, brought in by
two chairmen, with infinite approbation of the
audience.—P. W.

As, forced from wind-guns, lead itself can fly,[1]
And ponderous slugs cut swiftly through the
    sky;
As clocks to weight their nimble motion owe,
The wheels above urged by the load below;
Me Emptiness and Dulness could inspire,   185
And were my Elasticity and Fire.
Some Dæmon stole my pen (forgive th' offence)
And once betrayed me into common sense:
Else all my Prose and Verse were much the
    same;
This, prose on stilts; that, poetry fallen lame.
Did on the stage my Fops appear confined? 191
My life gave ampler lessons to mankind.
Did the dead letter unsuccessful prove?
The brisk Example never failed to move.
Yet sure had Heaven decreed to save the
    State,[2]   195
Heaven had decreed these works a longer date.
Could Troy be saved by any single hand,[3]
This grey-goose weapon must have made her
    stand.
What can I now? my Fletcher cast aside,[4]

---

[1] The thought of these four verses is found in a
poem of our Author's of a very date (namely, written
at fourteen years old, and soon after printed) to the
Author of a poem called *Successio.*—*Warburton.*

[2] " Me si cœlicolæ voluissent ducere vitam,
    Has mihi servassent sedes."—*Virg. Æn.* ii.—P.

[3]   "Si Pergama dextra
    Defendi possent, etiam hac defensa fuissent."—
                                Virg. ibid.—P.

[4] A familiar manner of speaking, used by modern
critics of a favourite author. Bays might as justly
speak thus of Fletcher, as a French wit did of Tully,
seeing his works in a library, " Ah! mon cher Cice-
ron! je le connois bien; c'est le même que Marc

Take up the Bible, once my better guide ? [1] 200
Or tread the path by venturous Heroes trod,
This Box my Thunder, this right hand my
    God ? [2]
Or chaired at White's amidst the Doctors sit,
Teach Oaths to Gamesters, and to Nobles Wit ?
Or bidst thou rather Party to embrace ?   205
(A friend to Party thou, and all her race ;
'Tis the same rope at different ends they twist ;
To Dulness Ridpath is as dear as Mist.) [3]
Shall I, like Curtius, desperate in my zeal,
O'er head and ears plunge for the common
    weal ?   210
Or rob Rome's ancient geese of all their
    glories,
And cackling save the Monarchy of Tories ? [4]

Tulle." But he had a better pride to call Fletcher
his own, having made so free with him.—P. W.

   [1] When, according to his father's intention, he had
been a *Clergyman*, or (as he thinks himself) a *Bishop*
of the Church of England.   Hear his own words :
" At the time that the fate of King James, the Prince
of Orange, and myself were on the anvil, Providence
thought fit to postpone mine, till theirs were determined ; but had my father carried me a month sooner
to the University, who knows but that purer fountain
might have washed my imperfections into a capacity
of writing, instead of Plays and annual Odes, Sermons
and Pastoral Letters ?"—*Apology for his Life*, c. iii.—
P. W.

   [2] " Dextra mihi Deus,'et telum quod missile libro."
        Virgil, of the Gods of Mezentius.—P. W.

   [3] George Ridpath, author of a Whig paper called
the Flying Post ; Nathaniel Mist, of a famous Tory
journal.—P.

   [4] Not out of any preference or affection to the
Tories.   For what Hobbes so ingenuously confesses
of himself, is true of all Party-writers whatsoever :
" That he defends the supreme powers, as the *Geese*

Hold—to the Minister I more incline;
To serve his cause, O Queen! is serving thine.
And see! thy very Gazetteers themselves give
    o'er,[1]   215
Ev'n Ralph repents,[2] and Henley writes no
    more.
What then remains? Ourself. Still, still re-
    main
Cibberian forehead,[3] and Cibberian brain.
This brazen Brightness, to the 'Squire so dear;
This polished Hardness, that reflects the
    Peer: 220
This arch Absurd, that wit and fool delights;
This Mess, tossed up of Hockley-hole[4] and
    White's;

by their *cackling* defended the Romans who held the
Capitol; for they favoured them no more than the
Gauls, their enemies, but were as ready to have
defended the Gauls if they had been *possessed of the
Capitol.*"—*Epist. Dedic. to the Leviathan.—War-
burton.*

   [1] A band of ministerial writers, hired at the price
mentioned in the note on Book ii. ver. 316; who, on
the very day their patron quitted his post, laid down
their paper, and declared they would never more
meddle in Politics.—P. W.

   [2] See Book iii. 165.

   [3] So, indeed, all the MSS. read; but I make no
scruple to pronounce them all wrong, the Laureate
being elsewhere celebrated by our Poet for his great
Modesty—modest Cibber. Read, therefore, at my
peril, *Cerberian forehead.* This is perfectly classical,
and, what is more, *Homerical:* the *Dog* was the
ancient, as the *Bitch* is the modern, symbol of impudence: (Κυνὸς ὄμματ' ἔχων, says Achilles to Agamem-
non) which, when in a superlative degree, may well
be denominated from *Cerberus,* the *Dog with three
heads.* But as to the latter part of this verse, *Cibberian brain,* that is certainly the genuine reading.—
Bentley.—Warburton. See Book iv. 532.

   [4] See Imitations of Horace, Bk. ii. Sat. i. 49.

Where Dukes and Butchers join to wreathe my
   crown,
At once the Bear and Fiddle of the town.   224
" O born in sin, and forth in folly brought ! [1]
Works damned, or to be damned ! (your
   father's fault)
Go, purified by flames ascend the sky,
My better and more christian progeny ! [2]
Unstained, untouched, and yet in maiden
   sheets ; [3]
While all your smutty sisters walk the streets.
Ye shall not beg, like gratis-given Bland,[4]   231
Sent with a Pass, and vagrant through the
   land ;
Not sail with Ward [5] to Ape-and-monkey
   climes,

[1] This is a tender and passionate Apostrophe to his
own works, which he is going to sacrifice, agreeable
to the nature of man in great affliction ; and reflecting,
like a parent, on the many miserable fates to which
they would otherwise be subject.—P.

[2] " It may be observable that my muse and my
spouse were equally prolific ; that the one was seldom
the mother of a Child, but in the same year the other
made me the father of a Play. I think we had a
dozen of each sort between us ; of both of which kinds
some *died* in their *Infancy*," &c.—*Life of C. C.*,
p. 217, 8vo edition.—P. W.

[3]   " Felix Priamëia virgo !
Jussa mori : quæ sortitus non pertulit ullos,
Nec victoris heri tetigit captiva cubile !
Nos, patria incensa, diversa per æquora vectæ," &c.
                      Virg. Æn. iii.—P.

[4] It was a practice so to give the Daily Gazetteer
and ministerial pamphlets (in which this B. was a
writer), and to send them *Post-free* to all the Towns
in the kingdom.—P. W. Dr. Bland, Provost of Eton.
See Epilogue to Satires, i. 75.

[5] " Edward Ward, a very voluminous poet in
Hudibrastic verse, but best known by the London

Where vile Mundungus trucks for viler
   rhymes :
Not sulphur-tipped, emblaze an Ale-house fire ;
Not wrap up Oranges, to pelt your sire !   236
O ! pass more innocent, in infant state,
To the mild Limbo of our Father Tate :
Or peaceably forgot, at once be blest
In Shadwell's [1] bosom with eternal Rest !   240
Soon to that mass of Nonsense to return,
Where things destroyed are swept to things
   unborn."
   With that, a Tear (portentous sign of
   Grace !)
Stole from the Master of the sevenfold Face :
And thrice he lifted high the Birth-day
   brand,[2]   245
And thrice he dropped it from his quivering
   hand ;
Then lights the structure, with averted eyes :
The rolling smoke involves the sacrifice.
The opening clouds disclose each work by
   turns :

Spy, in prose. He has of late years kept a public-
house in the City (but in a genteel way), and with his
wit, humour, and good liquor (ale), afforded his
guests a pleasurable entertainment, especially those
of the High Church party."—*Jacob, Lives of Poets,*
vol. ii. p. 225. Great numbers of his works were
yearly sold into the Plantations. Ward, in a book
called Apollo's Maggot, declared this account to be a
great falsity, protesting that his public-house was not
in the *City,* but in *Moorfields.—P.*

  [1] *Tate and Shadwell.* Two of his predecessors in the
Laurel.—*Warburton.*

  [2] Ovid, of Althæa on a like occasion, burning her
offspring.

    " Tum conata quater flammis imponere torrem,
    Cœpta quater tenuit."—*P.*

Now flames the Cid,[1] and now Perolla burns ;
Great Cæsar roars, and hisses in the fires ; 251
King John in silence modestly expires ;
No merit now the dear Nonjuror claims,[2]
Moliere's old stubble in a moment flames.
Tears gushed again, as from pale Priam's eyes,
When the last blaze sent Ilion to the skies.[3] 256

[1]   "Jam Deïphobi dedit ampla ruinam,
    Vulcano superante domus ; jam proximus ardet
    Ucalegon."—P.

In the first notes on the Dunciad it was said, that
this Author was particularly excellent at Tragedy.
" This (says he) is as unjust as to say I could not
dance on a Rope." But certain it is that he had
attempted to dance on this Rope, and fell most
shamefully, having produced no less than four Tragedies (the names of which the Poet preserves in these
few lines) ; the three first of them were fairly printed,
acted, and damned ; the fourth suppressed, in fear of
the like treatment.—P. W.

The Four Tragedies, by Cibber were " Ximena,"
which was founded on Corneille's " Cid," " Indamora
and Perolla," and " Cæsar in Egypt," all of which
were unsuccessful, and " King John," which was suppressed at first, but was acted in 1774.

[2] A Comedy threshed out of Molière's " Tartuffe,"
and so much the Translator's favourite, that he assures
us all our author's dislike to it could only arise from
disaffection to the *Government :*

" Qui méprise Cotin, n'estime point son Roi,
    Et n'a, selon Cotin, ni Dieu, ni foi, ni loi."—*Boil.*

He assures us, that " when he had the honour to kiss
his Majesty's hand upon presenting his dedication of
it, he was graciously pleased, out of his royal bounty,
to order him two hundred pounds for it. And this he
doubts not *grieved* Mr. P."—P. W.

[3] See Virgil, *Æn.* ii., where I would advise the
reader to peruse the story of Troy's destruction, rather
than in Wynkyn. But I caution him alike in both to
beware of a most grievous error, that of thinking it
was brought about by I know not what *Trojan
Horse ;* there never having been any such thing. For,

Roused by the light, old Dulness heaved the
    head,
Then snatched a sheet of Thulè [1] from her bed;
Sudden she flies, and whelms it o'er the pyre;
Down sink the flames, and with a hiss expire. 260
    Her ample presence fills up all the place ;
A veil of fogs dilates her awful face :
Great in her charms ! [2] as when on Shrieves and
    Mayors
She looks, and breathes herself into their airs.

first, it was not *Trojan*, being made by the *Greeks;*
and, secondly, it was not a *horse*, but a *mare.* This is
clear from many verses in Virgil :
    "Uterumque armato milite complent.
    Inclusos utero Danaos——"
Can a horse be said *utero gerere ?*   Again :
    "Uteroque recusso,
Insonuere cavæ.
    —— Atque utero sonitum quater arma dedere."
Nay, is it not expressly said,
    "Scandit fatalis machina muros
    Fœta armis."
How is it possible the word *fœta* can agree with a
horse ?   And, indeed, can it be conceived that the
chaste and virgin Goddess *Pallas* would employ herself in forming and fashioning the Male of that
species ?   But this shall be proved to a demonstration
in our Virgil Restored.—*Scribl.*—P.
    [1] An unfinished poem of that name, of which one
sheet was printed, many years ago, by Amb. Philips,
a northern author.   It is a usual method of putting
out a fire to cast wet sheets upon it.   Some critics
have been of opinion that this sheet was of the nature
of the Asbetos, which cannot be consumed by fire :
but I rather think it an allegorical allusion to the
coldness and heaviness of the writing.—P
    [2] "Alma parens confessa Deam ; qualisque videri
Cœlicolis, et quanta solet."—*Virg. Æn.* ii.
    "Et lætos oculis afflavit honores."—*Ibid. Æn.* i.—P.

She bids him wait her to her sacred Dome :[1] 265
Well pleased he entered, and confessed his
    home.
So Spirits ending their terrestrial race
Ascend, and recognise their Native Place.
This the Great Mother[2] dearer held than all
The clubs of Quidnuncs, or her own Guildhall :
Here stood her Opium, here she nursed her
    Owls, 271
And here she planned the Imperial seat of
    Fools.
    Here to her Chosen all her works she shews ;
Prose swelled to verse, verse loitering into
    prose :
How random thoughts now meaning chance to
    find, 275
Now leave all memory of sense behind :
How Prologues into Prefaces decay,
And these to Notes are frittered quite away :
How Index-learning turns no student pale,
Yet holds the eel of science by the tail : 280
How, with less reading than makes felons 'scape,
Less human genius than God gives an ape,
Small thanks to France, and none to Rome or
    Greece,

[1] Where he no sooner enters, but he reconnoitres
the place of his original ; as Plato says the spirits
shall, at their entrance into the celestial regions.—P.

[2] " Urbs antiqua fuit——
Quam Juno fertur terris magis omnibus unam
Posthabita coluisse Samo : hic illius arma,
Hic currus fuit : hic regnum Dea gentibus esse
(Si qua fata sinant) jam tum tenditque fovetque."
                     Virg. Æn. i.—P.

Magna mater, here applied to *Dulness*. The *Quidnuncs*, a name given to the ancient members of certain political clubs, who were constantly inquiring
Quid nunc? what news ?—P.

A vast, vamped, future, old, revived, new piece,
'Twixt Plautus, Fletcher, Shakespear, and
  Corneille,   285
Can make a Cibber, Tibbald,[1] or Ozell.[2]

[1] Lewis Tibbald (as pronounced) or Theobald (as
written) was bred an Attorney, and son to an
Attorney (says Mr. Jacob) of Sittenburn, in Kent.
He was Author of some forgotten Plays, Translations,
and other pieces. He was concerned in a paper called
the Censor, and a Translation of Ovid. "There is a
notorious Idiot, one hight Whachum, who, from an
under-spur-leather to the law, is become an under-
strapper to the Play-house, who hath lately burlesqued
the Metamorphoses of Ovid by a vile translation, &c.
This fellow is concerned in an impertinent paper called
the Censor."—Dennis Rem. on Pope's Hom. pp. 9,
10.—P. W.
[2] "Mr. John Ozell (if we credit Mr. Jacob) did go
to school in Leicestershire, where somebody left him
something to live on, when he shall retire from business. He was designed to be sent to Cambridge, in
order for priesthood; but he chose rather to be placed
in an office of accounts, in the City, being qualified
for the same by his skill in arithmetic, and writing the
necessary hands. He has obliged the world with
many translations of French plays."—Jacob, Lives of
Dram. Poets, p. 198.
  Mr. Jacob's character of Mr. Ozell seems vastly
short of his merits, and he ought to have further
justice done him, having since fully confuted all
Sarcasms on his learning and genius, by an advertisement of September 20, 1729, in a paper called the
Weekly Medley, &c. "As to my learning, this
envious Wretch knew, and everybody knows, that
the whole Bench of Bishops, not long ago, were pleased
to give me a purse of guineas, for discovering the
erroneous translations of the Common-prayer in
Portuguese, Spanish, French, Italian, &c. As for my
genius, let Mr. Cleland shew better verses in all Pope's
works, than Ozell's version of Boileau's Lutrin, which
the late Lord Halifax was so pleased with, that he
complimented him with leave to dedicate it to him,
&c. &c. Let him shew better and truer poetry in
the Rape of the Lock, than in Ozell's Rape of the

The Goddess then, o'er his anointed head,
With mystic words, the sacred Opium shed.
And lo! her bird (a monster of a fowl,
Something betwixt a Heideggre and Owl),[1] 290
Perched on his crown.   "All hail! and hail
    again,
My son : the promised land expects thy reign.
Know, Eusden thirsts no more for sack or
    praise ;
He sleeps among the dull of ancient days ;
Safe, where no Critics damn, no duns molest, 295
Where wretched Withers,[2] Ward, and Gildon[3]
    rest,

Bucket (*la Secchia rapita*).   And Mr. Toland and
Mr. Gildon publicly declared Ozell's translation of
Homer *to be*, as it was *prior*, so likewise *superior*
to Pope's.   Surely, surely, every man is free to deserve well of his country ! "—*John Ozell.*

We cannot but subscribe to such reverend testimonies as those of the *Bench of Bishops*, Mr. *Toland*,
and Mr. *Gildon.*—P.

Ozell translated Molière, Racine, Corneille, &c.   He
died in 1743.

[1] A strange bird from Switzerland, and not (as
some have supposed) the name of an eminent person,
who was a man of parts, and, as was said of Petronius,
Arbiter Elegantiarum.—P.—John James Heidegger
was Manager of the Opera House, and Master of the
Revels.

[2] George Withers was a great pretender to poetical
zeal, and abused the greatest personages in power,
which brought upon him *frequent correction.*   The
Marshalsea and Newgate were no strangers to him.—
Winstanley.—P.

[3] Charles Gildon, a writer of criticisms and libels of
the last age, bred at St. Omer's with the Jesuits ;
but, renouncing Popery, he published Blount's books
against the divinity of Christ, the Oracles of Reason,
&c.   He signalized himself as a critic, having written
some very bad Plays ; abused Mr. P. very scanda-
lously in an anonymous pamphlet of the Life of Mr.
Wycherly, printed by Curl ; in another called the

And high-born Howard,[1] more majestic sire,
With Fool of Quality completes the quire.
Thou, Cibber! thou, his Laurel shalt support,
Folly, my son, has still a Friend at Court.   300
Lift up your Gates, ye Princes, see him
   come !
Sound, sound ye Viols; be the Cat-call dumb !
Bring, bring the madding Bay, the drunken
   Vine ;
The creeping, dirty, courtly Ivy join.[2]
And thou! his Aid-de-camp, lead on my
   sons,   305
Light-armed with Points, Antitheses, and Puns.
Let Bawdry, Billingsgate, my daughters dear,
Support his front, and Oaths bring up the
   rear:
And under his, and under Archer's wing,
Gaming and Grub-street skulk behind the
   King.[3]   310

New Rehearsal, printed in 1714 ; in a third, entitled
the Complete Art of English Poetry, in two volumes ;
and others.—P.

[1] Hon. Edward Howard, author of the British
Princes, and a great number of wonderful pieces,
celebrated by the late Earls of Dorset and Rochester,
Duke of Buckingham, Mr. Waller, &c.—P.

[2]   "Quorum Imagines lambunt,
   Hederæ sequaces."—*Pers.*—P. W.

[3] When the Statute against Gaming was drawn up,
it was represented, that the King, by ancient custom,
plays at Hazard one night in the year ; and therefore
a clause was inserted, with an exception as to that
particular. Under this pretence, the Groom-porter
had a room appropriated to Gaming all the summer
the Court was at Kensington, which his Majesty
accidentally being acquainted of, with a just indignation prohibited. It is reported the same practice is
yet continued wherever the Court resides, and the

"O! when shall rise a Monarch all our own,[1]
And I, a Nursing-mother, rock the throne ;
'Twixt Prince and People close the Curtain
    draw,
Shade him from Light, and cover him from
    Law ;
Fatten the Courtier, starve the learned band, 315
And suckle Armies, and dry-nurse the land :
Till Senates nod to Lullabies divine,
And all be sleep, as at an Ode of thine."
    She ceased. Then swells the Chapel-royal
    throat :[2]
"God save King Cibber!" mounts in every
    note. 320
Familiar White's, "God save King Colley!"
    cries ;
"God save King Colley!" Drury-lane replies :
To Needham's quick the voice triumphal rode,
But pious Needham dropped the name of God :[3]

Hazard Table there open to all the professed gamesters
in town.

"Greatest and justest Sov'reign ! know you this ?
Alas ! no more than Thames' calm head can know
Whose meads his arms drown, or whose corn o'erflow."
          Donne to Queen Eliz.—P. W.

[1] Boileau, Lutrin, Chant. II. :
"Helas ! qu'est devenu ce tems, cet heureux tems,
Où les Rois s'honoroient du nom de Fainéans," &c.
                       —P. W.

[2] The voices and instruments used in the service of
the Chapel-royal being also employed in the performance of the Birth-day and New-year Odes.—P. W.
[3] A Matron of great fame, and very religious in her
way ; whose constant prayer it was, that she might
"get enough by her profession to leave it off in time,
and make her peace with God." But her fate was
not so happy ; for, being convicted and set in the
pillory, she was (to the lasting shame of all her great

Back to the Devil the last echoes roll,[1]   325
And " Coll ! " each butcher roars at Hockley-
hole.
So when Jove's block descended from on high
(As sings thy great forefather Ogilby)
Loud thunder to its bottom shook the bog,
And the hoarse nation croaked, "God save
King Log ! "[2]   330

Friends and Votaries) so ill-used by the populace, that
it put an end to her days.—P. W.
[1] The Devil Tavern, in Fleet-street, where these
Odes are usually rehearsed before they are performed
at Court. —P.
[2] See Ogilby's Æsop's Fables, where, in the story
of the Frogs and their King, this excellent hemistic is
to be found.
Our author manifests here, and elsewhere, a prodigious tenderness for the *bad writers.* We see he
selects the only good passage, perhaps, in all that
ever Ogilby writ ; which shows how candid and
patient a reader he must have been. What can be
more kind and affectionate than these words in the
preface to his Poems, where he labours to call up all
our humanity and forgiveness towards these unlucky
men by the most moderate representation of their
case that has ever been given by any author?
" Much may be said to extenuate the fault of bad
poets : What we call a *genius* is hard to be distinguished, by a man himself, from a prevalent inclination : and if it be never so great, he can at first
discover it no other way than by that strong pro-
pensity which renders him the more liable to be mistaken. He has no other method but to make the experiment by writing, and so appealing to the judgment of others : and if he happens to write ill (which
is certainly no sin in itself) he is immediately made
the object of ridicule ! I wish we had the humanity
to reflect that even the worst authors might endeavour
to please us, and in that endeavour, deserve something at our hands. We have no cause to quarrel
with them but for their obstinacy in persisting, and
even that may admit of alleviating circumstances.

For their particular friends may be either ignorant, or unsincere ; and the rest of the world too well-bred to shock them with a truth which generally their book-sellers are the first that inform them of."

But how much all indulgence is lost upon these people may appear from the just reflection made on their constant conduct, and constant fate, in the following Epigram :

" Ye little Wits, that gleamed awhile,
When Pope vouchsafed a ray,
Alas ! deprived of his kind smile,
How soon ye fade away !

" To compass Phœbus' car about,
Thus empty vapours rise ;
Each lends his cloud, to put him out,
That reared him to the skies.

" Alas ! those skies are not your sphere ;
There He shall ever burn :
Weep, weep, and fall ! for Earth ye were,
And must to Earth return."—P.

Two things there are, upon the supposition of which the very basis of all verbal criticism is founded and supported : the first, that an Author could never fail to use the *best word* on every occasion ; the second, that a critic cannot choose but know *which that is*. This being granted, whenever any word doth not fully content us, we take upon us to conclude, first, that the author could *never have used it ;* and, secondly, that he must have used *that very one* which we conjecture in its stead.

We cannot, therefore, enough admire the learned Scriblerus for his alteration of the text in the two last verses of the preceding book, which in all the former editions stood thus :

" Hoarse thunder to its bottom shook the bog,
And the loud nation croaked, God save King Log ! "

He has, with great judgment, transposed these two epithets ; putting *hoarse* to the nation, and *loud* to the thunder : and this being evidently the true read-ing, he vouchsafed not so much as to mention the former ; for which assertion of the just right of a Critic, he merits the acknowledgment of all sound Commentators.—P.

BOOK THE SECOND.

ARGUMENT.

The King being proclaimed, the solemnity is graced with public Games, and sports of various kinds : not instituted by the Hero, as by Æneas in Virgil, but for greater honour by the Goddess in person (in like manner as the games Pythia, Isthmia, &c., were anciently said to be ordained by the Gods, and as Thetis herself appearing, according to Homer, Odyss. xxiv., proposed the prizes in honour of her son Achilles). Hither flock the poets and critics, attended, as is but just, with their Patrons and Booksellers. The Goddess is first pleased, for her disport, to propose games to the Booksellers, and setteth up the Phantom of a Poet, which they contend to overtake. The Races described, with their divers accidents. Next, the game for a Poetess. Then follow the Exercises for the poets, of tickling, vociferating, diving : the first holds forth the arts and practices of Dedicators, the second of Disputants and fustian Poets, the third of profound, dark, and dirty Party-writers. Lastly, for the Critics, the Goddess proposes (with great propriety) an Exercise, not of their parts, but their patience, in hearing the works of two voluminous Authors, one in verse and the other in prose, deliberately read, without sleeping : the various effects of which, with the several degrees and manners of their operation, are here set forth; till the whole number, not of Critics only, but of spectators, actors, and all present, fall fast asleep; which naturally and necessarily ends the games.

BOOK II.

HIGH on a gorgeous seat, that far out-shone[1]
Henley's gilt tub,[2] or Fleckno's Irish throne,[3]
Or that where on her Curls the Public pours,[4]

[1] Parody of Milton, Book ii. :
"High on a throne of royal state, that far
Outshone the wealth of Ormus and of Ind,
Or where the gorgeous East with richest hand,
Showers on her Kings Barbaric pearl and gold,
Satan exalted sate."—P.

[2] The pulpit of a Dissenter is usually called a tub ;
but that of Mr. Orator Henley was covered with
velvet, and adorned with gold. He had also a fair
altar, and over it is this extraordinary inscription,
The Primitive Eucharist. See the history of this
person, Book iii.—P.

[3] Richard Fleckno was an Irish priest, but had laid
aside (as himself expressed it) the mechanic part of
priesthood. He printed some plays, poems, letters,
and travels. I doubt not our author took occasion to
mention him in respect to the Poem of Mr. Dryden,
to which this bears some resemblance, though of a
character more different from it than that of the
Æneid from the Iliad, or the Lutrin of Boileau from
the Défait des Bouts rimées of Sarazin.—P.

[4] Edmund Curl stood in the pillory at Charing Cross,
in March, 1727-8. "This (saith Edmund Curl) is a
false assertion—I had indeed the corporal punishment
of what the Gentlemen of the long Robe are pleased
jocosely to call *mounting the Rostrum* for one hour :
but that scene of action was not in the month of
March, but in *February.*" (*Curliad,* 12mo. p. 19)
And of *the History of his being tost in a Blanket,* he
saith, "Here, *Scriblerus !* thou leesеth in what thou
assertest concerning the blanket : it was not a *blanket,*
but a *rug.*"—p. 25. Much in the same manner Mr.
Cibber remonstrated, that his Brothers, at Bedlam,
mentioned Book i., were not *Brazen,* but *Blocks ;* yet

All-bounteous, fragrant Grains and Golden
    showers,
Great   Cibber   sate :   the   proud   Parnassian
    sneer,   5
The conscious simper, and the jealous leer,
Mix on his look : All eyes direct their rays
On him, and crowds turn Coxcombs as they
    gaze :
His Peers shine round him with reflected grace,
New edge their dulness, and new bronze their
    face.   10
So from the Sun's broad beam, in shallow urns
Heaven's twinkling Sparks draw light, and
    point their horns.
    Not with more glee, by hands pontific crowned,
With scarlet hats wide-waving circled round,
Rome in her Capitol saw Querno sit,[1]   15
Throned on seven hills, the Antichrist of wit.
    And now the Queen, to glad her sons, pro-
    claims,

our author let it pass unaltered, as a trifle that no way
altered the relationship.—*Scribl.*—P. W.

[1] Camillo Querno was of Apulia, who hearing the
great Encouragement which Leo X. gave to poets,
travelled to Rome with a harp in his hand, and sung
to it twenty thousand verses of a poem called Alexias.
He was introduced *as a Buffoon* to Leo, and promoted
to the honour of the *Laurel ;* a jest which the court
of Rome and the Pope himself entered into so far, as
to cause him to ride on an elephant to the Capitol,
and to hold a solemn festival on his coronation ; at
which it is recorded the Poet himself was so transported as to *weep for joy.*[1] He was ever after a constant frequenter of the Pope's table, drank abundantly,
and poured forth verses without number. PAULUS
JOVIUS, Elog. Vir. doct., cap. lxxxii. Some idea of
his poetry is given by Fam. Strada, in his Prolusions.
—P.

----

[1] See Life of C. C., chap. vi. p. 149.

By herald Hawkers, high heroic games.
They summon all her Race : an endless band
Pours forth, and leaves unpeopled half the
    land.   20
A motley mixture ! in long wigs, in bags,
In silks, in crapes, in Garters, and in Rags,
From drawing-rooms, from colleges, from
    garrets,
On horse, on foot, in hacks, and gilded chariots:
All who true Dunces in her cause appeared, 25
And all who knew those Dunces to reward.
    Amid that area wide they took their stand,
Where the tall may-pole once o'er-looked the
    Strand.
But now (so ANNE and Piety ordain)
A Church collects the saints of Drury-lane.[1] 30
    With Authors, Stationers obeyed the call,
(The field of glory is a field for all.)
Glory and gain, the industrious tribe provoke ;
And gentle Dulness ever loves a joke.
A Poet's form she placed before their eyes,[2] 35
And bade the nimblest racer seize the prize ;

[1] St. Mary-le-Strand, built by James Gibbs in
1717.
[2] This is what Juno does to deceive Turnus,
Æn. x. :

" Tum Dea nube cava, tenuem sine viribus umbram
In faciem Æneæ (visu mirabile monstrum !)
Dardaniis ornat telis, clypeumque jubasque
Divini assimilat capitis——
             —— Dat inania verba,
Dat sine mente sonum."

The reader will observe how exactly some of these
verses suit with their allegorical application here to a
Plagiary : there seems to me a great propriety in
this Episode, where such an one is imaged by a
phantom that eludes the grasp of the expecting Bookseller.— P.

No meagre, muse-rid mope, adust and thin,
In a dun night-gown of his own loose skin ;
But such a bulk as no twelve bards could raise,[1]
Twelve starv'ling bards of these degenerate
　　days.　　　　　　　　　　　　　　　　　40
All as a partridge plump, full-fed, and fair,
She formed this image of well-bodied air ;
With pert flat eyes she windowed well its
　　head ;
A brain of feathers, and a heart of lead ;
And empty words she gave, and sounding
　　strain,　　　　　　　　　　　　　　　　45
But senseless, lifeless ! idol void, and vain !
Never was dashed out, at one lucky hit,[2]
A fool, so just a copy of a wit ;
So like, that critics said, and courtiers swore,
A Wit it was, and called the phantom More.[3] 50

---

[1] " Vix illud lecti bis sex——
　　Qualia nunc hominum producit corpora tellus."
　　　　　　　　　　　　　　　Virg. Æn. xii.—P.

[2] Our author here seems willing to give some account of the possibility of *Dulness* making a Wit
(which could be done no other way than by *chance*).
The fiction is the more reconciled to probability, by
the known story of Apelles, who, being at a loss to
express the foam of Alexander's horse, dashed his
pencil in despair at the picture, and happened to do
it by that fortunate stroke.—P.

[3] Curl, in his Key to the Dunciad, affirmed this to
be James-Moore Smythe, Esq., and it is probable
(considering what is said of him in the *Testimonies*)
that some might fancy our author obliged to represent
this gentleman as a plagiary, or to pass for one himself. His case, indeed, was like that of a man I have
heard of, who, as he was sitting in company, perceived his next neighbour had stolen his handkerchief. " Sir (said the thief, finding himself detected),
do not expose me, I did it for mere want ; be so good
as to take it privately out of my pocket again and
say nothing." The honest man did so, but the other

All gaze with ardour : some a poet's name,
Others a sword-knot and laced suit inflame.
But lofty Lintot in the circle rose : [1]
" This prize is mine; who tempt it are my foes;
With me began this genius, and shall end." 55
He spoke : and who with Lintot shall contend ?
Fear held them mute. Alone, untaught to
    fear,

cried out, " See, gentlemen, what a thief we have
among us! look, he is stealing my handkerchief ! "
    The plagiarisms of this person gave occasion to the
following Epigram :

" More always smiles whenever he recites ;
He smiles (you think) approving what he writes.
And yet in this no vanity is shown ;
A modest man may like what's not his own."

This young Gentleman's whole misfortune was too
inordinate a passion to be thought a Wit.   Here is a
very strong instance attested by Mr. *Savage*, son of
the late Earl *Rivers*, who, having shown some verses
of his in manuscript to Mr. *Moore*, wherein Mr. Pope
was called *first of the tuneful train*, Mr. *Moore* the
next morning sent to Mr. *Savage* to desire him to give
those verses another turn, to wit, " That *Pope* might
now be the *first*, because *Moore* had left him unrivalled in turning his style to Comedy."   This was
during the rehearsal of the *Rival Modes*, his first and
only work ; the Town condemned it in the action,
but he printed it in 1726-7, with this modest motto,

" Hic cæstus, artemque repono."—P.

It appears from hence, that this is not the name of a
real person, but fictitious.   *Moore* from μῶρος, stultus,
μωρία, stultitia, to represent the folly of a plagiary.—
Scribl.—P. W.
    [1] We enter here upon the episode of the Book-
sellers : Persons, whose names being more known
and famous in the learned world than those of the
Authors in this poem, do therefore need less explanation.   The action of Mr. Lintot here imitates that of
Dares in Virgil, rising, just in this manner, to lay
hold on a *Bull*.   This eminent Bookseller printed the
Rival Modes before mentioned.—P.

Stood dauntless Curl;[1] "Behold that rival here!
The race by vigour, not by vaunts is won;
So take the hindmost, Hell,"[2] (he said) "and
　　run."　　　　　　　　　　　　　　　　60
Swift as a bard the bailiff leaves behind,[3]

[1] We come now to a character of much respect,
that of Mr. Edmund Curl. As a plain repetition of
great actions is the best praise of them, we shall only
say of this eminent man that he carried the Trade
many lengths beyond what it ever before had arrived
at, and that he was the envy and admiration of all
his profession. He possessed himself of a command
over all authors whatever; he caused them to write
what he pleased; they could not call their very *Names*
their own. He was not only famous among these;
he was taken notice of by the *State*, the *Church*, and
the *Law*, and received particular marks of distinction
from each.

It will be owned that he is here introduced with all
possible dignity. He speaks like the intrepid Diomed;
he runs like the swift-footed Achilles; if he falls, it
is like the beloved Nisus; and (what Homer makes
to be the chief of all praises) he is *favoured of the
Gods;* he says but three words, and his prayer is
heard; a Goddess conveys it to the seat of Jupiter;
though he loses the prize, he gains the victory; the
great Mother herself comforts him, she inspires him
with expedients, she honours him with an immortal
present (such as Achilles receives from Thetis, and
Æneas from Venus) at once instructive and pro-
phetical. After this he is unrivalled and triumphant.
—P.

[2] "Occupet extremum scabies; mihi turpe relinqui
　　est."
　　　　　　　　　　　　　　　　Hor. de Arte.—P.

[3] Something like this is in Homer, Il. x. ver. 220,
of Diomed. Two different manners of the same author
in his similes are also imitated in the two following;
the first, of the Bailiff, is short, unadorned, and (as
the Critics well know) from *familiar life;* the second,
of the Waterfowl, more extended, picturesque, and
from *rural life.* The 59th verse is likewise a literal
translation of one in Homer.—P.

He left huge Lintot, and out-stripped the wind.
As when a dab-chick waddles through the
   copse
On feet and wings, and flies, and wades, and
   hops;
So labouring on, with shoulders, hands, and
   head,[1]   65
Wide as a wind-mill, all his figure spread,
With arms expanded Bernard rows his state,[2]
And left-legged Jacob seems to emulate.
Full in the middle way there stood a lake,
Which Curl's Corinna[3] chanced that morn to
   make: 70
(Such was her wont, at early dawn to drop
Her evening cates before his neighbour's shop,)

[1]   "So eagerly the Fiend
O'er bog, o'er steep, through straight, rough, dense,
   or rare,
With head, hands, wings, or feet pursues his way,
And swims, or sinks, or wades, or creeps, or flies."
                             Milton, Book ii.—P.

[2] Milton, of the motion of the Swan,

         "—— rows
      His state with oary feet."

And Dryden, of another's,—*With two left legs.*—P.

[3] This name, it seems, was taken by one Mrs.
T——, who procured some private letters of Mr.
Pope, while almost a boy, to Mr. Cromwell, and sold
them without the consent of either of those Gentlemen to Curl, who printed them in 12mo. 1727. He
discovered her to be the publisher, in his Key, p. 11.
We only take this opportunity of mentioning the
manner in which those letters got abroad, which the
author was ashamed of as very trivial things, full not
only of levities, but of wrong judgments of men and
books, and only excusable from the youth and inexperience of the writer.—P.
   Cromwell gave Pope's letters to Mrs. Elizabeth
Thomas, who sold them to Curl.

Here fortuned Curl to slide ;[1] loud shout the
   band,
And "Bernard! Bernard!"[2] rings through all
   the Strand.
Obscene with filth[3] the miscreant lies be-
   wrayed,   ·   75
Fallen in the plash his wickedness had laid :
Then first (if Poets aught of truth declare)
The caitiff Vaticide conceived a prayer.

[1]   "Labitur infelix, cæsis ut forte juvencis
    Fusus humum viridesque super madefecerat her-
     bas—
    Concidit, immundoque fimo, sacroque cruore."
                  Virg. Æn. v. *of Nisus.*—P.

[2]   "Ut littus, Hyla, Hyla, omne sonaret."
                  Virg. Ecl. vi.—P.

[3] Though this incident may seem too low and base
for the dignity of an Epic poem, the learned very well
know it to be but a copy of Homer and Virgil ; the
very words ὄνθος and *fimus* are used by them, though
our poet (in compliance to modern nicety) has remarkably enriched and coloured his language, as well
as raised the versification, in this episode, and in the
following one of Eliza. If we consider that the exercises of his *authors* could with justice be no higher
than *tickling, chattering, braying,* or *diving,* it was
no easy matter to invent such games as were propor-
tioned to the meaner degree of *Booksellers.* In Homer
and Virgil, Ajax and Nisus, the persons drawn in
this plight are *Heroes ;* whereas here they are such
with whom it had been great impropriety to have
joined any but vile ideas ; besides the natural connection there is between Libellers and common Nui-
sances. Nevertheless I have heard our author own,
that this part of his poem was (as it frequently happens) what cost him most trouble and pleased him
least ; but that he hoped it was excusable, sin e
levelled at such as understand no delicate satire.
Thus the politest men are sometimes obliged to *swear,*
when they happen to have to do with porters and
oyster-wenches.— P.

"Hear, Jove! whose name my bards and I
   adore,
As much at least as any God's, or more;   80
And him and his if more devotion warms,
Down with the Bible, up with the Pope's Arms."[1]
   A place there is, betwixt earth, air, and seas,[2]
Where, from Ambrosia, Jove retires for ease.
There in his seat two spacious vents appear, 85
On this he sits, to that he leans his ear,
And hears the various vows of fond mankind;
Some beg an eastern, some a western wind:
All vain petitions, mounting to the sky,
With reams abundant this abode supply;   90
Amused he reads, and then returns the bills
Signed with that Ichor which from Gods distils.[3]
   In office here fair Cloacina[4] stands,
And ministers to Jove with purest hands.
Forth from the heap she picked her Votary's
    prayer,   95
And placed it next him, a distinction rare!
Oft had the Goddess heard her servant's call,
From her black grottos near the Temple-wall,
Listening delighted to the jest unclean
Of link-boys vile, and watermen obscene; 100

[1] The Bible, Curl's sign; the Cross-keys, Lintot's.
—P.

[2] See Lucian's Icaro-Menippus; where this fiction is
more extended.

"Orbe locus medio est, inter terrasque, fretumque,
Cœlestesque plagas."—*Ovid. Met.* xii.—P.

[3] Alludes to Homer, Iliad v. :

    ῥέε δ' ἄμβροτον αἷμα Θεοιο,
Ἰχὼρ, οἷός πέρ τε ῥέει μακάρεσσι Θεοῖσιν.

"A stream of nect'rous humour issuing flowed,
Sanguine, such as celestial sp'rits may bleed."
                Milton.—P.

[4] The Roman Goddess of the common sewers.—P.

Where as he fished her nether realms for Wit,[1]
She oft had favoured him, and favours yet.
Renewed by ordure's sympathetic force,
As oiled with magic juices for the course,[2]
Vigorous he rises; from the effluvia strong　105
Imbibes new life, and scours and stinks along;
Re-passes Lintot, vindicates the race,
Nor heeds the brown dishonours of his face.[3]
　And now the victor stretched his eager hand,
Where the tall Nothing stood, or seemed to
　　stand;　　110
A shapeless shade,[4] it melted from his sight,
Like forms in clouds, or visions of the night.
To seize his papers, Curl, was next thy care;
His papers light, fly diverse, tossed in air;[5]
Songs, sonnets, epigrams the winds uplift,　115
And whisk 'em back to Evans, Young, and
　　Swift.[6]
The embroidered suit at least he deemed his
　　prey;
That suit an unpaid tailor snatched away.[7]

[1] See the Preface to Swift's and Pope's Miscellanies.—P.
[2] Alluding to the opinion that there are ointments used by witches to enable them to fly in the air, &c. —P.
[3]　　　" Faciem ostentabat, et udo
　　Turpia membra limo."—*Virg. Æn.* v.—P.

[4]　　　　" Effugit imago
　Par levibus ventis, volucrique simillima somno."
　　　　　　　Virg. Æn. vi.—P.

[5] Virgil, *Æn.* vi. of the Sibyl's leaves,
　" Carmina—
　　　turbata volent rapidis ludibria ventis."—P.

[6] Some of those persons whose writings, epigrams, or jests he had owned.—P.
[7] This line has been loudly complained of in Mist,

No rag, no scrap, of all the bean, or wit.
That once so fluttered, and that once so writ. 120
  Heaven rings with laughter. Of the laughter
    vain,
Dulness, good Queen, repeats the jest again.
Three wicked imps, of her own Grub-street choir,
She decked like Congreve, Addison, and Prior;[1]
Mears, Warner, Wilkins run:[2] delusive thought!
Breval, Bond, Besaleel,[3] the varlets caught. 126

June 8, Dedic. to Sawney, and others, as a most in-
human satire on the *poverty of Poets*. But it is thought
our author would be acquitted by a jury of *Tailors*.
To me this instance seems unluckily chosen ; if it be
a satire on anybody, it must be on a bad *paymaster*,
since the person to whom they have here applied it
was a man of fortune. Not but poets may well be
jealous of so great a prerogative as *non-payment ;*
which Mr. Dennis so far asserts as boldly to pronounce that "if Homer himself was not in debt, it
was because nobody would trust him."—*Pref. to Rem.
on the Rape of the Lock*, p. 15.—P.
  [1] These authors being such whose names will reach
posterity, we shall not give any account of them, but
proceed to those of whom it is necessary. Besaleel
Morris was author of some satires on the translators
of Homer, with many other things printed in news-
papers.—"Bond writ a satire against Mr. P.—Capt.
Breval was author of the Confederates, an ingenious
dramatic performance to expose Mr. P., Mr. Gay,
Dr. Arb., and some ladies of quality," says Curl,
Key, p. 11.—P.
  [2] Booksellers, and Printers of much anonymous
stuff.—P.
  [3] I foresee it will be objected from this line that we
were in an error in our assertion on ver. 50 of this
book, that More was a fictitious name, since these
persons are equally represented by the poet as phantoms. So at first sight it may seem ; but be not
deceived, reader ; these also are not real persons. It
is true, Curl declares Breval, a captain, author of a
piece called The Confederates ; but the same Curl
first said it was written by Joseph Gay : Is his second

Curl stretches after Gay, but Gay is gone;
He grasps an empty Joseph for a John :[1]
So Proteus, hunted in a nobler shape,
Became, when seized, a puppy, or an ape. 130
   To him the Goddess : " Son ! thy grief lay down,
And turn this whole illusion on the town :[2]
As the sage dame, experienced in her trade,
By names of Toasts retails each battered jade ;
(Whence hapless Monsieur much complains at Paris 135
Of wrongs from Duchesses and Lady Maries;)[3]
Be thine, my stationer ! this magic gift;
Cooke shall be Prior,[4] and Concanen, Swift :[5]

assertion to be credited any more than his first ? He
likewise affirms Bond to be one who writ a satire on
our poet : But where is such a satire to be found?
where was such a writer ever heard of? As for
Besaleel, it carries forgery in the very name ; nor is
it, as the others are, a surname. Thou may'st depend
upon it, no such authors ever lived ; all phantoms.—
Scriblerus.—P.

  [1] Joseph Gay, a fictitious name put by Curl before
several pamphlets, which made them pass with many
for Mr. Gay's.—P.

  [2] It was a common practice of this bookseller to
publish vile pieces of obscure hands under the names
of eminent authors.—P.

  [3] Lady Mary Wortley Montagu. See Epilogue to
Satires, Dial. i. 112.

  [4] The man here specified writ a thing called The
Battle of Poets, in which Philips and Welsted were
the Heroes, and Swift and Pope utterly routed. He
also published some malevolent things in the British,
London, and Daily Journals ; and at the same time
wrote letters to Mr. Pope, protesting his Innocence.
His chief work was a translation of Hesiod, to which
Theobald writ notes and half-notes, which he carefully owned.—P.

  [5] In the first edition of this poem there were only
asterisks in this place, but the names were since

So shall each hostile name become our own,
And we too boast our Garth and Addison."[1] 140
    With that she gave him (piteous of his case,[2]
Yet smiling at his rueful length of face)[3]

inserted, merely to fill up the verse, and give ease
to the ear of the reader.—P. For Concanen, see
v. 299.

[1] Nothing is more remarkable than our author's
love of praising good writers. He has in this very
poem celebrated Mr. Locke, Sir Isaac Newton, Dr.
Barrow, Dr. Atterbury, Mr. Dryden, Mr. Congreve,
Dr. Garth, Mr. Addison; in a word, almost every
man of his time that deserved it; even Cibber himself (presuming him to be author of the Careless
Husband). It was very difficult to have that pleasure
in a poem on this subject, yet he has found means to
insert their panegyric, and has made even Dulness
out of her own mouth pronounce it. It must have
been particularly agreeable to him to celebrate Dr.
Garth, both as his constant friend, and as he was his
predecessor in this kind of satire.—P.

[2]   " Risit pater optimus illi.—
Me liceat casum misereri insontis amici—
Sic fatus, tergum Gætuli immane leonis," &c.
                                        Virg. Æn. v.—P.

[3] "The decrepid person or figure of a man are no
reflections upon his Genius: An honest mind will
love and esteem a man of worth, though he be de-
formed or poor. Yet the author of the Dunciad hath
libelled a person for his rueful length of face."—
Mist's Journal, June 8. This Genius and man of
worth, whom an honest mind should love, is Mr. Curl.
True it is, he stood in the pillory, an incident which
will lengthen the face of any man, though it were
ever so comely, therefore is no reflection on the
natural beauty of Mr. Curl. But as to reflections on
any man's face, or figure, Mr. Dennis saith excel-
lently: "Natural deformity comes not by our fault;
'tis often occasioned by calamities and diseases, which
a man can no more help than a monster can his deformity. There is no one misfortune, and no one
disease, but what all the rest of mankind are subject
to. [But the deformity of this Author is visible,

A shaggy Tap'stry,[1] worthy to be spread
On Codrus old, or Dunton's modern bed;[2]

present, lasting, unalterable, and peculiar to himself.
'Tis the Mark of God and Nature upon him, to give
us warning that we should hold no society with him,
as a creature not of our original, nor of our species;
and they who have refused to take this warning which
God and Nature have given them, and have, in spite
of it, by a senseless presumption, ventured to be familiar with him, have severely suffered, &c. 'Tis certain his original is not from Adam, but from the Devil,"
&c.—*Dennis, Character of Mr. P.*, 8vo, 1716.—P.
    Admirably it is observed by Mr. Dennis against
Mr. Law, p. 33, "That the language of Billingsgate
can never be the language of charity, nor consequently
of Christianity." I should else be tempted to use the
language of a Critic; for what is more provoking to
a commentator, than to behold his author thus por-
trayed? Yet I consider it really hurts not *him;*
whereas to call some others dull, might do them prejudice with a world too apt to believe it: therefore,
though Mr. D. may call another a *little ass* or a *young
toad*, far be it from us to call him a *toothless lion* or
an *old serpent*. Indeed, had I written these notes (as
was once my intent) in the learned language, I might
have given him the appellations of *balatro, calceatum
caput, scurra in triviis,* being phrases in good esteem
and frequent usage among the best learned; but in
our mother tongue, were I to tax any gentleman of
the Dunciad, surely it should be in words not to the
vulgar intelligible; whereby Christian charity, decency, and good accord among authors, might be
preserved.—*Scriblerus.*—P.
    [1] A sorry kind of Tapestry frequent in old Inns,
made of worsted or some coarser stuff; like that
which is spoken of by Donne—*Faces as frightful as
theirs who whip Christ in old hangings.* The imagery
woven in it alludes to the mantle of Cloanthus, in
Æn. v.—P.
    [2] Of Codrus the poet's bed, see Juvenal, describing
his *poverty* very copiously, *Sat.* iii. v. 103, &c.

        " Lectus erat Codro," &c.

But Mr. Concanen, in his dedication of the letters,

Instructive work! whose wry-mouthed por-
    traiture   145
Displayed the fates her confessors endure.
Earless on high, stood unabashed De Foe,[1]
And Tutchin flagrant from the scourge below.[2]
There Ridpath, Roper, cudgelled might ye
    view;[3]
The very worsted still looked black and blue. 150
Himself among the storied chiefs he spies,

advertisements, &c., to the author of the Dunciad,
assures us, "that Juvenal never satirized the Poverty
of Codrus"

John Dunton was a broken bookseller, and abusive
scribbler; he writ Neck or Nothing, a violent satire
on some minister of state, a libel on the Duke of
Devonshire and the Bishop of Peterborough, &c.—P.

Defoe was put in the pillory in 1703, for his
"Short way with Dissenters," but he did not lose
his ears. See bk. i. 109.

[1] John Tutchin, author of some vile verses, and of
a weekly paper called the Observator: he was sentenced to be whipped through several towns in the
west of England, upon which he petitioned King
James II. to be hanged. When that prince died in
exile, he wrote an invective against his memory,
occasioned by some humane elegies on his death. He
lived to the time of Queen Anne.—P.

See Macaulay's History of England, chap. v. (on
the "Bloody Assizes"): "A still more frightful sentence was passed on a lad named Tutchin, who was
tried for seditious words. . . . . The sentence was
that the boy should be imprisoned seven years, and
should, during that period, be flogged through every
market-town in Dorsetshire every year. . . . . As it
seemed highly improbable that the sentence would
ever be executed, the Chief Justice consented to remit
it, in return for a bribe which reduced the prisoner to
poverty."

[2] Authors of the Flying-post and Post-boy, two
scandalous papers on different sides, for which they
equally and alternately deserved to be cudgelled, and
were so.—P.

As, from the blanket, high in air he flies,[1]
And "Oh!" (he cried) "what street, what lane
   but knows
Our purgings, pumpings, blankettings, and
   blows ?
In every loom our labours shall be seen,   155
And the fresh vomit run for ever green!"[2]
   See in the circle next, Eliza placed,[3]
Two babes of love close clinging to her waist;[4]

[1] The history of Curl's being tossed in a blanket, and whipped by the scholars of Westminster, is well known.—P.

"Se quoque principibus permixtum agnovit Achivis—
Constitit, et lacrymans: Quis jam locus, inquit,
   Achate !
Quæ regio in terris nostri non plena laboris ?"
                Virg. Æn. i.—P.

[2] A parody on these lines of a late noble author [Lord Halifax]:

"His bleeding arm had furnished all their rooms,
And run for ever purple in the looms."—P.

[3] In this game is exposed, in the most contemptuous manner, the profligate licentiousness of those shameless scribblers (for the most part of that sex which ought least to be capable of such malice or impudence) who in libellous Memoirs and Novels reveal the faults or misfortunes of both sexes, to the ruin of public fame, or disturbance of private happiness. Our good poet (by the whole cast of his work being obliged not to take off the Irony) where he could not shew his indignation, hath shewn his contempt, as much as possible; having here drawn as vile a picture as could be represented in the colours of Epic poesy.—*Scriblerus.*—P.

Eliza Haywood. This woman was authoress of those most scandalous books called the Court of Carimania, and the New Utopia. For the *two babes of love*, see Curl, Key, p. 22.—P.

[4] "Cressa genus, Pholoë, geminique sub ubere nati."—*Virg. Æn.* v.—P.

Fair as before her works she stands confessed,
In flowers and pearls by bounteous Kirkall
     dressed.[1]   160
The Goddess then: "Who best can send on
     high
The salient spout, far streaming to the sky;
His be yon Juno of majestic size,
With cow-like udders, and with ox-like eyes.[2]
This China Jordan[3] let the chief o'ercome   165
Replenish, not ingloriously, at home."
     Osborne[1] and Curl accept the glorious strife,
(Though this his Son dissuades, and that his
     Wife.)
One on his manly confidence relies;

---

[1] *Kirkall*, the name of an engraver. Some of this
Lady's works were printed in four volumes in 12mo,
with her picture thus dressed up before them.—P.

[2] In allusion to Homer's Βοῶπις πότνια"Ηρη.—P.

[3] "Tertius Argolica hac galea contentus abito."
                                   Virg. Æn. v.

In the games of Homer, Iliad, xxiii., there are set
together, as prizes, a Lady and a Kettle, as in this
place Mrs. Haywood and a Jordan. But there the
preference in value is given to the Kettle, at which
Mad. Dacier is justly displeased. Mrs. H. is here
treated with distinction, and acknowledged to be the
more valuable of the two.—P.

[4] *Thomas Osborne*. A Bookseller in Gray's-Inn,
very well qualified by his impudence to act this part;
and therefore placed here instead of a less deserving
predecessor. This man published advertisements,
for a year together, pretending to sell Mr. Pope's
subscription books of Homer's Iliad at half the price:
Of which books he had none, but cut to the size of
them (which was Quarto) the common books in folio,
without Copper-plates, on a worse paper, and never
above half the value.—P. W.

Osborne was the bookseller whom Johnson was
said to have knocked down with a folio. See Bos-
well, under date of 1742.

One on his vigour and superior size.[1]　　170
First Osborne leaned against his lettered post;
It rose, and laboured to a curve at most.
So Jove's bright bow displays its watery round,
(Sure sign [2] that no spectator shall be drowned)
A second effort brought but new disgrace,　175
The wild Mæander washed the Artist's face:
Thus the small jet, which hasty hands unlock,
Spirts in the gardener's eyes who turns the cock.
Not so from shameless Curl; impetuous spread
The stream, and smoking flourished o'er his
　　head.　　180
So (famed like thee for turbulence and horns)
Eridanus his humble fountain scorns;[3]
Through half the heavens he pours the exalted
　　urn;
His rapid waters in their passage burn.

[1]　"Ille—melior motu, fretusque juventa;
　　Hic membris et mole valens."
　　　　　　　　　　　　　Virg. Æn. v.—P.
[2] The words of Homer, of the Rainbow, in Iliad, xi.:

ἅς τε Κρονίων
Ἐν νέφεϊ στήριξε, τέρας μερόπων ἀνθρώπων.

Que le fils de Saturn a fondez dans les nues,' pour
être dans tous les âges une signe à tous les mortels.—
Dacier.—P.
[3] Virgil mentions these two qualifications of Eridanus, Georg. iv.:

"Et gemina auratus taurino *cornua* vultu,
Eridanus, quo non alius per pinguia culta
In mare purpureum *violentior* influit amnis."

The Poets fabled of this river Eridanus, that it flowed
through the skies. Denham, Cooper's Hill:

"Heaven her Eridanus no more shall boast,
Whose fame in thine, like lesser currents lost;
Thy nobler stream shall visit Jove's abodes,
To shine among the stars, and bathe the Gods."
　　　　　　　　　　　　　　　　　—P.

Swift as it mounts, all follow with their eyes:
Still happy Impudence obtains the prize.   186
Thou triumph'st, Victor of the high-wrought
    day,
And the pleased dame, soft-smiling, lead'st
    away.
Osborne, through perfect modesty o'ercome,
Crowned with the Jordan, walks contented
    home.   190
But now for Authors nobler palms remain ;
" Room for my Lord ! " three jockeys in his
    train ;
Six huntsmen with a shout precede his chair :
He grins, and looks broad nonsense with a stare.
His Honour's meaning Dulness thus expressed,
" He wins this Patron, who can tickle best." 196
He chinks his purse, and takes his seat of
    state :
With ready quills the Dedicators wait ;
Now at his head the dexterous task commence,
And, instant, fancy feels the imputed sense ; 200
Now gentle touches wanton o'er his face,
He struts Adonis, and affects grimace :
Rolli the feather to his ear conveys,[1]
Then his nice taste directs our Operas :
Bentley his mouth with classic flattery opes,[2] 205

---

[1] *Paolo Antonio Rolli*, an Italian Poet, and writer
of many Operas in that language, which, partly by
the help of his genius, prevailed in England near
twenty years. He taught Italian to some fine Gentlemen who affected to direct the Operas.—P.

[2] Not spoken of the famous Dr. Richard Bentley,
but of one Tho. Bentley, a small critic, who aped his
uncle in a *little Horace*. The great one was intended
to be dedicated to the Lord Halifax, but (on a change
of the Ministry) was given to the Earl of Oxford ; for
which reason the little one was dedicated to his son
the Lord Harley.— P.

And the puffed orator bursts out in tropes.
But Welsted[1] most the Poet's healing balm
Strives to extract from his soft, giving palm ;
Unlucky Welsted ! thy unfeeling master,
The more thou ticklest, gripes his fist the faster.
  While thus each hand promotes the pleasing
    pain,   211
And quick sensations skip from vein to vein ;
A youth unknown to Phœbus,[2] in despair,
Puts his last refuge all in heaven and prayer.
What force have pious vows ! The Queen of
    Love   215
His sister sends, her votaress, from above.
As taught by Venus, Paris learnt the art
To touch Achilles' only tender part ;
Secure, through her, the noble prize to carry,
He marches off, his Grace's Secretary.   220
  " Now turn to different sports " (the Goddess
    cries)
" And learn, my sons, the wondrous power of
    Noise.

  [1] Leonard Welsted, author of The Triumvirate, or
a Letter in Verse from Palæmon to Celia at Bath,
which was meant for a satire on Mr. P. and some of
his friends, about the year 1718. He writ other
things, which we cannot remember. Smedley, in his
Metamorphosis of Scriblerus, mentions one, the Hymn
of a Gentleman to his Creator. And there was another in praise either of a Cellar or a Garret. You
have him again in Book iii. ver. 169.—P.
  [2] The satire of this Episode being levelled at the
base flatteries of authors to worthless wealth or greatness, concludes here with an excellent lesson to such
men : that although their pens and praises were as
exquisite as their conceit of themselves, yet (even in
their own mercenary views) a creature unlettered,
who serveth the passions, or pimpeth to the pleasures, of such vain, braggart, puffed Nobility, shall
with those patrons be much more inward, and of them
much higher rewarded.—Scriblerus.—P.

To move, to raise, to ravish every heart,
With Shakespear's nature, or with Jonson's art,
Let others aim: 'tis yours to shake the soul[1] 225
With Thunder rumbling from the mustard-
    bowl,[2]
With horns and trumpets now to madness swell,
Now sink in sorrows with a tolling bell;[3]
Such happy arts attention can command,
When fancy flags, and sense is at a stand. 230
Improve we these. Three Cat-calls be the bribe[4]
Of him, whose chattering shames the monkey-
    tribe:
And his this Drum, whose hoarse heroic bass
Drowns the loud clarion of the braying Ass."
    Now thousand tongues are heard in one loud
        din;   235
The monkey-mimics rush discordant in;
"Twas chattering, grinning, mouthing, jabber-
    ing all,

[1] " Excudent alii spirantia mollius æra,
    Credo equidem, vivos ducent de marmore vultus,
        &c.

    Tu regere imperio populos, Romane, memento,
    Hæ tibi erunt artes."—*Virgil, Æn.* vi.—P.

[2] The old way of making Thunder and Mustard
were the same; but since, it is more advantageously
performed by troughs of wood with stops in them.
Whether Mr. Dennis was the inventor of that im-
provement, I know not; but it is certain, that being
once at a Tragedy of a new author, he fell into a
great passion at hearing some, and cried, " 'Sdeath!
that is *my* thunder."—P.   Dennis, in his " Appius
and Virginia," introduced a new way of making
thunder, which was afterwards employed in " Mac-
beth."

[3] A mechanical aid to the Pathetic, not unuseful to
the modern writers of Tragedy.—P.

[4] Certain musical instruments used by one class of
Critics to confound the poets of the theatre.—P.

And Noise and Norton, Brangling and Breval,[1]
Dennis and Dissonance, and captious Art,
And Snip-snap short, and Interruption smart, 240
And Demonstration thin, and Theses thick,
And Major, Minor, and Conclusion quick.
" Hold ! " (cried the Queen) "a Cat-call each
    shall win ; [2]
Equal your merits ! equal is your din !
But that this well-disputed game may end, 245
Sound forth, my Brayers, and the welkin rend."
    As, when the long-eared milky mothers wait [3]
At some sick miser's triple-bolted gate,
For their defrauded, absent foals they make
A moan so loud, that all the guild awake ; 250
Sore sighs Sir Gilbert,[4] starting at the bray,
From dreams of millions, and three groats to pay.
So swells each wind-pipe ; Ass intones to Ass,
Harmonic twang ! of leather, horn, and brass ;
Such as from labouring lungs the Enthusiast
    blows, 255
High Sound, attempered to the vocal nose ;
Or such as bellow from the deep Divine ;
There, Webster ! pealed thy voice, and Whit-
field ! thine.[5]

[1] See ver. 415. J. Durant Breval, Author of a
very extraordinary Book of Travels, and some Poems.
See before, Note on ver. 126.—P.

[2] " Non nostrum inter vos tantas componere lites,
    Et vitula tu dignus, et hic."—*Virg. Ecl.* iii.—P.

[3] A simile with a long tail, in the manner of
Homer.—P.

[4] Sir Gilbert Heathcote. See Moral Essays, iii. 101.

[5] The one the writer of a Newspaper called the
Weekly Miscellany, the other a Field-preacher.—
Warburton.
    This couplet first appeared in 1742. George White-
field, the famous preacher, was born in 1714, and
died in 1770.

But far o'er all, sonorous Blackmore's strain;
Walls, steeples, skies, bray back to him again.[1]
In Tot'nam fields, the brethren, with amaze, 261
Prick all their ears up, and forget to graze;[2]
Long Chancery-lane[3] retentive rolls the sound,
And courts to courts return it round and round;
Thames wafts it thence to Rufus' roaring hall,
And Hungerford re-echoes bawl for bawl.   266
All hail him victor in both gifts of song,
Who sings so loudly, and who sings so long.[4]

---

[1] A figure of speech taken from Virgil:

" Et vox assensu nemorum ingeminata remugit."
                                    Georg. iii.

" He hears his numerous herds low o'er the plain,
While neighbouring hills *low* back to them again."
                                    Cowley.

The poet here celebrated, Sir R. B., delighted much in the word *bray*, which he endeavoured to ennoble by applying it to the sound of *Armour*, *War*, &c. In imitation of him, and strengthened by his authority, our author has here admitted it into Heroic poetry.—P.

[2] " Immemor herbarum quos est mirata juvenca."
                                    Virg. Ecl. viii.

The progress of the sound from place to place, and the scenery here of the bordering regions, Tottenham-fields, Chancery-lane, the Thames, Westminster-hall, and Hungerford-stairs, are imitated from Virgil, *Æn.* vii., on the sounding the horn of Alecto:

" Audiit et Triviæ longe lacus, audiit amnis
Sulphurea Nar albus aqua, fontesque Velini," &c.
                                    —P.

[3] The place where the offices of Chancery are kept. The long detention of Clients in that Court, and the difficulty of getting out, is humorously allegorized in these lines.—P.

[4] A just character of Sir Richard Blackmore, knight, who (as Mr. Dryden expresseth it)

" Writ to the rumbling of his coach's wheels;"

This labour past, by Bridewell all descend,
(As morning prayer and flagellation end) [1] 270

and whose indefatigable Muse produced no less than
six Epic poems: Prince and King Arthur, twenty
books; Eliza, ten; Alfred, twelve; The Redeemer,
six; besides Job, in folio; the whole Book of Psalms;
The Creation, seven books; Nature of Man, three
books; and many more. 'Tis in this sense he is
styled afterwards the *everlasting Blackmore*. Notwithstanding all which, Mr. Gildon seems assured
that "this admirable author did not think himself
upon the *same foot* with *Homer.*"—*Comp. Art of
Poetry*, vol. i. p. 108.

This gentleman, in his first works, abused the
character of Mr. Dryden; and, in his last, of Mr.
Pope, accusing him in very high and sober terms of
profaneness and immorality (Essay on Polite Writing,
vol. ii. p. 270), on a mere report from Edmund Curl
that he was author of a Travestie on the first Psalm.
Mr. Dennis took up the same report, but with the
addition of what Sir Richard had neglected, an *Argu-
ment to prove it;* which, being very curious, we shall
here transcribe. "It was he who burlesqued the
Psalm of David. It is *apparent* to me that Psalm
was burlesqued by a *Popish rhymester.* Let rhyming
persons who have been brought up *Protestants* be
otherwise what they will, let them be rakes, let them
be scoundrels, let them be *Atheists*, yet education
has made an invincible impression on them in behalf
of the sacred writings. But a *Popish rhymester* has
been brought up with a contempt for those sacred
writings; now shew me another *Popish rhymester*
but he." This manner of argumentation is usual
with Mr. Dennis; he has employed the same against
Sir Richard himself, in a like charge of *Impiety* and
Irreligion.—P.

[1] It is between eleven and twelve in the morning,
after church service, that the criminals are whipped
in Bridewell.—This is to mark punctually the *time*
of the day: Homer does it by the circumstance of
the Judges rising from court, or of the Labourers'
dinner; our author, by one very proper both to the
Persons and the *Scene* of his poem, which we may
remember commenced in the evening of the Lord

To where Fleet-ditch with disemboguing
    streams
Rolls the large tribute of dead dogs to Thames,
The king of dykes!¹ than whom no sluice of
    mud
With deeper sable blots the silver flood.
" Here strip, my children ! here at once leap in,
Here prove who best can dash through thick
    and thin,   276
And who the most in love of dirt excel,
Or dark dexterity of groping well.²
Who flings most filth, and wide pollutes around
The stream, be his the Weekly Journals bound;³
A pig of lead to him who dives the best;   281
A peck of coals a-piece shall glad the rest."⁴

Mayor's day : The first book passed in that *night ;*
the next *morning* the games begin in the Strand,
thence along Fleet-street (places inhabited by Booksellers), then they proceed by Bridewell towards
Fleet-ditch, and, lastly, through Ludgate to the City
and the Temple of the Goddess.—P.

  ¹ " Fluviorum rex Eridanus,
    —— quo non alius, per pinguia culta,
    In mare purpureum violentior influit amnis."
                           Virg.—P.

  ² The three chief qualifications of Party-writers :
to stick at nothing, to delight in flinging dirt, and to
slander in the dark by guess.—P.
  ³ Papers of news and scandal intermixed, on different sides and parties, and frequently shifting from
one side to the other, called the London Journal,
British Journal, Daily Journal, &c., the concealed
writers of which, for some time, were Oldmixon,
Roome, Arnall, Concanen, and others : persons never
seen by our author.—P.
  ⁴ Our indulgent Poet, whenever he has spoken of
any dirty or low work, constantly puts us in mind of
the *Poverty* of the offenders, as the only extenuation
of such practices. Let any one but remark, when a

In naked majesty Oldmixon stands,[1]
And Milo-like surveys his arms and hands;

Thief, a Pickpocket, an Highwayman, or a Knight of
the post are spoken of, how much our hate to those
characters is lessened, if they add a *needy* Thief, a
poor Pickpocket, an *hungry* Highwayman, a *starving*
Knight of the post, &c.—P.

[1] Mr. John Oldmixon, next to Mr. Dennis, the
most ancient Critic of our Nation; an unjust censurer of Mr. Addison in his prose Essay on Criticism,
whom, also, in his imitation of Bouhours (called the
Arts of Logic and Rhetoric), he misrepresents in plain
matter of fact; for, in page 45, he cites the Spectator
as abusing Dr. Swift by name, where there is not the
least hint of it; and in page 304, is so injurious as to
suggest that Mr. Addison himself writ that Tatler,
No. 43, which says of his own Simile, that "'Tis as
great as ever entered into the mind of man." "In
Poetry he was not so happy as laborious, and therefore characterized by the Tatler, No. 62, by the name
of *Omicron*, the *Unborn Poet.*"—*Curl, Key*, p. 13.
"He writ Dramatic works, and a volume of Poetry,
consisting of heroic Epistles, &c., some whereof are
very well done," saith that great Judge, Mr. Jacob,
in his Lives of Poets, vol. ii. p. 303.
In his Essay on Criticism, and the Arts of Logic
and Rhetoric, he frequently reflects on our author.
But the top of his character was a Perverter of
History, in that scandalous one of the Stuarts, in
folio, and his Critical History of England, two volumes,
octavo. Being employed by Bishop Kennet in publishing the Historians in his Collection, he falsified
Daniel's Chronicle in numberless places. Yet this
very man, in the Preface to the first of these books,
advanced a *particular fact* to charge three eminent
persons of falsifying the Lord Clarendon's History:
which fact has been disproved by Dr. Atterbury, late
Bishop of Rochester, then the only survivor of them;
and the particular part he pretended to be falsified,
produced since, after almost ninety years, in that
noble author's original manuscript. He was all his
life a virulent Party-writer for hire, and received his
reward in a small place, which he enjoyed to his
death.—P.

Then sighing, thus, "And am I now three-
   score ?[1]   285
Ah why, ye Gods! should two and two make
   four ? "
He said, and climbed a stranded lighter's
   height,
Shot to the black abyss, and plunged down-
   right.
The Senior's judgment all the crowd admire,
Who but to sink the deeper, rose the higher. 290
   Next Smedley dived:[2] slow circles dimpled
   o'er
The quaking mud, that closed, and oped no
   more.
All look, all sigh, and call on Smedley lost;[3]
" Smedley " in vain resounds through all the
   coast.
   Then * essayed;[4] scarce vanished out of
   sight,   295
He buoys up instant, and returns to light :

[1] " —— Fletque Milon senior, cum spectat inanes
Herculeis similes, fluidos pendere lacertos."
                               Ovid.—P.

[2] The person here mentioned, an Irishman, was
author and publisher of many scurrilous pieces, a
weekly Whitehall Journal, in the year 1722, in the
name of Sir James Baker; and particularly whole
volumes of Billingsgate against Dr. Swift and Mr.
Pope, called Gulliveriana and Alexandriana, printed
in octavo, 1728.—P.

[3] " Alcides wept in vain for Hylas lost,
Hylas, in vain, resounds through all the coast."
      Lord Roscom. Translat. of Virgil, Ecl. vi.—P.

[4] A gentleman of genius and spirit, who was secretly dipped in some papers of this kind, on whom
our poet bestows a panegyric instead of a satire, as
deserving to be better employed than in party quarrels and personal invectives.— P.   Aaron Hill, born
1685, died 1750, a voluminous dramatic writer.

He bears no token of the sabler streams,
And mounts far off among the Swans of
    Thames.
    True to the bottom see Concanen creep,[1]
A cold, long-winded native of the deep ;   300
If perseverance gain the Diver's prize,
Not everlasting Blackmore this denies :[2]
No noise, no stir, no motion canst thou make,
The unconscious stream sleeps o'er thee like a
    lake.
    Next plunged a feeble, but a desperate pack,
With each a sickly brother at his back :   306
Sons of a Day ![3] just buoyant on the flood,
Then numbered with the puppies in the mud.
Ask ye their names ? I could as soon disclose

[1] Mathew Concanen, an Irishman, bred to the law.
Smedley (one of his brethren in enmity to Swift), in
his Metamorphosis of Scriblerus, p. 7, accuses him of
"having boasted of what he had not written, but
others had revised and done for him." He was author
of several dull and dead scurrilities in the British and
London Journals, and in a paper called the Speculatist.
In a pamphlet, called a Supplement to the Profound, he dealt very unfairly with our Poet, not only
frequently imputing to him Mr. Broome's verses (for
which he might indeed seem in some degree accoun-
table, having corrected what that gentleman did), but
those of the Duke of Buckingham and others : To
this rare piece, somebody humorously caused him to
take for his motto, De profundis clamavi. He was
since a hired scribbler in the Daily Courant, where
he poured forth much Billingsgate against the Lord
Bolingbroke, and others ; after which this man was
surprisingly promoted to administer Justice and Law
in Jamaica.—P.

[2] " Nec bonus Eurytion prælato invidit honori," &c.
                                    Virg. Æn.—P.

[3] These were daily Papers, a number of which, to
lessen the expense, were printed one on the back of
another.—P. W.

The names of these blind puppies as of those.
Fast by, like Niobe (her children gone) [1]   311
Sits Mother Osborne, stupefied to stone ! [2]
And Monumental brass this record bears,
" These are,—ah no ! these were, the Gazet-
    teers ! "
Not so bold Arnall ; [3] with a weight of skull,
Furious he dives, precipitately dull.   316
Whirlpools and storms his circling arm invest,
With all the might of gravitation blest.
No crab more active in the dirty dance,
Downward to climb, and backward to advance.
He brings up half the bottom on his head, 321

[1] See the story in Ovid, Met. vii., where the
miserable Petrifaction of this old Lady is patheti-
cally described.—P. W.

[2] A name assumed by the eldest and gravest of
these writers, who at last, being ashamed of his
pupils, gave his paper over, and in his age remained
silent.—P. W.

[3] William Arnall, bred an Attorney, was a perfect
Genius in this sort of work. He began under twenty
with furious Party-papers ; then succeeded Concanen
in the British Journal. At the first publication of
the Dunciad, he prevailed on the Author not to give
him his due place in it, by a letter professing his
detestation of such practices as his Predecessor's.
But since, by the most unexampled insolence, and
personal abuse of several great men, the Poet's particular friends, he most amply deserved a niche in
the Temple of Infamy : Witness a paper, called the
Free Briton ; a Dedication, intituled, To the Genuine
Blunderer, 1732, and many others. He writ for hire,
and valued himself upon it ; not, indeed, without
cause, it appearing by the aforesaid Report that he
received "for Free Britons, and other writings, in
the space of *four years*, no less than *ten thousand
nine hundred and ninety-seven pounds, six shillings
and eightpence* out of the Treasury." But frequently,
through his fury or folly, he exceeded all the bounds
of his commission, and obliged his honourable Patron
to disavow his scurrilities.—P.

And loudly claims the Journals and the Lead.
The plunging Prelate,[1] and his ponderous
     Grace,[2]
With holy envy gave one Layman place.
When lo ! a burst of thunder shook the flood ;
Slow rose a form, in majesty of Mud ;   326
Shaking the horrors of his sable brows,
And each ferocious feature grim with ooze.
Greater he looks, and more than mortal stares;[3]
Then thus the wonders of the deep declares. 330
     First he relates, how sinking to the chin,
Smit with his mien, the Mud-nymphs sucked
     him in :
How young Lutetia, softer than the down,

[1] It having been invidiously insinuated that by
this title was meant a truly great Prelate, as re-
spectable for his defence of the present balance of
power in the *civil* constitution, as for his opposition
to no power at all, in the *religious;* I owe so much to
the memory of my deceased friend as to declare, that
when, a little before his death, I informed him of this
insinuation, he called it vile and malicious, as any
candid man, he said, might understand, by his having
paid a willing compliment to this very prelate in
another part of the poem.—*Warburton.*
     It was imagined he meant Bishop Sherlock. Sir
Robert Walpole, who was Sherlock's contemporary
at Eton, used to relate, that when some of the
scholars, going to bathe in the Thames, stood shivering on the bank, Sherlock plunged in immediately
over his head and ears.—*Warton.*
[2] The Archbishop of Canterbury, whether Wake,
who died in 1737, or Potter, who was Archbishop in
1743 (when this couplet first appeared), and who had
published some ponderous editions of Greek authors.
I think the meaning is that Walpole—the "one
Layman"—succeeded in diving even deeper in flattery
than Sherlock and the Archbishop.—*Courthope.*
[3] Virg. Æn. vi. of the Sibyl :
          " Majorque videri,
     Nec mortale sonans."—P.

Nigrina black, and Merdamante brown,
Vied for his love in jetty bowers below,   335
As Hylas fair was ravished long ago.[1]
Then sung, how shown him by the Nut-brown
   maids
A branch of Styx [2] here rises from the Shades,
That tinctured as it runs with Lethe's streams,
And wafting Vapours from the Land of
   Dreams,   340
(As under seas Alpheus' secret sluice
Bears Pisa's offerings to his Arethuse)
Pours into Thames: and hence the mingled
   wave
Intoxicates the pert, and lulls the grave:
Here brisker vapours o'er the Temple creep, 345

---

[1] Who was ravished by the water-nymphs, and
drawn into the river. The story is told at large by
Valerius Flaccus, lib. iii. Argon. See Virgil, Ecl. vi.
—P.

[2]   Οἵ τ' ἀμφ' ἱμερτὸν Τιταρήσιον ἔργ' ἐνέμοντο,
   Ὅς ῥ' ἐς Πηνειὸν προΐει καλλίρροον ὕδωρ.
   Οὐδ' ὅ γε Πηνειῷ συμμίσγεται ἀργυροδίνῃ,
   Ἀλλά τέ μιν καθύπερθεν ἐπιρρέει ἠΰτ' ἔλαιον·
   Ὅρκου γὰρ δεινοῦ Στυγὸς ὕδατός ἐστιν ἀπορρώξ.
                                    Hom. Il. ii. Catal.

Of the Land of Dreams, in the same region, he makes
mention, Odyss. xxiv. See also Lucian's True History. Lethe and the Land of Dreams allegorically
represent the Stupefaction and visionary Madness of
Poets, equally dull and extravagant. Of Alpheus's
waters gliding secretly under the sea of Pisa, to mix
with those of Arethuse in Sicily, see Moschus, Idyll.
viii., Virg. Ecl. x.

   "Sic tibi, cum fluctus subter labere Sicanos,
   Doris amara suam non intermisceat undam."

And again, Æn. iii. :

   " —— Alpheum fama est huc Elidis amnem
   Occultas egisse vias subter mare ; qui nunc
   Ore, Arethusa, tuo Siculis confunditur undis."—

There, all from Paul's to Aldgate drink and
   sleep.
Thence to the banks where reverend Bards
   repose,[1]
They led him soft ; each reverend Bard arose ;
And Milbourn chief,[2] deputed by the rest,|
Gave him the cassock, surcingle, and vest.   350
" Receive " (he said,) " these robes which once
   were mine,
Dulness is sacred in a sound divine."
He ceased, and spread the robe ; the crowd
   confess
The reverend Flamen in his lengthened dress.
Around him wide a sable Army stand,   355
A low-born, cell-bred, selfish, servile band,
Prompt or to guard or stab, to saint or damn,
Heaven's Swiss, who fight for any God, or
   Man.[3]
Through Lud's famed gates,[4] along the well-
   known Fleet,

[1] "Tum canit errantem Permessi ad flumina Gallum,
Utque viro Phœbi chorus assurrexerit omnis ;
Ut Linus hæc illi divino carmine pastor,
Floribus atque apio crines ornatus amaro,
Dixerit, Hos tibi dant calamos, en accipe, Musæ,
Ascræo quos ante seni," &c.—*Virg. Ecl.* vi.—P.

[2] Luke Milbourn, a Clergyman, the fairest of
Critics ; who, when he wrote against Mr. Dryden's
Virgil, did him justice in printing at the same time
his own translations of him, which were intolerable.
His manner of writing has a great resemblance with
that of the Gentlemen of the Dunciad against our
author, as will be seen in the Parallel of Mr. Dryden
and him. Appendix.—P. See Essay on Criticism,
v. 463.

[3] See Dryden's " Hind and Panther : "

" Those Swisses fight on any side for pay."
                      Warton.

[4] " King Lud repairing the City, called it after his

Rolls the black troop, and overshades the
  street;   360
'Till showers of Sermons, Characters, Essays,
In circling fleeces whiten all the ways :
So clouds, replenished from some bog below,
Mount in dark volumes, and descend in snow.
Here stopped the Goddess : and in pomp pro-
  claims   365
A gentler exercise to close the games.
  " Ye Critics ! in whose heads, as equal scales,
I weigh what author's heaviness prevails ;
Which most conduce to soothe the soul in
  slumbers,
My H—ley's periods,[1] or my Blackmore's
  numbers ;   370
Attend the trial we propose to make :
If there be man, who o'er such works can
  wake,
Sleep's all-subduing charms who dares defy,
And boasts Ulysses' ear with Argus' eye ;[2]
To him we grant our amplest powers to sit 375
Judge of all present, past, and future wit ;

own name, Lud's Town ; the strong gate which he
built in the west part, he likewise, for his own
honour, named Ludgate. In the year 1260, this gate
was beautified with images of Lud and other Kings.
Those images, in the reign of Edward VI., had their
Heads smitten off, and were otherwise defaced by
unadvised folks. Queen Mary did set new heads
upon their old bodies again. The 28th of Queen
Elizabeth the same gate was clean taken down, and
newly and beautifully builded, with images of Lud
and others, as afore."—*Stow's Survey of London.*—P.
Ludgate was pulled down in 1760.
  [1] The early editions, except the first, read " Henley's periods." The blank was afterwards restored,
so that the name " Hoadley " might be supplied, as
was originally intended. See note on v. 400.
  [2] See Hom. Odyss. xii. ; Ovid, Met. i.—P.

To cavil, censure, dictate, right or wrong ;
Full and eternal privilege of tongue."
   Three College Sophs,[1] and three pert Tem-
    plars came,
The same their talents, and their tastes the
    same ;   380
Each prompt to query, answer, and debate,[2]
And smit with love of Poesy and Prate.[3]
The ponderous books two gentle readers bring ;
The heroes sit, the vulgar form a ring.[4]
The clamorous crowd is hushed with mugs of
    Mum,[5]   385
'Till all, tuned equal, send a general hum.
Then mount the Clerks, and in one lazy tone
Through the long, heavy, painful page drawl
    on ;[6]

[1] At first "Three Cambridge Sophs;" and more properly as, I believe, the term is not used at Oxford. —*Wakefield.* "Soph" is a contraction of "Sophister," the old form of "Sophist." Second and third year men at Cambridge are called Junior and Senior Sophs.

[2] "Ambo florentes ætatibus, Arcades ambo,
  Et certare pares, et respondere parati."
                    Virg. Ecl. vi.—P.

[3] "Smit with the love of sacred song."
                         Milton.—P.

[4] "Consedere duces, et vulgi stante corona."
                    Ovid, Met. xiii.—P.

[5] Mum was a strong beer made at Brunswick, and so called from Christian Mumme, who first brewed it in 1492.

[6] "All these lines very well imitate the slow drowsiness with which they proceed. It is impossible to any one who has a poetical ear, to read them without perceiving the heaviness that lags in the verse, to imitate the action it describes. The simile of the Pines is very just, and well adapted to the subject;"

Soft creeping, words on words, the sense com-
pose ;
At every line they stretch, they yawn, they
doze.   390
As to soft gales top-heavy pines bow low
Their heads, and lift them as they cease to
blow :
Thus oft they rear, and oft the head decline,
As breathe, or pause, by fits, the airs divine ;
And now to this side, now to that they nod, 395
As verse, or prose, infuse the drowsy God.
Thrice Budgel aimed to speak, but thrice sup-
pressed [1]
By potent Arthur,[2] knocked his chin and
breast.
Toland and Tindal,[3] prompt at priests to jeer,

says an Enemy, in his Essay on the Dunciad, p. 21.
—P.

[1] Famous for his speeches on many occasions about
the South Sea scheme, &c. "He is a very ingenious
gentleman, and hath written some excellent Epi-
logues to plays, and one small piece on Love, which
is very pretty."—Jacob, Lives of Poets, vol. ii. p. 289.
But this gentleman since made himself much more
eminent, and personally well known to the greatest
statesmen of all parties, as well as to all the Courts of
Law in this nation.—P.
    Budgell committed suicide in 1737. He was a re-
lation of Addison, whom he accompanied to Ireland
as clerk : he afterwards rose to Under-Secretary of
State.—Carruthers. See Satires of Dr. Donne, iv.
51.

[2] Arthur Onslow, Speaker of the House of Commons.

[3] Two persons, not so happy as to be obscure, who
writ against the Religion of their Country. Toland,
the author of the Atheist's Liturgy, called Pan-
theisticon, was a spy, in pay to Lord Oxford. Tindal
was author of the Rights of the Christian Church,
and Christianity as old as the Creation.—P.

Yet silent bowed to *Christ's No kingdom here.*[1] 400
Who sate the nearest, by the words o'ercome,
Slept first; the distant nodded to the hum.
Then down are rolled the books; stretched
    o'er 'em lies
Each gentle clerk, and muttering seals his
    eyes.
As what a Dutchman plumps into the lakes,
One circle first, and then a second makes; 406
What Dulness dropped among her sons im-
    pressed
Like motion from one circle to the rest;
So from the mid-most the nutation spreads
Round and more round, o'er all the sea of
    heads.[2]   410
At last Centlivre felt her voice to fail;[3]
Motteux himself unfinished left his tale;[1]
Boyer the State, and Law the Stage gave
    o'er;[5]

[1] This is said by Curl, Key to Dunc., to allude to
a sermon of a reverend Bishop.—P. W.
    It alludes to Bishop Hoadley's sermon preached
before George I. in 1717, "On the Nature of the
Kingdom of Christ," which occasioned a long, ve-
hement, and learned debate known as the Bangorian
Controversy, of which See Hoadley was at that time
bishop.—*Wakefield.* Hoadley was afterwards Bishop
of Hereford, Salisbury, and Winchester, successively.

[2] " A waving sea of heads was round me spread,
    And still fresh streams the gazing deluge fed."
                    Blackm. Job.—P.

[3] Mrs. Susanna Centlivre, wife to Mr. Centlivre,
Yeoman of the Mouth to his Majesty. She writ
many plays and a Song (says Mr. Jacob, vol. i. p. 32)
before she was seven years old. She also writ a
Ballad against Mr. Pope's Homer, before he began
it.—P.
   [1] Peter Anthony Motteux, the translator of Don
Quixote. See Satires of Dr. Donne, iv. 50.
   [5] A. Boyer, a voluminous compiler of Annals,

Morgan [1] and Mandevil [2] could prate no more ;

Political Collections, &c. William Law, A.M., wrote
with great zeal against the Stage ; Mr. Dennis
answered with as great. Their books were printed
in 1726. Mr. Law affirmed, that " The Playhouse is
the temple of the Devil ; the peculiar pleasure of the
Devil ; where all they who go yield to the Devil ;
where all the laughter is a laughter among Devils ;
and all who are there are hearing Music in the very
Porch of Hell." To which Mr. Dennis replied, that
" There is every jot as much difference between a
true Play and one made by a Poetaster, as between
two religious books, the *Bible*, and the *Alcoran*."—P.
    The same Mr. Law is author of a book, entitled,
*An Appeal to all that doubt of or disbelieve the truth
of the Gospel*, in which he detailed a System of the
rankest Spinozism, for the most exalted Theology ;
and amongst other things as rare, has informed us of
this, that Sir Isaac Newton stole the principles of
his philosophy from one *Jacob Behman* [Boehm], a
German cobbler.—*Warburton.*
    [1] A writer against Religion, distinguished no other-
wise from the rabble of his tribe than by the pom-
pousness of his Title ; for having stolen his morality
from Tindal, and his philosophy from Spinoza, he calls
himself, by the courtesy of England, a *Moral Philosopher.*—*Warburton.*
    [2] This writer, who prided himself as much in the
reputation of an *Immoral Philosopher*, was author of
a famous book called *The Fable of the Bees ;* written
to prove that Moral Virtue is the invention of knaves,
and Christian Virtue the imposition of fools ; and
that Vice is necessary, and alone sufficient to render
Society flourishing and happy.—*Warburton.*
    Morgan was a Dissenting minister in Bristol, author
of the Moral Philosopher, 1737.—Bernard Mandeville
was a Dutchman by birth, but settled in England
when young, and practised as a physician until his
death, in 1733. His principal work, the Fable of the
Bees, or Private Vices made Public Benefits, was
doubly distinguished in being presented by the Grand
Jury of Middlesex as immoral and pernicious, and in
being answered by Pope's friend, Bishop Berkeley.—
Carruthers.

Norton,[1] from Daniel and Ostrœa[2] sprung, 415
Blessed with his father's front, and mother's
     tongue,
Hung silent down his never-blushing head ;
And all was hushed, as Folly's self lay dead.[3]
  Thus the soft gifts of Sleep conclude the
     day,
And stretched on bulks, as usual, Poets lay. 420
Why should I sing, what bards the nightly
     Muse
Did slumbering visit and convey to stews ;
Who prouder marched, with magistrates in
     state,
To some famed round-house, ever open gate !
How Henley lay inspired beside a sink,   425
And to mere mortals seemed a Priest in drink :[1]

---

[1] Norton De Foe, offspring of the famous Daniel.
Fortes creantur fortibus. One of the authors of the
Flying Post, in which well-bred work Mr. P. had
sometime the honour to be abused with his betters ;
and of many hired scurrilities and daily papers, to
which he never set his name.—P.

[2] The name of Ostrœa, meaning an oyster wench,
is borrowed from Gay's Trivia, iii. 185.—*Courthope.*

[3] Alludes to Dryden's verse in the Indian Emperor :

  " All things are hushed, as Nature's self lay dead."
                                   —P.

[1] This line presents us with an excellent moral,
that we are never to pass judgment merely by *ap-*
pearances ; a lesson to all men who may happen to
see a reverend Person in the like situation, not to
determine too rashly ; since not only the Poets frequently describe a Bard inspired in this posture,

(" On Cam's fair bank, where Chaucer lay inspired,"

and the like) but an eminent Casuist tells us, that
" if a priest be seen in any indecent action, we ought
to account it a deception of sight, or illusion of the

While others, timely, to the neighbouring
　　Fleet[1]
(Haunt of the Muses) made their safe retreat.

Devil, who sometimes takes upon him the shape of
holy men on purpose to cause scandal."—*Scriblerus.*
—P.

[1] A prison for insolvent Debtors on the bank of the
Ditch.—P.

BOOK THE THIRD.

ARGUMENT.

After the other persons are disposed in their proper places of rest, the Goddess transports the King to her Temple, and there lays him to slumber with his head on her lap : a position of marvellous virtue, which causes all the visions of wild enthusiasts, projectors, politicians, inamoratos, castle-builders, chemists, and poets. He is immediately carried on the wings of Fancy, and led, by a mad poetical Sibyl, to the Elysian shade, where, on the banks of Lethe, the souls of the dull are dipped by Bavius, before their entrance into this world : there he is met by the ghost of Settle, and by him made acquainted with the wonders of the place, and with those which he himself is destined to perform. He takes him to a Mount of Vision, from whence he shews him the past triumphs of the Empire of Dulness, then the present, and lastly the future : how small a part of the world was ever conquered by Science, how soon those conquests were stopped, and those very nations again reduced to her dominion. Then, distinguishing the Island of Great Britain, shews by what aids, by what persons, and by what degrees, it shall be brought to her Empire. Some of the persons he causes to pass in review before his eyes, describing each by his proper figure, character, and qualifications. On a sudden, the Scene shifts, and a vast number of miracles and prodigies appear, utterly surprising and unknown to the King himself, till they are explained to be the wonders of his own reign now commencing. On this subject Settle breaks into a congratulation, yet not unmixed with concern, that his own times were but the types of these. He prophesies how first the nation shall be overrun with Farces, Operas, and Shows ; how the throne of Dulness shall be advanced over the Theatres, and set up even at Court ; then how her sons shall preside in the seats of Arts and Sciences ; giving a glimpse, or Pisgah-sight, of the future Fulness of her Glory, the accomplishment whereof is the subject of the fourth and last book.

BOOK III.

But in her Temple's last recess enclosed,
On Dulness' lap the Anointed head reposed.
Him close she curtains round with Vapours
    blue,
And soft besprinkles with Cimmerian dew.
Then raptures high the seat of Sense o'erflow, 5
Which only heads refined from Reason know.
Hence, from the straw where Bedlam's Prophet
    nods,
He hears loud Oracles, and talks with Gods : [1]
Hence the Fool's Paradise, the Statesman's
    Scheme,
The air-built Castle, and the golden Dream, 10
The Maid's romantic wish, the Chemist's flame,
And Poet's vision of eternal Fame.
    And now, on Fancy's easy wing conveyed,
The King descending, views the Elysian Shade.
A slip-shod Sibyl [2] led his steps along,   15
In lofty madness meditating song ;
Her tresses staring from Poetic dreams,
And never washed, but in Castalia's streams.
Taylor, [3] their better Charon, lends an oar,

---

[1] " Et varias audit voces, fruiturque deorum
    Colloquio."—*Virg. Æn.* vii.—P.

[2] " Conclamat Vates——
    ——furens antro se immisit aperto."—*Virg.*—P.

[3] John Taylor, the Water-poet, an honest man,
who owns he learned not so much as the Accidence :
A rare example of modesty in a Poet !

    " I must confess I do want eloquence,
    And never scarce did learn my Accidence ;

(Once swan of Thames, though now he sings
   no more.) 20
Benlowes,[1] propitious still to blockheads, bows;
And Shadwell nods the Poppy on his brows.[2]
Here, in a dusky vale where Lethe rolls,[3]
Old Bavius sits,[4] to dip poetic souls,[5]

> For having got from *possum* to *posset*,
> I there was gravel'd, could no farther get."

He wrote fourscore books in the reign of James I.
and Charles I., and afterwards (like Edward Ward)
kept an Ale-house in Long-Acre. He died in 1654.
—P. W.
   Taylor was a waterman on the Thames. He died
in 1653. For a list of his numerous works, see
Lowndes' Bibliographers' Manual.
   [1] A country gentleman, famous for his own bad
Poetry, and for patronising bad Poets, as may be
seen from many Dedications of Quarles and others to
him. Some of these anagram'd his name, *Benlowes*,
into *Benevolus*; to verify which, he spent his whole
estate upon them.—P.
   [2] Shadwell took Opium for many years, and died
of too large a dose, in the year 1692.—P. W.

   [3] "——Videt Æneas in valle reducta
   Seclusum nemus——
   Lethæumque domos placidas qui prænatat am-
     nem, &c.
   Hunc circum innumeræ gentes," &c.
                 Virg. Æn. vi.—P.

   [4] Bavius was an ancient Poet, celebrated by Virgil
for the like cause as Bays by our author, though not
in so Christian-like a manner; for heathenishly it is
declared by Virgil of Bavius, that he ought to be
hated and *detested* for his evil works: *Qui Bavium
non* odit; whereas we have often had occasion to
observe our Poet's great *Good Nature* and *Merciful-*

   [5] Alluding to the story of Thetis dipping Achilles,
to render him impenetrable:

   " At pater Anchises penitus convalle virenti
   Inclusas animas, superumque ad lumen ituras,
   Lustrabat."—*Virg. Æn.* vi.—P.

And blunt the sense, and fit it for a skull   25
Of solid proof, impenetrably dull :
   Instant, when dipped, away they wing their
     flight,
Where Brown and Mears[1] unbar the gates of
     Light,[2]
Demand new bodies, and in Calf's array,
Rush to the world, impatient for the day.   30
Millions and millions on these banks he views,[3]
Thick as the stars of night, or morning dews,
As thick as bees o'er vernal blossoms fly,
As thick as eggs at Ward in pillory.[4]

ness through the whole course of this Poem.—*Scriblerus.*—P.
   Mr. Dennis warmly contends, that Bavius was no
inconsiderable author ; nay, that "He and Mævius
had (even in Augustus's days) a very formidable party
at Rome, who thought them much superior to Virgil
and Horace : For (saith he) I cannot believe they
would have fixed that eternal brand upon them, if
they had not been coxcombs in more than ordinary
credit."—*Rem. on Pr. Arthur*, part ii. c. i. An argu-
ment which, if this poem should last, will conduce to
the honour of the gentlemen of the Dunciad.—P.
  [1] Booksellers, Printers, for anybody. The allegory
of the souls of the dull coming forth in the form of
books, dressed in calf's leather, and being let abroad
in vast numbers by Booksellers, is sufficiently intelligible.—P.
  [2] An Hemistic of Milton.—P. Par. Lost, Book vi.
v. 4.
  [3] "Quam multa in silvis autumni frigore primo,
    Lapsa cadunt folia, aut ad terram gurgite ab alto
    Quam multæ glomerantur aves," &c.
                     Virg. Æn. vi.—P.
  [4] John Ward, of Hackney, Esq., member of Parliament, being convicted of forgery, was first expelled
the House, and then sentenced to the Pillory, on the
17th of February, 1727. Mr. Curl (having likewise
stood there) looks upon the mention of such a gentleman in a satire as a *great act of barbarity.—Key to*

Wondering he gazed : When lo ! a Sage
appears,   35
By his broad shoulders known, and length of
ears,
Known by the band and suit which Settle[1]
wore

the Dunciad, 3rd edit. p. 16. And another author
reasons thus upon it—*Durgen*, 8vo. pp. 11, 12: "How
unworthy it is of *Christian Charity* to animate the
rabble to abuse a *worthy man* in such a situation !
What could move the Poet thus to mention a *brave
sufferer*, a *gallant prisoner*, exposed to the view of
all mankind ! It was laying aside his *Senses*, it was
committing a *Crime*, for which the *Law is deficient*
not to punish him ; nay, a crime which *Man can
scarce forgive*, or *Time efface !* Nothing surely could
have induced him to it but being bribed by a great
Lady," &c. (to whom this brave, honest, worthy
gentleman was guilty of no offence but forgery, proved
in open court, &c.). But it is evident this verse could
not be meant of him ; it being notorious that no eggs
were thrown at that gentleman. Perhaps, therefore,
it might be intended of Mr. Edward Ward, the poet,
when he stood there.—P.

[1] Elkanah Settle was once a Writer in vogue, as
well as Cibber, both for Dramatic Poetry and Politics.
Mr. Dennis tells us that " he was a formidable rival
to Mr. Dryden, and that in the University of Cambridge there were those who gave him the *preference*."
Mr. Welsted goes yet further in his behalf : " Poor
Settle was formerly the *Mighty Rival* of Dryden ;
nay, for *many years*, bore his reputation *above* him."—
Pref. to his Poems, 8vo. p. 31. And Mr. Milbourn
cried out, " How little was Dryden able, even when
his blood run high, to defend himself against Mr.
Settle !"—*Notes on Dryd. Vir.*, p. 175. These are
comfortable opinions ! and no wonder some authors
indulge them.

He was author or publisher of many noted pamphlets in the time of King Charles II. He answered
all Dryden's political poems, and being cried up on
one side, succeeded not a little in his Tragedy of
the Empress of Morocco (the first that was ever
printed with Cuts).—P. W.

(His only suit) for twice three years before :
All as the vest, appeared the wearer's frame,
Old in new state ; another yet the same.   40
Bland and familiar as in life, begun
Thus the great Father to the greater Son.
   " Oh born to see what none can see awake !
Behold the wonders of the oblivious Lake.
Thou, yet unborn, hast touched this sacred
          shore ;   45
The hand of Bavius drenched thee o'er and
          o'er.
But blind to former, as to future fate,
What mortal knows his pre-existent state ?
Who knows how long thy transmigrating soul
Might from Bœotian to Bœotian roll ? [1]   50
How many Dutchmen she vouchsafed to thrid ?
Now many stages through old Monks she
          rid ?
And all who since, in mild benighted days,
Mixed the Owl's ivy with the Poet's bays ? [2]
As man's Mæanders to the vital spring   55
Roll all their tides ; then back their circles
          bring ;
Or whirligigs twirled round by skilful swain,
Suck the thread in, then yield it out again :
All nonsense thus, of old or modern date,
Shall in thee centre, from thee circulate.   60
For this our Queen unfolds to vision true

---

[1] Bœotia lay under the ridicule of the Wits formerly,
as Ireland does now ; though it produced one of the
greatest Poets, and one of the greatest Generals of
Greece :

         " Bœotum crasso jurares aere natum."
                              Horat. —P.

[2]   " —— Sine tempora circum,
Inter victrices hederam tibi serpere lauros."
                         Virg. Ecl. viii. —P.

Thy mental eye, for thou hast much to view :[1]
Old scenes of glory, times long cast behind
Shall, first recalled, rush forward to thy
    mind :
Then stretch thy sight o'er all her rising
    reign,   65
And let the past and future fire thy brain.
"Ascend this hill,[2] whose cloudy point com-
    mands
Her boundless empire over seas and lands.
See, round the Poles[3] where keener spangles
    shine,
Where spices smoke beneath the burning
    Line,   70
(Earth's wide extremes) her sable flag dis-
    played,
And all the nations covered in her shade.
" Far eastward cast thine eye, from whence
    the Sun

[1] This has a resemblance to that passage in Milton,
Book xi., where the Angel

" To noble sights from Adam's eye removed
The film ; then purged with Euphrasie and Rue
The visual nerve—*For he had much to see.*"

There is a general allusion, in what follows, to that
whole Episode.—P.
[2] The scenes of this Vision are remarkable for the
order of their appearance. First, from ver. 67 to 73,
those places of the globe are shown where Science
never rose ; then from ver. 74 to 83, those where she
was destroyed by *Tyranny:* from ver. 85 to 95, by
inundations of *Barbarians:* from ver. 96 to 106, by
Superstition. Then Rome, the Mistress of Arts, is
described in her degeneracy ; and lastly Britain, the
scene of the action of the poem ; which furnishes the
occasion of drawing out the Progeny of Dulness in
review.—*Warburton.*
[3] Almost the whole Southern and Northern con-
tinent wrapt in ignorance.—P

And orient Science their bright course begun :[1]
One god-like Monarch[2] all that pride con-
        founds,   75
He, whose long wall the wandering Tartar
        bounds ;
Heavens ! what a pile ! whole ages perish there,
And one bright blaze turns Learning into air.
  " Thence to the south extend thy gladdened
        eyes ;
There rival flames with equal glory rise,   80
From shelves to shelves see greedy Vulcan roll,
And lick up all their Physic of the Soul.[3]
How little, mark ! that portion of the ball,
Where, faint at best, the beams of Science fall :
Soon as they dawn, from Hyperborean skies 85
Embodied dark, what clouds of Vandals rise !
Lo ! where Mæotis sleeps, and hardly flows
The freezing Tanais through a waste of snows,[4]
The North by myriads pours her mighty sons,
Great nurse of Goths, of Alans, and of Huns !
See Alaric's stern port ! the martial frame   91
Of Genseric ! and Attila's dread name !
See the bold Ostrogoths on Latium fall ;
See the fierce Visigoths on Spain and Gaul !
See, where the morning gilds the palmy shore

[1] Our author favours the opinion that all Sciences
came from the Eastern nations.—P.
[2] Chi Ho-am-ti, Emperor of China, the same who
built the great wall between China and Tartary,
destroyed all the books and learned men of that
empire.—P.
[3] The Caliph, Omar I., having conquered Egypt,
caused his General to burn the Ptolemæan library,
on the gates of which was this inscription, ΨΥΧΗΣ
ΙΑΤΡΕΙΟΝ, the Physic of the Soul.—P.
[4] "I have been told that this was the couplet [in
all his works] by which he declared his own ear to be
most gratified. But the reason of this preference I
cannot discover."—Johnson, Life of Pope.

(The soil that arts and infant letters bore)¹   96
His conquering tribes the Arabian prophet
  draws,
And saving Ignorance enthrones by Laws.
See Christians, Jews, one heavy sabbath keep,
And all the western world believe and sleep.² 100
" Lo ! Rome herself, proud mistress now no
  more
Of arts, but thundering against heathen lore ; ³

¹ Phœnicia, Syria, &c., where Letters are said to
have been invented. In these countries Mahomet
began his conquests.—P.

² A modification of his Exemplar, Dryden, Epist.
xiv. :

> " Long time the sister-arts, in iron sleep
> A heavy sabbath did supinely keep."
> > *Wakefield.*

³ A strong instance of this pious rage is placed to
Pope Gregory's account. John of Salisbury gives a
very odd encomium of this Pope, at the same time
that he mentions one of the strangest effects of this
excess of zeal in him : " *Doctor sanctissimus ille
Gregorius, qui mellco prædicationis imbre totam
rigavit et inebriavit ecclesiam ; non modo Mathesin
jussit ab aula, sed, ut traditur a majoribus, incendio
dedit probatæ lectionis scripta, Palatinus quæcunque
tenebat Apollo.*" And in another place : " *Fertur
beatus Gregorius bibliothecam combussisse gentilem ;
quo divinæ paginæ gratior esset locus, et major autho-
ritas, et diligentia studiosior.*" Desiderius, Archbishop of Vienna, was sharply reproved by him for
teaching Grammar and Literature and explaining the
Poets ; because (says this Pope), " *In uno se ore cum
Jovis laudibus Christi laudes non capiunt: Et quam
grave nefandumque sit Episcopis canere quod nec Laico
religioso conveniat, ipse considera.*" He is said, among
the rest, to have burned Livy : " *Quia in superstitioni-
bus et sacris Romanorum perpetuo versatur.*" The
same Pope is accused by Vossius, and others, of
having caused the noble monuments of the old Roman
magnificence to be destroyed, lest those who came to

Her grey-haired Synods damning books un-
    read,
And Bacon trembling for his brazen head.[1]
Padua, with sighs, beholds her Livy burn,   105
And ev'n the Antipodes Virgilius mourn.
See, the Cirque falls, the unpillared Temple
    nods,
Streets paved with Heroes, Tiber choked with
    Gods:
'Till Peter's keys some christened Jove adorn,[2]
And Pan to Moses lends his pagan horn;   110
See graceless Venus to a Virgin turned,
Or Phidias broken, and Apelles burned.
   " Behold yon Isle, by Palmers, Pilgrims trod,
Men bearded, bald, cowled, uncowled, shod,
    unshod,
Peeled, patched, and piebald, linsey-wolsey
    brothers,   115
Grave Mummers! sleeveless some, and shirtless
    others.

Rome should give more attention to Triumphal
Arches, &c., than to holy things.—*Bayle, Dict.*—P.
  [1] " He probably means that Bacon trembled lest
the stories told about his making a brazen head for
the purposes of magic should be accepted against him
as good evidence."—*Courthope.* Roger Bacon, the
philosopher and mathematician, born 1214, died 1292.
  [2] After the government of Rome devolved to the
Popes, their zeal was for some time exerted in demo-
lishing the heathen Temples and Statues, so that the
Goths scarce destroyed more monuments of Antiquity
out of rage, than these out of devotion. At length
they spared some of the Temples, by converting them
to Churches; and some of the Statues, by modifying
them into the images of Saints. In much later times,
it was thought necessary to change the statues of
Apollo and Pallas, on the tomb of Sannazarius, into
David and Judith; the Lyre easily became a Harp,
and the Gorgon's head turned to that of Holofernes.
—P.

That once was Britain—Happy ! had she seen
No fiercer sons, had Easter never been.[1]
In peace, great Goddess, ever be adored ;
How keen the war, if Dulness draw the sword
Thus visit not thy own ! on this blest age   121
Oh spread thy Influence, but restrain thy Rage !
" And see, my son ! the hour is on its way,
That lifts our Goddess to imperial sway ;
This favourite Isle, long severed from her
    reign,   125
Dove-like, she gathers to her wings again.[2]
Now look through Fate ! behold the scene she
    draws ![3]
What aids, what armies to assert her cause ![4]
See all her progeny, illustrious sight !
Behold, and count them, as they rise to light.
As Berecynthia, while her offspring vie   131
In homage to the mother of the sky,
Surveys around her, in the blest abode,

[1] Wars in England, anciently, about the right time of celebrating Easter.—P.

" Et fortunatam, si nunquam armenta fuissent."
                 Virg. Ecl. vi.—P.

[2] This is fulfilled in the fourth book.—P.

[3] "Nunc age, Dardaniam prolem quæ deinde
    sequatur
Gloria, qui maneant Itala de gente nepotes,
Illustres animas, nostrumque in nomen ituras,
Expediam."—*Virg. Æn.* vi.—P.

[4] *i.e.* of Poets, Antiquaries, Critics, Divines, Free-thinkers. But as this Revolution is only here set on foot by the first of these classes, the Poets, they only are here particularly celebrated, and they only properly fall under the care and review of this Colleague of Dulness, the Laureate. The others, who finish the great work, are reserved for the fourth book, where the Goddess herself appears in full glory.—*Warburton.*

An hundred sons, and every son a God : [1]
Not with less glory mighty Dulness crowned 135
Shall take through Grubstreet her triumphant
   round ;
And her Parnassus glancing o'er at once,
Behold an hundred sons, and each a Dunce.
  "Mark first that youth who takes the fore-
   most place,[2]
And thrusts his person full into your face. 140
With all thy Father's virtues blessed, be born ![3]
And a new Cibber shall the stage adorn.
  "A second see, by meeker manners known,
And modest as the maid that sips alone ;
From the strong fate of drams if thou get
   free,[4]   145
Another Durfey, Ward ! shall sing in thee.

[1] " Felix prole virûm, qualis Berecynthia mater
  Invehitur curru Phrygias turrita per urbes,
  Læta deûm partu, centum complexa nepotes,
  Omnes cœlicolas, omnes supera alta tenentes."
               Virg. Æn. vi.—P.

[2] "Ille vides, pura juvenis qui nititur hasta,
  Proxima sorte tenet lucis loca."
               Virg. Æn. vi.—P.

[3] A manner of expression used by Virgil, *Ecl.* viii.

" Nascere ! præque diem veniens, age, Lucifer"——

As also that of *patriis virtutibus, Ecl.* iv.
  It was very natural to show to the Hero, before
all others, his own Son, who had already begun to
emulate him in his theatrical, poetical, and even
political capacities. By the attitude in which he
here presents himself, the reader may be cautioned
against ascribing wholly to the Father the merit of
the epithet *Cibberian*, which is equally to be understood with an eye to the Son.- P. W. See Book i. 31.

[4]   " ——si qua fata aspera rumpas,
    Tu Marcellus eris !—*Virg. Æn.* vi.—P.

Thee shall each ale-house, thee each gill-house
 mourn,[1]
And answering gin-shops sourer sighs return.
" Jacob, the scourge of Grammar, mark with
 awe,[2]
Nor less revere him, blunderbuss of Law.[3] 150
Lo P—p—le's brow,[4] tremendous to the town,
Horneck's fierce eye, and Roome's funereal
 frown.[5]

[1] " Te nemus Angitiæ, vitrea te Fucinus unda,
 Te liquidi flevere lacus."—*Virg. Æn.* vii.

Virgil again, *Ecl.* x.:

 " Illum etiam lauri, illum flevere myricæ," &c.—P.

[2] " This *Gentleman* is son of a *considerable Maltster*
of Romsey, in Southamptonshire, and bred to the
Law under a *very eminent Attorney:* Who, between
his *more laborious* studies, has *diverted* himself with
Poetry. He is a great admirer of Poets and their
works, which has occasioned him to try his genius
that way. He has writ in prose the *Lives* of the
Poets, Essays, and a great many Law-books, *The
Accomplish'd Conveyancer, Modern Justice,* &c."—
Giles Jacob of himself, *Lives of Poets,* vol. i. He
very grossly, and unprovoked, abused in that book
the author's friend, Mr. Gay.—P.

[3] " ——duo fulmina belli
 Scipiadas, cladem Libyæ !"—*Virg. Æn.* vi.—P.

[4] P—le [Popple] was the author of some vile plays
and pamphlets. He published abuses on our author
in a paper called The Prompter.—P.

[5] These two were virulent Party-writers, worthily
coupled together, and one would think prophetically,
since after the publishing of this piece, the former
dying, the latter succeeded him in *Honour* and *Employment.* The first was Philip Horneck, Author of a
Billingsgate paper called The High German Doctor.
Edward Roome was son of an Undertaker for Fune-
rals in Fleet-street, and writ some of the papers called
Pasquin, where, by malicious Inuendoes, he endeavoured to represent our Author guilty of malevolent

Lo sneering Goode,[1] half malice and half whim,
A fiend in glee, ridiculously grim.
Each Cygnet sweet, of Bath and Tunbridge
    race,   155
Whose tuneful whistling makes the waters
    pass :[2]
Each Songster, Riddler, every nameless name,
All crowd, who foremost shall be damned to
    Fame.
Some strain in rhyme; the Muses, on their
    racks,
Scream like the winding of ten thousand
    jacks;   160
Some free from rhyme or reason, rule or check,
Break Priscian's[3] head, and Pegasus's neck;

practices with a great man then under prosecution of
Parliament. Of this man was made the following
epigram :

    " You ask why Roome diverts you with his jokes,
    Yet if he writes, is dull as other folks?
    You wonder at it.—This, Sir, is the case,
    The jest is lost unless he prints his face."—P.

    [1] An ill-natured Critic, who writ a satire on our
Author, called *The mock Æsop*, and many anonymous
Libels in Newspapers for hire.—P.
    [2] There were several successions of these sort of
minor poets at Tunbridge, Bath, &c., singing the
praise of the Annuals flourishing for that season;
whose names, indeed, would be nameless, and therefore the poet slurs them over with others in general.
—P. W.
    Borrowed from Young's Universal Passion, Sat.
i. 277 :

    " Is there a man of an eternal vein,
    Who lulls the town in winter with his strain,
    At Bath in summer chants the reigning lass,
    And sweetly whistles as the waters pass?"
                       —*Warton.*

    [3] The Roman Grammarian; he flourished in the
6th century A.D.

Down, down they larum, with impetuous whirl,
The Pindars and the Miltons of a Curl.
" Silence, ye Wolves ! while Ralph to Cynthia
    howls,[1]   165
And makes night hideous [2]—Answer him, ye
    Owls !
" Sense, speech, and measure, living tongues
    and dead,
Let all give way, and Morris may be read.[3]
Flow, Welsted,[4] flow ! like thine inspirer, Beer,

[1] James Ralph, a name inserted after the first
editions, not known to our author till he writ a
swearing-piece called *Sawney*, very abusive of Dr.
Swift, Mr. Gay, and himself. These lines allude
to a thing of his, entitled *Night*, a Poem : This low
writer attended his own works with panegyrics in
the Journals, and once in particular praised himself
highly above Mr. Addison, in wretched remarks upon
that Author's Account of *English* Poets, printed in a
London Journal, September, 1728.—P.
    He was wholly illiterate, and knew no language,
not even *French*. Being advised to read the rules of
dramatic poetry before he began a play, he smiled
and replied, "*Shakespear* writ without rules." He
ended at last in the common sink of all such writers,
a political Newspaper, to which he was recommended
by his friend Arnal, and received a small pittance for
pay.— *Warburton.*

[2] " —— Visit thus the glimpses of the moon,
    Making Night hideous."—*Shakespear.*—P.

[3] *Besaleel*, see Book ii. [v. 126].—P.

[4] Of this author see the Remark on Book ii. v. 209.
But (to be impartial) add to it the following different
character of him :
    Mr. Welsted had, in his youth, raised so great
expectations of his future genius, that there was a
kind of struggle between the most eminent in the
two Universities which should have the honour of
his education. To *compound* this, he (*civilly*) became
a member of both, and after having passed some time
at the one, he removed to the other. From thence

Though stale, not ripe; though thin, yet never
    clear;   170
So sweetly mawkish, and so smoothly dull;
Heady, not strong; o'erflowing, though not
    full.[1]
"Ah Dennis![2] Gildon ah! what ill-starred
    rage

he returned to town, where he became the *darling
Expectation* of all the polite Writers, whose encouragement he acknowledged in his occasional poems,
in a manner that *will make no small part of the Fame*
of his protectors. It also appears from his Works,
that he was happy in the patronage of the most illustrious characters of the present age. Encouraged by
such a *Combination* in his favour, he published a book
of poems, some in the *Ovidian*, some in the *Horatian*
manner, in both which the most exquisite Judges
pronounce he even *rivalled his masters*. His Love
verses have rescued that way of writing from contempt. In his Translations, he has given us the very
soul and spirit of his author. His Ode—his Epistle—
his Verses—his Love tale—all, are the *most perfect
things in all poetry.*—Welsted of *Himself, Char. of
the Times,* 8vo. 1728, pp. 23, 24.—P.

    [1] Parody on Denham, *Cooper's Hill:*

"O could I flow like thee, and make thy stream
My great example, as it is my theme:
Though deep, yet clear; though gentle, yet not dull;
Strong without rage; without o'erflowing, full!"—P.

    [2] The reader, who has seen, through the course of
these notes, what a constant attendance Mr. Dennis
paid to our Author and all his works, may perhaps
wonder he should be mentioned but twice, and so
slightly touched, in this poem. But in truth he
looked upon him with some esteem, for having (more
generously than all the rest) *set his Name* to such
writings. He was also a very old man at this time.
By his own account of himself in Mr. *Jacob's Lives,*
he must have been above threescore, and happily
lived many years after. So that he was senior to Mr.
Durfey, who hitherto of all our Poets enjoyed the
longest bodily life.—P.

Divides a friendship long confirmed by age ?
Blockheads with reason wicked wits abhor; 175
But fool with fool is barbarous civil war.
Embrace, embrace, my sons! be foes no more![1]
Nor glad vile Poets with true Critics' gore.
" Behold yon Pair, in strict embraces joined ;[2]
How like in manners, and how like in mind !
Equal in wit, and equally polite,   181
Shall this a Pasquin, that a Grumbler write;
Like are their merits, like rewards they share,
That shines a Consul, this Commissioner.[3]
" But who is he, in closet close y-pent,[4]   185
Of sober face, with learned dust besprent ?

[1] Virg. Æn. vi. :

"—— Ne tanta animis assuescite bella,
Neu patriæ validas in viscera vertite vires :
Tuque prior, tu parce—sanguis meus ! "—P.

Expressly parodied from Dryden's version :

" Embrace again, my sons : be foes no more,
Nor stain your country with your children's gore."
                    —Wakefield.

[2] One of these was author of a weekly paper called
The Grumbler, as the other was concerned in another
called *Pasquin*, in which Mr. *Pope* was abused with
the Duke of *Buckingham* and Bishop of *Rochester*.
They also joined in a piece against his first undertaking to translate the *Iliad*, intituled *Homerides*,
by Sir *Iliad Doggrel*, printed 1715.—P.
    The pair were Thomas Burnet, third son of the
famous Bishop of Salisbury, and Colonel Ducket.
[3] Such places were given at this time to such sort
of Writers.—P. W.
    Burnet was consul at Lisbon ; Ducket a commis-
sioner of Excise.
[4] Virg. Æn. vi. questions and answers in this manner, of *Numa* :

" Quis procul ille autem ramis insignis olivæ,
Sacra ferens ?—nosco crines, incanaque menta,"
    &c.—P.

Right well mine eyes arede[1] the myster wight,[2]
On parchment scraps y-fed, and Wormius hight.[3]
To future ages may thy dulness last,
As thou preserv'st the dulness of the past! 190
" There, dim in clouds, the poring Scholiasts
    mark,
Wits, who, like owls,[4] see only in the dark,
A Lumberhouse of books in every head,
For ever reading, never to be read !
" But, where each Science lifts its modern
    type,   195
History her Pot, Divinity her Pipe,
While proud Philosophy repines to show,
Dishonest sight ! his breeches rent below ;
Embrowned with native bronze, lo ! Henley
    stands,[5]

[1] *Read*, or *peruse ;* though sometimes used for *counsel.*—P.

[2] Uncouth mortal.—P.

[3] Let not this name, purely fictitious, be conceited to mean the learned *Olaus Wormius;* much less (as it was unwarrantably foisted into the surreptitious editions) our own antiquary, Mr. *Thomas Hearne,* who had no way aggrieved our Poet, but, on the contrary, published many curious tracts which he hath to his great contentment perused.
" In Cumberland they say to *hight,* for to *promise,* or *vow ;* but HIGHT usually signifies, *was called ;* and so it does in the North even to this day, notwithstanding what is done in Cumberland."—*Hearne.*—P.

[4] These few lines exactly describe the right verbal critic : The darker his author is, the better he is pleased ; like the famous Quack Doctor, who put up in his bills, *he delighted in matters of difficulty.* Somebody said well of these men, that their heads were *Libraries out of order.*—P.

[5] J. Henley, the Orator : he preached on the Sundays upon Theological matters, and on the Wednesdays upon all other sciences. Each auditor paid one shilling. He declaimed some years against the greatest persons, and occasionally did our Author that honour.

Tuning his voice, and balancing his hands. 200
How fluent nonsense trickles from his tongue !

WELSTED, in Oratory Transactions, N. 1, published by
Henley himself, gives the following account of him :
" He was born at Melton Mowbray, in Leicestershire.
From his own Parish school he went to St. John's
College, in Cambridge. He began there to be uneasy;
for it *shocked* him to find he was *commanded to believe*
against his own judgment in points of Religion, Philosophy, &c., for his genius leading him freely to
dispute all propositions, and *call all points to account*,
he was impatient under those fetters of the free-born
mind. Being admitted to Priest's orders, he found
the examination very short and superficial, and that
it was not *necessary to conform to the Christian religion*, in order either to *Deaconship or Priesthood.*" He
came to town, and after having for some years been
a writer for Booksellers, he had an ambition to be so
for Ministers of state. The only reason he did not
rise in the Church, we are told, " was the envy of
others, and a disrelish entertained of him, because *he
was not qualified to be a compleat Spaniel.*" However, he offered the service of his pen to two great
men, of opinions and interests directly opposite ; by
both of whom being rejected, he set up a new Project, and styled himself the *Restorer of ancient
eloquence.* He thought " it as lawful to take a
licence from the King and Parliament at one place
as another ; at Hickes's hall, as at Doctors' Commons;
so set up his Oratory in Newport-market, Butcher-
row. There (says his friend) he had the *assurance* to
form a plan, which no mortal ever thought of ; he
had success against all opposition ; challenged his
adversaries to fair disputations, and *none would
dispute* with him ; writ, read, and studied twelve
hours a day ; composed three dissertations a week on
all subjects ; undertook to teach in *one year* what
schools and universities teach in *five;* was not terri-
fied by menaces, insults, or satires, but still procceded,
matured his bold scheme, and put the *Church* and
all that in danger."—*Welsted, Narrative in Orat.
Transact.*, N. 1.

After having stood some Prosecutions, he turned
his rhetoric to buffoonery upon all public and private
occurrences. All this passed in the same room ; where

How sweet the periods, neither said nor sung !
Still break the benches, Henley ! with thy strain,
While Sherlock, Hare, and Gibson preach in
    vain.[1]
Oh great Restorer of the good old Stage,   205
Preacher at once, and Zany of thy age !
Oh worthy thou of Egypt's wise abodes,
A decent priest, where monkeys were the gods!
But fate with butchers placed thy priestly stall,
Meek modern faith to murder, hack, and
    maul;   210
And bade thee live, to crown Britannia's praise,
In Toland's, Tindal's, and in Woolston's days.[2]
" Yet oh, my sons, a father's words attend :
(So may the fates preserve the ears you lend)
'Tis yours, a Bacon or a Locke to blame,   215
A Newton's genius, or a Milton's flame :

sometimes he broke jests, and sometimes that bread
which he called the *Primitive Eucharist.* This wonderful person struck Medals, which he dispersed as
Tickets to his subscribers : the device, a Star rising
to the meridian, with this motto, AD SVMMA ; and
below, INVENIAM VIAM AVT FACIAM. This man had
an hundred pounds a year given him for the secret
service of a weekly paper of unintelligible nonsense,
called the Hyp-Doctor.—P.
    Orator Henley published a piece called Oratory
Transactions, written by Mr. Welstede, spelt with
an *e* at the end, as an evasion, if Mr. Welsted should
call upon him for using his name, when he knew
nothing of the piece ; and that Pope could not but
know ; and yet he quotes Welsted in several places as
the author of these Oratory Transactions.—*Nichols's
Memoirs of Welsted.*
    [1] Bishops of Salisbury, Chichester, and London ;
whose Sermons and Pastoral Letters did honour to
their country as well as stations.—*Warburton.*
    [2] Of *Toland* and *Tindal,* see Book ii. [v. 399.]
Tho. Woolston was an impious madman, who wrote
in a most insolent style against the Miracles of the
Gospel, in the years 1726, &c.—P.

But oh ! with One, immortal One dispense;
The source of Newton's Light, of Bacon's Sense.
Content, each Emanation of his fires
That beams on earth, each Virtue he inspires,
Each Art he prompts, each Charm he can
    create,   221
Whate'er he gives, are given for you to hate.
Persist, by all divine in Man unawed,
But 'Learn, ye DUNCES ! not to scorn your
    God' "[1]
    Thus he, for then a ray of Reason stole   225
Half through the solid darkness of his soul;
But soon the cloud returned—and thus the
    Sire :
" See now, what Dulness and her sons admire!
See what the charms, that smite the simple
    heart
Not touched by Nature, and not reached by
    Art."   230
    His never-blushing head he turned aside,
(Not half so pleased when Goodman prophe-
    sied)[2]
And looked, and saw a sable Sorcerer rise,[3]

---

[1] "Discite justitiam moniti, et non temnere divos."
                                        Virg.—P.

[2] Mr. Cibber tells us, in his Life, p. 149, that
Goodman being at the rehearsal of a play, in which
he had a part, clapped him on the shoulder, and cried,
" If he does not make a good actor, I'll be d——d.
And (says Mr. Cibber) I make it a question whether
Alexander himself, or Charles XII. of Sweden, when
at the head of their first victorious armies, could feel
a greater transport in their bosoms than I did in
mine."—P. W.

[3] Dr. Faustus, the subject of a set of Farces, which
lasted in vogue two or three seasons, in which both
Playhouses strove to outdo each other for some years.
All the extravagances in the sixteen lines following
were introduced on the Stage, and frequented by

Swift to whose hand a winged volume flies :
All sudden, Gorgons hiss and Dragons glare, 235
And ten-horned fiends and Giants rush to war.
Hell rises, Heaven descends, and dance on
      Earth : [1]
Gods, imps, and monsters, music, rage, and
      mirth,
A fire, a jig, a battle, and a ball,
Till one wide conflagration swallows all.   240
      Thence a new world to Nature's laws un-
      known,
Breaks out refulgent with a heaven its own :
Another Cynthia her new journey runs,
And other planets circle other suns.[2]
The forests dance, the rivers upward rise, 245
Whales sport in woods, and dolphins in the
      skies ; [3]
And last, to give the whole creation grace,
Lo ! one vast Egg produces human race.[4]
      Joy fills his soul, joy innocent of thought ;
' What power,' he cries, ' what power these
      wonders wrought ? '   250
" Son, what thou seek'st is in thee ! [5] Look,
      and find
Each monster meets his likeness in thy mind.

persons of the first quality in England, to the twen-
tieth and thirtieth time.—P.
    [1] This monstrous absurdity was actually repre-
sented in Tibbald's Rape of Proserpine.—P.
    [2] " —— solemque _suum, sua_ sidera norunt."
                              Virg. Æn. vi.—P.
    [3] " Delphinum sylvis appingit, fluctibus aprum."
                              Hor.—P.
    [4] In another of these Farces Harlequin is hatched
upon the stage out of a large Egg.—P.
    [5] " Quod petis in te est——
      ——Ne te quæsiveris extra."—_Pers._—P.

Yet would'st thou more? In yonder cloud
    behold,
Whose sarsenet skirts are edged with flamy
    gold,
A matchless youth! his nod these worlds
    controls,   255
Wings the red lightning, and the thunder
    rolls.[1]
Angel of Dulness, sent to scatter round
Her magic charms o'er all unclassic ground : [2]
Yon stars, yon suns, he rears at pleasure higher,
Illumes their light, and sets their flames on
    fire.   260
Immortal Rich![3] how calm he sits at ease
'Mid snows of paper, and fierce hail of pease ;
And proud his Mistress' orders to perform,
Rides in the whirlwind, and directs the storm.
    "But lo! to dark encounter in mid air   265
New wizards rise ; I see my Cibber there!
Booth in his cloudy tabernacle shrined.[4]

[1] Like Salmoneus in _Æn._ vi. :
   "Dum flammas Jovis, et sonitus imitatur Olympi.
   —— nimbos, et non imitabile fulmen,
   Ære et cornipedum cursu simulabat equorum."—P.

[2] Alludes to Mr. Addison's verse, in the praises of
Italy :
   "Poetic fields encompass me around,
   And still I seem to tread on classic ground."

As ver. 264 is a parody on a noble one of the same
author in The Campaign ; and ver. 259, 260, on two
sublime verses of Dr. Y.—P.
   See Young's Epistle to Lord Lansdowne, verses
474, 475.
   [3] Mr. John Rich, Master of the Theatre Royal in
Covent-garden, was the first that excelled in this
way.—P.
   [4] _Booth_ and _Cibber_ were joint managers of the
Theatre in Drury-lane.—P.

On grinning dragons thou shalt mount the
    wind.[1]
Dire is the conflict, dismal is the din,
Here shouts all Drury, there all Lincoln's-
    inn ; [2]   270
Contending Theatres our empire raise,
Alike their labours, and alike their praise.
" And are these wonders, Son, to thee un-
    known ?
Unknown to thee ?   These wonders are thy
    own.   274
These Fate reserved to grace thy reign divine,
Foreseen by me, but ah ! withheld from mine.
In Lud's old walls though long I ruled, re-
    nowned
Far as loud Bow's stupendous bells resound ;
Though my own Aldermen conferred the bays,
To me committing their eternal praise,   280
Their full-fed Heroes, their pacific Mayors,
Their annual trophies, and their monthly wars : [3]
Though long my Party built on me their
    hopes,[4]

---

[1] In his Letter to Mr. P., Mr. C. solemnly declares
this not to be *literally true*. We hope, therefore, the
reader will understand it *allegorically* only.—P. W.
   [2] The Duke's Theatre, in Portugal-street, Lincoln's
Inn Fields.
   [3] *Annual trophies*, on the Lord Mayor's day ; and
monthly wars in the Artillery-ground.—P.
   [4] Settle, like most Party-writers, was very uncertain in his political principles. He was employed to
hold the pen in the *Character* of a *popish successor*,
but afterwards printed his *Narrative* on the other
side. He had managed the ceremony of a famous
Pope-burning on November 17, 1680, then became a
trooper in King James's army, at Hounslow-heath.
After the Revolution he kept a booth at Bartholomew-
fair, where, in the droll called *St. George for England*,
he acted in his old age in a Dragon of green leather

For writing Pamphlets, and for roasting Popes;
Yet lo! in me what authors have to brag on!
Reduced at last to hiss in my own dragon. 286
Avert it, Heaven! that thou, my Cibber, e'er
Should'st wag a serpent-tail in Smithfield fair!
Like the vile straw that's blown about the
　　streets,
The needy Poet sticks to all he meets,　　290
Coached, carted, trod upon, now loose, now
　　fast,
And carried off in some Dog's tail at last.
Happier thy fortunes! like a rolling stone,
Thy giddy dulness still shall lumber on,
Safe in its heaviness, shall never stray,　　295
But lick up every blockhead in the way.
Thee shall the Patriot, thee the Courtier taste,[1]
And every year be duller than the last.
Till raised from booths, to Theatre, to Court,
Her seat imperial Dulness shall transport. 300
Already Opera prepares the way,
The sure fore-runner of her gentle sway :
Let her thy heart, next Drabs and Dice, engage,
The third mad passion of thy doting age.
Teach thou the warbling Polypheme to roar,[2] 305

of his own invention ; he was at last taken into the
Charter-house, and there died, aged sixty years.—P.
　　Carruthers points out that Settle was born in 1648,
and died in the Charter-house in 1724. He was therefore seventy-six at the time of his death.
　　[1] It stood in the first edition with blanks, * * and
* *. Concanen was sure "they must needs mean
nobody but *King GEORGE* and *Queen CAROLINE;*
and said he would insist it was so, till the poet cleared
himself by filling up the blanks otherwise, agreeably
to the context, and consistent with his *allegiance.*"—
*Pref. to a Collection of Verses, Essays, Letters, &c.,
against Mr. P.,* printed for A. Moor, p. 6.—P.
　　[2] He translated the Italian Opera of Polifemo ; but
unfortunately lost the whole jest of the story. The

And scream thyself as none e'er screamed be-
fore !
To aid our cause, if Heaven thou canst not
bend,
Hell thou shalt move ; for Faustus is our
friend :
Pluto with Cato thou for this shalt join,
And link the Mourning Bride to Proserpine.¹
Grubstreet ! thy fall should men and Gods
conspire,   311
Thy stage shall stand, ensure it but from Fire.²
Another Æschylus appears ! ³ prepare
For new abortions, all ye pregnant fair !
In flames, like Semele's, be brought to bed,⁴ 315
While opening Hell spouts wild-fire at your
head.

Cyclops asks Ulysses his *name*, who tells him his
name is *Noman:* After his eye is put out, he roars
and calls the brother Cyclops to his aid. They inquire,
who has hurt him? he answers, *Noman;* whereupon
they all go away again. Our ingenious translator
made Ulysses answer, *I take no name,* whereby all
that followed became unintelligible. Hence it appears
that Mr. Cibber (who values himself on subscribing
to the English Translation of Homer's Iliad) had not
that merit with respect to the Odyssey, or he might
have been better instructed in the Greek *Pun-nology.*
—P. W.

¹ Names of miserable Farces, which it was the
custom to act at the end of the best Tragedies, to
spoil the digestion of the audience.—P.

² In Tibbald's Farce of Proserpine, a corn-field was
set on fire : whereupon the other play-house had a
barn burnt down for the recreation of the spectators.
They also rivalled each other in showing the burnings
of hell-fire, in Dr. Faustus.—P.

³ It is reported of Æschylus, that when his tragedy
of the Furies was acted, the audience were so terri-
fied, that the children fell into fits, and the big-bellied
women miscarried.—P.

⁴ See Ovid, Met. iii.—P.

" Now, Bavius, take the poppy from thy brow,
And place it here ! here all ye Heroes bow !
This, this is he, foretold by ancient rhymes :
The Augustus born to bring Saturnian times.[1]
Signs following signs lead on the mighty
    year !   321
See ! the dull stars roll round and re-appear.
See, see, our own true Phœbus wears the bays !
Our Midas sits Lord Chancellor of Plays !
On Poets' Tombs see Benson's titles writ ![2] 325
Lo ! Ambrose Philips is preferred for Wit ![3]

[1] " Hic ver, hic est! tibi quem promitti sæpius audis,
    Augustus Cæsar, divum genus ; aurea condet
    Secula qui rursus Latio, regnata per arva
    Saturno quondam."—*Virg. Æn.* vi.

Saturnian here relates to the age of *Lead*, mentioned
Book i. ver. 28.—P.

[2] W——m Benson (Surveyor of Buildings to his
Majesty King George I.) gave in a report to the Lords,
that their House and the Painted Chamber adjoining
were in immediate danger of falling. Whereupon the
Lords met in a committee to appoint some other place
to sit in, while the house should be taken down. But
it being proposed to cause some other builders first to
inspect it, they found it in very good condition. The
Lords, upon this, were going upon an address to the
King against Benson, for such a misrepresentation ;
but the Earl of Sunderland, then Secretary, gave
them an assurance that his Majesty would remove
him, which was done accordingly. In favour of this
man, the famous Sir Christopher Wren, who had been
Architect to the Crown for above fifty years, who
built most of the Churches in London, laid the first
stone of St. Paul's, and lived to finish it, had been
displaced from his employment at the age of near
ninety years.—P.

In 1737 Benson erected a monument to Milton in
Westminster Abbey, and inscribed his own name on
it as founder.—*Courthope.*

[3] " He was (saith Mr. JACOB) one of the wits at
Button's, and a justice of the peace." But he hath
since met with higher preferment in Ireland : and a

See under Ripley rise a new Whitehall,[1]
While Jones' and Boyle's united Labours fall;[2]
While Wren with sorrow to the grave descends;
Gay dies unpensioned with a hundred friends;[3]

much greater character we have of him in Mr. Gildon's
Complete Art of Poetry, vol. i. p. 157. "Indeed he
confesses, he dares not set him *quite on the same foot
with Virgil*, lest it should *seem* flattery; but he is
much mistaken if posterity does not afford him a
greater esteem than he *at present enjoys.*" He endeavoured to create some misunderstanding between our
Author and Mr. Addison, whom also soon after he
abused as much. His constant cry was, that Mr. P.
was an *Enemy to the Government;* and in particular
he was the avowed author of a report very indus-
triously spread, that he had a hand in a party-paper
called the *Examiner:* a falsehood well known to those
yet living, who had the direction and publication of
it.—P.

[1] See Moral Essays, iv. 18.
[2] At the time when this poem was written, the
banqueting-house of Whitehall, the church and
piazza of Covent-garden, and the palace and chapel
of Somerset-house, the works of the famous Inigo
Jones, had been for many years so neglected, as to
be in danger of ruin. The portico of Covent-garden
church had been just then restored and beautified at
the expense of the Earl of Burlington; who at the
same time, by his publication of the designs of that
great Master and Palladio, as well as by many noble
buildings of his own, revived the true taste of Archi-
tecture in this Kingdom.—P.

[3] See Mr. Gay's fable of the *Hare and many Friends.*
This gentleman was early in the friendship of our
author, which continued to his death. He wrote
several works of humour with great success, the
Shepherd's Week, Trivia, the What-d'ye-call-it,
Fables; and lastly, the celebrated Beggar's Opera;
a piece of satire which hit all tastes and degrees of
men, from those of the highest quality to the very
rabble: That verse of Horace,

"Primores populi arripuit, populumque tributim,"

could never be so justly applied as to this.. The vast

Hibernian Politics, O Swift! thy fate; [1]   331
And Pope's, ten years to comment and translate. [2]

success of it was unprecedented, and almost incredible: What is related of the wonderful effects of the
ancient music or tragedy hardly came up to it: So-
phocles and Euripides were less followed and famous.
It was acted in London sixty-three days, uninter-
rupted; and renewed the next season with equal
applauses. It spread into all the great towns of
England, was played in many places to the thirtieth
and fortieth time, at Bath and Bristol fifty, &c. It
made its progress into Wales, Scotland, and Ireland,
where it was performed twenty-four days together:
It was last acted in Minorca. The fame of it was
not confined to the author only; the ladies carried
about with them the favourite songs of it in fans;
and houses were furnished with it in screens. The
person who acted Polly, till then obscure, became
all at once the favourite of the town; her pictures
were engraved, and sold in great numbers; her life
written, books of letters and verses to her published; and pamphlets made even of her sayings and
jests.

Furthermore, it drove out of England, for that
season, the Italian Opera, which had carried all
before it for ten years. That idol of the Nobility and
people, which the great Critic Mr. Dennis by the
labours and outcries of a whole life could not over-
throw, was demolished by a single stroke of this
gentleman's pen. This happened in the year 1728.
Yet so great was his modesty, that he constantly
prefixed to all the editions of it this motto, *Nos hæc
novimus esse nihil.*—P.

[1] See Book i. v. 26.—P. W.
[2] The author here plainly laments that he was so
long employed in translating and commenting. He
began the Iliad in 1713, and finished it in 1719. The
edition of Shakespear (which he undertook merely
because nobody else would) took up near two years
more in the drudgery of comparing impressions,
rectifying the Scenery, &c., and the Translation of
half the Odyssey employed him from that time to
1725.—P.

" Proceed, great days ! till Learning fly the
    shore,
Till Birch shall blush with noble blood no
    more,
Till Thames see Eton's sons for ever play,   335
Till Westminster's whole year be holiday,
Till Isis' Elders reel, their pupils sport,
And Alma Mater lie dissolved in Port ! "
   " Enough ! enough ! " the raptured Monarch
    cries ;
And through the Ivory Gate the Vision flies.[1] 340

[1] " Sunt geminæ Somni portæ ; quarum altera fertur
Cornea, qua veris facilis datur exitus umbris ;
Altera candenti perfecta nitens elephanto,
Sed falsa ad cœlum mittunt insomnia manes."
                   Virg. Æn. vi.—P.

BOOK THE FOURTH.

ARGUMENT.

The Poet being, in this Book, to declare the Completion of the Prophecies mentioned at the end of the former, makes a new Invocation; as the greater Poets are wont when some high and worthy matter is to be sung. He shews the Goddess coming in her Majesty, to destroy Order and Science, and to substitute the Kingdom of the Dull upon earth. How she leads captive the Sciences, and silenceth the Muses; and what they be who succeed in their stead. All her Children, by a wonderful attraction, are drawn about her, and bear along with them divers others, who promote her Empire by connivance, weak resistance, or discouragement of Arts; such as Half-wits, tasteless Admirers, vain Pretenders, the Flatterers of Dunces, or the Patrons of them. All these crowd round her; one of them, offering to approach her, is driven back by a Rival, but she commends and encourages both. The first who speak in form are the Geniuses of the Schools, who assure her of their care to advance her Cause, by confining Youth to Words, and keeping them out of the way of real Knowledge. Their Address, and her gracious Answer; with her Charge to them and the Universities. The Universities appear by their proper Deputies, and assure her that the same method is observed in the progress of Education. The speech of Aristarchus on this subject. They are driven off by a band of young gentlemen returned from Travel with their Tutors: one of whom delivers to the Goddess, in a polite oration, an account of the whole Conduct and Fruits of their Travels: presenting to her at the same time a young Nobleman perfectly accomplished. She receives him graciously, and endues him with the happy quality of Want of Shame. She sees loitering about her a number of Indolent Persons, abandoning all business and duty, and dying with laziness: To these approaches the Antiquary Annius, intreating her to make them Virtuosos, and assign them over to him: But Mummius, another Antiquary, complaining

of his fraudulent proceeding, she finds a method to
reconcile their difference. Then enter a Troop of people
fantastically adorned, offering her strange and exotic
presents: Amongst them, one stands forth and demands justice on another, who had deprived him of
one of the greatest Curiosities in nature: but he
justifies himself so well, that the Goddess gives them
both her approbation. She recommends to them to
find proper employment for the Indolents before mentioned, in the study of Butterflies, Shells, Birds'-
nests, Moss, &c., but with particular caution not to
proceed beyond Trifles, to any useful or extensive
views of Nature, or of the Author of Nature. Against
the last of these apprehensions, she is secured by a
hearty Address from the Minute Philosophers and
Free-thinkers, one of whom speaks in the name of
the rest. The Youth, thus instructed and principled,
are delivered to her in a body by the hands of Silenus:
and then admitted to taste the Cup of the Magus,
her High Priest, which causes a total oblivion of all
Obligations, divine, civil, moral, or rational. To
these her Adepts she sends Priests, Attendants, and
Comforters, of various kinds; confers on them Orders
and Degrees; and then, dismissing them with a
speech, confirming to each his Privileges, and telling
what she expects from each, concludes with a Yawn
of extraordinary virtue; The Progress and Effects
whereof on all Orders of men, and the Consummation
of all, in the Restoration of Night and Chaos, conclude the Poem.

BOOK IV.[1]

YET, yet a moment, one dim Ray of Light
Indulge, dread Chaos, and eternal Night![2]
Of darkness visible so much be lent,
As half to shew, half veil the deep Intent.[3]
Ye Powers! whose Mysteries restored I sing, 5
To whom Time bears me on his rapid wing,
Suspend a while your Force inertly strong,[4]
Then take at once the Poet and the Song.
Now flamed the Dog-star's unpropitious ray,
Smote every Brain, and withered every Bay; 10

[1] This book may properly be distinguished from
the former, by the name of the GREATER DUNCIAD,
not so indeed in size, but in subject; and so far contrary to the distinction anciently made of the *Greater*
and *Lesser Iliad*. But much are they mistaken who
imagine this Work in any wise inferior to the former,
or of any other hand than of our Poet; of which I
am much more certain than that the *Iliad* itself was
the work of *Solomon*, or the *Batrachomuomachia* of
Homer, as *Barnes* hath affirmed.—*Bentley.*—P. W.

[2] Invoked, as the Restoration of their Empire is
the Action of the Poem.—P. W.

[3] This is a great propriety, for a dull Poet can
never express himself otherwise than by *halves*, or
imperfectly.—*Scriblerus.*—P. W.

I understand it very differently; the Author in this
work had indeed a *deep intent*; there were in it
Mysteries or ἀπόρρητα which he durst not fully reveal,
and doubtless in divers verses (according to Milton)

"—— more is meant than meets the ear."
                    —*Bentley.*—P. W.

[4] Alluding to the *Vis inertiæ of Matter*, which,
though it really be no Power, is yet the fountain of
all the qualities and attributes of that sluggish Sub-
stance.—P. W.

III.   R

Sick was the Sun, the Owl forsook his bower,
The moon-struck Prophet felt the madding
    hour:
Then rose the Seed of Chaos, and of Night,
To blot out Order, and extinguish Light,[1]
Of dull and venal[2] a new World to mould,[3] 15
And bring Saturnian days of Lead and Gold.[4]
    She mounts the Throne: her head a Cloud
        concealed,
In broad Effulgence all below revealed;
('Tis thus aspiring Dulness ever shines)
Soft on her lap her Laureate son reclines.[5]   20
    Beneath her footstool, Science groans in
        Chains,[6]

[1] The two great ends of her mission; the one in
quality of daughter of *Chaos*, the other as daughter
of *Night*. *Order* here is to be understood extensively,
both as civil and moral; the distinctions between
high and low in Society, and true and false in Indivi-
duals: *Light*, as intellectual only, Wit, Science,
Arts.—P. W.

[2] The Allegory continued; *dull* referring to the
extinction of light or Science; *venal*, to the destruction of Order, or the truth of things.—P. W.

[3] In allusion to the Epicurean opinion, that from
the dissolution of the natural World into Night and
Chaos, a new one should arise; this the Poet alluding
to, in the production of a new moral World, makes it
partake of its original Principles.—P. W.

[4] *i.e.* dull and venal.—P. W.

[5] With great judgment it is imagined by the Poet,
that such a colleague as Dulness had elected, should
sleep on the Throne, and have very little share in the
Action of the Poem. Accordingly, he hath done little
or nothing from the day of his anointing; having
passed through the second book without taking part
in anything that was transacted about him; and
through the third in profound sleep. Nor ought this,
well considered, to seem strange in our days, when so
many *King-consorts* have done the like.—*Scriblerus.*
—P. W.

    We are next presented with the pictures of those

And Wit dreads Exile, Penalties, and Pains.
There foamed rebellious Logic, gagged and
　　bound,
There, stripped, fair Rhetoric languished on
　　the ground ;
His blunted Arms by Sophistry are borne,　25
And shameless Billingsgate her Robes adorn.
Morality, by her false Guardians drawn,
Chicane in Furs, and Casuistry in Lawn,
Gasps, as they straiten at each end the cord,
And dies, when Dulness gives her Page the
　　word.[1]　　　　　　　　　　　　　　　　30
Mad Máthesis[2] alone was unconfined,
Too mad for mere material chains to bind,
Now to pure Space lifts her ecstatic stare,
Now running round the Circle, finds it square.[3]
But held in ten-fold bonds the Muses lie,　35
Watched both by Envy's and by Flattery's eye :[4]

whom the Goddess leads in captivity. *Science* is only
depressed and confined so as to be rendered useless ;
but *Wit* or *Genius*, as a more dangerous and active
enemy, punished, or driven away : *Dulness* being
often reconciled in some degree with Learning, but
never upon any terms with Wit. And accordingly it
will be seen that she admits something *like* each
Science, as Casuistry, Sophistry, &c., but nothing
like *Wit*, *Opera* alone supplying its place.—P. W.
　[1] There was a Judge of this name, always ready to
hang any man that came before him, of which he was
suffered to give a hundred miserable examples during
a long life, even to his dotage.—P. W.
　See Imitations of Horace, Book ii. Sat. i. 82, and
Epilogue to Satires ii. 159.
　[2] Alluding to the strange Conclusions some Mathematicians have deduced from their principles, concerning the *real Quantity of Matter*, the *Reality of
Space*, &c.—P. W.
　[3] Regards the wild and fruitless attempts of *squar-
ing the circle*.—P. W.
　[4] One of the misfortunes falling on Authors, from

There to her heart sad Tragedy addressed
The dagger wont to pierce the Tyrant's breast;
But sober History restrained her rage,
And promised Vengeance on a barbarous age. 40
There sunk Thalia, nerveless, cold, and dead,
Had not her Sister Satire held her head:
Nor could'st thou, CHESTERFIELD![1] a tear refuse,
Thou wept'st, and with thee wept each gentle
    Muse.
When lo! a Harlot form soft sliding by,[2] 45
With mincing step, small voice, and languid
    eye:
Foreign her air, her robe's discordant pride
In patch-work fluttering, and her head aside:

the *Act* for subjecting *Plays* to the power of a *Licenser*,
being the false representations to which they were
exposed, from such as either gratified their envy to
merit, or made their court to Greatness, by pervert-
ing general reflections against vice into libels on
particular Persons.—P. W.

[1] This Noble Person, in the year 1737, when the
Act aforesaid was brought into the House of Lords,
opposed it in an excellent speech (says Mr. *Cibber*),
"with a lively spirit and uncommon eloquence." This
speech had the honour to be answered by the said
Mr. *Cibber*, with a lively spirit also, and in a manner
very uncommon, in the 8th chapter of his *Life and
Manners.—Bentley.—P. W.

For Chesterfield, see Epilogue to Satires, ii. 84.

[2] The attitude given to this Phantom represents
the nature and genius of the *Italian* Opera: its
affected airs, its effeminate sounds, and the practice
of patching up these Operas with favourite songs,
incoherently put together. These things were supported by the subscriptions of the Nobility. This
circumstance, that OPERA should prepare for the
opening of the grand Sessions, was prophesied of
in Book iii. v. 301:

"Already Opera prepares the way,
The sure fore-runner of her gentle sway."—P. W.

By singing Peers up-held on either hand,
She tripped and laughed, too pretty much to
　　stand；　　　　　　　　　　　　　　　50
Cast on the prostrate Nine a scornful look,
Then thus in quaint Recitativo spoke.
"O *Cara! Cara!* silence all that train :
Joy to great Chaos !　[1] let Division reign : [2]
Chromatic tortures soon shall drive them
　　hence,[3]　　　　　　　　　　　　　　55
Break all their nerves, and fritter all their
　　sense :
One Trill shall harmonize joy, grief, and rage,
Wake the dull Church, and lull the ranting
　　Stage ; [4]
To the same notes thy sons shall hum, or
　　snore,
And all thy yawning daughters cry, *encore.*　60

[1] *Joy to Great Cæsar.*—The beginning of a famous
old song [by Durfey].—*Warburton.*
[2] Alluding to the false taste of playing tricks in
Music with numberless divisions, to the neglect of
that harmony which conforms to the sense, and applies
to the Passions.　Mr. *Handel* had introduced a great
number of hands and more variety of Instruments
into the Orchestra, and employed even drums and
cannon to make a fuller Chorus ; which proved so
much too manly for the fine Gentlemen of his age,
that he was obliged to remove his Music into *Ireland.*
After which they were reduced, for want of Com-
posers, to practise the patchwork above mentioned.
—P. W.
[3] That species of the ancient music called the *Chromatic,* was a variation and embellishment, in odd
irregularities, of the *Diatonic* kind.　They say it was
invented about the time of *Alexander,* and that the
Spartans forbad the use of it, as languid and effeminate.—*Warburton.*
[4] *i. e.* Dissipate the *devotion* of the one by light and
wanton airs ; and subdue the *pathos* of the other by
recitative and sing-song.—*Warburton.*

Another Phœbus, thy own Phœbus, reigns,[1]
Joys in my jigs, and dances in my chains.
But soon, ah soon, Rebellion will commence,
If Music meanly borrows aid from Sense.
Strong in new Arms, lo! Giant HANDEL stands,
Like bold Briareus, with a hundred hands;   66
To stir, to rouse, to shake the soul he comes,
And Jove's own Thunders follow Mars's Drums.
Arrest him, Empress; or you sleep no more—"
She heard, and drove him to the Hibernian
    shore.   70
    And now had Fame's posterior trumpet
    blown,[2]
And all the Nations summoned to the Throne.
The young, the old, who feel her inward sway,
One instinct seizes, and transports away.
None need a guide, by sure attraction led,[3]   75
And strong impulsive gravity of Head:[4]

---

[1] "Tuus jam regnat Apollo."—*Virg.*
Not the ancient *Phœbus*, the God of Harmony, but
a modern *Phœbus* of *French* extraction, married to
the Princess *Galimathia*, one of the handmaids of
Dulness, and an assistant to Opera. Of whom see
Bouhours, and other Critics of that nation.—*Scrible-*
rus.—P. W.
[2] *Posterior*—viz., her *second* or *more certain* Report;
unless we imagine this word *posterior* to relate to
the position of one of her trumpets, according to
Hudibras:

    "She blows not both with the same Wind,
    But one before and one behind;
    And therefore modern Authors name
    One good, and t'other evil Fame."—P. W.

[3] The sons of Dulness want no instructors in study,
nor guides in life. They are their own masters in all
Sciences, and their own Heralds and introducers into
all places.—P. W.
[4] Ver. 76 to 101. It ought to be observed that here
are three classes in this assembly. The first of men

None want a place, for all their Centre found,
Hung to the Goddess, and cohered around.
Not closer, orb in orb, conglobed are seen
The buzzing Bees about their dusky Queen. 80
   The gathering number, as it moves along,
Involves a vast involuntary throng,
Who gently drawn, and struggling less and
    less,
Roll in her Vortex, and her power confess.
Not those alone who passive own her laws, 85
But who, weak rebels, more advance her cause.
Whate'er of dunce in College or in Town
Sneers at another, in toupee[1] or gown;
Whate'er of mongrel no one class admits,
A wit with dunces, and a dunce with wits. 90
   Nor absent they, no members of her state,
Who pay her homage in her sons, the Great;
Who, false to Phœbus,[2] bow the knee to Baal;
Or impious, preach his word without a call.
Patrons, who sneak from living worth to
    dead, 95
Withhold the pension, and set up the head;
Or vest dull Flattery in the sacred Gown;
Or give from fool to fool the Laurel crown.

absolutely and avowedly dull, who naturally adhere
to the Goddess, and are imaged in the simile of the
Bees about their Queen. The second involuntarily
drawn to her, though not caring to own her influence;
from ver. 81 to 90. The third, of such as, though
not members of her state, yet advance her service
by flattering Dulness, cultivating mistaken talents,
patronizing vile scribblers, discouraging living merit,
or setting up for wits, and men of taste in arts they
understand not; from ver. 91 to 101.—P. W.
   [1] The fashionable curl on the top of the head.
   [2] Spoken of the ancient and true *Phœbus;* not the
French Phœbus, who hath no chosen Priests or Poets,
but equally inspires any man that pleaseth to sing or
preach.—*Scriblerus.*—P. W.

And (last and worst) with all the cant of wit,
Without the soul, the Muse's Hypocrite.   100
  There marched the bard and blockhead, side
    by side,
Who rhymed for hire, and patronized for pride.
Narcissus,[1] praised with all a Parson's power,
Looked a white lily sunk beneath a shower.
There moved Montalto with superior air;[2] 105
His stretched-out arm displayed a volume fair;
Courtiers and Patriots in two ranks divide,
Through both he passed, and bowed from side
    to side:
But as in graceful act, with awful eye
Composed he stood, bold Benson thrust him
    by:[3]   110
On two unequal crutches propped he came,
Milton's on this, on that one Johnston's name.
The decent Knight retired with sober rage,
Withdrew his hand, and closed the pompous
    page.
But (happy for him as the times went then)[1]

  [1] Lord Hervey, praised by Dr. Conyers Middleton,
in his dedication of the Life of Cicero.—*Warton.* See
Prologue to the Satires, v. 305.
  [2] An eminent person, who was about to publish a
very pompous Edition of a great Author, *at his own
expense.*—P. W.
  Sir Thomas Hanmer, Speaker of the House of Commons from 1713 to 1715. He published an edition of
Shakespear in 6 vols. 4to, 1744.
  [3] This man endeavoured to raise himself to Fame
by erecting monuments, striking coins, setting up
heads, and procuring translations, of *Milton;* and
afterwards by as great a passion for *Arthur Johnston,*
a *Scotch* physician's version of the Psalms, of which
he printed many fine Editions. See more of him,
Book iii. v. 325.—P. W.
  [1] Ver. 115, &c. These four lines were printed in a
separate leaf by Mr. Pope in the last edition, which
he himself gave, of the Dunciad, with directions to

Appeared Apollo's Mayor and Aldermen,　116
On whom three hundred gold-capped youths
　　await,
To lug the ponderous volume off in state.
　　When Dulness, smiling—" Thus revive the
　　Wits! [1]
But murder first, and mince them all to bits;
As erst Medea (cruel, so to save!)　　　　121
A new Edition of old Æson gave; [2]
Let standard-authors, thus, like trophies borne,

the printer to put this leaf into its place as soon as
Sir T. H.'s Shakespear should be published.—*B.*

" B." is perhaps Bowyer, the printer. The lines are
not in the edition of 1743. Warburton had a quarrel
with Sir Thomas Hanmer, the " decent knight," rela-
tive to Sir Thomas's edition of Shakespear. Warburton
charged the knight with making an unauthorized use
of his emendations on the text of Shakespear, while
the knight, on the other hand, charged Warburton
with a desire to produce a " paltry edition," with the
view of getting " a greater sum of money by it."
The result, said Warburton, was that Sir Thomas
" applied to the University of Oxford, and was at the
expense of his purse in procuring cuts for this edition,
and at the expense of his reputation in employing a
number of my emendations on the text, without my
knowledge or consent; and his behaviour was what
occasioned Mr. Pope's perpetuating the memory of
the Oxford edition of Shakespear in the Dunciad."—
Carruthers.

[1] The Goddess applauds the practice of tacking the
obscure names of Persons not eminent in any branch
of learning to those of the most distinguished Writers;
either by printing *editions* of their works with impertinent alterations of their Text, as in the former
instances, or by setting up *Monuments* disgraced
with their own vile names and inscriptions, as in the
latter.—P. W.

[2] Of whom Ovid (very applicable to these restored
authors),
　　　　　　" Æson *miratur,*
Dissimilemque animum *subiit.*"—P. W.

Appear more glorious as more hacked and torn.
And you, my Critics! in the chequered shade,
Admire new light through holes yourselves
   have made.[1]   126
" Leave not a foot of verse, a foot of stone,
A Page, a Grave, that they can call their
   own;[2]
But spread, my sons, your glory thin or thick,
On passive paper, or on solid brick.   130
So by each Bard an Alderman shall sit,[3]
A heavy Lord shall hang at every Wit,
And while on Fame's triumphal Car they ride,
Some Slave of mine be pinioned to their side."
   Now crowds on crowds around the Goddess
   press,   135
Each eager to present the first Address.
Dunce scorning Dunce beholds the next
   advance,
But Fop shews Fop superior complaisance.
When lo! a Spectre rose, whose index-hand
Held forth the virtue of the dreadful wand;[4]
His beavered brow a birchen garland wears, 141

[1] " The Soul's dark cottage, battered and decayed,
   Lets in new light, through chinks that time has
   made."—*Waller.*—*Warburton.*

[2] For what less than a Grave can be granted to a
dead author? or what less than a Page can be allowed
a living one?—P. W.
   Pagina, not *Pedissequus.* A Page of a Book, not
a Servant, Follower, or Attendant; no Poet having
had a *Page* since the death of Mr. Thomas Durfey.—
Scriblerus.—P. W.
[3] Vide the *Tombs of the Poets*, Editio Westmonas-
teriensis.—P. W. Alluding to the monument erected
for Butler by Alderman Barber.—*Warburton.*
[4] A Cane usually borne by Schoolmasters, which
drives the poor Souls about like the wand of Mercury.
—*Scriblerus.*—P. W.

Dropping with Infants' blood, and Mothers'
    tears.[1]
O'er every vein a shuddering horror runs;
Eton and Winton shake through all their Sons.
All Flesh is humbled, Westminster's bold
    race   145
Shrink, and confess the genius of the place:[2]
The pale Boy-Senator yet tingling stands,
And holds his breeches close with both his
    hands.[3]
    Then thus.   "Since Man from beast by
        Words is known,
Words are Man's province, Words we teach
    alone.   150
When Reason doubtful, like the Samian letter,[4]
Points him two ways, the narrower is the better.
Placed at the door of Learning, youth to guide,[5]

---

[1] "First Moloch, horrid King, besmeared with blood
Of human sacrifice, and parents' tears."
                                        Milton.—P.

[2] Alluding to Dr. Busby, the famous headmaster of
Westminster School. from 1640 to 1695.

[3] An effect of fear somewhat like this is described
in the viith Æneid :

    "Contremuit nemus——
    Et trepidæ matres pressere ad pectora natos ;"

nothing being so natural in any apprehension as to
lay close hold on whatever is supposed to be most in
danger.—*Scriblerus.*—P. W.

[4] The letter Y, used by Pythagoras as an emblem
of the different roads of Virtue and Vice.

    "Et tibi quæ Samios diduxit litera ramos."
                                        Pers.—P. W.

[5] This circumstance of the *Genius Loci* (with that
of the Index-hand before) seems to be an allusion to
the *Table of Cebes*, where the Genius of human Nature
points out the road to be pursued by those entering

We never suffer it to stand too wide.
To ask, to guess, to know, as they com-
    mence,   155
As Fancy opens the quick springs of Sense,
We ply the Memory, we load the brain,
Bind rebel Wit, and double chain on chain,
Confine the thought, to exercise the breath ;[1]
And keep them in the pale of Words till death.
Whate'er the talents, or howe'er designed, 161
We hang one jingling padlock[2] on the mind :
A Poet the first day he dips his quill;
And what the last ? A very Poet still.
Pity ! the charm works only in our wall,   165
Lost, lost too soon in yonder House or Hall.[3]
There truant WYNDHAM every Muse gave o'er,
There TALBOT sunk, and was a Wit no more !
How sweet an Ovid, MURRAY was our boast !
How many Martials were in PULTENEY lost ![4] 170
Else sure some Bard, to our eternal praise,
In twice ten thousand rhyming nights and
    days,

into life. Ὁ δὲ γέρων ὁ ἄνω ἑστηκὼς, ἔχων χάρτην τινὰ
ἐν τῇ χειρὶ, καὶ τῇ ἑτέρᾳ ὥσπερ δεικνύων τι, οὗτος Δαίμων
καλεῖται, &c.—P. W.

    [1] By obliging them to get the classic poets by heart,
which furnishes them with endless matter for Conversation and Verbal amusement for their whole lives.
—P. W.

    [2] For youth being used like Pack-horses and beaten
on under a heavy load of Words, lest they should
tire, their instructors contrive to make the Words
jingle in rhyme or metre.—P. W.

    [3] Westminster-hall and the House of Commons.—
Warburton.

    [4] Sir William Wyndham, Chancellor of the Exche-
quer; Charles Lord Talbot, Lord Chancellor; Murray,
Lord Mansfield ; and Pulteney, Earl of Bath.   See
Epilogue to the Satires, ii. 84, 88, and Imitations of
Horace, Book ii. Ep. ii. 134, and Book i. Ep. vi.

Had reached the Work, the All that mortal
   can ;
And South beheld that Master-piece of Man."[1]
" Oh " (cried the Goddess) " for some pedant
   Reign !   175
Some gentle JAMES, to bless the land again ;[2]
To stick the Doctor's Chair into the Throne,
Give law to Words, or war with Words alone,
Senates and Courts with Greek and Latin rule,
And turn the Council to a Grammar School !
For sure, if Dulness sees a grateful Day,   181
'Tis in the shade of Arbitrary Sway.
O ! if my sons may learn one earthly thing,
Teach but that one, sufficient for a King ;
That which my Priests, and mine alone, main-
   tain,   185
Which as it dies, or lives, we fall, or reign :
May you, my Cam and Isis, preach it long !
'The RIGHT DIVINE of Kings to govern wrong.' "
   Prompt at the call, around the Goddess roll
Broad hats, and hoods, and caps, a sable shoal :

---

[1] Viz., an *Epigram*, The famous Dr. *South* declared a perfect Epigram to be as difficult a performance as an Epic Poem. And the Critics say,
"an Epic Poem is the greatest work human nature
is capable of."—P. W.

[2] Wilson tells us that this King, *James I.*, took
upon himself to teach the Latin tongue to Car, Earl
of Somerset ; and that Gondomar, the Spanish Ambas-
sador, would speak false Latin to him, on purpose
to give him the pleasure of correcting it, whereby he
wrought himself into his good graces.
   This great prince was the first who assumed the title
of *Sacred Majesty*, which his loyal clergy transferred
from *God* to *him*. "The principles of Passive Obedience
and Non-resistance (says the author of the Dissertation
on Parties, Letter 8) which before his time had skulked
perhaps in some old Homily, were talked, written,
and preached into vogue in that inglorious reign."—
P. W.

Thick and more thick the black blockade
    extends,   191
A hundred head of Aristotle's friends.[1]
Nor wert thou, Isis! wanting to the day,
[Though Christ-church long kept prudishly
    away.][2]
Each staunch Polemic, stubborn as a rock, 195
Each fierce Logician, still expelling Locke,[3]
Came whip and spur, and dashed through thin
    and thick
On German Crouzaz, and Dutch Burgersdyck.[4]
As many quit the streams that murmuring fall
To lull the sons of Margaret and Clare-hall,[5] 200

[1] The Author, with great propriety, hath made
these who were so *prompt, at the call* of Dulness, to
become preachers of the Divine Right of Kings, to be
the *friends* of *Aristotle;* for this philosopher, in his
politics, hath laid it down as a principle, that some
men were by nature made to serve, and others to
command.—*Warburton.*

[2] This line is doubtless spurious, and foisted in by
the impertinence of the Editor; and, accordingly,
we have put it between Hooks. For I affirm this
College came as early as any other, by its *proper
Deputies:* nor did any College pay homage to Dulness
in its *whole body.—Bentley.—* P. W.

An allusion to Bentley's quarrel with Boyle and
other Christ Church men about the authenticity of the
Epistles of Phalaris.

[3] In the year 1703, there was a meeting of the heads
of the University of Oxford to censure Mr. Locke's
Essay on Human Understanding, and to forbid the
reading it. —P. W.

Locke was deprived of his studentship at Christ
Church for political reasons, and before his " Essay "
was published. He was not expelled.

[4] John Peter de Crousaz, a famous philosopher and
mathematician, born 1663, died 1748. Francis Burgersdyck, author of a treatise on Logic, and Professor
at the University of Leyden, born 1590, died 1629.

[5] The river Cam, running by the walls of these

Where Bentley late tempestuous wont to sport
In troubled waters, but now sleeps in Port.[1]
Before them marched that awful Aristarch ;
Ploughed was his front with many a deep
    Remark :
His Hat, which never vailed to human pride,
Walker [2] with reverence took, and laid aside. 206
Low bowed the rest : He, kingly, did but nod,[3]
So upright Quakers please both Man and God.[4]
" Mistress ! dismiss that rabble from your
    throne :
Avaunt—is Aristarchus yet unknown ? [5]   210

Colleges, which are particularly famous for their skill
in disputation.—P. W.

  [1] Viz., " Now retired into harbour, after the tem-
pests that had long agitated his society." So Scriblerus. But the learned Scipio Maffei understands it
of a certain wine called Port, from Oporto, a city of
Portugal, of which this Professor invited him to drink
abundantly.—Scip. Maff. De Compotationibus Academ-
icis.—P. W.

Bentley's long war with the Authorities of Trinity
College and the University came to an end in 1738.

  [2] John Walker, Vice-Master of Trinity College,
Cambridge, while Bentley was Master. He was the
associate and friend of the " awful Aristarch " in all
his contests classical and personal.—Carruthers.

  [3] Milton :

      " —— He, kingly, from his State
    Declined not."—P.

  [4] The Hat-worship, as the Quakers call it, is an
abomination to that sect : yet, where it is necessary
to pay that respect to man (as in the Courts of Justice
and Houses of Parliament), they have, to avoid offence,
and yet not violate their conscience, permitted other
people to uncover them.—P. W.

  [5] A famous Commentator, and Corrector of Homer,
whose name has been frequently used to signify a
complete Critic. The compliment paid by our author
to this eminent Professor, in applying to him so great
a name, was the reason that he hath omitted to com-

Thy mighty Scholiast, whose unwearied pains
Made Horace dull, and humbled Milton's
 strains.
Turn what they will to Verse, their toil is vain,
Critics like me shall make it Prose again.
Roman and Greek Grammarians! know your
 Better; [1]   215
Author of something yet more great than
 Letter:
While towering o'er your Alphabet, like Saul,
Stands our Digamma, and o'ertops them all. [2]
 " 'Tis true, on Words is still our whole
 debate,
Dispute of *Me* or *Te* [3] of *aut* or *at;*   220

ment on this part, which contains his own praises.
We shall therefore supply that loss to our best ability.
—*Scriblerus.*—P. W.

 "—— Sic notus Ulysses?"—*Virg.*
 " Dost thou not feel me, Rome?"
                          Ben Jonson.—P.

 [1] Imitated from Propertius, speaking of the Æneid:

 " Cedite, Romani scriptores, cedite Graii !
 Nescio quid majus nascitur Iliade."—P.

 [2] Alludes to the boasted restoration of the Æolic
Digamma, in his long projected Edition of Homer.
He calls it *something more than Letter*, from the
enormous figure it would make among the other
letters, being one Gamma set upon the shoulders of
another.—P. W.
 " Bentley's printer having no better method of
representing the Digamma than by a Roman capital
F, gave occasion to Pope's allusion to its towering
size."—*Monk's Life of Bentley,* quoted by *Courthope.*
 [3] It was a serious dispute, about which the learned
were much divided, and some treatises written : Had
it been about *Meum* or *Tuum* it could not be more
contested, than whether at the end of the first Ode of
Horace, to read, Me *doctarum hederæ præmia fron-
tium,* or Te *doctarum hederæ.*—*Scriblerus.*—P. W.

To sound or sink, in *cano*, O or A,
Or give up Cicero to C or K.[1]
Let Freind affect to speak as Terence spoke,
And Alsop never but like Horace joke;[2]
For me, what Virgil, Pliny may deny,   225
Manilius or Solinus shall supply:[3]
For Attic Phrase in Plato let them seek,
I poach in Suidas for unlicensed Greek.
In ancient Sense if any needs will deal,
Be sure I give them Fragments, not a Meal;
What Gellius or Stobæus hashed before,[4]   231
Or chewed by blind old Scholiasts o'er and o'er.[5]
The critic Eye, that microscope of Wit,
Sees hairs and pores, examines bit by bit:
How parts relate to parts, or they to whole, 235
The body's harmony, the beaming soul,
Are things which Kuster, Burman, Wasse shall
    see,[6]

[1] Grammatical disputes about the manner of pronouncing Cicero's name.—*Warburton.*

[2] Dr. Robert Freind, Master of Westminster School, and Canon of Christ-church. Dr. Anthony Alsop, a happy imitator of the Horatian style.—P. W.

[3] Some Critics having had it in their choice to comment either on Virgil or Manilius, Pliny or Solinus, have chosen the worse author, the more freely to display their critical capacity.—P. W. Alluding to Bentley's Edition of Manilius.

[4] *Suidas, Gellius, Stobæus.* The first, a Dictionary-writer, a collector of impertinent facts and barbarous words; the second, a minute Critic; the third, an author, who gave his Common-place book to the public, where we happen to find much Mince-meat of old books.—P. W.

[5] These taking the same things eternally from the mouth of one another.—P. W.

[6] Men of real and useful erudition.—*Warton.* Küster edited Suidas. Wasse was a Fellow of Queen's College, Cambridge, and edited Sallust and Thucydides. Burman was a scholar of Utrecht.

When Man's whole frame is obvious to a *Flea*.
" Ah, think not, Mistress ! more true Dulness
        lies
In Folly's Cap, than Wisdom's grave disguise.
Like buoys, that never sink into the flood,   241
On Learning's surface we but lie and nod.
Thine is the genuine head of many a house,
And much Divinity without a Νοῦς.
Nor could a BARROW work on every block,   245
Nor has one ATTERBURY spoiled the flock.[1]
See ! still thy own, the heavy Canon roll,[2]
And Metaphysic smokes involve the Pole.
For thee we dim the eyes, and stuff the head
With all such reading as was never read :   250
For thee explain a thing till all men doubt it,
And write about it, Goddess, and about it:
So spins the silk-worm small its slender store,
And labours till it clouds itself all o'er.
" What though we let some better sort of
        fool   255
Thrid every science, run through every school ?

---

[1] Isaac Barrow, Master of Trinity ; Francis Atterbury, Dean of Christ-church : both great Geniuses
and eloquent Preachers; one more conversant in the
sublime Geometry, the other in classical Learning;
but who equally made it their care to advance the
polite Arts in their several Societies.—P. W.
    Dr. Isaac Barrow, the celebrated theologian and
mathematician, born 1630, died 1677.
[2] Canon here, if spoken of *Artillery*, is in the plural
number ; if of the *Canons of the House*, in the singular, and meant only of *one :* in which case I suspect
the *Pole* to be a false reading, and that it should be
the *Poll* or *Head* of that Canon. It may be objected.
that this is a mere *Paronomasia*, or *Pun*.   But what
of that ? Is any figure of Speech more apposite to our
gentle Goddess, or more frequently used by her and
her Children, especially of the University?—*Scriblerus.*—P. W.

Never by tumbler through the hoops was shown
Such skill in passing all, and touching none ;[1]
He may indeed (if sober all this time)
Plague with Dispute, or persecute with Rhyme.
We only furnish what he cannot use,   261
Or wed to what he must divorce, a Muse :
Full in the midst of Euclid dip at once,
And petrify a Genius[2] to a Dunce :
Or set on Metaphysic ground to prance,   265
Show all his paces, not a step advance.
With the same CEMENT, ever sure to bind,
We bring to one dead level every mind.
Then take him to develop, if you can,
And hew the Block off,[3] and get out the Man.
But wherefore waste I words? I see advance 271
Whore, Pupil, and laced Governor from France.
Walker ! our hat "— nor more he deigned to
    say,
But, stern as Ajax' spectre, strode away.[4]
In flowed at once a gay embroidered race, 275
And tittering pushed the Pedants off the place :[5]
Some would have spoken, but the voice was
    drowned
By the French horn, or by the opening hound.

[1] These two verses are verbatim from an epigram
of Dr. Evans, of St. John's College, Oxford ; given to
my father twenty years before the *Dunciad* was written.—*Warton.*

[2] Those who have no Genius, employed in works of
imagination ; those who have, in abstract sciences.—
P. W.

[3] A notion of Aristotle, that there was originally in
every block of marble a Statue, which would appear
on the removal of the superfluous parts.—P. W.

[4] See Homer, Odyss. xi., where the Ghost of Ajax
turns sullenly from Ulysses.—*Scriblerus.*—*Warburton.*

[5] " Rideat et pulset lasciva decentius ætas."
                                        Hor.—P. W.

The first came forwards, with as easy mien,
As if he saw St. James's [1] and the Queen.   280
When thus the attendant Orator [2] begun,
" Receive, Great Empress! thy accomplished
    Son :
Thine from the birth, and sacred from the rod,
A dauntless infant! never scared with God.[3]
The Sire saw, one by one, his Virtues wake :
The Mother begged the blessing of a Rake. 286
Thou gav'st that Ripeness, which so soon began,
And ceased so soon, he ne'er was Boy, nor
    Man,[4]
Through School and College, thy kind cloud
    o'ercast,
Safe and unseen the young Æneas passed : [5] 290

[1] Reflecting on the disrespectful and indecent
Behaviour of several forward young persons in the
presence, so offensive to all serious men, and to none
more than the good Scriblerus.—P. W.

[2] The Governor above-said. The Poet gives him
no particular name ; being unwilling, I presume, to
offend or do injustice to any, by celebrating one only
with whom this character agrees, in preference to so
many who equally deserve it.—*Scriblerus.*— P. W.

[3] "—— sine Dis animosus infans."—*Hor.*—P.

[4] Nature hath bestowed on the human species two
states or conditions, *Infancy* and *Manhood.* Wit
sometimes makes the *first* disappear, and *Folly* the
latter ; but true Dulness annihilates *both.* For want
of *apprehension* in Boys, not suffering that conscious
ignorance and inexperience which produce the awkward bashfulness of youth, makes them *assured ;* and
want of *imagination* makes them *grave.* But this
gravity and *assurance,* which is beyond *boyhood,* being
neither wisdom nor knowledge, do never reach to
manhood.—*Scriblerus.*—W.

[5] See Virg. *Æn.* i. :

    " At Venus obscuro gradientes aëre sepsit,
    Et multo nebulæ circum Dea fudit amictu,

Thence bursting glorious, all at once let down,
Stunned with his giddy 'larum half the town.
Intrepid then, o'er seas and lands he flew:
Europe he saw, and Europe saw him too.
There all thy gifts and graces we display,   295
Thou, only thou, directing all our way!
To where the Seine, obsequious as she runs,
Pours at great Bourbon's feet her silken sons;
Or Tiber, now no longer Roman, rolls,
Vain of Italian Arts, Italian Souls: 300
To happy Convents, bosomed deep in vines,
Where slumber Abbots, purple as their wines:
To Isles of fragrance, lily-silvered vales,[1]
Diffusing languor in the panting gales:
To lands of singing or of dancing slaves,   305
Love-whispering woods, and lute-resounding
        waves.
But chief her shrine where naked Venus keeps,
And Cupids ride the Lion of the Deeps;[2]
Where, eased of Fleets, the Adriatic main
Wafts the smooth Eunuch and enamoured
        swain.   310
Led by my hand, he sauntered Europe round,
And gathered every Vice on Christian ground;
Saw every Court, heard every King declare
His royal Sense of Operas or the Fair;

Cernere ne quis eos;—1. neu quis contingere possit;
2. Molirive moram;—aut 3. veniendi poscere causas."

Where he enumerates the causes why his mother
took this care of him—to wit: 1. That nobody might
touch or correct him; 2. Might stop or detain him;
3. Examine him about the progress he had made, or
so much as guess why he came there.—P. W.

    [1] Tuberoses.—P. W.
    [2] The winged Lion, the Arms of Venice. This Re-
public, heretofore the most considerable in Europe for
her Naval Force and the extent of her Commerce, now
illustrious for her *Carnivals.*—P. W.

The Stews and Palace equally explored,   315
Intrigued with glory, and with spirit whored ; ,
Tried all *hors-d'œuvres*, all *liqueurs* defined,
Judicious drank, and greatly-daring dined ; [1]
Dropped the dull lumber of the Latin store,
Spoiled his own language, and acquired no
          more ;   320
All Classic learning lost on Classic ground ;
And last turned *Air*, the Echo of a Sound ! [2]
See now, half-cured, and perfectly well-bred,
With nothing but a Solo in his head ; [3]
As much Estate, and Principle, and Wit,   325
As Jansen, Fleetwood, Cibber, shall think fit ; [4]

[1] It being indeed no small risk to eat through those
extraordinary compositions, whose disguised ingre-
dients are generally unknown to the guests, and
highly inflammatory and unwholesome.—P. W.
  [2] Yet less a Body than Echo itself; for Echo reflects
Sense or *Words* at least, this Gentleman, only *Airs*
and *Tunes:*

  "—— Sonus *est, qui vivit in* illo."—*Ovid, Met.*

So that this was not a Metamorphosis either in one
or the other, but only a Resolution of the Soul into
its true Principles ; its real Essence being Harmony,
according to the doctrine of Orpheus, the Inventor of
Opera, who first performed to a select assembly of
Beasts.—*Scriblerus.—Warburton.*
  [3] With nothing but a *Solo?* Why, if it be a *Solo*,
how should there be anything else ? Palpable tauto-
logy ! Read boldly an *Opera*, which is enough of
conscience for such a head as has lost all its Latin.—
Bentley.—P. W.
  [4] Three very eminent persons, all Managers of
Plays; who, though not Governors by profession,
had, each in his way, concerned themselves in the
Education of Youth, and regulated their Wits, their
Morals, or their Finances, at that period of their age
which is the most important, their entrance into the
polite world. Of the last of these, and his talents for
this end, see Book i. v. 199, &c.—P. W.
  Fleetwood was manager of Drury-lane Theatre from

Stolen from a Duel, followed by a Nun,
And, if a Borough choose him not, undone;[1]
See, to my country happy I restore
This glorious Youth, and add one Venus more.
Her too receive (for 'her my soul adores)   331
So may the sons of sons of sons of whores[2]
Prop thine, O Empress! like each neighbour
    Throne,
And make a long Posterity thy own."
Pleased, she accepts the Hero and the Dame, 335
Wraps in her Veil, and frees from sense of
    Shame.
Then looked, and saw a lazy, lolling sort,
Unseen at Church, at Senate, or at Court,
Of ever-listless Loiterers, that attend
No Cause, no Trust, no Duty, and no Friend. 340
Thee too, my Paridel![3] she marked thee there,
Stretched on the rack[4] of a too easy chair,
And heard thy everlasting yawn confess
The Pains and Penalties of Idleness.
She pitied! but her Pity only shed   345
Benigner influence on thy nodding head.

1734 to 1745.   For Jansen, see Satires of Dr. Donne,
ii. 88.
   [1] Members of Parliament were privileged from
arrests for debt.

   [2] "Et nati natorum, et qui nascentur ab illis."
                                        Virg.—P.

   [3] The Poet seems to speak of this young gentleman
with great affection. The name is taken from Spenser,
who gives it to a _wandering Courtly 'Squire_, that
travelled about for the same reason for which many
young Squires are now fond of travelling, and especially to _Paris._—P. W.

   [4]   "Sedet, æternumque sedebit,
       Infelix Theseus, Phlegyasque miserrimus omnes
       Admonet."—_Virg._—P.

But Annius, crafty Seer, with ebon wand,[1]
And well-dissembled emerald on his hand,
False as his Gems, and cankered as his Coins,[2]
Came, crammed with capon, from where Pollio
   dines.   350
Soft, as the wily Fox is seen to creep,
Where bask on sunny banks the simple sheep,
Walk round and round, now prying here, now
   there,
So he; but pious, whispered first his prayer.
  " Grant, gracious Goddess! grant me still to
   cheat,[3]   355
O may thy cloud still cover the deceit![4]
Thy choicer mists on this assembly shed,
But pour them thickest on the noble head.
So shall each youth, assisted by our eyes,
See other Cæsars, other Homers rise;   360
Through twilight ages hunt the Athenian
   fowl,

---

[1] The name taken from Annius, the Monk of
Viterbo, famous for many impositions and forgeries
of ancient manuscripts and inscriptions, which he
was prompted to by mere vanity; but our Annius
had a more substantial motive.—P. W.   Sir Andrew
Fountaine.—*Warton.*

[2] Sir Andrew Fountaine had a famous collection of
coins and antiquities.   He was a friend of Swift, and
succeeded Sir Isaac Newton as Warden of the Mint
in 1727.

Pollio, in the next line, was said by Walpole to
mean Lord Burlington.

[3] Some read *skill*, but that is frivolous, for Annius
hath that skill already; or if he had not, *skill*
were not wanting to cheat such persons.—*Bentley.*
—P. W.

[4]   "——Da, pulchra, Laverna,
  Da mihi fallere——
  Noctem peccatis et fraudibus objice nubem."
                  Hor.—P.

Which Chalcis Gods, and mortals call an Owl,[1]
Now see an Attys, now a Cecrops[2] clear,
Nay, Mahomet! the Pigeon at thine ear;
Be rich in ancient brass, though not in gold, 365
And keep his Lares, though his house be sold;
To headless Phœbe his fair bride postpone,
Honour a Syrian Prince above his own;
Lord of an Otho, if I vouch it true;
Blest in one Niger, till he knows of two."[3]　370
　Mummius o'erheard him;[4] Mummius, Fool-
　renowned,[5]
Who like his Cheops stinks above the ground,[6]

[1] The Owl stamped on the reverse on the ancient money of Athens.

　"Which *Chalcis* Gods, and mortals call an *Owl*,"

is the verse by which Hobbes renders that of Homer,

Χαλκίδα κικλήσκουσι Θεοί, ἄνδρες δὲ Κύμινδιν.—P. W.

[2] The first King of Athens, of whom it is hard to suppose any Coins are extant; but not so improbable as what follows, that there should be any of Mahomet, who forbade all Images; and the story of whose pigeon was a monkish fable. Nevertheless, one of these Annius's made a counterfeit medal of that Impostor. now in the collection of a learned Nobleman.—P. W.

[3] Compare the Epistle to Addison.

[4] This name is not merely an allusion to the Mummies he was so fond of, but probably referred to the Roman General of that name, who burned Corinth, and committed the curious Statues to the Captain of a Ship, assuring him, "that if any were lost or broken, he should procure others to be made in their stead:" by which it would seem (whatever may be pretended) that Mummius was no Virtuoso.—P. W.

　Warton says that Dr. Mead was meant, but he is certainly mistaken. Courthope thinks Woodward was referred to. See Satires of Dr. Donne, iv. 30, and Epistle to Addison, v. 41.

[5] A compound epithet in the Greek manner, *renowned by Fools*, or *renowned for making Fools*.—P.

[6] A King of Egypt, whose body was certainly to

Fierce as a startled Adder, swelled, and said,
Rattling an ancient Sistrum at his head :
" Speak'st thou of Syrian Princes ? ¹ Traitor
    base !   375
Mine, Goddess ! mine is all the horned race.
True, he had wit, to make their value rise ;
From foolish Greeks to steal them, was as wise;
More glorious yet, from barbarous hands to keep,
When Sallee Rovers chased him on the deep. 380
Then taught by Hermes, and divinely bold,
Down his own throat he risked the Grecian gold,

be known, as being buried alone in his Pyramid, and
is therefore more genuine than any of the Cleopatras.
This Royal Mummy, being stolen by a wild Arab, was
purchased by the Consul of Alexandria, and transmitted to the Museum of Mummius ; for proof of
which he brings a passage in Sandys's Travels, where
that accurate and learned Voyager assures us that he
saw the Sepulchre empty, which agrees exactly (saith
he) with the time of the theft above mentioned. But
he omits to observe that Herodotus tells the same
thing of it in his time.—P. W.
  ¹ The strange story following, which may be taken
for a fiction of the poet, is justified by a true relation
in Spon's Voyages. Vaillant (who wrote the History
of the Syrian Kings as it is to be found on medals)
coming from the Levant, where he had been collect-
ing various coins, and being pursued by a Corsair of
Sallee, swallowed down twenty gold medals. A sudden Bourasque freed him from the Rover, and he got
to land with them in his belly. On his road to
Avignon he met two Physicians, of whom he demanded
assistance. One advised purgations, the other vomits.
In this uncertainty he took neither, but pursued his
way to Lyons, where he found his ancient friend, the
famous Physician and Antiquary, Dufour, to whom
he related his adventure. Dufour first asked him
whether the medals were of the higher Empire? He
assured him they were. Dufour was ravished with
the hope of possessing such a treasure : he bargained
with him on the spot for the most curious of them,
and was to recover them at his own expense.—P. W.

Received each Demi-God,[1] with pious care,
Deep in his entrails—I revered them there,
I bought them, shrouded in that living shrine,
And at their second birth, they issue mine." 386
" Witness, great Ammon ! by whose horns I
   swore," [2]
(Replied soft Annius) " this our paunch before
Still bears them, faithful ; and that thus I eat,
Is to refund the Medals with the meat.   390
To prove me, Goddess ! clear of all design,
Bid me with Pollio sup as well as dine :
There all the Learn'd shall at the labour stand,
And Douglas lend his soft, obstetric hand." [3]
   The Goddess smiling seemed to give consent ;
So back to Pollio, hand in hand, they went. 396
   Then thick as Locusts blackening all the
      ground,
A tribe, with weeds and shells fantastic crowned,
Each with some wondrous gift approached the
      Power,
A Nest, a Toad, a Fungus, or a Flower.   400
But far the foremost, two, with earnest zeal,
And aspect ardent to the Throne appeal.
   The first thus opened : " Hear thy suppliant's
      call,
Great Queen, and common Mother of us all !
Fair from its humble bed I reared this Flower,

[1] They are called Θεοί on their coins.—P. W.
[2] Jupiter Ammon is called to witness, as the father
of Alexander, to whom those Kings succeeded in the
division of the Macedonian Empire, and whose *Horns*
they wore on their Medals.—P. W.
[3] A Physician of great learning and no less taste ;
above all, curious in what related to *Horace*, of whom
he collected every Edition, Translation, and Comment, to the number of several hundred volumes.—
P. W.
   Dr. James Douglas, a famous anatomist. He died
in 1742.

Suckled, and cheered, with air, and sun, and
  shower,   406
Soft on the paper ruff its leaves I spread,
Bright with the gilded button tipped its head;
Then throned in glass, and named it CAROLINE:[1]
Each maid cried, Charming! and each youth,
  Divine!   410
Did Nature's pencil ever blend such rays,
Such varied light in one promiscuous blaze?
Now prostrate! dead! behold that Caroline:
No maid cries, Charming! and no youth, Divine!
And lo the wretch! whose vile, whose insect
  lust   415
Laid this gay daughter of the Spring in dust.
Oh punish him, or to the Elysian shades
Dismiss my soul, where no Carnation fades!"
He ceased and wept. With innocence of mien,
The Accused stood forth, and thus addressed the
  Queen.   420
  "Of all the enamelled race,[2] whose silvery
  wing

[1] These verses are translated from Catullus, Epith. :
"Ut flos in septis secretus nascitur hortis,
Quam mulcent aurae, firmat Sol, educat imber,
Multi illum pueri, multae optavere puellae :
Idem quum tenui carptus defloruit ungui,
Nulli illum pueri, nullae optavere puellae," &c.
It is a compliment which the Florists usually pay
to Princes and great persons, to give their names to
the most curious flowers of their raising : Some have
been very jealous of vindicating this honour, but none
more than that ambitious Gardener at Hammersmith,
who caused his Favourite to be painted on his Sign,
with this inscription, "This is My Queen Caroline."
—P. W.
[2] The Poet seems to have an eye to Spenser, Muio-
potmos :
  "Of all the race of silver-winged Flies
  Which do possess the Empire of the Air."—P.

Waves to the tepid Zephyrs of the spring,
Or swims along the fluid atmosphere,
Once brightest shined this child of Heat and
    Air.
I saw, and started from its vernal bower,   425
The rising game, and chased from flower to
    flower.
It fled, I followed ;¹ now in hope, now pain ;
It stopped, I stopped ; it moved, I moved again.
At last it fixed, 'twas on what plant it pleased,
And where it fixed, the beauteous bird I seized :
Rose or Carnation was below my care ;   431
I meddle, Goddess ! only in my sphere.
I tell the naked fact without disguise,
And, to excuse it, need but shew the prize ;
Whose spoils this paper offers to your eye,   435
Fair even in death ! this peerless *Butterfly*."
" My sons !" (she answered) " both have done
    your parts :
Live happy both, and long promote our arts !
But hear a Mother, when she recommends
To your fraternal care our sleeping friends.²   440
The common Soul, of Heaven's more frugal
    make,
Serves but to keep fools pert, and knaves awake :
A drowsy Watchman, that just gives a knock,
And breaks our rest, to tell us what's o'clock.
Yet by some object every brain is stirred :   445
The dull may 'waken to a humming-bird ;
The most recluse, discreetly opened, find
Congenial matter in the Cockle-kind ;
The mind, in Metaphysics at a loss,

---

¹   "—— I started back,
    It started back ; but pleased I soon returned,
    Pleased it returned as soon."—*Milton.*—P.

² Of whom, see verse 345 above. — P. W.

May wander in a wilderness of Moss;[1]   450
The head that turns at super-lunar things,
Poised with a tail, may steer on Wilkins' wings.[2]
" O ! would the Sons of Men[3] once think
     their Eyes
And Reason given them but to study *Flies!*
See Nature in some partial narrow shape,   455
And let the Author of the Whole escape :
Learn but to trifle ; or, who most observe,
To wonder at their Maker, not to serve ! "
" Be that my task " (replies a gloomy Clerk,[4]

---

[1] Of which the Naturalists count I cannot tell how many hundred species.—P. W.

[2] One of the first Projectors of the Royal Society ; who, among many enlarged and useful notions, entertained the extravagant hope of a possibility to fly to the Moon ; which has put some volatile Geniuses upon making wings for that purpose.—P. W.

Dr. John Wilkins, Master of Trinity College, Cambridge, and afterwards Bishop of Chester. He wrote a book entitled " The Discovery of a New World; or a discourse tending to prove that 'tis probable there may be another habitable World in the Moon ; with a discourse concerning the possibility of a passage thither," published in 1638.

[3] This is the third speech of the Goddess to her Supplicants, and completes the whole of what she had to give in instruction on this important occasion, concerning Learning, Civil Society, and Religion. In the first speech, verse 119, to her Editors and conceited Critics, she directs how to deprave Wit and discredit Fine Writers. In her second, verse 175, to the Educators of Youth, she shows them how all civil duties may be extinguished, in that one doctrine of Divine hereditary Right. And in this third, she charges the Investigators of Nature to amuse themselves in trifles, and rest in second causes, with a total disregard of the first. This being all that Dulness can wish, is all she needs to say ; and we may apply to her (as the Poet hath managed it) what hath been said of true Wit, that *She neither says too little, nor too much.*—P. W.

[4] The Epithet *gloomy* in this line may seem the

Sworn foe to Mystery, yet divinely dark ;   460
Whose pious hope aspires to see the day
When Moral Evidence shall quite decay,[1]
And damns implicit faith, and holy lies,
Prompt to impose, and fond to dogmatize :)
" Let others creep by timid steps, and slow,   465
On plain Experience lay foundations low,
By common sense to common knowledge bred,
And last, to Nature's Cause through Nature led.
All-seeing in thy mists, we want no guide,
Mother of Arrogance, and Source of Pride !   470
We nobly take the high Priori Road,[2]

same with that of *dark* in the next. But *gloomy*
relates to the uncomfortable and disastrous condition
of an irreligious Sceptic ; whereas *dark* alludes only
to his puzzled and embroiled Systems.—P. W.

[1] Alluding to a ridiculous and absurd way of some
Mathematicians, in calculating the gradual decay of
Moral Evidence by mathematical proportions: according to which calculation, in about fifty years it will be
no longer probable that Julius Cæsar was in Gaul, or
died in the Senate-House. See *Craig's Theologiæ
Christianæ Principia Mathematica.* But as it seems
evident that facts of a thousand years old, for instance,
are now as probable as they were five hundred years
ago, it is plain that if in fifty more they quite disappear, it must be owing, not to their Arguments, but
to the extraordinary power of our Goddess ; for whose
help therefore they have reason to pray.—P. W.

[2] Those who, from the effects in this visible world,
deduce the Eternal Power and Godhead of the First
Cause, though they cannot attain to an adequate idea
of the Deity, yet discover so much of him, as enables
them to see the End of their Creation, and the means
of their Happiness : whereas they who take this high
Priori Road (such as Hobbes, Spinoza, Des Cartes,
and some better Reasoners), for one that goes right,
ten lose themselves in Mists, or ramble after Visions,
which deprive them of all sight of their end, and
mislead them in the choice of wrong means.—P. W.

An oblique censure of Dr. S. Clarke's "Demonstration of the Being and Attributes of God."—*Wakefield.*

And reason downward, till we doubt of God;
Make Nature still¹ encroach upon his plan ;
And shove him off as far as e'er we can :
Thrust some Mechanic Cause into his place ; 475
Or bind in Matter, or diffuse in Space,²
Or, at one bound o'erleaping all his laws,
Make God Man's Image, Man the final Cause,
Find Virtue local, all Relation scorn,
See all in *Self*,³ and but for self be born :   480
Of nought so certain as our *Reason* still,⁴
Of nought so doubtful as of *Soul* and *Will*,
Oh hide the God still more ! and make us
      see,
Such as Lucretius drew,⁵ a God like Thee :

¹ This relates to such as, being ashamed to assert
a mere Mechanic Cause, and yet unwilling to forsake
it entirely, have had recourse to a certain *Plastic
Nature, Elastic Fluid, Subtile Matter*, &c.—P. W.
² The first of these Follies is that of Des Cartes ;
the second of Hobbes ; the third of some succeeding
philosophers.—P. W.
³ Here the Poet, from the errors relating to a Deity
in natural Philosophy, descends to those in moral.
Man was made according to *God's Image*; this false
Theology, measuring his attributes by ours, makes
God after *Man's Image*. This proceeds from the im-
perfection of his *Reason*. The next, of imagining
himself the final Cause, is the effect of his *Pride* : as
the making Virtue and Vice arbitrary, and Morality
the imposition of the Magistrate, is of the *Corruption*
of his *heart*. Hence he centres everything in *himself*.
The Progress of Dulness herein differing from that of
Madness ; one ends in *seeing all in God*, the other in
seeing all in Self.- P. W.
¹ Of which we have most cause to be diffident. *Of
nought so doubtful as of Soul and Will :* two things
the most self-evident, the existence of our Soul, and
the freedom of our Will.—P. W.
⁵ Lib. i. ver. 57 :

  "Omnis enim per se Divam natura necesse est
  Immortali ævo *summa cum pace* fruatur,

Wrapped up in Self, a God without a Thought,
Regardless of our merit or default.
Or that bright Image to our fancy draw,[1]
Which Theocles in raptured vision saw,[2]
While through Poetic scenes the GENIUS roves,
Or wanders wild in Academic Groves;   490
That NATURE our Society adores,
Where Tindal dictates, and Silenus snores."[3]
  Roused at his name, up rose the bousy Sire,
And shook from out his Pipe the seeds of fire ;[4]
Then snapped his box, and stroked his belly
  down :   495
Rosy and reverend, though without a Gown.
Bland and familiar to the throne he came,
Led up the Youth, and called the Goddess
  Dame :
Then thus: " From Priest-craft happily set free,
Lo! every finished Son returns to thee :   500
First slave to Words,[5] then vassal to a Name,

> *Semota* ab nostris rebus, *summotaque* longe—
> Nec bene pro *meritis* capitur, nec tangitur *ira ;*"

from whence the two verses following are translated,
and wonderfully agree with the character of our
Goddess.—*Scriblerus.*—P. W.

[1] *Bright Image* was the title given by the later
Platonists to that Vision of *Nature* which they had
formed out of their own fancy, so bright, that they
called it Ἀὔτοπτον Ἀγαλμα, or the *Self-seen Image,*
i.e. seen by its own light.—*Scriblerus.*—*Warburton.*

[2] Referring to Shaftesbury's " Characteristics."

[3] Silenus was an Epicurean Philosopher, as appears
from Virgil, Eclog. vi., where he sings the principles
of that philosophy in his drink.—P. W.

By Silenus he means Thomas Gordon, the translator of Tacitus, who published the *Independent Whig.*
—*Warton.*

[4] The Epicurean language, *Semina rerum,* or Atoms.
Virg. Eclog. vi., *Semina ignis- semina flammæ.*—
P. W.

[5] A recapitulation of the whole Course of modern

III.   T

Then dupe to Party; child and man the same;
Bounded by Nature, narrowed still by Art,
A trifling head, and a contracted heart.
Thus bred, thus taught, how many have I seen,
Smiling on all, and smiled on by a Queen ?[1] 506
Marked out for Honours, honoured for their
      Birth,
To thee the most rebellious things on earth :
Now to thy gentle shadow all are shrunk,
All melted down in Pension, or in Punk !   510
So K* so B** sneaked into the grave,[2]
A Monarch's half, and half a Harlot's slave.
Poor W**[3] nipped in Folly's broadest bloom,
Who praises now ? his Chaplain on his Tomb.
Then take them all, oh take them to thy breast !
Thy Magus, Goddess! shall perform the rest." 516
    With that a WIZARD OLD his Cup extends;
Which whoso tastes, forgets his former friends,[4]

Education described in this book, which confines
Youth to the study of *Words* only in Schools; subjects them to the authority of *Systems* in the Universities; and deludes them with the names of *Party
distinctions* in the World. All equally concurring to
narrow the understanding, and establish slavery and
error in Literature, Philosophy, and Politics. The
whole finished in modern Free-thinking; the completion of whatever is vain, wrong, and destructive to
the happiness of mankind, as it establishes *Self-love*
for the sole Principle of Action.—P. W.
    [1] *i.e.* This Queen or Goddess of Dulness.—*Scrible-
rus.—Warburton.*
    [2] Carruthers, and after him Courthope, conjecture
that the Duke of Kent and Lord Berkeley are meant.
    [3] Philip Duke of Wharton. See Moral Essays,
179.
    [4] Homer of the Nepenthe, Odyss. iv.:

Αὐτίκ' ἄρ' εἰς οἶνον βάλε φάρμακον, ἔνθεν ἔπιον
Νηπενθές τ' ἀχολόν τε, κακῶν ἐπίληθον ἁπάντων.

The cup of Self-love, which causes a total oblivion
of the obligations of Friendship or Honour; and of

Sire, Ancestors, Himself.   One casts his eyes
Up to a *Star*, and, like Endymion, dies :   520
A *Feather*, shooting from another's head,
Extracts his brain ; and Principle is fled ;
Lost is his God, his Country, everything ;
And nothing left but Homage to a King ! [1]
The vulgar herd turn off to roll with Hogs, 525
To run with Horses, or to hunt with Dogs ;
But, sad example ! never to escape
Their Infamy, still keep the human shape. [2]
But she, good Goddess, [3] sent to every child
Firm Impudence, or Stupefaction mild ;   530
And straight succeeded, leaving shame no room,
Cibberian forehead, or Cimmerian gloom. [4]

the Service of God or our Country ; all sacrificed to
Vain-glory, Court-worship, or the yet meaner consi-
derations of Lucre and brutal Pleasures.   From ver.
520 to 528.—P. W.

   [1] So strange as this must seem to a mere English
reader, the famous Mons. de la Bruyère declares it to
be the character of every good Subject in a Monarchy:
" Where (says he) *there is no such thing as Love of
our Country*, the Interest, the Glory, and Service
of the *Prince*, supply its place."—*De la République*,
chap. x.—P. W.

   [2] The effect of the Magus's Cup, by which is allegorized a *total* corruption of heart, are just contrary
to that of Circe, which only represents the *sudden*
plunging into pleasures.   Hers, therefore, took away
the shape, and left the human mind ; his takes away
the mind, and leaves the human shape.— *Warburton*.

   [3] The only comfort people can receive, must be
owing in some shape or other to Dulness ; which
makes some stupid, others impudent, gives self-
conceit to some, upon the flatteries of their depen-
dents, presents the false colours of interest to others,
and busies or amuses the rest with idle pleasures or
sensuality, till they become easy under any infamy.
Each of which species is here shadowed under allegorical persons.—P. W.

   [4] *i.e.* She communicates to them of her own virtue,
or of her Royal Colleague's.   The *Cibberian forehead*

Kind Self-conceit to some her glass applies,
Which no one looks in with another's eyes :
But as the Flatterer or Dependant paint,   535
Beholds himself a Patriot, Chief, or Saint.
  On others Interest her gay livery flings,
Interest, that waves on Party-coloured wings :
Turned to the Sun, she casts a thousand dyes,
And, as she turns, the colours fall or rise.   540
  Others the Syren Sisters warble round,
And empty heads console with empty sound.
No more, alas! the voice of Fame they hear,
The balm of Dulness trickling in their ear.[1]
Great C**, H**, P**, R**, K*,[2]   545

being to fit them for self-conceit, self-interest, &c.,
and the *Cimmerian gloom* for the pleasures of Opera
and the Table.—*Scriblerus.—Warburton.*
  [1] The true *Balm of Dulness*, called by the Greek
Physicians Κολακεία, is a *Sovereign* remedy against
Inanity, and has its poetic name from the Goddess
herself. Its ancient Dispensators were *her Poets;* and
for that reason our Author, Book ii. v. 207, calls it
the Poet's healing balm : but it is now got into as
many hands as Goddard's Drops or Daffy's Elixir. It
is prepared by the *Clergy,* as appears from several
places of this poem ; and by v. 534, 535, it seems as
if the *Nobility* had it made up in their own houses.
This, which *Opera* is here said to administer, is but a
spurious sort. See my Dissertation on the *Silphium*
of the Ancients.—*Bentley.—Warburton.*
  [2] In the first editions the line stands :
      " Great Shades of **, **, **, **, *,"
which Walpole fills up thus :
      " Great Shades of Cowper, Raymond, Harcourt,
        King."
Croker (quoted by Courthope) says that the line as
it now stands is filled up in Wilkes' MS. notes as
follows :
      " Great Cowper, Parker, Raymond, Harcourt,
        King:"
and adds that Harcourt, Cowper, Parker, and King

Why all your Toils? your Sons have learned
　to sing.
How quick Ambition hastes to ridicule!
The Sire is made a Peer, the Son a Fool.
On some, a Priest succinct in amice white
Attends; all flesh is nothing in his sight!　550
Beeves, at his touch, at once to jelly turn,
And the huge Boar is shrunk into an Urn:
The board with specious miracles he loads,[1]
Turns Hares to Larks, and Pigeons into Toads.
Another (for in all what one can shine?)　555
Explains the *Sève* and *Verdeur* of the Vine.[2]

were Lord Chancellors, and Raymond Lord Chief
Justice. The whole passage refers to the Italian
Opera.

[1] Scriblerus seems at a loss in this place. *Speciosa
miracula* (says he), according to Horace, were the
monstrous fables of the Cyclops, Læstrygons, Scylla,
&c. What relation have these to the transformation
of hares into larks, or of pigeons into toads? I shall
tell thee. The Læstrygons spitted men upon spears,
as we do larks upon skewers; and the fair pigeon
turned to a toad is similar to the fair virgin Scylla
ending in a filthy beast. But here is the difficulty,
why pigeons in so shocking a shape should be brought
to a table? Hares, indeed, might be cut into larks
at a second dressing, out of frugality: yet that seems
no probable motive, when we consider the extrava-
gance before mentioned of dissolving whole Oxen and
Boars into a small vial of Jelly; nay, it is expressly
said, that *all Flesh is nothing in his sight*. I have
searched in Apicius, Pliny, and the Feast of Trimal-
chio, in vain: I can only resolve it into some myste-
rious superstitious Rite, as it is said to be done by a
Priest, and soon after called a *Sacrifice*, attended (as
all ancient sacrifices were) with *Libation* and *Song*.—
Scriblerus.

This good Scholiast, not being acquainted with
modern Luxury, was ignorant that these were only
the miracles of *French Cookery*, and that particularly
pigeons en crapeau were a common dish.—P. W.

[2] French Terms relating to wines, which signify

What cannot copious Sacrifice atone?
Thy Truffles, Perigord! thy Hams, Bayonne!
With French Libation, and Italian Strain,
Wash Bladen white, and expiate Hays's stain.[1]
KNIGHT lifts the head, for what are crowds
    undone,   561
To three essential Partridges in one?[2]
Gone every blush, and silent all reproach,
Contending Princes mount them in their Coach.

    Next, bidding all draw near on bended knees,
The Queen confers her *Titles* and *Degrees.*   566
Her children first of more distinguished sort,
Who study Shakespear at the Inns of Court,
Impale a Glow-worm, or Vertù profess,
Shine in the dignity of F.R.S.   570
Some, deep Free-Masons, join the silent race,
Worthy to fill Pythagoras's place:
Some Botanists, or Florists at the least,

their flavour and poignancy. St. Evremont has a very pathetic letter to a *Nobleman in Disgrace*, advising him to seek comfort in a *good table*, and particularly to be attentive to *these qualities* in his champagne.— P. W.

[1] Names of Gamesters. Bladen is a black man. ROBERT KNIGHT, Cashier of the South Sea Company, who fled from England in 1720 (afterwards pardoned in 1742). These lived with the utmost magnificence at Paris, and kept open tables frequented by persons of the first Quality of England, and even by Princes of the blood of France.—P. W.

Colonel Martin Bladen was a man of some literature, and translated Cæsar's *Commentaries.* I never could learn that he had offended Pope.—*Warton.*

[2] Two dissolved into quintessence to make sauce for the third. The honour of this invention belongs to France, yet has it been excelled by our native luxury, a hundred squab Turkeys being not unfrequently deposited in one pie in the bishopric of Durham; to which our Author alludes in verse 593 of this work.—P. (Omitted in Edition of 1751.)

Or issue Members of an Annual feast.
Nor pass the meanest unregarded, one   575
Rose a Gregorian, one a Gormogon.[1]
The last, not least in honour or applause,
Isis and Cam made DOCTORS of her LAWS.[2]
    Then, blessing all, " Go, Children of my care!
To Practice now from Theory repair.   580
All my commands are easy, short, and full :
My Sons! be proud, be selfish, and be dull.
Guard my Prerogative, assert my Throne :
This Nod confirms each Privilege your own.[3]
The Cap and Switch be sacred to his Grace;[4] 585
With Staff and Pumps the Marquis lead the
    Race ;
From Stage to Stage the licensed Earl may
    run,[5]

    [1] A sort of Lay-brothers, *Slips* from the Root of the
Freemasons.—P. W.
    [2] Pope refused the degree of D.C.L. at Oxford
because the University did not at the same time
confer the degree of D.D. on Warburton.
    [3] This speech of Dulness to her Sons at parting may
possibly fall short of the Reader's expectations ; who
may imagine the Goddess might give them a Charge
of more consequence, and, from such a Theory as is
before delivered, incite them to the practice of something more extraordinary than to personate Running-
Footmen, Jockeys, Stage-Coachmen, &c.
    But if it be well considered that whatever inclina-
tion they might have to do mischief, her sons are
generally rendered harmless by their inability ; and
that it is the common effect of Dulness (even in her
greatest efforts) to defeat her own design ; the Poet, I
am persuaded, will be justified, and it will be allowed
that these worthy persons, in their several ranks, do
as much as can be expected from them.—P. W.
    [4] The Duke of Devonshire. The Marquis in the
next line is his son the Marquis of Hartington.—
Courthope.
    [5] The Earl of Salisbury, who took the property of
a Stage Coach and drove it himself.—*Walpole.*

Paired with his Fellow-Charioteer the Sun ;
The learned Baron Butterflies design,
Or draw to silk Arachne's subtile line ;[1]   590
The Judge to dance his brother Serjeant call ;[2]
The Senator at Cricket urge the Ball ;
The Bishop stow (Pontific Luxury !)
An hundred Souls of Turkeys in a pie ;
The sturdy Squire to Gallic masters stoop,   595
And drown his Lands and Manors in a Soupe.
Others import yet nobler arts from France,
Teach Kings to fiddle,[3] and make Senates dance.
Perhaps more high some daring son may soar,
Proud to my list to add one Monarch more ! 600
And nobly conscious, Princes are but things
Born for First Ministers, as Slaves for Kings,
Tyrant supreme ! shall three Estates command,
And MAKE ONE MIGHTY DUNCIAD OF THE LAND !"
     More she had spoke, but yawned—All Nature
          nods :   605
What Mortal can resist the Yawn of Gods ?[4]

     [1] This is one of the most ingenious employments
assigned, and therefore recommended only to Peers
of Learning. Of weaving Stockings of the Webs of
Spiders, see the Phil. Trans.—P. W.
     [2] Alluding, perhaps, to that ancient and solemn
Dance, entitled A Call of Serjeants.—P. W.
     [3] An ancient amusement of Sovereign Princes,
viz., Achilles, Alexander, Nero ; though despised by
Themistocles, who was a Republican.—Make Senates
dance, either after their Prince, or to Pontoise, or
Siberia.— P. W. See Moral Essays iii. 44.
     [4] This verse is truly Homerical ; as is the conclu-
sion of the Action, where the great Mother composes
all, in the same manner as Minerva at the period of
the Odyssey. It may, indeed, seem a very singular
Epitasis of a Poem to end as this does with a Great
Yawn ; but we must consider it as the Yawn of a
God, and of powerful effects. It is not out of nature ;
most long and grave Counsels concluding in this very
manner : nor without authority, the incomparable

Churches and Chapels instantly it reached; [1]
(St. James's first, for leaden G—— [2] preached)
Then catched the Schools ; the Hall scarce kept
　awake ;
The Convocation gaped, but could not speak : 610
Lost was the Nation's Sense, nor could be found,
While the long solemn Unison went round :
Wide, and more wide, it spread o'er all the realm ;
Ev'n Palinurus nodded at the Helm : [3]
The Vapour mild o'er each Committee crept ;
Unfinished Treaties in each Office slept ;　　616
And Chiefless Armies dozed out the Campaign ;

Spenser having ended one of the most considerable of
his works with a *Roar;* but then it is the *Roar of a
Lion*, the effects whereof are described as the Catas-
trophe of the Poem.—P. W.

[1] The Progress of this Yawn is judicious, natural,
and worthy to be noted. First it seizeth the Churches
and Chapels ; then catcheth the Schools, where, though
the boys be unwilling to sleep, the Masters are not ;
next Westminster-hall, much more hard indeed to
subdue, and not totally put to silence, even by the
Goddess ; then the Convocation, which though
extremely desirous to speak, yet cannot : even the
House of Commons, justly called the Sense of the
Nation, is *lost* (that is to say *suspended*) during
the Yawn (far be it from our Author to suggest it
could be lost any longer !), but it spreadeth at large
all over the rest of the Kingdom, to such a degree,
that Palinurus himself (though as incapable of sleeping as Jupiter) yet noddeth for a moment : the effect
of which, though ever so momentary, could not but
cause some relaxation, for the time, in all public
affairs.—*Scriblerus.*—P. W.

[2] Dr. Gilbert, Bishop of Salisbury (afterwards
Archbishop of York). He had never given Pope any
particular offence, but he had attacked Dr. King, of
Oxford, whom Pope respected.—*Warton.*

[3] Young's *Universal Passion*, Sat. vii. 225 :

　" What felt thy Walpole, pilot of the realm !
　Our Palinurus slept not at the helm."
　　　　　　　　　　　　　　—*Wakefield.*

And Navies yawned for Orders on the Main.[1]
O Muse! relate (for you can tell alone,
Wits have short Memories,[2] and Dunces none,)
Relate, who first, who last resigned to rest ;   621
Whose Heads she partly, whose completely,
   blessed ;
What Charms could Faction, what Ambition
   lull,
The Venal quiet, and entrance the Dull ;
'Till drowned was Sense, and Shame, and Right,
   and Wrong—   625
O sing, and hush the Nations with thy Song!
    *   *   *   *

In vain, in vain,—the all-composing Hour

---

[1] These verses were written many years ago, and may be found in the State Poems of that time. So that Scriblerus is mistaken, or whoever else have imagined this Poem of a fresher date.—P. W.

From a poem by Halifax on Orpheus and Margarita :

   " And when the tawny Tuscan raised her strain,
   Rook furls his sails, and dozes on the main :
   Treaties unfinished in the office sleep,
   And Shovel yawns for orders on the deep."
              —*Wakefield.*

[2] This seems to be the reason why the Poets, whenever they give us a Catalogue, constantly call for help on the Muses, who, as the Daughters of *Memory*, are obliged not to forget anything. So Homer, Iliad ii. :

   Πληθὺν δ' οὐκ ἂν ἐγὼ μυθήσομαι οὐδ' ὀνομήνω,
   Εἰ μὴ 'Ολυμπιάδες Μοῦσαι, Διὸς αἰγιόχοιο
   Ουγατέρες, μνησαίαθ'.

And Virgil, Æn. vii. :

   " Et meministis enim, Divæ, et memorare potestis:
   Ad nos vix tenuis famæ perlabitur aura."

But our Poet had yet another reason for putting this task upon the Muse, that, all besides being *asleep*, she only could relate what passed. — *Scriblerus.*—P. W.

Resistless falls : the Muse obeys the Power.
She comes ! she comes ! the sable Throne behold [1]
Of Night primæval, and of Chaos old !   630
Before her, Fancy's gilded clouds decay,
And all its varying Rain-bows die away.
Wit shoots in vain its momentary fires,
The meteor drops, and in a flash expires.
As one by one, at dread Medea's strain,   635
The sickening stars fade off the ethereal plain ;
As Argus' eyes,[2] by Hermes' wand oppressed,
Closed one by one to everlasting rest;
Thus at her felt approach, and secret might,
Art after Art goes out, and all is Night.   640
See skulking Truth to her old cavern fled,[3]
Mountains of Casuistry heaped o'er her head !
Philosophy, that leaned on Heaven before,
Shrinks to her second cause, and is no more ;
Physic of Metaphysic begs defence,   645
And Metaphysic calls for aid on Sense !
See Mystery to Mathematics fly !
In vain ! they gaze, turn giddy, rave, and die.
Religion blushing veils her sacred fires,
And unawares Morality expires.   650
Nor public Flame, nor private, dares to shine ;

---

[1] The sable Thrones of Night and Chaos, here represented as advancing to extinguish the light of the
Sciences, in the first place blot out the colours of
Fancy, and damp the fire of *Wit*, before they proceed
to their greater work.—*Warburton.*

[2] " Et quamvis sopor est oculorum parte receptus,
   Parte tamen vigilat——
         ——Vidit Cyllenius omnes
   Succubuisse oculos," etc.—*Ovid, Met.* i.—P.

[3] Alluding to the saying of Democritus, that Truth
lay at the bottom of a deep well, from whence he had
drawn her : though Butler says, *He first put her in,
before he drew her out.*- P.

Nor human Spark is left, nor Glimpse divine!
Lo! thy dread Empire, CHAOS! is restored;
Light dies before thy uncreating word;
Thy hand, great Anarch! lets the curtain fall;
And universal Darkness buries All.   656

BY THE AUTHOR.
A DECLARATION.

Whereas certain Haberdashers of Points and Particles, **being instigated by the spirit** of Pride, **and assuming to themselves the name of Critics and Restorers, have taken upon them to adulterate the common and current sense of our** Glorious Ancestors, Poets of this Realm, **by clipping, coining, defacing the images, mixing their own base alloy, or otherwise falsifying the same; which they publish, utter, and vend as genuine: The said haberdashers having no right thereto, as neither heirs, executors, administrators, assigns, or in any** sort related to such **Poets, to all or any of them:** Now We, **having carefully revised this** our Dunciad, **beginning**[1] **with the words** The Mighty Mother, **and ending with the words** buries All, **containing the entire sum of** One thousand seven hundred and fifty-four verses, **declare every word, figure, point, and comma of this impression to be authentic: And do therefore strictly enjoin and forbid any person or persons whatever to erase, reverse, put between hooks, or by any other means, directly or indirectly, change**

---

[1] Read thus confidently, instead of "beginning with the word *books*, and ending with the word *flies*," as formerly it stood: read also, "containing the entire sum of one thousand, seven hundred, and fifty-six verses," instead of "one thousand and twelve lines;" such being the initial and final words, and such the true and entire contents of this poem.

Thou art to know, reader! that the first edition thereof, like that of Milton, was never seen by the Author (though living and not blind). The Editor himself confessed as much in his Preface: and no two poems were ever published in so arbitrary a manner. The Editor of this had as boldly suppressed whole passages, yea the entire last book, as the Editor of Paradise Lost, added and augmented. Milton himself gave but ten books, his editor twelve; this author gave four books, his editor only three. But we have happily done justice to both; and presume we shall live, in this our last labour, as long as in any of our others.—*Bentley.*—P.

or mangle any of them. And we do hereby earnestly exhort all our brethren to follow this our Example, which we heartily wish our great Predecessors had heretofore set, as a remedy and prevention of all such abuses. Provided always, that nothing in this Declaration shall be construed to limit the lawful and undoubted right of every subject of this Realm, to judge, censure, or condemn, in the whole or in part, any Poem or Poet whatsoever.

> Given under our hand, at London, this third day of January, in the year of our Lord One thousand, seven hundred, thirty and two.

Declarat' cor' me,
JOHN BARBER, *Mayor.*

APPENDICES.

I.

PREFACE

PREFIXED TO THE FIVE FIRST IMPERFECT EDITIONS OF

THE DUNCIAD,

IN THREE BOOKS, PRINTED AT DUBLIN AND LONDON,

IN OCTAVO AND DUODECIMO, 1727.

THE PUBLISHER [1] TO THE READER.

T will be found a true observation, though somewhat surprising, that when any scandal is vented against a man of the highest distinction and character, either in the state or in literature, the

---

[1] Who he was is uncertain ; but Edward Ward tells us, in his preface to Durgen, "that most judges are of opinion this preface is not of English extraction, but Hibernian," &c. He means it was written by Dr. Swift, who, whether publisher or not, may be said in a sort to be author of the poem. For when he, together with Mr. Pope (for reasons specified in the preface to their Miscellanies), determined to own the most trifling pieces in which they had any hand, and to destroy all that remained in their power ; the first sketch of this poem was snatched from the fire by Dr. Swift, who persuaded his friend to proceed in it, and to him it was therefore inscribed. But the occasion of printing it was as follows :

There was published in those Miscellanies, a Treatise of the

public in general afford it a most quiet reception ; and the larger part accept it as favourably as if it were some kindness done to themselves : whereas if a known scoundrel or blockhead but chance to be touched upon, a whole legion is up in arms, and it becomes the common cause of all scribblers, booksellers, and printers whatsoever.

Not to search too deeply into the reason hereof, I will only observe as a fact, that every week for these two months past, the town has been perse-cuted with[1] pamphlets, advertisements, letters, and weekly essays, not only against the wit and writings, but against the character and person of Mr. Pope. And that of all those men who have received pleasure from his works, which by modest computation may be about[2] a hundred thousand

Bathos, or Art of Sinking in Poetry, in which was a chapter, where the species of bad writers were ranged in classes, and initial letters of names prefixed, for the most part at random. But such was the number of poets eminent in that art, that some one or other took every letter to himself. All fell into so violent a fury, that for half a year, or more, the common news-papers (in most of which they had some property, as being hired writers) were filled with the most abusive falsehoods and scurrilities they could possibly devise ; a liberty no ways to be wondered at in those people, and in those papers, that, for many years, during the uncontrolled licence of the press, had aspersed almost all the great characters of the age ; and this with impunity, their own persons and names being utterly secret and obscure. This gave Mr. Pope the thought, that he had now some opportunity of doing good, by detecting and dragging into light these common enemies of mankind ; since, to invalidate this universal slander, it sufficed to show what contemptible men were the authors of it. He was not without hopes, that by manifesting the dulness of those who had only malice to recommend them ; either the booksellers would not find their account in employing them, or the men themselves, when discovered, want courage to proceed in so unlawful an occupation. This it was that gave birth to the Dunciad ; and he thought it an happiness, that by the late flood of slander on himself, he had acquired such a peculiar right over their names as was necessary to his design.—P.

[1] See the list of those anonymous papers, with their dates and authors annexed, inserted before the poem.--P.

[2] It is surprising with what stupidity this preface, which is almost a continued irony, was taken by those authors. All such passages as these were understood by Curl, Cook, Cibber, and others, to be serious. Hear the Laureate (Letter to Mr.

in these kingdoms of England and Ireland (not to mention Jersey, Guernsey, the Orcades, those in the new world, and foreigners who have translated him into their languages), of all this number not a man hath stood up to say one word in his defence.

The only exception is the [1] author of the following poem, who doubtless had either a better insight into the grounds of this clamour, or a better opinion of Mr. Pope's integrity, joined with a greater personal love for him, than any other of his numerous friends and admirers.

Farther, that he was in his peculiar intimacy, appears from the knowledge he manifests of the most private authors of all the anonymous pieces against him, and from his having in this poem attacked [2] no man living, who had not before printed, or published, some scandal against this gentleman.

How I came possessed of it, is no concern to the reader; but it would have been a wrong to him had I detained the publication; since those names which are its chief ornaments die off daily so fast, as must render it too soon unintelligible, If it provoke the author to give us a more perfect edition, I have my end.

Who he is I cannot say, and (which is a great

Pope, p. 9): "Though I grant the Dunciad 'a better poem of its kind than ever was writ; yet, when I read it with those vainglorious encumbrances of notes and remarks upon it, &c.—it is amazing, that you, who have writ with such masterly spirit upon the ruling passion, should be so blind a slave to your own, as not to see how far a low avarice of praise," &c. (taking it for granted that the notes of Scriblerus and others were the author's own).—P.

[1] A very plain irony, speaking of Mr. Pope himself.—P.

[2] The publisher in these words went a little too far; but it is certain that whatever names the reader finds that are unknown to him, are of such; and the exception is only of two or three, whose dulness, impudent scurrility, or self-conceit, all mankind agreed to have justly entitled them to a place in the Dunciad —P.

III. U

pity) there is certainly [1] nothing in his style and
manner of writing which can distinguish or discover him : for if it bears any resemblance to
that of Mr. Pope, 'tis not improbable but it might
be done on purpose, with a view to have it pass
for his.   But by the frequency of his allusions to
Virgil, and a laboured (not to say affected) short-
ness in imitation of him, I should think him more
an admirer of the Roman poet than of the Grecian,
and in that not of the same taste with his friend.

1 have been well informed, that this work was
the labour of full [2] six years of his life, and that
he wholly retired himself from all the avocations
and pleasures of the world, to attend diligently to
its correction and perfection ; and six years more
he intended to bestow upon it, as it should seem
by this verse of Statius which was cited at the
head of his manuscript :

> *Oh mihi bissenos multum vigilata per annos,*
> *Duncia !* [3]

Hence also we learn the true title of the poem ;
which with the same certainty as we call that of
Homer the Iliad, of Virgil the Æneid, of Camoens

[1] This irony had small effect in concealing the author. The
Dunciad, imperfect as it was, had not been published two days
but the whole town gave it to Mr. Pope.—P.

[2] This also was honestly and seriously believed by divers
gentlemen of the Dunciad. J. Ralph, preface to Sawney : "We
are told it was the labour of six years, with the utmost assiduity
and application : it is no great compliment to the author's
sense, to have employed so large a part of his life," &c. So also
Ward, Pref. to Durgen : "The Dunciad, as the publisher very
wisely confesses, cost the author six years' retirement from all
the pleasures of life : though it is somewhat difficult to conceive, from either its bulk or beauty, that it could be so long in
hatching, &c. But the length of time and closeness of application were mentioned to prepossess the reader with a good
opinion of it."—P.

They just as well understood what Scriblerus said of the
poem.—P.

[3] The prefacer to Curl's Key, p. 3, took this word to be really
in Statius : " By a quibble on the word *Duncia*, the *Dunciad* is
formed." Mr. Ward also follows him in the same opinion.—P.

the Lusiad, we may pronounce, could have been, and can be no other than

THE DUNCIAD.

It is styled Heroic, as being doubly so; not only with respect to its nature, which according to the best rules of the ancients, and strictest ideas of the moderns, is critically such; but also with regard to the heroical disposition and high courage of the writer, who dared to stir up such a formidable, irritable, and implacable race of mortals.

There may arise some obscurity in chronology from the names in the poem, by the inevitable removal of some authors, and insertion of others in their niches. For whoever will consider the unity of the whole design, will be sensible, that the poem was not made for these authors, but these authors for the poem. I should judge that they were clapped in as they rose, fresh and fresh, and changed from day to day; in like manner as when the old boughs wither, we thrust new ones into a chimney.

I would not have the reader too much troubled or anxious, if he cannot decipher them; since, when he shall have found them out, he will probably know no more of the persons than before.

Yet we judged it better to preserve them as they are, than to change them for fictitious names; by which the satire would only be multiplied, and applied to many instead of one. Had the hero, for instance, been called Codrus, how many would have affirmed him to have been Mr. T., Mr. E., Sir R. B., &c.; but now all that unjust scandal is saved by calling him by a name, which by good luck happens to be that of a real person.

II.

A LIST OF BOOKS, PAPERS, AND VERSES,

IN WHICH OUR AUTHOR WAS ABUSED, BEFORE THE

PUBLICATION OF THE

DUNCIAD;

WITH THE TRUE NAMES OF THE AUTHORS.

REFLECTIONS Critical and Satyrical on a late Rhapsody, called An Essay on Criticism. By Mr. Dennis, printed by B. Lintot, price 6*d*.

A New Rehearsal, or Bays the younger; containing an Examen of Mr. Rowe's plays, and a word or two on Mr. Pope's Rape of the Lock. Anon. (By Charles Gildon.) Printed for J. Roberts, 1714, price 1*s*.

Homerides, or a Letter to Mr. Pope, occasioned by his intended translation of H mer. By Sir Iliad Dogrel. (Tho. Burnet and G. Ducket, Esquires.) Printed for W. Wilkins, 1715, price 9*d*.

Æsop at the Bear Garden ; a Vision, in imitation of the Temple of Fame. By Mr. Preston. Sold by John Morphew, 1715, price 6*d*.

The Catholic Poet, or Protestant Barnaby's Sorrowful Lamentation ; a Ballad about Homer's Iliad. By Mrs. Centlivre and others, 1715, price 1*d*.

An Epilogue to a Puppet-Show at Bath, concerning the said Iliad. By George Ducket, Esq. Printed by E. Curl.

A Complete Key to the What d'ye call it. Anon. (By Griffin, a player, supervised by Mr. Th——.) Printed by J. Roberts, 1715.

A True Character of Mr. P. and his Writings, in a Letter to a Friend. Anon. (Dennis.) Printed for S. Popping, 1716, price 3d.

The Confederates ; a Farce. By Joseph Gay. (J. D. Breval.) Printed for R. Burleigh, 1717, price 1s.

Remarks upon Mr. Pope's Translation of Homer; with two Letters concerning the Windsor Forest and the Temple of Fame. By Mr. Dennis. Printed for E. Curl, 1717, price 1s. 6d.

Satyrs on the Translators of Homer, Mr. P. and Mr. T. Anon. (Bez. Morris.) 1717, price 6d.

The Triumvirate; or, a Letter from Palæmon to Celia at Bath. Anon. (Leonard Welsted.) 1711, folio, price 1s.

The Battle of Poets; an Heroic Poem. By Tho. Cooke. Printed for J. Roberts, folio, 1725.

Memoirs of Lilliput. Anon. (Eliza Haywood.) Octavo, printed in 1727.

An Essay on Criticism, in Prose. By the Author of the Critical History of England. (J. Oldmixon.) Octavo, printed 1728.

Gulliveriana and Alexandriana; with an ample Preface and Critique on Swift and Pope's Miscellanies. By Jonathan Smedley. Printed by J. Roberts. Octavo, 1728.

Characters of the Times ; or, an Account of the Writings, Characters, &c., of several Gentlemen libelled by S—— and P——, in a late Miscellany. Octavo, 1728.

Remarks on Mr. Pope's Rape of the Lock, in Letters to a Friend. By Mr. Dennis. Written in 1724, though not printed till 1728. Octavo.

VERSES, LETTERS, ESSAYS, OR

ADVERTISEMENTS

IN THE PUBLIC PRINTS.

British Journal, Nov 25, 1727. A Letter on Swift and Pope's Miscellanies. (Writ by M. Concanen.)

Daily Journal, March 18, 1728. A Letter by Philo-mauri. James Moore-Smythe.

Id. March 29. A Letter about Thersites ; accusing the author of disaffection to the Government. By James Moore-Smythe.

Mist's Weekly Journal, March 30. An Essay on the Arts of a Poet's sinking in reputation ; or, a Supplement to the Art of Sinking in Poetry. (Supposed by Mr. Theobald.)

Daily Journal, April 3. A Letter under the name of Philo-ditto. By James Moore-Smythe.

Flying Post, April 4. A Letter against Gulliver and Mr. P. By Mr. Oldmixon.

Daily Journal, April 5. An Auction of Goods at Twickenham. By James Moore-Smythe.

The Flying Post, April 6. A Fragment of a Treatise upon Swift and Pope. By Mr. Oldmixon.

The Senator, April 9. On the Same. By Edward Roome.

Daily Journal, April 8. Advertisement by James Moore-Smythe.

Flying Post, April 13. Verses against Dr. Swift, and against Mr. P——'s Homer. By J. Oldmixon.

Daily Journal, April 23. Letter about the Translation of the Character of Thersites in Homer. By Thomas Cooke, &c.

Mist's Weekly Journal, April 27. A Letter of Lewis Theobald.

Daily Journal, May 11. A Letter against Mr. P. at large. Anon. (John Dennis.)

All these were afterwards reprinted in a pamphlet, entitled A Collection of all the Verses, Essays, Letters, and Advertisements occasioned by Mr. Pope and Swift's Miscellanies, prefaced by Concanen, Anonymous, octavo, and printed for A. Moore, 1728, price 1s. Others of an elder date, having lain as waste paper many years, were, upon the publication of the Dunciad, brought out, and their authors betrayed by the mercenary booksellers (in hope of some possibility of vending a few) by advertising them in this manner :— " The Confederates, a Farce. By Captain Breval (for which he was put into the Dunciad). An Epilogue to Powel's Puppet-Show. By Col. Ducket (for which he is put into the Dunciad). Essays, &c. By Sir Richard Blackmore. (N.B. It was for a passage of this book that Sir Richard was put into the Dunciad.)" And so of others.

AFTER THE DUNCIAD, 1728.

An Essay on the Dunciad. Octavo, printed for J. Roberts. (In this book, p. 9, it was formally declared, " That the complaint of the aforesaid libels and advertisements was forged and untrue; that all mouths had been silent, except in Mr. Pope's praise; and nothing against him published, but by Mr. Theobald.")

Sawney, in Blank Verse, occasioned by the Dunciad; with a Critique on that Poem. By J. Ralph (a person never mentioned in it at first, but inserted after). Printed for J. Roberts. Octavo.

A Complete Key to the Dunciad. By E. Curl. 12mo, price 6*d.*

A second and third edition of the same, with additions. 12mo.

The Popiad. By E. Curl. Extracted from J. Dennis, Sir Richard Blackmore, &c. 12mo, price 6*d.*

The Curliad. By the same E. Curl.

The Female Dunciad. Collected by the same Mr. Curl. 12mo, price 6*d.* With the Metamorphosis of P. into a Stinging-Nettle. By Mr. Foxton. 12mo.

The Metamorphosis of Scriblerus into Snarlerus. By J. Smedley. Printed for A. Moore. Folio, price 6*d.*

The Dunciad Dissected. By Curl and Mrs. Thomas. 12mo.

An Essay on the Taste and Writings of the Present Times. Said to be writ by a Gentleman of C. C. C., Oxon. Printed for J. Roberts. Octavo.

The Arts of Logic and Rhetoric, partly taken from Bouhours, with new Reflections, &c. By John Oldmixon. Octavo.

Remarks on the Dunciad. By Mr. Dennis. Dedicated to Theobald. Octavo.

A Supplement to the Profund. Anon. (By Matthew Concanen.) Octavo.

Mist's Weekly Journal, June 8. A long Letter, signed W. A. Writ by some or other of the Club of Theobald, Dennis, Moore, Concanen, Cooke, who for some time held constant weekly meetings for these kind of performances.

Daily Journal, June 11. A Letter, signed Philo-Scriblerus, on the name of Pope.—Letter to Mr.

Theobald, in verse, signed B. M. (Bezaleel Morris), against Mr. P——. Many other little Epigrams about this time in the same papers. By James Moore, and others.

Mist's Journal, June 22. A Letter by Lewis Theobald.

Flying Post, August 8. Letter on Pope and Swift.

Daily Journal, August 8. Letter charging the Author of the Dunciad with Treason.

Durgen : a Plain Satire on a Pompous Satirist. By Edward Ward, with a little of James Moore.

Apollo's Maggot in his Cups. By E. Ward.

Gulliveriana Secunda. Being a Collection of many of the Libels in the Newspapers, like the former volume, under the same title, by Smedley. Advertised in the Craftsman, Nov. 9, 1728, with this remarkable promise, that " *any thing* which *any body* should send as Mr. Pope's or Dr. Swift's, should be inserted and published as theirs."

Pope Alexander's Supremacy and Infallibility Examined, &c. By George Ducket and John Dennis. Quarto.

Dean Jonathan's Paraphrase on the Fourth Chapter of Genesis. Writ by E. Roome. Folio, 1729.

Labeo. A paper of Verses by Leonard Welsted which after came into One *Epistle*, and was published by James Moore. Quarto, 1730. Another part of it came out in Welsted's own name, under the just title of Dulness and Scandal. Folio, 1731.

There have been since published :

Verses on the Imitator of Horace. By a Lady (or between a Lady, a Lord, and a Court-'Squire). Printed for J. Roberts. Folio.

An Epistle from a Nobleman to a Doctor of Divinity, from Hampton-court (Lord H——y). Printed for J. Roberts also. Folio.

A Letter from Mr. Cibber to Mr. Pope. Printed for W. Lewis in Covent-garden. Octavo.

III.

ADVERTISEMENT

TO THE FIRST EDITION WITH NOTES, IN QUARTO, 1729.

It will be sufficient to say of this edition, that the reader has here a much more correct and complete copy of the DUNCIAD than has hitherto appeared. I cannot answer but some mistakes may have slipped into it, but a vast number of others will be prevented by the names being now not only set at length, but justified by the authorities and reasons given. I make no doubt, the author's own motive to use real rather than feigned names, was his care to preserve the innocent from any false application ; whereas, in the former editions, which had no more than the initial letters, he was made, by keys printed here, to hurt the inoffensive ; and (what was worse) to abuse his friends, by an impression at Dublin.

The commentary which attends this poem was sent me from several hands, and, consequently, must be unequally written ; yet will have one advantage over most commentaries, that it is not made upon conjectures, or at a remote distance of time. And the reader cannot but derive one pleasure from the very obscurity of the persons it treats of, that it partakes of the nature of a secret, which most people love to be let into, though the men or the things be ever so inconsiderable or trivial.

Of the *persons* it was judged proper to give some account : for since it is only in this monument that they must expect to survive (and here survive they will, as long as the English tongue shall remain such as it was in the reigns of Queen Anne and King George), it seemed but humanity to bestow a word or two upon each, just to tell what he was, what he writ, when he lived, and when he died.

If a word or two more are added upon the chief offenders, 'tis only as a paper pinned upon the breast, to mark the enormities for which they suffered; lest the correction only should be remembered, and the crime forgotten.

In some articles it was thought sufficient barely to transcribe from Jacob, Curl, and other writers of their own rank, who were much better acquainted with them than any of the authors of this comment can pretend to be. Most of them had drawn each other's characters on certain occasions ; but the few here inserted are all that could be saved from the general destruction of such works.

Of the part of Scriblerus I need say nothing ; his manner is well enough known, and approved by all but those who are too much concerned to be judges.

The Imitations of the Ancients are added to gratify those who either never read, or may have forgotten them, together with some of the parodies and allusions to the most excellent of the Moderns. If, from the frequency of the former, any man think the poem too much a Cento, our poet will

but appear to have done the same thing in jest
which Boileau did in earnest, and upon which Vida,
Fracastorius, and many of the most eminent Latin
poets, professedly valued themselves.

IV.

ADVERTISEMENT

TO THE FIRST EDITION OF THE FOURTH BOOK OF THE DUNCIAD, WHEN PRINTED SEPARATELY IN THE YEAR 1742.

WE apprehend it can be deemed no injury to
the author of the three first books of the Dunciad,
that we publish this fourth.   It was found merely
by accident, in taking a survey of the library of a
late eminent nobleman ; but in so blotted a condition, and in so many detached pieces, as plainly
showed it to be not only incorrect but unfinished.
That the author of the three first books had a design to extend and complete his poem in this
manner, appears from the dissertation prefixed to
it, where it is said that the design is more extensive, and that we may expect other episodes to
complete it : and from the declaration in the argu-
ment to the third book, that the accomplishment
of the prophecies therein would be the theme
hereafter of a greater Dunciad.   But whether or
no he be the author of this, we declare ourselves
ignorant.   If he be, we are no more to be blamed
for the publication of it than Tucca and Varius for
that of the last six books of the Æneid, though
perhaps inferior to the former.

If any person be possessed of a more perfect

copy of this work, or of any other fragments of it, and will communicate them to the publisher, we shall make the next edition more complete: in which we also promise to insert any criticisms that shall be published (if at all to the purpose) with the names of the authors ; or any letters sent us (though not to the purpose) shall yet be printed, under the title of *Epistolæ Obscurorum Virorum ;* which, together with some others of the same kind, formerly laid by for that end, may make no unpleasant addition to the future impressions of this poem.

V.

ADVERTISEMENT

TO THE COMPLETE EDITION OF 1743.

I HAVE long had a design of giving some sort of Notes on the works of this poet. Before I had the happiness of his acquaintance, I had written a commentary on his Essay on Man, and have since finished another on the Essay on Criticism. There was one already on the Dunciad, which had met with general approbation ; but I still thought some additions were wanting (of a more serious kind) to the humorous notes of Scriblerus, and even to those written by Mr. Cleland, Dr. Arbuthnot, and others. I had lately the pleasure to pass some months with the author in the country, where I prevailed upon him to do what I had long desired, and favour me with his explanation of several passages in his works. It happened, that just at that juncture was published a ridiculous book

against him, full of personal reflections, which
furnished him with a lucky opportunity of im-
proving this poem, by giving it the only thing it
wanted, a more considerable hero. He was always
sensible of its defect in that particular, and owned
he had let it pass with the hero it had, purely for
want of a better ; not entertaining the least expectation that such an one was reserved for this post
as has since obtained the Laurel : but since that had
happened, he could no longer deny this justice
either to him or the Dunciad.

And yet I will venture to say, there was another
motive which had still more weight with our
author; this person was one who, from every
folly (not to say vice) of which another would be
ashamed, has constantly derived a vanity ; and
therefore was the man in the world who would least
be hurt by it.   W. W.

VI.

ADVERTISEMENT

PRINTED IN THE JOURNALS, 1730.

WHEREAS, upon occasion of certain pieces relating to the gentlemen of the Dunciad, some have been willing to suggest, as if they looked upon them as an abuse : we can do no less than own, it is our opinion, that to call these gentlemen bad authors is no sort of abuse, but a great truth. We cannot alter this opinion without some reason ; but we promise to do it in respect to every person who thinks it an injury to be represented as no wit, or poet, provided he procures a certificate of his being really such, from any three of his companions in the Dunciad, or from Mr. Dennis singly, who is esteemed equal to any three of the number.

VII.

A PARALLEL OF THE CHARACTERS

OF

MR. DRYDEN AND MR. POPE.

AS DRAWN BY CERTAIN OF THEIR CONTEMPORARIES.

MR. DRYDEN.

His Politics, Religion, Morals.

MR. DRYDEN is a mere renegado from monarchy, poetry, and good sense.[1]   A true republican son of monarchical Church.[2]   A republican atheist.[3] Dryden was from the beginning an ἀλλοπρόσαλλος, and I doubt not will continue so to the last.[4]

In the poem called Absalom and Achitophel are notoriously traduced, the King, the Queen, the Lords and Gentlemen, not only their honourable persons exposed, but the whole Nation and its Representatives notoriously libelled. It is *scandalum magnatum*, yea of Majesty itself.[5]

He looks upon God's gospel as a foolish fable, like the Pope, to whom he is a pitiful purveyor.[6] His very Christianity may be questioned.[7]   He ought to expect more severity than other men, as

---

[1] Milbourn on Dryden's Virgil, 8vo, 1698, p. 6.   (The references throughout are Pope's.)
[2] Page 38.   [3] Page 192.   [4] Page 8.
[5] Whip and Key, 4to, printed for R. Janeway, 1682.   Preface.
[6] Ibid.   [7] Milbourn, p. 9.

VII.

A PARALLEL OF THE CHARACTERS

OF

MR. POPE AND MR. DRYDEN.

AS DRAWN BY CERTAIN OF THEIR CONTEMPORARIES.

MR. POPE.

His Politics, Religion, Morals.

Mr. POPE is an open and mortal enemy to his country and the commonwealth of learning.[1] Some call him a popish whig, which is directly inconsistent.[2] Pope, as a papist, must be a tory and highflyer.[3] He is both a whig and tory.[4]

He hath made it his custom to cackle to more than one party in their own sentiments.[5]

In his Miscellanies the persons abused are, the King, the Queen, his late Majesty, both Houses of Parliament, the Privy-Council, the Bench of Bishops, the Established Church, the present Ministry, &c. To make sense of some passages, they must be construed into Royal Scandal.[6]

He is a Popish Rhymester, bred up with a contempt of the Sacred Writings.[7] His religion allows him to destroy heretics, not only with his pen, but with fire and sword ; and such were all

[1] Dennis's Remarks on the Rape of the Lock, Preface, p. xii.
[2] Dunciad dissected.   [3] Pref. to Gulliveriana.
[4] Dennis, Character of Mr. Pope.
[5] Theobald, Letter in Mist's Journal, June 22, 1728.
[6] List at the end of a Collection of Verses, Letters, Advertisements. 8vo. Printed for A. Moore, 1728, and the Preface to it, p. 6.
[7] Dennis's Remarks on Homer, p. 27.

III.   X

he is most unmerciful in his reflectious on others.[1]
With as good right as his Holiness, he sets up for
poetical infallibility.[2]

Mr. DRYDEN only a Versifier.

His whole Libel is all bad matter beautified
(which is all that can be said of it) with good
metre.[3] Mr. Dryden's genius did not appear in
anything more than his versification, and whether
he is to be ennobled for that only, is a question.[4]

Mr. DRYDEN's Virgil.

Tonson calls it Dryden's Virgil, to show that
this is not that Virgil so admired in the Augustean
age; but a Virgil of another stamp, a silly, impertinent, nonsensical writer.[5] None but a Bavius,
a Mævius, or a Bathyllus, carped at Virgil; and
none but such unthinking vermin admire his
translator.[6] It is true, soft and easy lines might
become Ovid's Epistles or Art of Love—but Virgil,
who is all great and majestic, &c., requires strength
of lines, weight of words, and closeness of expressions; not an ambling Muse running on Carpet-
ground, and shod as lightly as a Newmarket-racer.
He has numberless faults in his author's meaning,
and in propriety of expression.[7]

Mr. DRYDEN understood no Greek nor Latin.

Mr. Dryden was once, I have heard, at Westminster School: Dr. Busby would have whipped
him for so childish a paraphrase.[8] The meanest

[1] Milbourn, p. 175.
[2] Page 39.
[3] Whip and Key, Preface.
[4] Oldmixon, Essay on Criticism, p. 84.
[5] Milbourn, p. 2.
[6] Page 35.
[7] Page 22, and 192.
[8] Page 72.

those unhappy wits whom he sacrificed to his accursed Popish principles.[1] It deserved vengeance to suggest that Mr. Pope had less infallibility than his namesake at Rome.[2]

Mr. Pope only a Versifier.

The smooth numbers of the Dunciad are all that recommend it, nor has it any other merit.[3] It must be owned that he hath got a notable knack of rhyming and writing smooth verse.[4]

Mr. Pope's Homer.

The Homer which Lintot prints, does not talk like Homer, but like Pope; and he who translated him, one would swear, had a hill in Tipperary for his Parnassus, and a puddle in some bog for his Hippocrene.[5] He has no admirers among those who can distinguish, discern, and judge.[6]

He hath a knack at smooth verse, but without either genius or good sense, or any tolerable knowledge of English. The qualities which distinguish Homer are the beauties of his diction, and the harmony of his versification. But this little author, who is so much in vogue, has neither sense in his thoughts, nor English in his expressions.[7]

Mr. Pope understood no Greek.

He hath undertaken to translate Homer from the Greek, of which he knows not one word, into English, of which he understands as little.[8] I

1 Pref. to Gulliveriana, p. 11.
2 Dedication to the Collection of Verses, Letters, &c. p. 9.
3 Mist's Journal of June 8, 1728.
4 Character of Mr. P., and Dennis on Homer.
5 Dennis's Remarks on Pope's Homer, p. 12.
6 Ibid. p. 14.
7 Character of Mr. P., p. 17, and Remarks on Homer, p. 91
8 Dennis's Remarks on Homer, p. 12.

pedant in England would whip a lubber of twelve for construing so absurdly.[1] The translator is mad, every line betrays his stupidity.[2] The faults are innumerable, and convince me that Mr. Dryden did not, or would not, understand his author.[3] This shows how fit Mr. D. may be to translate Homer ! A mistake in a single letter might fall on the printer well enough, but εἴχωρ for ἰχὼρ must be the error of the author. Nor had he art enough to correct it at the press.[4] Mr. Dryden writes for the court ladies. He writes for the ladies, and not for use.[5]

The translator puts in a little burlesque now and then into Virgil, for a ragout to his cheated subscribers.[6]

Mr. DRYDEN tricked his Subscribers.

I wonder that any man, who could not but be conscious of his own unfitness for it, should go to amuse the learned world with such an undertaking ! A man ought to value his reputation more than money, and not to hope that those who can read for themselves will be imposed upon merely by a partially and unseasonably celebrated name.[7] Poetis quidlibet audendi shall be Mr. Dryden's motto, though it should extend to picking of pockets.[8]

Names bestowed on Mr. DRYDEN.

AN APE.—A crafty Ape, dressed up in a gaudy gown—Whips put into an Ape's paw, to play pranks with—None but Apish and Papish brats will heed him.[9]

AN ASS.—A Camel will take upon him no more burden than is sufficient for his strength, but there is another beast that crouches under all.[10]

---

[1] Milbourn, p. 203.   [2] Page 78.   [3] Page 206.   [4] Page 19.
[5] Page 144, 190.   [6] Page 67.   [7] Page 192.
[8] Page 125.   [9] Whip and Key, Pref.   [10] Milbourn, p. 105.

wonder how this gentleman would look, should it
be discovered that he has not translated ten verses
together in any book of Homer with justice to the
poet, and yet he dares reproach his fellow-writers
with not understanding Greek.[1] He has stuck so
little to his original as to have his knowledge in
Greek called in question.[2] I should be glad to
know which it is of all Homer's excellences which
has so delighted the ladies, and the gentlemen
who judge like ladies.[3]

But he has a notable talent at burlesque; his
genius slides so naturally into it, that he hath
burlesqued Homer without designing it.[4]

Mr. POPE tricked his Subscribers.

'Tis indeed somewhat bold, and almost prodigious, for a single man to undertake such a
work: But 'tis too late to dissuade by demonstra-
ting the madness of the project. The subscribers'
expectations have been raised in proportion to
what their pockets have been drained of.[5] Pope
has been concerned in jobs, and hired out his name
to booksellers.[6]

Names bestowed on Mr. POPE.

AN APE.—Let us take the initial letter of his
christian name, and the initial and final letters
of his surname, viz. A P E, and they give you
the same Idea of an Ape as his Face,[7] &c.

AN ASS.—It is my duty to pull off the Lion's
skin from this little Ass.[8]

1 Daily Journal of April 23, 1728.
2 Suppl. to the Profund, Pref.
3 Oldmixon, Essay on Criticism, p. 66.
4 Dennis's Remarks, p. 28.
5 Homerides, p. 1, &c.
6 British Journ., Nov. 25, 1727.
7 Dennis, Daily Journal, May 11, 1728.
8 Dennis's Rem. on Hom. pref.

A Frog.—Poet Squab endued with Poet Maro's Spirit! An ugly, croaking kind of Vermin, which would swell to the bulk of an ox.[1]

A Coward.—A Clineas or a Damætas, or a Man of Mr. Dryden's own courage.[2]

A Knave.—Mr. Dryden has heard of Paul, the Knave of Jesus Christ; and, if I mistake not, I've read somewhere of John Dryden, Servant to his Majesty.[3]

A Fool.—Had he not been such a self-conceited Fool.[4]—Some great Poets are positive blockheads.[5]

A Thing.—So little a Thing as Mr. Dryden.[6]

[1] Milbourn, p. 11.   [2] Page 176.
[3] Page 57.   [4] Whip and Key, Pref.
[5] Milbourn, p. 34.   [6] Ibid. p. 35.

A Frog.—A squab, short Gentleman—a little creature that, like the Frog in the Fable, swells, and is angry that it is not allowed to be as big as an ox.[1]

A Coward.—A lurking, way-laying coward.[2]

A Knave.—He is one whom God and nature have marked for want of common honesty.[3]

A Fool.—Great Fools will be christened by the names of great Poets, and Pope will be called Homer.[4]

A Thing.—A little abject Thing.[5]

1 Dennis's Rem. on the Rape of the Lock, pref. p. 9.
2 Char. of Mr. P. p. 3.   3 Ibid.
4 Dennis's Rem. on Homer, p. 37.   5 Ibid. p. 8.

INDEX OF PERSONS

CELEBRATED IN THIS POEM.

(The first Number shows the Book, the second the Verse.)

INDEX OF MATTERS

CONTAINED IN THIS POEM AND NOTES.

(The first Number denotes the Book, the second the Verse and Note on it. Test. Testimonies.

END OF VOL. III.

www.ingramcontent.com/pod-product-compliance
Lightning Source LLC
Chambersburg PA
CBHW060519030726